# Making the Match

# MAKING THE MATCH

## A RIVER RAIN NOVEL

### KRISTEN ASHLEY

Making the Match

A River Rain Novel

By Kristen Ashley

Copyright 2022 Kristen Ashley

ISBN: 978-1-957568-01-0

Published by Blue Box Press, an imprint of Evil Eye Concepts, Incorporated

# BOOK DESCRIPTION

Making the Match
A River Rain Novel, Book 4
By Kristen Ashley

From *New York Times* bestselling author Kristen Ashley comes the new book in her River Rain Series, *Making the Match*.

Decades ago, tennis superstar Tom Pierce and "It Girl" Mika Stowe met at a party.

Mika fell in love. Tom was already in love with his wife. As badly as Tom wanted Mika as a friend, Mika knew it would hurt too much to be attracted to this amazing man and never be able to have him.

They parted ways for what they thought would be forever, only to reconnect just once, when unspeakable tragedy darkens Mika's life.

Years later, the impossible happens.

A time comes when they're both unattached.

But now Tom has made a terrible mistake. A mistake so damaging to the ones he loves, he feels he'll never be redeemed.

Mika has never forgotten how far and how fast she fell when she met him, but Tom's transgression is holding her distant from reaching out.

There are matchmakers in their midst, however.

And when the plot has been unleashed to make that match, Tom and Mika are thrown into an international intrigue that pits them against a Goliath of the sports industry.

Now they face a massive battle at the same time they're navigating friendship, attraction, love, family, grief, redemption, two very different lives lived on two opposite sides of a continent and a box full of kittens.

# ABOUT KRISTEN ASHLEY

Kristen Ashley is the *New York Times* bestselling author of over eighty romance novels including the *Rock Chick, Colorado Mountain, Dream Man, Chaos, Unfinished Heroes, The 'Burg, Magdalene, Fantasyland, The Three, Ghost and Reincarnation, The Rising, Dream Team* and *Honey* series along with several standalone novels. She's a hybrid author, publishing titles both independently and traditionally, her books have been translated in fourteen languages and she's sold over five million books.

Kristen's novel, *Law Man*, won the *RT Book Reviews* Reviewer's Choice Award for best Romantic Suspense, her independently published title *Hold On* was nominated for *RT Book Reviews* best Independent Contemporary Romance and her traditionally published title *Breathe* was nominated for best Contemporary Romance. Kristen's titles *Motorcycle Man, The Will*, and *Ride Steady* (which won the Reader's Choice award from *Romance Reviews*) all made the final rounds for Goodreads Choice Awards in the Romance category.

Kristen, born in Gary and raised in Brownsburg, Indiana, was a fourth-generation graduate of Purdue University. Since, she has lived in Denver, the West Country of England, and she now resides in Phoenix. She worked as a charity executive for eighteen years prior to beginning her independent publishing career. She now writes full-time.

Although romance is her genre, the prevailing themes running through all of Kristen's novels are friendship, family and a strong sisterhood. To this end, and as a way to thank her readers for their support, Kristen has created the Rock Chick Nation, a series of programs that are designed to give back to her readers and promote a strong female community.

The mission of the Rock Chick Nation is to live your best life, be true to your true self, recognize your beauty, and last but definitely not least, take your sister's back whether they're at your side as friends and family or if they're thousands of miles away and you don't know who they are.

The programs of the RC Nation include Rock Chick Rendezvous, weekends Kristen organizes full of parties and get-togethers to bring the sisterhood together, Rock Chick Recharges, evenings Kristen arranges for women who have been nominated to receive a special night, and Rock Chick Rewards, an ongoing program that raises funds for nonprofit women's organizations Kristen's readers nominate. Kristen's Rock Chick Rewards have donated hundreds of thousands of dollars to charity and this number continues to rise.

You can read more about Kristen, her titles and the Rock Chick Nation at KristenAshley.net.

# ALSO BY KRISTEN ASHLEY

**Rock Chick Series:**

*Rock Chick*

*Rock Chick Rescue*

*Rock Chick Redemption*

*Rock Chick Renegade*

*Rock Chick Revenge*

*Rock Chick Reckoning*

*Rock Chick Regret*

*Rock Chick Revolution*

*Rock Chick Reawakening*

*Rock Chick Reborn*

**The 'Burg Series:**

*For You*

*At Peace*

*Golden Trail*

*Games of the Heart*

*The Promise*

*Hold On*

**The Chaos Series:**

*Own the Wind*

*Fire Inside*

*Ride Steady*

*Walk Through Fire*

*A Christmas to Remember*

*Rough Ride*

*Wild Like the Wind*

*Free*

*Wild Fire*

*Wild Wind*

**The Colorado Mountain Series:**

*The Gamble*

*Sweet Dreams*

*Lady Luck*

*Breathe*

*Jagged*

*Kaleidoscope*

*Bounty*

**Dream Man Series:**

*Mystery Man*

*Wild Man*

*Law Man*

*Motorcycle Man*

*Quiet Man*

**Dream Team Series:**

*Dream Maker*

*Dream Chaser*

*Dream Bites Cookbook*

*Dream Spinner*

**The Fantasyland Series:**

*Wildest Dreams*

*The Golden Dynasty*

*Fantastical*

*Broken Dove*

*Midnight Soul*

*Gossamer in the Darkness*


**The Honey Series:**

*The Deep End*

*The Farthest Edge*

*The Greatest Risk*


**The Magdalene Series:**

*The Will*

*Soaring*

*The Time in Between*


**Moonlight and Motor Oil Series:**

*The Hookup*

*The Slow Burn*


**The River Rain Series:**

*After the Climb*

*Chasing Serenity*

*Taking the Leap*


**The Three Series:**

*Until the Sun Falls from the Sky*

*With Everything I Am*

*Wild and Free*

*Complicated*

*Loose Ends*

*Fast Lane*

# AUTHOR'S NOTE AND ACKNOWLEDGEMENTS

Thank you to Donna Perry for being my reading buddy and crying as hard as I did at Mika's poems.

A shout of gratitude to my River Rain Team on Facebook (please see more detail on all the goodness I received from my Team at the end of the book).

And thank you to my Aunt Patty Stiles who, when she heard of the passing of my beloved Uncle Mike, reached out and called him as he was. An American Original. I told her I was going to steal that, but even if I did, I need to give her the credit for defining one of the many things that made him so damned special.

And last but not least, to the kickass team at Blue Box Press, Liz Berry, MJ Rose and Jillian Stein, thank you for being, ever and always, so damned awesome! And this includes Kim Guidroz for having it so ridiculously together, and Asha Hossain for bringing such beautiful covers to life!

# DEDICATION

This book is dedicated to the memory of my Uncle Mike Mahan.

A True American Original.

# PROLOGUE

## THE GOOD ONE

*Corey*

ecades ago...

HE DIDN'T THINK HE'D GAIN ENTRY.

But when he knocked, the door opened, and one of the groomsmen looked at him, then glanced over his shoulder, he heard the familiar deep voice call, "Let him in."

Corey entered and saw immediately that the groom had prepared for Corey's visit.

As, of course, he would.

He was not stupid.

Corey knew he'd prepared because, with a nod and a look, but not a word, all the groomsmen filed out.

Corey did not see joyous-wedding-day expressions on their faces when each man caught his eye as he left the room.

That wasn't about them having any apprehension about what was to happen that day or the woman their friend was about to tie the rest of his life to.

It was because they all detested Corey and perhaps knew why he was there.

Or they thought they did.

His face void of expression, Corey met every eye.

He was used to this, especially with the male gender. Men never knew what to do when another man was in their orbit who was smarter than them in a way they'd never equal him— and worse for them, richer just the same.

Especially ones with huge egos like these men had.

And on that thought, the door closed behind the last and Corey turned to Tom Pierce.

"I know," Tom started. "If I hurt her—"

"I will have her."

Tom's mouth snapped shut and his eyes, annoyingly always filled with wit and intelligence, turned shrewd.

Another annoying thing about Tom Pierce?

Not only was he the most talented tennis player on the planet—a player who turned that wit and intelligence against opponents so that he not only prevailed through physical prowess, he outthought them.

(As an aside, this was, to Corey's way of thinking, worse than someone humiliating you after serving an ace, then doing it again, and again, and then again, something Pierce did often—his serve was, as one of his rivals put it, like trying to return a bullet.)

He was also one of the most handsome men on the planet.

He was not built like a tennis player. He was built like a football player, his tall body packed with power. This being what made his serve so terrifying, not to mention his return.

Dark hair.

Dark eyes.

Classic looks, square jaw, strong chin, high cheekbones.

The first time Corey heard his name was overhearing office talk. Someone's assistant was talking about "that tennis guy, Pierce," who "looks like JFK, Jr., but more handsome."

When Corey saw a photo of him, he noted she was not wrong.

When Genny phoned him and said, "Corey, I think I've met the man I'm going to marry," and that man was Tom Pierce, Corey's heart cracked in two.

Last, when Corey had met Tom, he knew what Genny knew.

She would never truly be his.

But Pierce would always be hers.

And he'd be happy with that.

As to the matter at hand...

"You would not be the first to break her, or the best," Corey jibed.

Pierce, damn the man, didn't give him anything. Not a sneer, a flinch, or even an eye twitch, his ability to hold his own against Corey was something else he didn't like about the guy.

Corey carried on, "I put her together before, I'll put her together again."

At that, Pierce spoke.

"Let's not pretend that's what you're angling for."

"And what am I angling for?" Corey pushed.

It was a mistake.

His first for so long, he didn't realize it, not then.

"You hope this will crash and burn, like she and Holloway crashed and burned, because you hope she'll eventually give up on men she actually wants and settle for one she doesn't want, but he wants her."

Truly.

Corey hated this man.

"Are you saying you don't want her?" he goaded, purposefully misinterpreting what Pierce said.

Pierce drew in a very long breath.

He let it out, speaking slowly.

"What I'll make very clear right now is, what I want, what Genny wants, our marriage and the family we'll create is none of your business, Szabo. I will hurt her, and I'll hate it, but it'll happen. She'll hurt me, and she'll hate it, but it'll happen. None of that will be your business. We will fight. We will make up. We will wonder if we made the right choice. We'll remember that we absolutely did. We will repeat all of this time and again until we're both dead. And in between times, there will be love that never dies and commitment that will never break. And not one fucking bit of it will have one fucking thing to do with you."

It was Corey who was quiet then. He needed to be. He had to take that time to fortify his defenses.

"Am I heard?" Pierce prompted.

"I'm important to her," Corey replied.

"I know you are, that's why I'll put up with you," Pierce retorted.

Corey grew silent again.

"Have I made myself clear, Szabo?" Pierce pressed.

"You will hurt her. Your kind always do."

"I'm not him."

"No," Corey spat, his tone and the expression he allowed to come over his face underlined his words. "You are not."

Pierce's eyes slightly narrowed.

"You still love him," he said quietly.

He was talking about Duncan.

Duncan Holloway.

The man who broke Genny's heart.

"He's my best friend."

"He tore her apart."

"And this is why my best friend is no longer in my life. I had to choose. I chose her. I will always choose her, Pierce. And I will always be at her side."

"You may always be in her life, but you've never been at her side, Szabo. And you never will. It's only now you won't because I'll be there."

*That* was the blow that penetrated.

"Yeah," Pierce whispered, not missing he'd drawn blood.

They stood there, staring at each other.

And then it happened.

Never.

Not once since he'd graduated college had he lost such a duel, professionally, cerebrally, creatively or romantically.

So it was no wonder he tasted ash as he broke Tom Pierce's gaze, turned and walked out the door.

That ash nearly choked him forty-five minutes later when Imogen Swan, the woman Corey Szabo loved down to his bones, became the lawfully wedded wife of a man who would become one of the greatest tennis players of all time, known for his physical prowess on the court, but most especially, his intelligence.

Tom Pierce.

---

## Tom

*A FEW YEARS LATER...*

"IT'S...I DON'T KNOW WHAT IT IS."

"It's bullshit, that's what it is. It's the creation of a useless woman desperately trying to prove she has something more than long legs, a beautiful head of hair and a golden snatch."

"Jesus, Andrew."

"Am I wrong?"

"I don't know, but Christ."

"I don't agree. It makes me feel..."

"Yeah? It makes you feel? Feel what?"

"I don't know...something."

"Well, that's a stellar recommendation for it. Wouldn't buy it for my house, though, and not just because it's butt-ugly."

Tom, the last to have a turn, stepped away from the microscope.

He'd slid two slides under it, slides with white bits stuck between them, and you could only read what they said under the microscope.

The two slides he'd read said SKY and BROTHERHOOD.

He didn't know what he felt either, except he wanted to see what the other five slides said, and then maybe he'd understand.

A new voice, one he'd never heard, entered their conversation.

"It's an homage."

Tom turned and…

Shit.

Mika Stowe stood there.

The woman whose art show they were right then attending.

And whose piece Andrew was right then trashing.

"Or derivative," she went on, uncrossing her arms from her chest and pressing her hands into the front pockets of her faded jeans. "Depending on how you want to look at it."

No one said a word, and he didn't know how he knew, but it was because he understood, as they all did, she'd heard everything they'd said.

She took a step toward them, stopped and spoke on.

"John Lennon went to an art show and there, he saw *Ceiling Painting*. He was in a bad way, significantly depressed. He climbed the ladder at that show, looked through the magnifying glass, and read the word on the ceiling. It said 'Yes.' If it hadn't said yes, if it hadn't said something positive, even John himself didn't know what consequence that would have had on his life. He needed the positivity of that word. And he got it. So he climbed off the ladder and asked to meet the artist. That artist was Yoko Ono."

Holy hell.

Tom didn't know that.

Mika wasn't done.

"There's a lot of controversy around Yoko, mostly, obviously, based in sexism and racism, of course."

Tom pressed his lips together, because she was right, but Andrew grunting didn't come as a surprise, and Tom was torn between thinking her honesty in the face of Andrew's assholery was hilarious or wishing like fuck he was nowhere near the man when this situation came about.

Tom didn't know Andrew all that well, except that he was an excellent tennis player and could be a good guy.

But he could also be a colossal ass.

Andrew had tagged along with their group because Patsy was seeing him, and everyone liked Patsy.

"But no matter how you feel about Yoko," Mika continued, "or the love affair of John and Yoko, one inalienable truth is that if John had not met Yoko that day, there would be no 'Imagine.' Yoko herself said that if nothing else, the union of her and John gave the world that song, and the message in that song, and that was meant to be. As that's the best song of the twentieth century, and the message is the most profound a song has ever delivered, you can't argue it."

"I could argue it," Andrew stated.

This fucking guy.

"Bud," Tom said under his breath.

When he muttered his one word, Mika turned her gaze to Tom, and it stayed there for an uncomfortably long time.

She eventually returned to Andrew.

"You could argue what?"

"That song is the best of the twentieth century."

"Name a better one," she challenged.

Andrew either couldn't, or he wasn't fast enough, though she did give him time before she again shifted her gaze to Tom.

"The other words are 'dreamer,' 'join,' 'us,' 'sharing' and 'life,'" she said softly, staring right in his eyes.

Once she'd said that, she walked away.

"Well, at least she wasn't obvious by adding 'Imagine,'" Rod mumbled.

"Probably would have sucked you off in the cloakroom, man, you just asked for it," Andrew said to Tom.

Tom clenched his teeth.

"There a reason you have to be such a huge dick on too frequent of occasions?" Rod asked.

"Yeah, Andrew. As you know, he's *very* married," Patsy snapped.

"*She* didn't care." Andrew jerked his head in the direction Mika had walked away. "She was gagging for it."

"No," Tom said slowly. "She was thinking we were a bunch of

dumb jocks who didn't understand the point she was trying to make with her piece. And she was right."

"We're not here to write a dissertation on her *art*." Andrew said the last word like it tasted bad. "We're here because we're in town for that charity thing and because we like Terence Ladrelle's music, and she's banging Ladrelle, and we thought he'd be here too," Andrew pointed out, incorrectly.

At least, that wasn't why Tom was there, though he did like Ladrelle's music.

It was that Mika Stowe might be the current It Girl, muse to musicians and artists and photographers, party girl and budding style icon.

But she seemed interesting, and Tom was interested in what she had to say through her art.

And from what he'd seen so far of her showing, the microscope now being his favorite part, he felt it proved she was.

"I'm here to see what she's wearing," Miranda whispered to Patsy. "And only she could make jeans and a glittery top, with bare feet, look couture."

"Word," Patsy replied.

"You do her, don't let it get to Ladrelle," Andrew advised Tom. "I bet you can take care of yourself, but Ladrelle is right out of the ghetto."

Tom saw so much red, he had to blink.

"For fuck's sake," Rod bit out.

Miranda lifted her hand, and after dropping her pointer, middle, ring and pinkie finger on her thumb as she spelled the word, "D. O. N. E. Done," she stormed away.

"I know this ugly is from you trying it on with her, and she told you to go fuck yourself, and you obviously couldn't take that hit to your manhood, which is majorly unappealing. But the rest of it is a dealbreaker," Patsy declared. "So now I'll jump on that action and also tell you to go fuck yourself."

With that, she followed Miranda.

"Looks like you're not gonna get laid tonight," Rod noted to Andrew, watching Patsy go. "Or ever again, at least with Patsy."

"Are you serious?" Tom was also addressing Andrew. "The reason you're acting like such an ass is because you crashed and burned with Mika Stowe?"

"That used pussy?" Andrew scoffed.

Tom studied him.

Yeah.

He was being an ass because he'd wanted her, and she hadn't wanted him.

But also, he was just an asshole.

"Done," Tom said quietly to his friend who he was glad was more like an acquaintance, because Tom was not bluffing.

He was done.

And then he, too, walked away.

---

SEVERAL WEEKS LATER...

HE DIDN'T SEEK IT OUT, BUT WHEN HE NOTICED IT IN PASSING IN ONE OF Genny's magazines, he read the review of Mika's showing.

It was scathing.

So much so, Tom stood still, holding the magazine in hand, rereading the words because they were so far from what he'd experienced (outside Andrew's horseshit), he couldn't reconcile it.

There was mystery in her show. Poignancy. Thoughtfulness. Hope. Nothing in it was classically beautiful, but all of it made you think.

Which was what art was.

Or at least that was what Tom thought it was.

IT WAS THE FIRST TIME HE NOTICED HOW MIKA, AND AS AN EXTENSION of her and what she'd said about Yoko Ono, others in the present and in the past, were dismissed.

It would not be the last.

------

*Several years after that...*

THE LOOK SHE GAVE HIM COULD HAVE STRIPPED THE WALLPAPER FROM the walls.

"Do you know Mika?"

"We haven't formally met," Tom told his hostess of the evening, Eleanor Ellington, a pompous woman he didn't like all that much, but she loved tennis, and she personally funded ten scholarships to Tom's summer camp. Scholarships that included strict criteria which boiled down to one statement she'd made when she'd first offered the money.

*"Arthur can't be the only one, now can he?"*

"Well, Mika, this is Tom Pierce, normally escort to our darling Imogen Swan, who could not attend this evening," Eleanor purred. Mika's expression cleared as she smiled broadly at the introduction, all the while Tom grimaced and shook his head. "He also knows how to play tennis. Tom, this is Mika, she is, quite simply"—she floated a hand through the air—"*everything.*"

Tom dipped his chin to Mika.

She treated him to an expression like she was rolling her eyes, without rolling her eyes.

"Tom is flying solo tonight, as are you, my darling," Eleanor said to Mika. "So allow him to entertain you. I'm sure he's capable of doing that for at least half an hour. And then we'll sit for dinner, I will seat you close to the brilliance and humor that is me, and you will be saved." She finished on, "Tra la," and drifted away.

"Apparently, we're partners for the evening," Tom noted when they were alone.

"She's seventy-eight. She's lived her whole life thinking that a woman alone needs some sort of companion or guard, if she doesn't have a significant other, that significant other's priority purpose, according to Eleanor, being acting as a companion and guard," Mika replied. "However, I can assure you that I'm perfectly capable of maneuvering this evening without your aid."

"I didn't say you weren't," Tom pointed out.

"What *I'm* saying is you shouldn't feel like you need to stick around. It's one of my least favorite things to do, mingling. But I'll be fine."

"Maybe I've heard quite a bit about you and want to get to know you."

"Maybe *your wife* doesn't want you to get to know me."

"Maybe my wife knows I love her down to my soul, so she understands I can have a conversation with another woman, and even be friends with her, without getting jealous or territorial because she knows I would never go there," Tom drawled.

That shut her up.

"Jesus, does every man you meet hit on you?" he asked.

Her gaze moved through the room, she lifted a hand, pointed and shared, "That one over there hasn't."

Tom looked in the direction she was pointing to see literary critic and nonagenarian Niall Greenaway asleep in an armchair.

Tom burst out laughing.

"And I know a fair few homosexuals who aren't interested in me, though some of them are interested in my closet, which, perversely, I find far more threatening because I carefully curated that closet and even one piece purloined I would consider the end of the world," she continued.

Tom kept laughing.

When he finished, he noted, "Genny isn't here because Genny's pregnant with our third and the doctor doesn't want her traveling. As for me, I couldn't get out of this because my camp kids need Eleanor's scholarships, and Eleanor needs me to kiss her ass. So I'm here, rather than where I should be. With my wife."

"Poor you," she murmured, lifting a pink drink in a coupe glass to her lips.

He knew all about pink drinks and coupe glasses, so he felt his lips twitching.

"Pink Lady?" he asked.

"Mary Pickford," she answered.

"I've never heard of that."

"Rum, pineapple, cherry liqueur, grenadine. Sublime."

Tom made a face.

"Let me guess. Bourbon," she surmised.

"Not just, though I like bourbon. It's that I don't go too sweet."

She said nothing.

Which meant, for some reason he didn't understand, he carried on, "Tart. Bitter. Smoky. Okay. Sweet, not so much."

"Fascinating," she whispered, and if they hadn't spoken of what they'd just spoken of, he might have thought she was flirting.

Tom maneuvered them out of that lane.

"Maybe we should address the fact that Andrew Winston is an asshole," he suggested.

That was when she laughed.

Watching her do it was when Tom got it.

Sure, she was attractive. Tall and rounded with a head of golden-blonde hair that could be described as nothing short of extraordinary. She also had an interesting face. Not beautiful, not pretty, *interesting*, with a statement nose, broad lips with a stretched bow up top and brutally honest aquamarine eyes.

On a certain level, he always got why she was attached to some of the most important people of any given moment. It was her unusual looks and how well she carried them. She also had a flair for fashion and clothes looked good on her, or she had acute skill in picking clothes that did.

Most of all, there always seemed something held back with her.

Mystery was hard to deny, it drew you in, and the longer it took to get answers, the more hooked you got.

But it was this, that throaty laugh, the wide mouth exposing perfect teeth and highlighting how full and magnificent her lips were, her eyes lighting to the point they sparkled.

This was not only why she was attached to the most important people of any given moment, it was why she landed the most coveted men of any given moment.

It was, last, the first time since he'd met Genny that he wondered what it would feel like to kiss a woman.

No.

With Mika, he wondered what it would be like to taste her.

"You didn't say anything," she spoke, thankfully taking his mind from that last thought. "When your friend was off on one at the gallery, you didn't say anything. I was worried you were like him. And I was disappointed. I knew who you were, and I thought I knew that on a deeper level, after what you did for your wife."

Tom was confused. "What I did for my wife?"

"That casting couch thing. How you nipped that in the bud." When he silently stared at her, she assured, "It's quiet, Tom, but you must know it got around."

"You're the only one who's ever mentioned it to me."

Her head tipped to the side. "Does that upset you?"

"I don't really give a fuck how many people know that degenerate got called on his bullshit. What I give a fuck about is if it affects my wife and her career, because she's worked very hard to get where she is."

She righted her head and decreed, "So you're a good one. So far, I've only met three. Not including the gays, that is. The gays rocket the numbers into scores."

"Sorry?"

"A good guy, Tom," she explained.

"I hope so."

"Did you like my piece?"

She was talking about her microscope.

"I hadn't decided," he admitted. "I hadn't been able to view all seven of the slides."

"Seven," she said in a strange voice.

"Yes, seven. Aren't I right? There were seven slides?"

"There were, it just touches me that was what? Two, three years ago? One piece in an installation of thirty, and all the life you've lived in between, and you still remember there were seven slides."

"Join. Sharing. Sky. Brotherhood. Dreamer. And..."

"Life and us," she said softly.

"Sorry, I forgot the last two," he muttered.

"No, five out of seven isn't bad."

"But I would have liked it, if Andrew hadn't been acting like he was, and I'd been able to experience it without that negativity."

Constant eye contact from Mika, always, including when she said, "He's not a good guy."

"I learned that at the gallery."

"No, Tom, he is *not* a good guy."

More eye contact, heavy with meaning, before he murmured, "Fuck."

"Indeed."

"You?" he asked, remembering how Patsy noted he'd made a pass at Mika.

She shook her head.

"Someone you know."

She nodded her head.

"Should I...is there something I should do?" he inquired.

Now there was eye contact, but she was blinking.

"Do?" she queried.

"I'm on the circuit, as is he...but even if I wasn't."

"Tom, stop."

"What?"

"Stop."

"Why?"

"Because you're happily married, and I am not."

He shut up.

"There's nothing you can do anyway," she went on. "It's up to her, and sadly, I don't think she has the courage. I don't blame her. If she breathed a word, him and the machine around him would chew her up and spit her out. The caliber of your sponsors is impressive, but his aren't shoddy."

Tom felt his neck getting hot.

"It's a long road we're on, and while we traverse it, we have to pave the way so the women can speak," she noted.

"I'll keep an eye," Tom stated, the words so heavy, they landed like stones, so she couldn't have missed it.

And she didn't.

"He doesn't do it out in the open."

Very slowly, Tom repeated, "I'll keep an eye. And an ear."

For a moment, she said nothing.

Then she repeated, "Yes. You're a good one."

---

*SEVERAL HOURS LATER...*

ELEANOR'S DINNER WAS DONE, AND CONSIDERING THE FACT THAT MIKA and he were younger than anyone there by approximately forty years, after a hurried digestif, the end of dinner ended the party.

This meant now they were in a bar and Mika was laughing.

"It sounds like you're going to need to keep an eye on her," she noted.

They were talking about his oldest, Chloe.

"She's a pistol," he agreed. "Just like her grandmother, which both relieves me, because she'll suck the marrow out of life and I love that for her, and terrifies me, because she'll stop at nothing to suck the marrow out of life, no matter who she has to steamroll to do it."

Mika just smiled at him.

"And Matt is her opposite," he continued. "Quiet. Watchful. At first, I thought it was because Chloe overshadowed him. She's such a big personality, his couldn't shine through. But that's just how he is. It's almost a blessing for him. Chloe can grab all the attention, which means he can be off on his own, doing his thing."

"I can't say I know you very well, but that doesn't seem very much like you. Your boy. You're very outgoing."

"Matt's not like anybody, except..."

When Tom trailed off, she prompted, "Except?"

He didn't want to say it, but he did. "His Uncle Corey. He's a lot like Corey."

Her brows drew down over her eyes. "Corey? Corey Szabo?"

"Yes," Tom said shortly.

"I sense you two aren't the best of friends, like he is with your wife."

"I tolerate him. She adores him."

"Which is why you tolerate him."

Tom nodded.

She smiled at him again.

Then she announced, "It's at this juncture I'm going to say something I don't want to say. Because I want to meet your wife. I'm a fan of her work, she's a very talented actress, but also, it's beautiful, how your face changes when you speak of her. And I want to meet the woman who would make a man like you look like that when she's in his thoughts and on his lips. I want to meet your children, they sound wonderful. I want to know you more, I want to be your friend, Tom. I want you in my life. But I'm afraid we're not going to be friends, you and I."

Tom was so stunned by this unexpected and unwanted declaration, he felt his body jerk with the blow of hearing it.

"Sorry...what?" he asked.

"I'm attracted to you."

Tom said nothing.

"Very," she added a modifier.

Tom remained silent.

"I know you won't go there," she carried on. "I certainly won't go there. But it's such that it'll hurt. And I suspect, the longer I know you, the more that ache will grow."

"Jesus, Mika," he whispered, the compliment registering warmth, but the loss of her coated that warmth in a cold that was bitter.

And he barely knew her.

But she was just that phenomenal.

She shrugged.

He didn't like this decision. "I would never, and if you would never, then..."

"Tom." She wrapped a hand around his forearm, her fingers long and thin with tapered, perfectly lacquered nails at the tips. "I'm already half in love with you. This night has been perfect. Let's have it, having become friends, and staying friends, all that happy, with none of the hurt."

"You'll find somebody and then we can—"

"I've found a lot of somebodies, but not one like you."

She let him go, took hold of her Mary Pickford and held it his way.

With no choice, he lifted his vodka tonic.

And he didn't like it, but he did it.

They clinked, and with it, before they really began, their end was struck.

And Tom understood the ache she meant.

Because she was attractive, even if he wasn't attracted to her in that way.

But he still missed her now that she was gone.

———

*A YEAR AND A HALF LATER...*

HE HAD TO FORCE HIMSELF TO WAIT A WHOLE WEEK.

Then he used the number his agent acquired for him and called.

It was not a surprise she didn't pick up.

He left a message.

It was a surprise that, within an hour, she called back.

"Tom?" she asked after he said hello.

"Honey," he whispered.

He heard her breath catch, then he heard the sobs.

She wasn't hiding it and she wasn't holding back.

He knew her, but he didn't.

Still, he knew that was so very Mika.

It took a while, but finally, through sniffles, she said, "He wielded drumsticks, not a racket, but he was like you."

"I'm so fucking sorry, Mika."

"I'm pregnant, Tom."

At this news, as a husband, but mostly as a father, he felt a vicious burn sear through his innards.

"Shit," he bit off.

"No one knows. I'm only ten weeks along."

"I won't say anything."

"She'll never know her—"

Her voice cracked, and she lost it again.

He waited, his throat tight.

Genny walked in while he did.

When he glanced her way, with one look at his face, his wife knew who he was talking to and she came right to him, fitted herself to his body and wrapped her arms around.

In his ear, Mika got it together again.

"It's incredibly lovely you called."

"Of course. If you need anything—"

"The only thing I need is him, so…"

"Yeah," he said gently.

"Be happy, Tom."

"It doesn't seem like it now, Mika, but it's good he left you with her, or him. Trust me, it's the best thing in the world."

"I already know that. And it's a her. That's what he wanted. So she has to be."

"Right."

"Thanks for calling."

"Chin up."

Mika said nothing, no reply, no goodbye.

She just disconnected.

Tom looked down at his pretty wife with her sad eyes as she stared up into her husband's face.

"Is she a mess?" she asked.

"Yes," he stated the obvious.

Her gaze slid to his chin as she mumbled, "I can't even imagine."

He couldn't either.

Pete "Rollo" Merriman, the drummer for The Pissed-Off Hippies, had been in the wrong place at the wrong time when someone hit the truck in front of him and the cargo of steel sheets lashed to the back had come untethered.

Merriman had been decapitated.

Mika and Merriman had been married four months. According to anyone, both in the know and through gossip channels, they were a love match.

Like Tom and Genny.

And the photographic evidence played that positive, something Tom had paid attention to hopefully, for Mika.

They weren't smitten. She wasn't his muse.

She was the love of his life.

And he was her world.

So, yes.

He couldn't imagine.

"She's pregnant," he told Genny.

He took her weight as it slumped into him.

"Oh God," she breathed.

"Yeah."

"And thank God," she said.

Tom let that go a beat, feeling it for all its heaviness and joy, doing that pulling his wife closer.

And then he said, "Yeah."

---

Not too long ago...

·  ·  ·

When he looked through the peephole to see who was at the door, since no one knew where he was, even his children, he still was unsurprised at who he saw.

The man had his ways.

That happened when you were the richest being on the planet.

But Tom thought it was better to get it over with now than deal with his shit later.

He opened the door, looked the man in the eyes, then stepped away, leaving it up to Szabo to catch the door before it closed, then enter.

Szabo did this.

Tom went back to his glass of vodka.

Szabo savored the moment he'd been waiting for for nearly thirty years, not speaking for a long time.

Tom finished his vodka and poured another. Only then did he turn to lift the bottle Szabo's way.

It was the first time he'd looked at him since he came in.

Szabo hadn't taken a seat, and the expression on his face was unexpected.

Tom ignored it.

"Drink?" he offered.

"You know I don't drink, Tom," Szabo said quietly.

Tom put the bottle down and the ice clinked when he picked up the very full glass.

He walked to the couch in the cottage at the Biltmore where he was staying, a space that would be his home for the foreseeable future since he and Genny had agreed to a divorce and he had moved out.

He folded into the couch, raised his glass and rounded it in the air.

"Let's have it," he invited.

"I hate this," Szabo said.

There it was.

The expression on his face.

"For Genny," Tom surmised.

"For Genny. For the kids." Pause then, "For you."

"Right," Tom muttered dubiously and sucked back some vodka.

"Tom—"

"She won't have you," Tom informed him.

"I know," Szabo replied. There was sadness in his tone, resignation, and Tom felt his eyes narrow.

"The great Corey Szabo giving up?"

"You can't have missed that the time came when I stopped disliking you and started to think of you as family."

Tom was staggered.

"I can have missed it because I did," he returned.

Szabo nodded, let that go and moved on.

"Yes, I was pissed when I found out you cheated."

"I'm sure you were," Tom sneered, no doubt now, just derision, because he suspected Szabo was thrilled Tom had fucked up so incalculably.

Szabo took in a breath.

Then he snapped, "What the fuck were you thinking?"

"If I knew that, don't you think I would have shared that with *my wife* so maybe she could find her way past this, and we could move on...together?"

"Fuck that, Tom, and fuck *you* for saying that shit. Come on. You adored her."

"More than you."

Szabo's face pinched.

"Admit it, you know it, don't you? You know I loved her more than you," Tom pushed.

"Which makes your actions all the more perplexing," Szabo shot back, not quite admitting it, not quite denying it.

"She left me."

"She didn't leave you," Szabo countered. "She ended the marriage."

"No, Corey, she left me *while* we were married. And it's the biggest fucking copout a cheater can drag into a marriage to blame it on the woman he betrayed, but there it is. She checked out of our marriage. I did all I knew how to do to figure out what was going on. I gave her some space. I asked her what was up. I asked again. And again. I tried to reignite our intimacy. I asked her to go away with me, take a vacation from our lives, find each other again. I got frustrated and impatient and tried to coax it out of her through arguments. And when I admitted I stepped out on her, that was when she reengaged, though that wasn't why I did it. We had therapy, but how do I say any of that shit to her?"

"I can understand your dilemma because that's exactly what it is. A pile of complete, stinking shit," Szabo derided.

"Yup," Tom agreed, and took another sip of his drink.

"*Christ, Tom!*" Szabo exploded. "Fucking another woman?"

"I was going to leave her."

Szabo shot stick straight and stared, mouth hanging open.

Tom wished he was in the mood to take a picture. He sensed Corey Szabo had looked like that never in his life.

Not ever.

Flabbergasted.

As much as he'd like to cherish that look, he didn't.

In that moment, he preferred what was steeping in ice.

"I should have left her," Tom murmured into his glass and took another sip. When he was done, he rested the drink on his thigh, looked back at Szabo and repeated, "I should have left her. My weakness wasn't fucking another woman. My weakness was not leaving my wife before I did it."

"I disagree," Szabo said in a strangled voice.

"Phoenix is okay, better than LA. I'd prefer one of the Carolinas or Florida. And when I say that, I mean I'd *vastly* prefer the East Coast."

They'd moved to Phoenix not long ago. It was what Genny wanted.

It wasn't what Tom wanted.

They talked, he made his feelings known. She was done with LA. He didn't know what was going on with her, she wasn't sharing, but one thing he did know was that he wanted her to be happy, he wanted her to be happy with him, so they moved.

"I didn't want to live in a condo," he continued. "I am not at all a condo type of man."

And he wasn't. Even though she already knew this, he nevertheless shared that with Genny. She put her foot down. *"The kids are all but gone, Tom, what are we going to do with a huge house when the kids are gone? It's a waste. We're not wasteful."*

And he wanted her to be happy, so they got a huge condo instead.

"I've hated LA since we moved into our first house there," he went on.

"You have a mouth, why didn't you—?"

Tom cut him off.

"I hate those fucking awards dinners and shows and premieres. Genny does too. They make her tense. They pick apart your outfits. Your shoes. Hair. The fucking jewelry you were given to wear. The best dressed lists. The worst dressed lists. Dissecting you like you're not a human being. The glee in their hate is despicable. Even if she never landed on the worst dressed lists, her friends did, and you hurt when someone you care about hurts. They ask questions. You know how it is. 'How do you and Tom keep the spark in your marriage, Imogen?' Like it's their fucking business."

"Tom—"

"She hates it, I hate it more. Always did. Having to go through it and watching her have to do the same."

"Seems you married the wrong woman then."

Tom shook his head. "You love someone, you put up with a lot of shit you hate."

"This is fucked up," Szabo hissed. "Excuses. You're a grown man, Tom."

Tom ignored that.

"I'm on her arm during those, Corey. Didn't you notice? I don't think she did. I drop everything. Even if there's a tournament I'm calling, I fly to get to her and fly redeye to get back to my seat at the desk in front of the camera for the next day's matches. We're talking hauling ass from Melbourne or Paris or London. I did that not because she wanted me there. I did it because she *needed* me there. So I was there. Hell and high water, I got my ass in a fucking tux and stood at her side doing something she hated and something I detested, smiling while I did it. When I'm doing my thing, though, Corey, when

has Genny dropped everything to be with me? When I'm kissing ass
to raise money for my camp or doing my bit for the girls, if Genny's
filming, she's on set and not with me. Rod joked a couple of years ago,
I'm known as the Lone Wolf. He wasn't wrong, I was alone so often,
but only when it was something that mattered to me. Something that
had to do with my interests and my career. He didn't mean it ugly, but
when he said it, it got under my skin."

"And you didn't talk to your wife about it?"

"Of course I did."

"And Genny, *our* Genny, told you to fuck off?"

"*My* Genny was shocked I didn't understand the way it was in her
business after all these years. She was *hurt* that I was hurt. And in the
beginning, I didn't mind. Then it got old and one-sided, and I did. In
the end, she's right. It was her business, it was what she had to do to
maintain her career, and I knew it. Men have been doing that same
thing for centuries, and no one questions it. But she was also wrong."

"So your response was to fuck someone that wasn't her," Szabo
stated scathingly.

"No, I got even more hurt when she pulled away and stayed away
and I lived in a city I hated, because she needed to live there. Then
moved to a city I didn't want to move to, into a home I didn't like,
because she wanted to move here. Then she wasn't working as much,
but she still didn't step to my side. She threw herself into our kids,
who were grown, for fuck's sake, and took a break from her marriage
without actually taking a break from her marriage."

"But *she* didn't fuck someone else."

"No, you're right. She didn't. But I wished she did. God's honest
truth. Because I would have understood that. Silence. Distance. When
she's sleeping beside me in our bed. That I did not get."

"Did you address this in therapy?"

Tom nodded and took another sip from his drink.

"And what did she say about pulling away?"

"It was what that fucked-up place does to women's heads. It's what
happens to them when they aren't twenty-five anymore. It took her to
her knees."

"And you didn't get that?"

"How could I if she didn't give it to me?"

"But she did, in therapy. When it was too late," Corey surmised.

"She did. In therapy. When I'd made it too late," Tom confirmed.

"And you didn't explain your issues to her, not even through therapy?"

"Not fully. It makes it sound like I think it's her fault I had an affair. And it isn't."

"You're right, it isn't." Szabo leaned back. "So that's your Scylla and Charybdis. You had a beef. You can't share your beef. Because it might be a beef, but it doesn't explain what you did."

Since that was precisely it, Tom had no reply.

It was then, Szabo sat on the very edge of a chair across from Tom.

He leaned forward.

And urgently, he said, "Tell her, Tom."

Tom stared at Genny's best friend, a man she'd known since she was eight, the closest person to her outside her family and Tom.

They were a miracle, those two. Kids from a small town in the Midwest. He became the richest man in the world, brilliant, genius at computers, anything tech, *and* business. The Midas Touch. She became the most famous woman in the world, beautiful, sweet, talented, smart, and one of the best actresses of her generation.

The third of their friendship posse from that small town, the one who broke their hearts...he didn't do so badly either.

But Szabo was also the man who loved her, not more than Tom, but too much for Tom ever to have been comfortable with.

In other words, this earnestness was a shock.

And he didn't trust it.

"It'll make things worse, and you know it," he replied.

"It might help her understand," Szabo suggested.

"Again, *I* don't even know why I did it."

"Not about what you did, but about where you were, and where you both need to be."

"She needs space."

"You need to fight for her."

"I know my wife, and she needs space."

"Tom, I'm telling you. Listen to me right now. *You need to fight for her.*"

Something about that made Tom's skin feel strange. He wasn't certain what it was. The tone. The words. The odd look on Szabo's face.

Or all of it.

It wasn't like he was giving advice.

It was like he was issuing an order.

"Are you going to fight for her?" Szabo pressed.

"I know my wife, Corey. Therapy didn't work not because of what I didn't share, because even if I did share it, she's not in a place to hear it. I have to wait. So I'll wait."

They stared at each other over the coffee table.

And then Szabo said something that snaked down Tom's spine.

"So be it."

He stood.

Tom stood.

Szabo moved to the door.

Tom moved with him.

He turned and looked at Tom.

"I didn't always like you, but I always admired you. Even when I didn't want to. But then, I started liking you. And now…" His gaze grew intent. "Now, Tom, I care about you deeply. You. Not Genny. Not the family. *You.* And this hurts."

Tom didn't like that either.

There was something wrong about it.

"Corey—"

Szabo cut him off with a nod and a statement.

A statement that was uttered almost like a wish.

Or a plan.

"You'll be happy again."

After he delivered that, he walked out the door.

It was the last time Tom saw him.

Within a few months, Corey Szabo blew his brains out.

And set his plans into motion.

When he did, Tom didn't stand a chance.

Then again, he'd refused a direct order.

And that was what happened when you defied Corey Szabo.

---

*SOME TIME LATER...*

WHEN THE CALL CAME THROUGH, SINCE HE DIDN'T KNOW THE NUMBER, he didn't take it.

They left a voicemail.

He had all sorts of shit going down, most of it surrounding the YouTube gossipmonger Elsa Cohen and Corey's bitch of an ex, so he didn't bother listening to it or clearing it. Not for weeks.

When that time came, and he was set to listen to the first few seconds before he trashed it, and he heard Mika's voice for the first time in nearly two decades, he did not trash it.

He listened.

And he wished he didn't.

"So you aren't one of the good ones. I'm gutted. Absolutely."

That was it.

All she said.

Genny and her PR team had spun it so no one outside immediate family knew the truth.

But Tom knew in that instant that Mika knew it.

And Tom had recently realized he'd lost his wife forever.

So he was unable to handle the blow of knowing he'd lost Mika too.

# CHAPTER 1

## THE MEET

*Chloe*

*N*ow...

I SAW IT. AND WHEN I DID, I THOUGHT I GOT IT.

She didn't live in a condo or penthouse.

Her house was just like Dad's.

It was in a different development. However, like Dad's, it was a golf course community. Clearly, HOA rules stated no cars allowed to park on the streets, because the streets were vehicle free. The gated neighborhood was filled with different homes, though all had picture perfect landscaping, and all were one story.

There was a lot of white.

White houses.

White vehicles in the drives.

White golf carts zipping around.

I pulled into her driveway so she wouldn't get slammed with an HOA notice.

She was standing in the door before I was fully up her walk.

Very slender. Blonde. Pretty.

Susan Shepherd.

The woman my father had an affair with, an occurrence that tore apart my family.

Although I'd seen pictures, laying eyes on her in the flesh, I saw that she did not remind me of my mom. Both were blonde, but Susan was thinner. There was a hard edge to her my mother could never have, I knew, because Mom had been through a lot, and she didn't have it.

*En fin*, Susan's expression wasn't just closed.

It was boarded away.

I'd need a crowbar to get behind that.

Nevertheless, I was me, always up for a challenge, so I didn't miss a step as I walked up to her house.

She didn't close the door to me.

She also didn't bar the door with her body.

Last, she didn't welcome me.

She simply disappeared into the shadows of the house.

But she left the door ajar.

I took that as my invitation and followed her in.

The temperature was cool inside. The area spacious. The décor screamed *"Interior Designer!"* with very little personal flair to go with it.

Not much shocked me, but that did.

My father might not do personal flair, but he did do personality.

And her great room hinted at no personality.

Her voice was as hard-edged as the rest of her, even as she asked, "Would you like a drink, or is this not that type of visit?"

"I'm not certain what type this visit is," I admitted.

"That makes two of us," she replied.

She gave me a top to toe and again, I read nothing on her face.

"Do you drink iced tea?" she queried.

"No," I answered.

"Diet Coke?"

"No."

She didn't put more effort into it, just lifted her brows.

"Espresso?" I requested.

She shook her head and mumbled, "Californians."

She then turned and disappeared around a massive fireplace.

I was not often uncertain of what to do, but in that moment, I was. Did I follow her?

See, I'd received my report from Uncle Corey's lieutenant or spy or henchman or whatever Rhys Vaughan was.

Honestly, I was angry at Uncle Corey for a lot of things, primarily him taking himself from me, from all of us.

But the man knew how to leave an inheritance.

How many girls could say, after his death, their uncle left them a secret operative?

Rhys Vaughan had been thorough in looking into Susan Shepherd. However, he didn't end his report with something useful. Say, a conclusion.

Perhaps, *She's a tough broad, but good deep down. She'll make your father happy.*

Or alternately, *She's a total bitch. Stay away.*

Thus, I was there, in the home of the woman who slept with my dad even though she had to know he was very married, seeing as probably most everyone on the planet knew that fact. At least those that had access to Western media.

I decided to follow her. She wasn't giving warm vibes, but I was an excellent judge of character, and no one was completely closed off (not even Uncle Corey, and he was the best I knew at that kind of thing).

Eventually, she'd give something away.

Her kitchen was as pristine and gorgeous and lifeless as her great room.

And she might have an issue with Californians, but she had an espresso maker, as well as a lovely, all-white espresso cup and saucer.

In other words, she wasn't a complete philistine.

I knew she knew I'd followed her.

She didn't say anything, nor did she look at me.

I walked to her island and stood there, resting my hand on it, watching her watch the machine spit out a stream of life's blood.

She hadn't filled a glass of iced tea for herself. She also didn't leave the espresso to pour herself one.

So I was to have a drink, perhaps because she was from Indiana, and she might spontaneously combust if she didn't offer the famed Hoosier Hospitality.

But she wasn't going to make herself a drink because we were not two gals sitting down for a chat.

Message received.

When the machine completed its task, she put the cup in its saucer, turned, came to stand opposite the island from me and slid it across the counter my way.

"Cream?" she asked.

"No," I answered.

"It was me," she stated.

I said nothing.

She did.

"I deserve whatever you're here to dish out. I didn't chase him. I'm a lot of things, and not many of them are all that great, but I've learned to accept myself as who I am. That said, I have lines I don't cross. At least, I do now. And that's one of them. We started as friends. I wasn't in the accepting-myself-for-who-I-was part then, and your dad helped me with that. In return, I listened to him, because at the time, he needed someone to listen...and hear the things he had to say. My feelings grew stronger, and I made the first move. I took it there. It was me."

"Apparently, he didn't rebuff you."

She shook her head, but not to deny my comment.

"I'm sorry, you may think you deserve the details, but you don't, unless your father decides he wants to give them to you. Do what you came here to do. Say what you came to say. I earned whatever that is. But your father's still your father and that's off-limits. At least through me."

"He needed someone to listen?" I asked.

Another shake of her head.

"You're an adult. I know what you've been doing. Cal called from back home. He told me someone came around, asking questions. You've been looking into me. I don't have a private investigator doing it, like you do. But I looked into you too. It isn't hard to find things about you. I knew you had someone before I saw that ring on your finger. I know who he is. Your father spoke of you, not much. That wasn't who we were to each other. But I know he loves you. I don't know the nature of your relationship with him. What I suspect is, there are things in your life that are not his business unless you make them his business. I'd also suspect that he expects the same."

"Fair enough," I murmured, still unable to get a lock on her.

I gave myself some time to keep trying while lifting the espresso cup to my lips.

She had good coffee.

And the aforementioned espresso maker.

Both pluses.

She was a plain talker, something else I liked.

I put the cup back in the saucer.

"Do you see him?" I inquired.

"Never."

I found this hard to believe. They lived ten minutes from each other.

"Never?" I pressed.

She looked me square in the eye.

"I have lived an entire life of regret. I have done things to balm hurts that simply created more hurt, mine and for others. What happened with your father was the last."

Obviously, she could be honest.

So could I.

"He's lonely, and I don't like the woman he's seeing."

That mask that was soldered to her face finally cracked, and out of it leaked surprised confusion.

"I'm sorry?"

"Paloma," I said. "I don't know what it is. She seems perfectly fine. Maybe that's it. She's perfectly fine. She's perfectly everything. She's perfectly perfect. It's disturbing."

She still did not hide her shock. "You came here to tell me that?"

"I came here to ask why, if whatever he had with you was something worth risking his family for, you two aren't together?"

For a second, she appeared beyond confused. She seemed completely thrown.

Then, stiltedly, she queried, "You...came...you...I..."

I helped her out.

"He should be with you."

Her eyes went round. "You want me to be with your father?"

"He must have felt deeply for you. That's who he is. He would never have done what he'd done if he didn't."

She let that sit a beat before she decided it safe to agree. "He did."

"He did? Or he does?"

"We've ended our relationship. It's done. I haven't seen him in years. I only spoke to him when that gossip person had your mother's friend's ex on her show to assure him I won't say a word. I would never, not ever do that to Tom."

"I know."

Her eyes went squinty. "Your PI."

"Yes."

"Well, that particular information he shared is accurate."

"There was also the fact that you didn't come forward after the situation with Elsa Cohen and Samantha Wheeler on Elsa's gossip show. Not like you talked to that reporter after you were kidnapped by Dennis Lowe."

She winced, as she would.

And I was off my game. I should never have brought it up. The entire situation was horrible, and she'd been in the eye of the storm. Being in the clutches of a serial killer, it had to be terrifying.

I hadn't come here to make her feel bad.

I'd come here to find some way to make my father happy.

"I didn't mean it that way," I said quietly.

She eyed me suspiciously, as she would since what I said did sound like an accusation. "All right."

"Susan—"

"Susie."

"Susie, have you met Paloma?"

"No."

"Do you know who she is?"

"She was a supermodel, and as you know since you know about Lowe, I didn't live in a cave until I met your dad. So yes. I know who she is."

"I don't like her for him."

"I'm sorry, Chloe. I care about Tom. I hope your concerns aren't valid. But I'm not sure I know what to do about them."

"If you needed him, he'd come."

Her hair shook, such was her surprise at my words.

And then she burst out laughing.

I didn't find anything funny.

"I'm not joking."

"Christ," she pushed out, her mirth still uncontrolled. "Yes, you are."

"Do you know how much it took for me to come here?"

Still smiling, she asked, "And you came here to try to get me together with Tom?"

"He chose you over my mother."

The amusement swept from her face, and she said softly, "No. No, he didn't. He made a mistake. After thirty years of being so perfectly perfect, anyone paying attention might find it troubling, he had a moment of weakness, and he did the wrong thing."

Um.

No.

"Are you saying my mother wasn't paying attention?"

"I'm saying I was."

I closed my mouth.

"He did the wrong thing. *We* did the wrong thing. He didn't choose me over your mother. He loves her still. Even though they've both moved on to other people."

I continued my silence.

Susie spoke.

"I...as you can tell, I'm stunned you came here to say what you just said. But as I mentioned, he loves her still. He loves you and your brother and sister more than his own life. Can you imagine me sitting down to Thanksgiving with Matt?"

Matt would burn the dining room table to cinders before he'd sit down to Thanksgiving dinner with Susan Shepherd.

Uncharacteristically of me, I hadn't thought of that.

I scrunched my nose.

"Yeah," she agreed. "Even if Tom wanted to take it there, he's a good man, a man I could love, I wouldn't take it there. I wouldn't, and take note, because this is the first selfless thing I've done in my entire life...I wouldn't because Tom would tie himself into knots to make me happy, that's the man he is, but he wouldn't have happiness for himself. Not unless you all welcomed me, and that includes Imogen. And I wouldn't do that to him. He deserves better. When he moves on, he must find someone that isn't tainted. Someone you kids will accept. Someone Imogen will accept. And someone that makes him completely happy. That will never be me."

She lifted her hand and waved it my way before she continued talking.

"I'm not saying you all wouldn't be polite. But your father deserves more than that, surely."

He did.

Surely.

*Zut.*

Now what was I going to do about Dad?

And Paloma?

I downed the rest of the espresso.

It was excellent, but I should have asked for cream.

"How...*disturbed* are you about this woman?"

At her question, I got out of my head and came back into the room.

"I love Bowie," I told her.

"Bowie?" she asked.

"Duncan. People close to him call him Bowie. But I mean Duncan. Duncan Holloway. Mom's man."

She nodded. She knew Duncan. Probably knew him before because he was semi-famous. But with Mom being Mom, now everyone knew him because they were together.

I explained what I meant.

"I know my parents are never going to get back together, and I'm okay with that."

"All right."

"Dad can do his own thing," I began.

Something changed in her face when I said that, but the way it did, I knew I couldn't ask after it, because whatever was behind that was about Dad. And she wouldn't tell me.

Therefore, I continued, "But he's better in a relationship. That said, he's not better with Paloma."

"I don't understand what you're saying."

"He's going through the motions. I don't know. You're right. Some of his life is off-limits to me. I'm not his best bud. He doesn't confide everything to me. Maybe it's because Mom's moved on and he feels like he needs a partner to even things out. To try to communicate to me and Matt and Sasha that he's okay. Maybe I should stop worrying, it's good he has company. Or maybe he's settling for whatever came his way, because he feels guilty, and he doesn't think he deserves someone who will truly make him happy."

I took a deep breath.

And then I finished, "Or maybe it's something darker. Like, he feels so guilty, he's punishing himself by finding someone who doesn't make him happy."

Her shoulders straightened, which I read as concern.

I took heart in that and kept going.

"I'm not being catty or bratty when I say she's not smart. She's flown around the world time and again. She's met some of the world's most interesting people. And she has no conversation. She's very pretty. She dresses very well. She listens like she's hearing you, and yet you know by that vacancy behind her eyes she's wondering what face mask she should apply before bed. She laughs at the right times and stops laughing exactly when she should. She's like a robot."

Susie's face was paling.

First, something inside me shifted, seeing how genuinely she cared about my dad.

But also, this misery-loves-company thing fortified me.

So I continued.

"Dad's a world-renowned tennis player. When he retired, he earned his doctorate in medicine and set up a practice on top of his contract with the network doing commentary on the big tournaments. He reads. He travels. He sees movies. He cooks and goes to restaurants. He still plays tennis, and he plays golf, and he has his tennis camp, and he volunteers for Trail Blazer. Outside of being perfectly turned out and standing at his side when he needs her to do that, the only thing I've ever seen Paloma do is sit out in the sun with her phone, scrolling Instagram, or leafing through the latest copy of *Vogue*, or worse, setting up a 'Hanging by Tom's pool' selfie."

Susie stood, wan and motionless, staring at me.

And I again took heart, having someone to talk to about this, because it was clear she found it as alarming as I did.

I couldn't talk to Matt, who was healing his breach with Dad, but he wasn't ready to go here. And not our baby sister, Sasha, because she was dealing with her own thing, that thing, frustratingly, something she had yet to share.

Thus, I kept at it with Susie.

"There are times when they're together that I see him drifting, like he's replaying a tennis match in his head or arranging his to-do list. He's not engaged. Not with her. And it's come to the point sometimes, by extension, not with us when we're together. And still, she's there. He hasn't ended it. In fact, she's around more than she used to be. And frankly, Susie, it's beginning to scare me."

"Mika Stowe," she blurted.

My head jerked. "Sorry?"

"Mika Stowe. She's unattached, and your father admires her. A lot."

"Mika Stowe? The artist, poet, documentarian, novelist, and all-around ridiculously cool renaissance woman?"

She nodded and there was energy behind that nod.

My heart felt lighter than it had in months.

"We were talking about regrets," she told me. "He was helping me come to terms with mine. And he said one of his was that he'd met Mika, after he'd married Imogen, and they'd clicked. Not that way, but still, as it happens sometimes, it was also kind of in that way. But Mika was single, Tom was not. She couldn't have him, and she knew that would hurt. So she disallowed a friendship. Tom told me he regretted letting her do that. He felt he'd missed something important in his life, not having her in it. But more, he felt she missed something too, not having him. Especially when her life took such a tragic turn. So yes..." She took a big breath and concluded, "Mika Stowe."

We looked at each other over her island, but I didn't see her.

My heart had taken flight.

There was quite a bit of attention swirling around Mika Stowe of late.

In fact, for the last few years, the rediscovery of her in the wake of the latest wave of feminism had her at the forefront in arts, entertainment and the news as people reevaluated who she was in pop culture, and how important of a role she'd played.

Even before this, when I ran across a book of her poetry in high school, and experienced the brutally honest beauty of it, I'd become a fan, then sought and devoured everything she did.

Mom had watched one of her documentaries with me, and now I remembered she said, "I never met her, but your father did, and he really liked her."

I didn't know why I'd never asked Dad about it.

But now...

Mika Stowe and Tom Pierce.

A vision of them together formed in my mind.

Okay now...

*That* worked.

When I came back to myself and saw the look on Susie's face, it made me smile.

And my smile was wide.

What sealed the deal?

Susie smiled back.

And hers might have been wider than mine.

# CHAPTER 2

## THE COURIER

*Rhys*

$S$he lived so rural, he had to use an ATV and high-powered binoculars.

But he caught it.

The courier arriving and walking between the low adobe walls that started wide and curved inward to her front door.

Her opening that door, signing for the large envelope, the courier moving away and the target looking down at the envelope before the door closed behind her.

He watched the courier drive away.

Rhys then turned his attention to his phone.

He pulled up an app he'd already programmed for what he needed it to do.

He watched patiently.

It took her forty-five minutes before she made the call.

That either indicated she was thorough in reading what had been sent to her, or she was indecisive about whether or not to make the call.

With what Rhys had learned about Michelle Jillian "Mika" Stowe, it was the former.

Her call was lasting some time, which was advantageous.

He brought up his own texts and typed one in.

*It's begun.*

Chloe Pierce sent a one-word reply.

*Excellent.*

# CHAPTER 3

## THE PEDESTAL

### *Mika*

"Oh my God, you're freaking me out. I've never seen you this indecisive. Just call him and stop being weird."

That was my daughter.

I'd raised her like I wanted to raise her, because I was a single parent, and I could.

I'd also raised her like I thought Rollo would raise her, because I needed to give her that. For me. For her.

For Rollo.

That said, even though Rollo would have been adorably, but ridiculously permissive, and likely spoil her to shit, she'd had structure as a kid. There were rules. Bedtimes. Picking up after herself. Getting her homework done. Things like that.

But there were freedoms too.

Lots of them.

And one thing I worked at particularly was I wanted her to feel open to talk to me about anything. Open and that no matter how busy I might seem, how into one of my projects I was, I wanted her to know she was always my priority, and I'd always have time to listen.

I probably would have felt the same if she were a boy, but I definitely needed that since she was a girl.

I didn't want some bitchy mean girl bullying her, and Cadence not feeling it was important enough to interrupt me so she could tell me.

I didn't want some boy pressuring her into something she didn't want, and Cadence feeling awkward confiding that in me.

Or something worse, and she didn't think she could share it with me.

This meant I checked the judgment (and it was hard, I had a fair few opinions about everything, but my daughter and how she behaved and the type of person I hoped she would become was top of that list). I listened. I tried to be supportive when necessary, neutral when requested, offering wisdom when needed. But generally I was open to anything she wanted to give me without there being a downside for her.

This bred her saying it like it was.

Or it could be she came by that naturally, because that was a lot like her dad.

And a lot like me.

On the other hand, I couldn't tell her I didn't want to phone Tom Pierce because I was pissed as shit at him for turning out to be an asshole.

He'd polluted the fantasy.

He was the last one standing, after Rollo was gone.

And then he fell.

But he'd said something to me years ago. And since I cut ties with him and we only spoke that once, after Rollo died, I didn't know if what I took as a promise, he kept.

And now, I needed to know if he kept that promise.

Last, and worst, the conversation would best be had in person. Shit like this was real. It was extreme. And I wasn't paranoid, but I had my share of attention, especially lately, now that the Millennials and Gen Z were discovering me.

Better safe than sorry.

"Mom, if this guy knows something, it's doing the right thing to drag him in. Even if he doesn't want to be in. But I'm looking him up..."

And she was, I could see. Cadence was scrunched in our pillowy couch, knees up, heels in the seat with her laptop wedged between her body and her thighs.

"...and he looks like he's a decent guy. Maybe even a super decent one. I'm skimming this op-ed he wrote about USA Gymnastics' and Michigan State's responsibility in regard to the Larry Nassar situation, and he didn't pull any punches. So he might even be, like, *unicorn* decent."

Yes.

He *seemed* to be like that.

On paper and he talked a fair game too.

One thing I learned early, but somehow forgot when it came to Tom Pierce: Looks could be deceiving.

But this wasn't about Tom. Or me. Or me and Tom, which never was, never could be and now I'd never allow it to be.

It was about something a whole lot bigger.

After a big sigh that garnered an even bigger grin from Cadence, I left my daughter where she was, went up to my studio and phoned him.

I thought I'd have to leave a message because he'd be busy seeing patients or hobnobbing with world-class athletes or hanging around while Paloma Friedrichsen got a pedicure.

Okay, that last was bitchy.

But what was he thinking, going from Imogen Swan to Paloma?

I'd had occasion to be around Paloma far too frequently in my life, and the woman had two modes. First was Cut A Bitch if she felt the vaguest indication you might stand between her and something she wanted. Second, Vacuous Arm Candy, but only vacuous so she wouldn't do anything to annoy the man she had her fangs sunk into so she could bask in the light of his fame. This was, until she found another wealthier, more famous man she wanted to bleed (and bang).

Paloma Friedrichsen was one of most coldly calculating females I'd ever run across. I couldn't believe Tom fell for her crap.

Then again, I was realizing I didn't know Tom at all. I had read him completely wrong in our very brief acquaintance.

But that was on me.

However, in that moment, Tom was doing none of these things I thought would keep him from answering his phone, or if he was, he had time to take a call.

Because he picked up within three rings.

"Mika?"

Well, hell.

He knew who was calling which meant he'd programmed me in.

And he'd done that after I left that shitty message on the heels of that Elsa Cohen/Samantha Wheeler fiasco.

What did I do with that?

And worse, a friend of mine, who was a tennis fan, and just a man fan, said she taped Tom's commentaries and listened to them while she was masturbating.

"I know what the face looks like," she'd said. "But for me, I close my eyes and listen, because it's about *that voice.*"

She was not wrong.

Tom Pierce looked good *and* sounded good.

Smooth and easy.

Maybe that was how he bamboozled me twenty years ago.

"Tom," I replied.

"Is everything okay?"

*No.* I thought. *A dude like you is seeing a scheming cow, and no longer with your interesting, talented wife and the mother of your children. So, yeah. No, everything is not okay.*

"Mika?" he called.

"Something has come to my attention, Tom, and I need to talk to you about it," I told him.

"All right." His vibe was startled, but still friendly.

"Do you have time soon to meet up?"

"Meet up?"

Damn.

This was the biggest part of this whole thing that I didn't want to do.

I did it anyway.

"Come over to my place for a coffee."

He chuckled and regrettably, that was wildly attractive too.

"I live in Phoenix, Mika. I'd have to catch a plane to come to your place in New York for coffee."

"I'm not at my brownstone. I'm at my place in the desert. It's about half an hour outside Cave Creek."

He didn't immediately reply, but when he did, it was incredulous.

"You have a place in Arizona?"

For the most part, I kept this knowledge under wraps. However, when the small number of people I told heard it, this was mostly their response.

Me having a home in Arizona was like Fran Leibowitz quitting smoking, that was how synonymous I'd become with the Big Apple.

And it made sense, that city was my addiction, my life had been there, much of my art centered around there.

But I'd needed new horizons.

Broader ones.

"Sometimes I need space to do my thing," I told him.

"Right," he murmured.

"Coffee, Tom. Do you have time?"

"This is out of the blue."

Now he was fishing.

Why couldn't he just say yes and come over, for fuck's sake?

"I'm not asking you to my place to seduce you, Mr. Pierce. I have no interest in that and we both know why."

Sadly, my tone wasn't as modulated as I would have liked, nor were my words as carefully chosen.

Then again, I was never good at that kind of thing.

"But it's important," I finished.

Again, he didn't reply immediately, and his voice held caution when he did, which wasn't a surprise, considering I was speaking to him for the first time in years, asking him for coffee and not being very nice about it.

"Can you give me a hint?"

"It's about Andrew Winston."

"Andrew?"

"Are you friendly with him?" I asked, and if he was, there was another promise of him that bit the dust.

"Other than smiling while telling him to go fuck himself over a net as I shook his hand after I beat him, I haven't spoken to him since we were at your show."

I was stupidly thrilled to hear that.

I instantly buried that feeling and mumbled, "Then maybe you aren't the person I need to talk to."

The problem was, I wasn't into sports. It wasn't like I detested them. I just didn't find them interesting. True, of the many professional sports to pick from, tennis was one of the most interesting, I still didn't follow it because I not only didn't care, I didn't have time to do stuff I didn't care about.

(That said, I didn't follow it *now*, since Tom was no longer playing. I oh so totally watched it then, but only his matches.)

Back in the day, I'd known a number of women who dated sports stars. I'd also come into contact with a number of sports stars.

But that was a long time ago.

I'd lost my husband, had a kid and shifted my focus.

Those circles still courted me, but in the interim, I'd earned the privilege to pick and choose who got my time. Though, I'd always done that anyway.

I just learned to be choosier.

And people like Paloma Friedrichsen and Andrew Winston didn't get my time.

So Tom Pierce was my only in with that.

At least in tennis.

"He left tennis years before I did, Mika," Tom kept talking. "And he burned a lot of bridges when he left, not to mention before."

Interesting.

"So I'm not sure he's even coaching and pretty much everyone has lost track of him," he concluded.

Someone hadn't lost track of him, and that someone was whoever sent me that envelope I got earlier that day.

And that was another thing.

Why was *I* getting that envelope?

Was it because of Luna?

"Tomorrow," he went on.

"Sorry?"

"Tomorrow. Text me your address. Tomorrow. Ten o'clock."

"Don't you have patients to see?"

The words fell out of my mouth before I could stop them.

What he did with his time was none of my business.

I didn't even care.

Which was totally a lie.

Amendment: I didn't *want* to care.

Guess I was still hanging on to traces of the illusion of who Tom Pierce used to be to me.

Even as much as I didn't want to care, I'd always admired he'd earned his medical degree after he'd retired from tennis.

Then again, he'd insisted on earning his undergraduate degree before he'd turned pro. He'd been a popular phenom on the junior circuit, gaining celebrity not only because of his game, but because of his looks. But then he'd quit the junior tour after he graduated high school in order to go to college (and play tennis there). When players were turning pro at seventeen and eighteen, or even earlier, the fact he had the talent he'd had, and he'd waited until he was twenty-one to go pro, it blew everyone's mind.

After meeting him, and being so drawn to him, I'd learned everything I could about Tom Pierce, and that had blown my mind too.

At the time, all the pundits had said it was a huge mistake. He was wasting his best tennis years in a classroom, when he could return to the classroom later. But he'd never get back those years of strength and stamina to play tennis.

All the pundits turned out wrong.

If he'd decided to do that for a strategic purpose, it was also a stroke of brilliance. Because once he hit the pros, he'd blown through that too.

Like a cyclone.

"My practice is part-time," he shared. "I only have a few patients of my own, I'm choosy when I take on new ones, and for the most part, my office hours are to fill in for my partners when I'm in town so they can have a break."

Only Tom Pierce would practice medicine in a way it seemed like a hobby.

"Oh," I said.

"So yes, I can come over tomorrow."

"Fine. Great. I'll text you my address."

"She's ready to come forward."

"Pardon?"

"Your friend, or the person you knew. Now that things have changed, shifted, it's safer, she's ready to come forward."

But of course, even after all these years, Tom did not forget I mentioned what I did, even ambiguously, about Luna.

His guess wasn't on the nose, but it was close.

"We need to talk about it in person."

"Text me," he ordered, and strangely, my nipples tingled.

Okay…

What was *that*?

I was not a woman who got off on being ordered around by a guy.

Shit.

"Will do. See you tomorrow."

I was about to ring off when I heard him call, "Mika?"

"Yes?"

"I'm glad you phoned."

Now, how did I respond to that?

"See you tomorrow, Tom."

He sounded amused, which sucked, when he said, "Tomorrow, Mika."

I ended the call thinking, my whole life, I'd been surrounded by powerful, fascinating, attractive, talented men, and for the most part they were all assholes.

I jumped when I heard Cadence's voice.

"Is there a reason you had to hole up in your studio all alone to talk to a tennis stud?"

I took her in.

She didn't look like me at all.

She had Rollo's dark, wild curls. He'd been tall and bulky. She had a body like his mother's: average height and slender (which was totally not me). She had his dark eyes and olive cast to her skin and that nice line to her nose. She tanned in a blink, and it was beautiful.

Sometimes, when she was a little kid, I would bury my face in her curls and I'd swear, they smelled just like Rollo's.

Then the years passed, and I wasn't sure I remembered it right. I'd had him so little time, did I make that up?

It didn't matter, that smell went away, it became all Cadence, so even that part of Rollo was lost to me.

Still, she was so very him in so many ways, I had that. I held on to that.

And I held on to the other thing my husband left me. That frisson inside that I felt the first second I laid eyes on him, and it remained when he was gone. Where it lived in me was the part of me he owned, and I was never going to give it to another.

That didn't mean, if I fancied a fuck, I didn't have one. I did. I'd also had a few affairs that lasted longer than a night. And I had a few men who were fuck buddies who I could call on to take care of business.

Not one of them had I brought into Cadence's life.

Hell, in any meaningful way, none of them had been in *my* life.

My daughter was eighteen now, and after those agonizing years long ago when she came to understand the concept of having a daddy, and it dawned on her others had one, but she did not, she didn't give me any impression she had missed a man like that in her life.

Until recently.

She'd begun doing weird shit, like right now, staring at me hopefully after I had a private conversation with a "tennis stud."

I sensed this was because she was eighteen. She was graduating next May. And after that, she'd be gone.

Which petrified me.

Because first, I was a mother and that shit happened when you were a mom, no matter how cool of a mom you were. And I imagined myself one of the coolest moms there was (though Cadence might argue that, at least on occasion).

But mostly it was because she wanted to work for a place like Judge Oakley and Hale Wheeler's Trail Blazer program.

And not just that.

She also wanted to follow in her father's footsteps and be a drummer (and she was a damn good one, and I knew music, so I wasn't prejudiced (much)). She wrote songs as well (and those were damn good too, Lorde-esque meanderings, but there were tinges of Taylor's storytelling and honesty in Cadence's stuff).

But it wasn't just that either.

She further wanted to be a veterinarian, both the "Tame stuff, Mom, in an office. But also, wild stuff, like *Dr. Oakley Yukon Vet.*" (Which was something else to be petrified about, because Dr. Oakley jumped out of planes and was known to be rushed by musk ox.)

And then there was backpacking through Europe, "Just, you know, to see what's up with that."

Also, her desire to film a *Travels with My Father* type of thing, except it would be *Adventures with My Mother* because she wanted to drag me along and make a movie about it.

In other words, she was her mother's daughter, but she had no plan. She hadn't applied to any schools. She hadn't nailed anything down.

She was just going to "You know, let the universe guide me, like it did you."

My mother, if she was alive, which sadly she was not, would bust a gut laughing at that. I could hear her voice cackling, "The pigeons have come home to roost! Finally."

This because I put Mom through the same thing.

My father, who was alive, sadly, because he was an asshole, probably would have lots to say not only about the scope and ambiguity of Cadence's plans, but also the actual plans, none of which, except the veterinarian part, he'd approve of.

Since I didn't talk to him, I had no idea what any of those things he had to say were.

Therefore, now, I sensed Cadence understood that I'd soon be alone.

And although I'd tried to hide it from her, I sensed she knew I still missed her father like an ache. She knew because I could be immortal and live thousands of years, and I'd pine for him to touch his live wire to that frisson that hummed in me, and I'd pine for that until everything blinked out of existence and there was nothing but oblivion.

So now, my guess was, she didn't want me to be alone.

And considering the fact she knew I was heterosexual, she was angling for me to find a man.

That was not going to happen.

And if it should, it sure as hell would not be with Tom Pierce.

"I don't know him very well," I told her. "I only met him a couple of times. But the last time I spoke to him, he'd done something to upset me, and I phoned and shared how disappointed I was in him. I wasn't sure how he'd respond to me contacting him, and if it got ugly, I didn't want you to overhear."

"Did it get ugly?"

Fodder for thought, because no, he didn't make it ugly in the slightest. But I wasn't going to allow myself to chew on that.

"No."

"What did he do to upset you?"

"Just man stuff many men do."

"Like what?"

"Like, we're not going to talk about what."

"Mom."

"Cadence," I said softly. "I met him a couple of times, but I liked him very much in those times. We really connected. I thought he was a tremendous individual. When someone like that disappoints you, it stings. And I'm sorry, but how it stings is private."

"So he fell off your pedestal."

I froze, which was no surprise, considering fierce cold was sweeping through me.

"I'm not sure that's how it went, baby," I replied.

"You met him a couple of times and you thought he was a 'tremendous individual.' No one knows if someone is tremendous if they don't truly know them, which means spending time with them." She made a scoffing noise and decreed, "Pedestal city. By the way, Mom, those pedestals come in one size and the top is only a couple of inches wide. No matter how hard they try, no one can stay balanced up there. Everyone forced on one falls off."

With that, my eighteen-year-old sage of an offspring turned and glided out of my studio, and I was thinking I really, really, really should not have let her travel with me. And I really, really, really should have made her go to bed when I had my friends over, or threw my parties, rather than letting her mingle with so many adults. And I really, really, really should not have let her do that semester abroad in Sweden, or that summer cooking course in France.

She was eighteen going on sixty.

And considering I was forty-eight, that made her older and wiser than me.

My alternatives were her being a brat, checked out, into drugs, doing something that might get her arrested or pregnant, or focusing all her energies on being popular.

Not great choices.

Still, in that moment, I was wondering if one of those would have been better.

Because she'd just clobbered me.

# CHAPTER 4

## THE FEELING IS MUTUAL

*Tom*

Idiotically eager to get there, considering she'd made it clear he wasn't her favorite person, when he arrived, Tom found Mika's home was white adobe, and it had a wide, but not tall, footprint.

And even though there was a lot of it, there wasn't even a hint of vegetation that wasn't native. Cacti, succulents, mesquite, palo verde and desert willow trees—all Arizona, all arid, no need for irrigation, not a blade of grass to be found.

There were also well-placed rocks dotting the space that looked natural, as if the house was built among them, but was likely not.

The curved drive at the front was covered in a fine, golden-sand-colored gravel that matched the landscape.

The windows of the home were framed and beamed in wood, boxy and paned, except a large picture one to the right of her front door, which was one big sheet of glass.

As an entity, Mika's house managed to be out of the way, private, unassuming, yet attractive and impressive.

In other words, it seemed she hadn't lost her touch.

Tom parked, got out and walked down the middle of the low fence that started wide along the front of the home, but it curved narrow to the wood-framed glass front door, the path seamlessly shifting from gravel to travertine because they both were the same color.

There was something welcoming about the entry, the closing in of the fence toward the front door being like a beacon, inviting you in.

He knocked, both looking forward to seeing Mika again, and not.

Even if he'd disappointed her, he still thought the world of her, and he was glad she'd phoned. Now the seal had been broken, it might give him a chance—not to explain, that wasn't hers to have—but to get them to a different place where at the very least, she didn't think he was an ass.

And he thought there was hope that she'd called him in the first place. If you were done with someone, you were just done, no matter what you might want from them. There were always other ways to get what you needed.

But whatever she had to say about Andrew was probably not good, and he wasn't looking forward to that.

Tom could see her approaching through the glass of the door.

Not Mika.

Her daughter.

Rollo Merriman's daughter.

And he was taken aback at how much she looked like her father.

He was wondering if that was a balm for Mika, or a bite, as the young woman opened the door.

"Hey," she greeted enthusiastically, her brown eyes alive.

Not the reception he was expecting from anyone in that house.

"Hey there, I'm Tom. I'm here to see your mom."

"I know who you are," she replied, stepping aside and opening the door wider as she did, doing this still talking. "Mom's in her studio talking to her agent and refusing an offer to sit down with *60 Minutes* or *20/20* or some Netflix executive who has some documentarian they want Mom to film testimonials for about her life."

By this time, he was in a small entryway with beams running across the ceilings, terracotta tiled floors, those tiles cutting through a curved adobe staircase off to the side that had a wrought-iron banister with lazy curls adorning the end.

She was closing the door behind him.

He was surprised the home had a second story.

Mika's daughter continued to speak as she explained the mystery of the second floor.

This was because she led him down six steps into a room with an extraordinary adobe fireplace complete with high hearth and built-in mantle, all this snug inside sloping adobe walls. The fireplace being the focal point of the room, the hearth was decorated with bright blooms in a bottle-glass vase and wide-matted, colorful photographs of pictures of Mika with her daughter.

A cushiony couch faced this, a long table behind it, end tables beside it, a wooden rocking chair to one side, and off the room, he could see parts of a dining room table.

But that was it.

No TV.

No excess of décor.

It was welcoming and comforting and interesting and surprising and warm and not overdone.

All Mika.

"Like, after her saying no a bazillion times," the daughter was sharing, "she's suddenly going to change her mind. Uh…*hello*. The reason she's so cool is she doesn't do lame, fame-hungry things like that."

"No," he agreed. "She doesn't."

She stopped and pinned him with a very astute stare.

"You don't either."

She knew he was coming, obviously.

And now, just as obviously, he knew she'd looked into him.

"I'm in front of a camera or at a microphone enough in my life, I don't need more."

"Yeah," she said and admitted, "I'm not into tennis."

"Not everybody is."

"Mom and me, we aren't sports people."

"That's okay."

"I know. But, you know, it's weird."

"Not being a sports person?" he asked.

"No, *being* one. I can get it, in a way. I've had PE. What they do is hard. And there aren't that many who do it as well as the people who do it for those massive amounts of money. But it's got kind of this weird...*lemming* quality about it. I mean, have you heard about some of the crap that goes down at those soccer games in England?"

She pulled her shoulders forward, released them, and didn't wait for him to respond to her question before she kept talking.

"It's important to care about something. Have loyalty. But going ga-ga, even harming or fighting other people about a team where the players are there, then they're traded somewhere else, the coaches mean nothing unless they win, and the owners make huge-ass amounts of money off you, and that's all they care about? I don't know. It seems there are a lot of better things to give your money and time to. You know?"

"Like what?" Tom asked, thinking, at her age, her answer would not be anything like what it was.

"Books. Music. A hiking trail. Frank Capra movies. Cooking the perfect risotto. Or hamburger, if you're not into risotto. Figuring out how to take a great selfie, getting the focus right, the angle, the lighting, the framing. Or, you know, like going out and *playing* those games you like to watch other people play so much."

And, clearly, she was also very sharp.

"I can't say I disagree," he replied.

An easy smile came to her lips, and she said, "Cool. Then I saw *Ted Lasso* and I made Mom watch it."

He wasn't following her jump between topics, so he asked, "Sorry?"

"Mom isn't into TV. She's too busy doing stuff. It's kinda annoying, because, you know, it's the golden age of TV. She's missing all of it. She's never seen *Insecure*. Can you believe that?"

Tom fought back a smile. "I have to admit, I haven't either."

"Well, of course not. You're a dude. And you're a white dude. So I wouldn't expect you to. Though, you should. It'd give you insights into women. And people need to hear Black voices. And support Black women."

"Agreed," he replied.

"But also, it's just funny. And real. And I like all the clothes."

"Right," he murmured, still fighting his smile.

"But I made Mom watch *Ted Lasso*. She loved it by the way."

Tom tried not to paint broad strokes in anything in life, but he felt he could safely say he didn't want to know the person who didn't love *Ted Lasso*.

"In a world divided, *Ted Lasso* is universal," he said.

"Totally," she replied.

He didn't fight back that smile before he said, "Your name is Cadence, am I right?"

She nodded. "Sorry, I didn't introduce myself. It's weird. Everyone knows Mom, but not a lot of people know me, even some people she knows. She was rabid about that. Especially with the whole, you know…"

She flitted a hand, an expression he didn't like drifted over her face, and her posture grew awkward, something that didn't suit her at all, but she kept talking.

"*Way* I came into this world."

"Yes," he said softly. "I can imagine just how much your mom needed to protect you after that."

Her acute gaze refocused on him, and she shook off her awkwardness.

"She named me Cadence because Dad declared I was a girl and that was what I was going to be called. I'm glad he did. I have the best name of anybody I know."

Damn, but he loved the confidence. This young woman liking something about herself and not having a qualm sharing that she did. He'd seen too many girls—younger, and her age, and women who were far older, even top-notch athletes—who struggled with accepting themselves, even just small parts of themselves.

Cadence was a breath of fresh air.

"You have a very cool name," he concurred.

"You named your daughters Chloe and Sasha. Those are super-cool names too. And Chloe is rad, being rich and famous and still running a socially responsible business. I try not to buy anything from anywhere that isn't socially responsible. But it's hard because there aren't very many of them. People need to get with the program."

He liked her so much, now he couldn't stop smiling.

"I can't argue that."

"And Chloe's engaged to Judge Oakley, and he's the grooviest guy on the planet, you know, for a super binary guy. But he's groovy in everything he does. The closest groovy thing next to Judge being all-around groovy is Tom Holland lip syncing to 'Umbrella,' which was not binary at all. But it was totally hot. Have you seen that?"

Tom nodded. "I have."

She lifted a hand with her wrist limp and shook out a snap.

"It was lit. Didn't you think it was lit?"

"It was definitely lit."

"Yeah." She looked beyond him and called, "Hey, Mom."

Suddenly, Tom felt like he'd been punched in the chest, his breath not coming easy.

Dragging some in, he turned and saw Mika standing there.

She was wearing a kaftan dress with a low V at the neck, draping sleeves and a string through an empire waist that gathered the material. The print on a black background was mostly reds, oranges and pinks with bright accents of green and blue and turquoise. She had some flat, embroidered mules on her feet. And her still-golden hair was up in a messy knot on top of her head.

Even though she was dressed like she was hanging around the house, she wore makeup. Mostly neutral but with black cat's-eye, drawing focus to her eyes and the startling sea-blue color of the iris. She had some delicate chain bracelets at her wrists and a number of piercings in her ears, with studs or small hoops running up the shell, and dangling beads coming from the lobe.

She looked the picture of what a poet, photographer, novelist, filmmaker would look like. An easy style that was not unique, but she made it that way.

She was also still one of the most attractive women he'd ever laid eyes on.

In fact, he'd go so far as saying she was in the top two, vying for number one.

"Tom," she greeted.

"Mika," he replied, and then was surprised yet again in his short visit to her home.

He saw a soft pink rise in her cheeks, the kind a woman got when she felt nervous or didn't know what to do with flattery, something he hadn't offered, unless she caught it in his gaze.

She looked to her daughter and ordered, "Scram, kid."

"I need coffee," Cadence declared.

"You need to get to the library. You wanted this freedom, your teachers challenged you to earn it. You've got work to do, sister. A lot of it."

"I'll make coffee with you guys and take one with me."

"You can buy one and tip someone with money we have, and they need."

Cadence did an eye roll. "You're the only person I know who uses the excuse to spend money so other people can have it."

"I don't earn it to sit on it and I don't earn it to leave it to you. By the time I'm gone, you better be earning your own."

"Yeah, I better. Because you'll have spent all yours, and I'll be taking care of you," Cadence retorted.

Mika smiled, but said, "Get out."

Cadence turned to Tom. "See what I have to deal with?"

"What freedom is your mom talking about?" he asked.

"I'm still in school," she told him. "Back home. In New York. It's a weird, hippie, progressive school that, of course, costs a million dollars a semester, so, like, less than a percent of the population can afford to go there, which is totally liberal, is it not?"

Tom started laughing at her cheeky, self-aware sarcasm.

"It doesn't cost a million dollars a semester," Mika said on a sigh.

Grinning with him but ignoring her mom, Cadence continued, "Mom wanted to come out here and work, I wanted to come with her.

So I struck a deal with my teachers so I could come with. I've got all the credits I need to graduate anyway. I'm doing college courses now. So they piled it on me, since I'm independently studying. I've got, like, I don't know, fifty papers to write before we go home after spring break."

It was February.

"Sounds like you need to get to the library," he noted.

"You can get everything you need on the Internet," she retorted.

"You can also get distracted on the Internet and end up not studying and instead, getting in some Twitter war with some neanderthal who uses the only thing he has going for him, his opposable thumbs, to type rubbish into the hive mind of social media. *Go to the library,*" Mika commanded.

"Why do you have to be cool and with it and understand what a waste of time social media is and how your daughter's brain doesn't focus unless all distractions are taken away?" Cadence whined as she trudged toward the entryway.

"Your lot in life, I fear, my dearest," Mika replied, caught Cadence as she would pass, and kissed the side of her head before she let her go.

"See you later, Tom," Cadence called after she disappeared into the entry.

"Nice to meet you, Cadence," he called back.

His smile for Cadence was still at his mouth when he turned his attention to her mother.

She was frowning and offering, "Coffee?"

"Sure."

She moved to him, past him, and he followed.

Her kitchen was more white adobe, including that substance enclosing the fan over the range. The beamed ceilings were here too, as well as creamy white cabinets, most of the upper ones without doors so you could see an impressive stoneware collection in French gray, cobalt and cream.

"I can make you just about anything," she said. "Like mother like daughter, Cadence replaced the blood in her veins with java at around the age of sixteen. So we have it all."

"I'll have whatever you're making for yourself."

She wasn't looking at him as she busied herself between the machine, fridge and at the cupboard getting some mugs.

Tom went to the island, which was a contrast stainless steel with a butcher block top that worked great in the space, cutting the native southwest and giving a hint of contemporary so the top-of-the-line appliances didn't clash with the rest, which looked molded by hand.

Since she'd lapsed into silence, he began.

"It's good to see you."

She didn't agree.

Instead, she chose to say, "You look well."

"I am, thanks."

He didn't have a view of her full face, but he thought he saw her lip curl.

Obviously, that meant it was time to tackle it.

"Maybe we should clear the air," he suggested.

"It's unnecessary," she replied, setting the machine to running and turning to him. "What we have to talk about has nothing to do with us."

"There isn't an us, Mika. You made that happen," he reminded her.

"And it turned out it was good I did," she returned.

He wouldn't get angry, even though he didn't deserve that.

He'd fucked up, but the people that hurt who mattered were not standing in this room, and she made it that way.

If she had allowed them to be friends, she might or might not understand, but at the very least, she'd have a right to have a reaction.

Now, she didn't.

"Can I ask why you feel entitled to be upset with me about something that doesn't have anything to do with you?" he queried.

"Really, we should talk about what I asked you to come here to talk about. It's important. This isn't."

"I disagree."

"Okay then."

She leaned back against the counter and put the apples of her palms on it, getting comfortable to slap him with her honesty.

And then she launched in, no hesitation, slapping him with her honesty.

"You put on a good show, drew me in. So much, I barely knew you, but still, I missed you, Tom. All these years. Especially during certain parts of that time where I really needed someone strong and good to lean on. But in the end, it was just a show."

He shook his head. "Mika, you have no idea what you're talking about."

"So, no matter what the spin doctors said when you and Imogen scrambled to contain the damage after Corey Szabo's ex went for his throat, even though the man was well past sustaining whatever wound she wished to inflict, and she used you two as her in with the gossip machine? Hollywood's most perfect marriage didn't end because you fucked around on your wife?"

He reminded himself he was not there to get angry.

Or explain.

"You can't have lived all your years thinking that's all there is to the end of a marriage. What I'd like to understand is why you think I owe you an explanation."

"It wasn't me who wanted to talk about this."

"I can't help you with the other, whatever that is, unless we get past this."

"Now, I disagree."

"I've not seen or spoken to Andrew in at least twenty years, Mika. Whatever it is you heard about him, I'm not an attorney. I'm not a judge. I'm not a counselor. I'm not a journalist. So maybe you need to do some introspection to understand why it is you called me and requested I show in person at your home, and perhaps come to the understanding what we're discussing right now is why you did it."

He was trying not to get angry, it was difficult, and he knew she was struggling with impatience as well.

He also knew with what he'd just said, she lost that struggle.

"You don't know me well enough to claim an understanding of my motivations," she spat.

And he didn't drive all the way out beyond Cave Creek to have a woman spit words at him.

"You're right, I don't," he returned, and done with this, leaned into the island, which meant leaning toward her, and he went on, "Because the woman *I* thought I'd met, the woman *I* missed, because she took away her friendship the same night she gave it, would not call a man when he was at his lowest. When he'd fucked up and lost the most precious thing in his life. When he was down in a way it took everything he had to pull himself out of bed in the mornings, because he knew it was all his to own, what he did, and what he lost. And then kick him in the teeth without knowing *that first hint* of what the fuck was going on. I disappointed you, Mika? Well, honey, the feeling is mutual."

He turned and walked to the kitchen door but twisted back to see her staring at him, her cheeks again colored, but this time he didn't know if it was embarrassment, because he'd hit home, or anger, because she didn't want to admit that he'd hit home.

"My sense is, you've learned something hideous about Andrew. You're right, that's important. I'm involved in USTA, so if they need to be informed, I can facilitate that. I know smart, thoughtful journalists who will be gentle with victims and thorough in telling stories. I also know attorneys who take care of their clients, even as they go for the throat in a courtroom. I can help. But I'm too pissed at you right now to talk about it. I'll get you some names, and I'll do some introductions, if that becomes necessary. But for now, I'm going to go. You have a lovely home and an amazing daughter. It's good to see you healthy, and what a wonderful job you did with your girl. Live well and be well, Mika."

And, before their conversation degenerated any further, finished with what he had to say, Tom walked out of her white adobe, got into his car and drove away.

# CHAPTER 5

## THE CALL

*Mika*

*I* was fiddling in my studio.
Not working.
Fiddling.

I'd immersed myself in a project I knew would go nowhere. I didn't even know why I was doing it.

It began with starting to write when I'd heard Tom Pierce and Imogen Swan were getting a divorce. Free-form thoughts. Essays.

This was around the time it hit me that soon, my daughter would be finishing school and deciding what was next for her life.

Not long later, I'd begun to organize the pictures. Categorize them. Put them with the pieces I was writing. The musings. The poems.

Then came Elsa Cohen's interview with Samantha Wheeler, and something broke in me.

The project shifted, took a different shape.

And I'd gone into overdrive, leaving Cadence at home with the oversight of Nora and a couple of Cadence's best friends' parents, heading to Arizona for large chunks of time, going out for long walks on my property, spending hours photographing a single wildflower.

I glanced down at the workbench, caught sight of the picture of that wildflower, and right beside it, the photo I took of Rollo on his back on my couch with his big hands wrapped around my cat Bow's belly.

Rollo's fingers were so long, they ran up her sides all the way to her spine. She was kneading his chest. His bearded chin was dipped into his throat. They were staring at each other eye to eye.

Christ, my man could thrash a drum, but his touch was so fucking gentle.

Unable to sit with that thought for long, I shifted my attention to Bow.

She'd adored him. He'd stolen her from me the first time he'd come over. I'd left the bed to go to the bathroom after we'd made love, and when I came back, she was curled into him, his fingers massaging her neck, her eyes were slits, and she was purring.

On his side, wide, furry chest exposed, head in his hand, Rollo had looked up at me with those dancing brown eyes and said, "I like your cat."

It was the most beautiful thing I'd ever seen.

Maybe that was when I fell in love with him.

Before he came into my life, I'd had Bow for five years.

When he didn't come home, a few days later, she darted out the door. She'd never done that. Not in five years.

I knew she took off to find him.

I searched desperately. Asked everyone I knew to help me. Put up fliers. Called shelters.

But I never saw her again.

In my heart I knew she was still searching.

But eventually, she found him.

As the ache started to form, my phone went, and that was indication of how off I was.

When I worked, I put it on do not disturb without fail. Unless

Cadence was out and I needed to be able to get a call if she needed me, there were no exceptions to the do not disturb rule.

Now, Cadence was home, not in her bedroom. Unless she was going to school, she did hours like me, up when she was up, sleeping when she was tired, and she had her own area outside her room. She called it her "space." It was part study room, part game room, part music room and part art room.

That night, I purposefully had not activated the do not disturb on my phone.

I was waiting for Tom to call.

No, I was hoping he'd call.

Why?

Because I was too proud to call him. Something I should do since I'd been a bitch.

He was correct, his life was none of my business and it was me who'd made it that way. I didn't have a right to be angry or disappointed. I also didn't have a right to call him unexpectedly, ask him to come all the way out to my home (which wasn't far from Phoenix, but it wasn't close), and when he got here, be a bitch to him.

Furthermore, for my own peace of mind I'd cut ties with him way back in the day, but I still considered him a friend. And if a female friend had a marriage end because she'd had an affair, and she'd shared with me about it, I would have listened at first without judgment. I might not have agreed with her course of action, but I would have listened. And if there was a deeper issue behind it, and she was hurt, even if she'd done that to herself, I would have commiserated.

I knew all this.

I still couldn't get past my stubborn pride in order to phone him and apologize.

A failing.

The call wasn't from Tom.

It was Nora.

I picked up the phone and saw she wanted FaceTime.

I gave it to her and greeted her with, "It's one in the morning there."

"Yes, and it's eleven there and you still look like you could step out on a red carpet. I hate you."

Nora, on the other hand, had bedhead and a shiny face from her nighttime moisturizer because she was back in New York and in bed.

"You can't sleep?" I asked my closest friend.

Nora was Eleanor Ellington's youngest daughter.

She was eight years older than me, and she was her mother of a new generation. A society dame loaded with old money who lunched, sat on boards, raised money, and popped out children for the husband who divorced her for a younger model, a man she actively detested beyond rationality, and he deserved it.

Now, she dated the "dregs" (her words), who would "have me in my advanced state of decay" (also her words, and further a lie, she was gorgeous). And she spent what was left of her time at spas, shopping for things she didn't need, traveling to places where she could shop for more shit she didn't need, going to the ballet (which she loved), the opera (which she loathed, but her family had been a patron for four generations, so it was ingrained), and either in person or on the phone with her girlfriends, doggedly complaining about everything that annoyed her.

Which was pretty much everything.

She also slept terribly, which helped our friendship because I had no routine, no schedule. As noted, I was up when I was up, I slept when I slept. And as such, the chances were good anytime she wanted me, even in the dead of night, even when I was in her time zone and it was late, I would pick up the phone when she called.

"I'm done trying to sleep. I'm becoming Martha Stewart. She sleeps four hours a night. I'm getting up. I'm making muffins. I'm going to start an empire at fifty-six, making muffins and arranging flowers and turning compost."

"You live in an apartment on Central Park West. What are you going to do with compost?"

"I have a place in the Hamptons, stupid. Remember?"

I smiled. "Ah, right. Silly me. I forgot."

"I'll drag it up there. Or I'll tell Alyona to drag it up there."

"You might want to ask Alyona if there's flour in the house. You'll need that to make muffins."

She assumed a mock-horrified face. "*Muffins* have *gluten*? The horror!"

I started laughing.

"Well, that's out," she said through my laughter.

"Perhaps you can take up knitting."

"And give myself arthritis?"

"Does knitting give you arthritis?"

"I've no idea. Doesn't doing blindingly boring things eventually cause physical maladies?"

God, I loved this woman.

"You could try reading," I suggested.

"Stop attempting to sort my problems and tell me something exciting. What's happening with you?"

"Tom Pierce came by today."

Her phone jostled as she sat straighter in bed.

"Say that again," she demanded.

"Tom Pierce came by today."

"Oh, good Lord. Did you tackle him? Did you have sex on the kitchen floor? Or get all muddy doing it by your pottery wheel?"

"I don't have a pottery wheel."

"Shush, darling. Mother's fantasizing."

"We fought," I shared.

Her lips turned down in an exaggerated frown any mime would kill for before she asked, "You what?"

"We fought. I was bitchy to him. He didn't like it. He threw it in my face and walked out."

"Can we step back two dozen paces, and you explain why that fine specimen of a man walked in in the first place?"

I took a deep breath and reminded myself this was Nora. She knew so much dirt on so many people, starting with her mother sharing things from days of yore that would bring down the most powerful families in America (and a variety of western European countries besides), to Nora amassing her own nuggets along the way.

As every Ellington had done before, she'd parcel those out to her own children (if she hadn't done that already), then take what she knew to her grave.

Therefore, I had no hesitation in baring all. Sharing about meeting Tom years ago and liking him. Tom standing in my kitchen essentially admitting by omission of any denial that he'd cheated on his wife. And the contents of that envelope I got which was enough to blacken the life of Andrew Winston for the rest of it, even if the statute of limitations had run out (I'd checked) on his heinous crimes.

But further, his largest sponsor risked much more if anyone knew the lengths they'd gone to keep things quiet.

I finished this with sharing I'd called Tom to talk to him about Winston and giving details of what had happened earlier that day.

"Right, darling, first," she began when I stopped speaking, "when you tell Mother this kind of thing, you warn her beforehand to go pour herself a gin and tonic."

"Sorry," I mumbled, grinning at her.

"Second, there are a variety of manners of justice. That blackguard having the world know he's a rapist is one, even if he serves no time. But more, Core Point Athletics needs to be brought to its knees. So I agree with you, you must do something with this information you've been given."

Which brought to mind...

"And that's another thing, Nora. Why did *I* get that envelope?"

"We can ponder that later," she decreed. "The next point we must discuss is addressing and assessing why *did* you call Tom Pierce?"

I'd considered this at length for the rest of the morning after he left, the afternoon and into the evening.

"I don't know," I said.

Or lied.

"Mika, please," she drawled.

She knew I was lying.

"He's in tennis. Winston was a pro player. They were on the circuit at the same time. And Tom told me years ago that he'd keep an eye on him. I wanted to know if he'd seen or heard anything from back then to corroborate what was in that envelope."

"Is what was in that envelope in question?"

I shook my head. "It seems thorough. I obviously haven't called any of the women, but there were copies of emails, transcripts of phone calls and interviews. Bank transfers. Signed NDAs. If it isn't real, I can't begin to imagine why someone would create such an elaborate ruse, or why they'd drag me into it. Unless they had it in for Winston. However, that still doesn't explain why they've gotten me involved. But I do know Winston is of that bent. I know because he's done it before to a friend of mine."

She nodded, and noted, "Now, let's explore why you're so personally affronted by Tom Pierce straying from Imogen Swan."

"I thought he was a good guy," I pointed out.

"There are too few of those, as we know," she commiserated. "But Mika, you're aware I rarely tread cautiously, however, I promise you I am when I say...he's right. What happened between him and his wife is not really any of your concern. Am I unaware of you having a close friendship with Imogen Swan?"

I shook my head, my stomach pitching, because I'd already processed this.

And I knew she was right.

"I haven't even met her."

"Then what does it have to do with you?"

"I liked him," I explained. Lamely.

"So did my mother. She called him The Bee's Knees, and if you didn't read the capitalization of that title in how I said it, please take note. She adored him. She'd never let him know that because that was her way. I was her child and she never let *me* know it, except for the day she took me aside and said, 'Dearest, I've changed my will. You're getting my Fabergé egg. I've noticed how particularly drawn to it you are.' And up until that point, I hadn't known she'd noticed she'd borne and birthed me. I thought she thought I was our housekeeper's daughter who kept getting underfoot."

I started laughing again because that was pure Eleanor.

Though, she'd loved Nora to pieces.

Eleanor had two zones. She'd be fascinated with you, and show it, and she was actually fascinated with you (how she was with me). Or she'd openly disdain you, and the more disdainful she was, the more she adored you (how she was with Nora, and back when she introduced him, Tom).

She often said about Nora, "That child does me in. She's just *too much*."

And she did think Nora was too much, all of it good.

Nora was not unaware of that.

It was an odd way to show affection, but affection was shown. I knew this because Nora was the same way with her mom and her kids. She loved her mother, and when Eleanor passed, Nora was inconsolable.

On the flipside, when Eleanor acted like she liked you or she was polite to you, that was when you should be wary. In those cases, she either thought you were not worthy of her time, or you were a walking abomination and she'd eviscerate you behind your back.

Again, in that, Nora was just like her mother.

"She would not have blinked at him straying from his wife. It wouldn't change her feelings for him in the slightest," Nora continued.

"Her generation was taught to ignore men's indiscretions," I pointed out.

"She still had opinions and was far more unforgiving and judgmental than even me. I know" —she closed and opened her eyes slowly while she dipped her chin humbly—"hard to believe. But it's true. But no man, or woman for that matter, is made by one thing they did or one mistake they made. Charles Lindberg did something considered at the time outrageously heroic. But later, when he opened his mouth on matters of grave import, he proved he was not. Neither of these instances made him, and depending on your viewpoint, if you don't take in the whole, one or the other could define him, when they do not. Is Pierce a serial philanderer?"

He'd said he'd "fucked up" and he had to own that. He was open about it, honest to the point it was raw.

But the way he said it made it sound like a one-off. Not "I'd been fucking up" or "I'd been taking my marriage for granted" or "I'd spent years betraying my wife" or anything that would make it seem like it was an ongoing thing.

He talked like it was an incident. Singular.

And the pain he was signaling seemed more concentrated. Not like he'd been fucking around and got found out, but that he'd fucked up, he definitely owned that fuckup, and was mired in his regret.

I still answered, "I don't think so."

"Then, Mika—"

"He was married to her for over twenty years."

"And again," she shot back immediately, "how is this your business?"

"Because when I heard they were divorcing, I thought I had a chance at happiness again."

Nora's eyes went wide as saucers.

"So there you go," I continued. "That's it. Years ago, your mom introduced us, and we spent an evening together, talking and connecting. This was before I met Rollo. I felt something with Tom. I felt like he saw me. I felt like he got me. Not many people did back then. He listened. He was interesting. He was funny. He was beautiful to look at. He was beautiful to listen to. He was so *unlike* any of the men I'd been around it was almost startling. He was the exact opposite of my father. I didn't want the night to end. I wanted him to make love to me. I wanted to wake up next to him. I wanted to make him breakfast. I wanted to watch him play tennis. I wanted him to read my poetry and tell me what he thought. But he was married, so I couldn't have any of that. I didn't rediscover that feeling until I met Rollo. And I was going to give it some time, let Tom get over the split, then I was going to try to connect with him again."

"Mika," she said softly.

"So yes, when I figured out he'd fucked around on his wife, all that beauty that was him that I held in my heart and the hope that maybe I could reconnect with him and we could discover what we couldn't have was dead before I'd even attempted to breathe life into it. And it pissed me off."

"And of course you let him know that rather than saying, 'Now tell me, what have you been doing the last two decades? Don't leave anything out!' Then giving him the chance to explain. After that come to terms with the fact he's human after all. And *then* having sex with him at your pottery wheel."

"Nora—"

"Listen to me," she hissed.

And I blinked at her tone.

She carried on.

"You and I started to become friends around the time you were falling in love with Rollo. I went to your wedding. I loved him for the man he was and for you. But he's been gone a long time, and I'm tired of watching you put obstacle upon obstacle in your own damned way so you won't ever have to stop worshipping at the altar of Rollo Merriman."

"Nora," I breathed, winded by her words, shocked.

She'd never spoken like this.

Ever.

"He loved you, God, Christ, Mika, what he had for you was once-in-a-lifetime love. I know. Because I know a lot of people and I've lived a lot of life, and I've only ever seen it once. What I saw between the two of you. I can't even begin to imagine the strength it would take to carry on after the loss of something that enormous. That beautiful. And I don't wish to be insensitive, truly. I adore you and I'd never want to hurt you. However, I must point out the obvious. It's been years. You must *move on*."

Damn it.

I was getting angry.

Because I'd built the life I wanted after we lost Rollo. I did it with consideration and purpose. I'd had a number of relationships before him, I'd been with a number of men after he was gone. And I wasn't going to settle for anything less than some version of what I had with him.

And I'd felt that with only two men in my life.

My husband.

And Tom Pierce.

In the meantime, I wasn't miserable. I wasn't unfulfilled. Sure, I was still grieving, but I'd never stop. That wasn't unnatural. I'd talked to counselors about it. I still grieved my mother too. It was how anyone dealt with loss. The pain was paralyzing in the beginning, and the pain never really lessened.

It was like a chronic illness that wouldn't kill you, but it had no treatment.

You just learned how to live with it.

But I knew me. I knew what I wanted. I waited to find it in Rollo. I knew I couldn't be happy with anything else.

And I knew I wasn't going to introduce my daughter to it either.

"I don't want to move on," I snapped.

"No kidding?" she snapped back.

"And if I did, it wouldn't be with Tom Pierce."

"Because you've decided he's not perfect enough to stand up to the memory of Rollo."

"Because he's taken again. He's seeing Paloma Friedrichsen."

Nora said nothing. She didn't even move. And there was a look on her face that pained me.

Then I saw covers flying.

"Nora," I called.

A bright light shone on my screen before I saw racks of clothes.

"Nora!" I semi-yelled.

Her face came into view, and she appeared to be retching.

"Oh my God, are you all right?" I asked.

"I'm going to have to...*fly* over *New Jersey.*"

Was she being funny?

Why was she being funny?

I knew one thing, I wasn't laughing.

"What are you talking about?" I demanded.

"Paloma fucked Roland."

My lungs squeezed.

Roland Castellini was her ex-husband and the father of her children.

"*What?*" I forced out.

"*Way* back when. I was pregnant with Allegra. It was his first peccadillo. At least it was the first that I knew of. I discovered his perfidy. He apologized profusely, claimed some issues within himself he promised he'd work on. Also, as per him, there were problems with our marriage, obviously, because it couldn't be just that he was a toxic piece of shit. Though, that last would bear out to be the truth. At the time I forgave him. We went to counseling. He said he'd never do it again. He did it many agains until I ousted him."

Allegra was her first child of three.

"Oh my God," I breathed, horrified.

"How taken is he?" she demanded to know.

Now she was asking about Tom.

"I've no clue. He and I talked for maybe five minutes before I pissed him off enough to leave. But I think he's been with her for a while."

"I'll set some moles to digging. It doesn't matter. We're breaking them up. And then you're going to extract your head from your ass so you can make your move."

Now I wasn't breathing at all.

"I can't talk anymore," she decided. "I have to pack while in full drama. I've never had occasion to do that, but I've been wanting to do it forever. Obviously, I'll leave when I can either charter a jet, or make certain whatever flight I'm on is nonstop and has those seats that recline into beds. So packing in full drama is moot. I'm doing it anyway. But what is it? A thirty-hour flight to Phoenix?"

"It's five," I said hurriedly. "Now, Nora—"

"It's hot there, right? I should dig into my Mediterranean cruise and Portofino sections of my wardrobe? Yes?"

"It's hot in the summer. It's February. Now it gets chilly at night, but it's usually in the seventies during the day. But, Nora—"

"Good Lord, how do you wear fur in the winter?"

"No one wears fur or *should* wear fur. Now, *listen to me, Nora.*"

All I saw was her face because she brought her phone close to it.

"I'm not going to listen to you because you're going to say something lamebrained and annoying. I'll text you with my arrival details. Don't worry, I'll hire a car to take me to you. Have a bedroom ready for me. One with an en suite, darling, or I'll complain quite a bit, but I won't go to a hotel because I can't ride your ass if you're not doing what I want if I'm at a hotel. And none of that almond milk or coconut milk or any of that nonsense. The milk I drink comes from an *udder*. But be sure it's no more than two percent. I haven't had milk over two percent since my mother sat me down when I was seven and had our housekeeper demonstrate the powers of a girdle but cautioned me never to get to the point of needing one."

I really hoped that wasn't true.

But I suspected it was.

"Nora—"

Again, she cut me off.

"Mika, my dearest, I have never known anyone who lives their life with no excuses, no explanations, they are who they are and do what they please when and with whom, except you. But when you were talking about how Tom Pierce made you feel, for the first time since I've known you, I saw fear in your eyes. The *good* kind. The kind that's mingled with hope. So if you think I'm not coming to you as soon as I can extremely comfortably do it, you're high. Bonus, I get a semblance of vengeance by scheming to take that bitch's man. In short, wild horses couldn't keep me from Phoenix. And you know it."

I said not a word.

Because I knew it.

She smiled a contented smile. "See you tomorrow, probably. Kisses and hugs."

She made a smoochy face then disappeared from my phone.

Well, one good thing, Cadence cherished Nora. She'd be beside herself Nora was coming out.

Another good thing, all the bedrooms were en suite, and in the unlikely event that Nora would one day come out, that occurrence now coming true, I'd been sure my guest room afforded every luxury.

As for me…
I was stubborn.
And I was proud.
But I didn't procrastinate.
I needed to apologize to Tom.
And now I needed to warn him what was coming.

# CHAPTER 6

## THE KITTENS

*Tom*

om tossed the ball up in the air.

And then put everything he had into whacking the fuck out of it, sending it over the net.

It skimmed the center service line then slammed into the chain link fence, embedding itself there.

There were four of his balls embedded in the fence.

That was his mood that morning.

Another few dozen balls were littering the area in front of the fence. He had half a bucket left, sitting beside him on the baseline.

He was practicing his serve.

He should be calling Mika, apologizing for acting like a child, and getting the details about whatever she had on Andrew so he could help her decide what to do about it.

Actually, first, he should be calling Paloma and embarking on the difficult conversation that included explaining that he didn't feel they were at a place in their relationship where he was ready for them to move in together.

And further explaining that he didn't feel they'd ever get to that place.

Neither call was something he was chomping at the bit to do, which was why he was taking his foul mood out on a court.

Unusually for him, he was procrastinating.

The moving-in-together proposal was Paloma's, something that caught him off guard.

She lived in New York, though she spent quite a bit of time in LA and Europe, mostly in Spain with her mother, or Denmark, with her father.

Phoenix was not on her normal trajectory.

However now, she'd visit when she was going to or leaving LA. And if he thought about it, which he hadn't until she made her request, those visits had been coming more frequently lately.

But the fact that she wanted to move there, into his house, with him, was not something he was expecting.

And he felt like an ass, because he was assuming she was where he was in their relationship, and clearly, that was not the case.

He enjoyed her company. When they spent time together, it was good, easy, undemanding. They had some of the same friends and some of the same interests, which was always beneficial when you spent time with someone.

But it wasn't serious.

She was company, not a partner. He wouldn't even describe her as a companion in the strictest sense of that concept.

When they were apart, they texted sparingly, spoke on the phone even less, simply remaining in touch and loosely connected. For the most part, their relationship was one contacting the other because there was an event, and they'd fallen into a pattern of attending those together, or they were going to be in the same town, and they were arranging to see one another.

And that time together was spent having sex, going out to dinner when Tom didn't want to cook because Paloma simply didn't cook, and him doing his thing while she did hers at a spa or Scottsdale Fashion Square or sitting with a magazine by his pool.

He thought he was company for her as well. Their paths crossed when there was a reason for them to cross or they were in one or the other's zone.

And nothing more.

They'd never even discussed the concept exclusive, because that wasn't where at least he thought they were heading.

Further, there was no passion. Nothing deep nor meaningful. She wasn't a deep person. Some people weren't and that didn't make them bad people, it was just not the kind of person that Tom would commit to. They'd shared some history, but no hopes or desires, regrets, dreams.

She was an only child with no children, and considering she was fifty-one years old, would likely not be starting a family.

And she'd been in his life for nearly a year, and he didn't know if she'd ever wanted a child, or even if she'd hit menopause. She'd side-stepped his question about family when he'd asked, and thinking it might be a sensitive question, he didn't ask again. And she kept personal things to herself like they'd just started seeing each other, rather than them being comfortable around each other.

Which, Tom felt, said a lot about their relationship. Not everyone was free with using the bathroom with the door open or asking their man to go out and buy them tampons or stowing some in his bathroom should the need arise or sharing they didn't need them anymore. But all were certainly indicators of what level of intimacy you felt you had with a lover.

She was a good person, however. Attentive, quiet, pleasant. She was beautiful to look at and good in bed, the last in a practiced way that was enjoyable, but never fiery or explosive. Not only in the way he responded to her, but in the way she responded to him.

To end, he liked her, he'd enjoyed the time they spent together, but moving in together was out of the question.

He didn't love her. He wasn't going to fall in love with her. And because of these things, he certainly wasn't going to live with her.

Though, as perplexing as it was that she'd make the request to take their relationship to a different level, because she'd given no sign her feelings ran any deeper than his did, he was avoiding having that uncomfortable conversation.

He was because, at this juncture, it should include him ending their relationship.

If she was at that place and he was not and further knew he never would be, the best thing he could do for her was end it.

He intended to do that.

He just was not looking forward to it.

Though, he should sort himself out, especially considering he'd decided to go to a public court, rather than the one at his club, and he now had an audience. And he was acting less like he was practicing his serve and more like he wanted to murder someone with a tennis ball.

A young, gangly Black kid, maybe ten years old, was watching him.

The kid was so young, he wasn't even born when Tom was competing.

Still, he didn't hide he was watching, and Tom took every opportunity he was afforded to turn kids on to physical fitness, especially tennis.

In a second, he'd pull himself together and ask if he was interested in serving a few. And since the kid was carrying a racket, maybe they could do a volley.

With this in mind, he set up the serve and followed through, running forward with the momentum of his swing.

That was when he saw it.

A kitten tripping and rolling over some of his spent tennis balls.

Not a cat.

A kitten, a tiny one, apparently out by itself on a public tennis court.

He stared at it, feeling a prickle at the back of his neck as he watched it move.

He turned his head to the kid and pointed at the animal.

"That kitten yours?"

The kid was studying Tom's bucket of balls, but when Tom called, he looked to where Tom was pointing.

Back to Tom, "No, sir!"

Tom returned his attention to the cat, which had rolled off a ball onto its side.

Then he approached.

He was close before the kitten saw him, and when it did, it made for its escape.

Tom didn't stalk or give any indication of menace. He set his racket down, moved slowly, watching the animal's gait, which was ungainly, stumbling. Likely because it was a very young kitten, but also, Tom suspected, due to something worse.

The animal rounded the fence, and Tom did too.

It made its way over the browned, winter grass toward a line of shrubs.

Tom followed it.

That was when he saw the box pushed under the shrubs.

Which was when he stopped fucking around.

The kitten was in no shape to outrun him, and it didn't. Tom scooped him up and became instantly alarmed as he felt the weight of the cat, which couldn't be much more than a pound, and the obvious protrusion of ribs against his palm.

He moved swiftly to the overturned box, crouched and peered inside.

"Shit," he whispered, turned and shouted to the kid who was still watching him. "Hey! Can you come here?"

The kid started jogging, but Tom returned his attention to the box. Carefully, he reached in and felt around the pile of unmoving fur.

There were three of them, all of them had pulses, all very weak.

And none of them even mewed when they felt his touch.

Even if he found some way to get them water, they were too feeble to drink it.

But they needed fluids immediately.

"Holy crap," the kid said when he arrived.

"You have a phone, bud?" Tom asked.

"Yeah," the kid answered.

"Great," Tom said, and held the kitten he had toward the boy.

"Hold him a sec. I've got to turn this box. Then I want you to look up the nearest twenty-four-hour vet hospital."

"'Kay." The kid took the kitten, and immediately muttered, "He's like holding a feather."

Frighteningly true.

Carefully, arranging the cats as he moved the box, Tom righted it.

He took the kitten from the kid and placed it with the others, lifting up the box as he came out of his crouch.

"There's a place on Shea," the kid said, head tipped down to his phone. "It's ten minutes from here."

Tom was striding quickly to where he'd set his stuff, the kid following and giving him details on the hospital.

"What's your name?" he asked when the kid stopped talking.

"Clay," he answered.

"Great, Clay. Now, program my number into your phone."

Tom was at his bag. He put the box down, shrugged on his jacket, nabbed his phone, tossed the bag over his shoulder, grabbed his water bottle, all while Clay programmed his number in as Tom gave it to him.

"Will you do something for me?" he asked, picking up the box and beginning to move.

"You want me to pick up your balls and grab your racket?" Clay offered.

Tom had forgotten about them.

"Yes, that'd be great. But first, can you look around and see if there are any other kittens who might have gotten out of this box? Litters can be larger than this, I want to make sure we got them all, but I don't have time to look. These cats need care immediately. If you find one, call me. Then, yes, if you could take care of my gear, I'd appreciate it. I'll arrange to get it from you later. All right?"

"Yes, sir."

They were at his Jaguar I-Pace and Tom was gingerly putting the box in the front seat. He then unscrewed the top of his water bottle, wedged it into the corner of the box, and filled it with water.

He was right, the three who'd remained in the box didn't move, the ginger who was out on the court headed right to it.

"Are they going to be okay?" Clay asked.

His guess, no. Maybe the one who'd gotten out. He was in far better shape than the others. However, the other three were skimming the line. Malnourished and alarmingly dehydrated, their pulses were so faint, he'd be surprised if they survived the ride to the hospital.

"We'll hope," he murmured, closed the door and looked down at the kid. "Thanks, bud."

"No problem, Mr. Pierce."

He felt surprise the kid knew him, but he just gave him a distracted smile and rounded the hood.

He dumped his bag in the back seat, got behind the wheel, started up and headed to the hospital.

On the way, he phoned his daughter Sasha, because if any of those cats managed to pull through, he'd need to be set up. And since she had nothing better to do, she could get to the pet store for him.

The last he'd heard from her, which was the day before, she wasn't up in the mountains with her mother and Bowie. She was at her mother's condo in Phoenix.

She didn't pick up.

Tom felt his mouth tighten.

It was early Saturday morning, not yet nine o'clock, but she was probably still in bed asleep.

This was indicative of a number of concerns he had about his youngest. It was a weekend, it was, for some, still early, but she wasn't a teenager. She was also not in school. And she had no job.

There was really no reason for her to be up, she had nothing pressing to do.

But it was still time to be up and doing something.

And that was at the height of his concerns for his youngest.

She did nothing.

When he got her voicemail, he said, "Call me the minute you get this, Sasha. It's important," and he disconnected.

He drove to the hospital and hustled the box into reception.

When the receptionist saw him, her mouth dropped open.

Not everyone was a tennis fan, but most everyone was an Imogen Swan fan, so he'd had that kind of response his entire adult life.

He ignored it, set the box on the counter in front of her and said, "I found these kittens by the public tennis courts. All of them need IV fluids immediately. I'll take responsibility for them. Please, all efforts to save, not euthanize."

She was up and she glanced into the box.

Within half a second, she grabbed hold and hurried into the back.

He stepped away from the desk, pulled out his phone, and noticed two people in the waiting room.

One had a lethargic Boston terrier on her lap, the other had a black, domestic shorthair in a cat carrier on the seat beside her.

Both were women.

Both were staring at him.

He nodded to them, stepped to some empty seats on the other side of the room that were in front of a window, and he looked to the parking lot, pulling out his phone.

In an effort to contain his fury that anyone would be heartless enough to shove a box of kittens anywhere, it didn't matter where, rather than making certain they had care, attention and sustenance, he started to call his daughter again.

While he was in the middle of that, another call came in.

Hoping it wasn't Clay with news of another kitten, but thinking that was a possibility, he took the call without looking to see who it was.

"Pierce," he answered.

"Tom?"

Damn.

It was Mika.

Unexpected and he was pleased to hear from her, but now was not the time.

"Mika, I—"

His phone buzzed.

"Hang on," he said. "I'm getting another call. I'm at the vet with an emergency, and I might have to take it."

"Okay, I'll—"

He didn't wait to hear what she had to say, he took the call.

"Pierce."

"Mr. Pierce. It's Clay. I found another kitten."

Goddamn it.

He started toward the door. "Okay, Clay, I'll be there in—"

"No, I called my mom. She came to the courts with Dad. We got it and Mom and me are on our way there."

"Right, Clay. Good. I'll see you when you get here."

"Dad's grabbing your balls and racket and he'll bring them when he comes. Is that okay?"

"Perfect, Clay. You're a hero."

"I don't think...I don't think..." Clay was suddenly stammering, and Tom heard a woman say, "Give me your phone, baby." Then he had Clay's mother. "Hi, Tom. I'm Priscilla."

"Hello, Priscilla."

"The kitten isn't in good shape, Tom. Brayton says it's breathing, but I'm not sure it'll make it to the hospital."

"I'll warn them, Priscilla."

"We'll get there as soon as we can."

"Great, see you when you get here."

"'Bye."

She was gone.

The receptionist hadn't come back to her desk, so Tom moved through the door to the exam rooms at the back. He found his way to a large treatment area where they had the four kittens on an exam table. They'd already arranged heated blankets for them to lie on, and it was all hands on deck inserting lines, something that had to be excruciatingly difficult, getting those into tiny, dehydrated kitten veins.

"Hey, you can't be back...holy Moses," the vet said, catching sight then staring at him.

"Another kitten is coming in. It was separated, probably exposed, and it might be in worse shape than these," he informed them.

"Grab another bag," the vet ordered the receptionist, who hustled to some storage, then she was back to Tom. "We have our hands full. Bring it back when it arrives?"

He nodded and left them to it.

As he went, his phone made a noise.

He looked at it and realized Mika was still waiting.

He reengaged the call and put it to his ear.

"Sorry," he said to her. "Got a call another kitten was found."

"What?"

"I was at some public courts and found a box of deserted kittens. They're in bad shape. A kid was there, and while I took the box to the vet, I asked him to look to see if there were more from the litter that was dumped. He found one. He and his mom are bringing it in."

"Where are you?"

"A twenty-four-hour vet hospital on Shea."

"Are you sticking around?"

Was he sticking around?

What kind of question was that?

"I'm responsible for these animals now, Mika," he bit off.

"All right," she said softly.

"We need to talk but I'll call you later."

He was currently outside the front door, waiting for Clay and Priscilla.

"I'll let you go then."

"I'll call you later."

"Right, Tom. Later."

"Later."

He disconnected.

Priscilla and Clay showed, Clay getting out of the car holding a tiny kitten like it was priceless porcelain, but what it definitely was, was the runt of the litter.

Tom approached, and Clay pulled back protectively.

He read that for what it was.

"Okay, bud, let me just touch him, all right?" he asked.

"She's a her," Clay informed him.

"Okay, can I check her pulse?"

Clay nodded.

Priscilla moved close to them.

Tom wrapped two fingers around the miniscule chest.

At first he was worried, then he felt it, so faint, it was almost not there.

No time to waste.

"Let's get her in," he ordered.

He let Clay take her to the treatment space.

The vet nor the techs said anything as Tom moved Clay out of the way, and they stood side by side and watched them get to work.

"She's not gonna make it, is she?" Clay whispered.

"You want her to make it?" Tom asked.

"Yeah. Like, she's super cute and she weighs like, *nothing*. Not fair she doesn't get to grow big."

"I'll tell you something I know about animals. They feel things from humans. They understand us. They communicate with us. They sense things from us. They know stuff. And she knows you're rooting for her. So, since you saved her, I suspect she'll give it all she's got to stick with us."

The vet took the earpieces of her stethoscope from her ears, glanced at him, then to the door, indication he needed to move Clay out.

Fuck.

Tom took the hint and said, "We have to give them space to do their jobs."

It was clear Clay didn't want to go, but he let Tom lead him back to the waiting room.

The woman with the cat asked, "How are they doing?"

Tom shook his head.

She frowned.

Clay sat by his mom, Tom sat by Clay.

Five minutes later, Clay's dad walked in, Tom knew, because Clay jumped up, moved to him, and the man opened his arms.

Clay walked into them.

"How's it going?" he murmured to his son.

"I don't know, Dad. She's so *teeny*."

Father's arms held fast.

Tom stood too and made his way over.

As Clay tucked himself into his dad's side, Tom offered his hand.

"Tom Pierce."

"I know, man. I'm Brayton Davis."

"Pleasure," Tom said.

"You could say that," Davis replied, his lips twitching, his hold on his boy tight. "Got your stuff in my car."

"Appreciated."

"Not a problem. Though, I 'spect I should have taken a minute to stop by the pet store and get a litter box before I showed."

Clay looked up at his dad at that. "I don't think she's gonna make it, Dad."

Brayton looked down at his boy. "What kind of talk is that, son?"

Clay slumped into his father.

They meandered back to the chairs and sat.

The receptionist returned to her desk and said, "The vet will be out in a bit to talk to you."

Tom wasn't looking forward to that, at least not about Clay's girl kitty.

The Boston was called back.

The black cat was called back.

A pittie mix came and checked in.

Then a flop-eared bunny.

The pittie mix was called back.

Tom, Clay, Priscilla and Brayton sat and waited.

Tom was about to offer to go get them coffee and donuts when the door opened, and Mika and Cadence shocked the shit out of him by walking in.

He glanced at Cadence, giving her a small smile, but stared at her mother.

No kaftan today.

Faded jeans that had not been ripped in a factory, the split in the knee was from actual wear, and there were paint splotches and other stains on them. A mushroom-colored tank over which was a loosely knitted cardigan that fell down at the back to her ankles. It was patterned in a variety of rust and cream stripes and had wide sleeves. She was wearing slip-on flat sandals made with a bunch of beaded or metallic or braided bands, the same over her big toe. One necklace at her neck. Her array of earrings from lobe up the shell of her ear. Her golden hair was piled up again, but now there was a pattered scarf wrapped around, framing her face.

She looked born in State 48, tall, curvy, gorgeous, with her shining eyes searching his, open, concerned, gentle.

Not only seeing her, but seeing the way she was looking at him, Tom felt the jagged edges of his morning smooth out.

She came to him, but Cadence rushed him.

"Any word?" Cadence asked.

"Not yet, honey," he told her, getting up from his chair.

"It's been a long time. Hasn't it been a long time?" She whirled to her mom. "We live, like, a gazillion miles away. It's been a long time."

"She's an animal lover," Mika said to Tom.

"I deduced that," he replied.

"Hey," Cadence said to the Davis family, giving them a wide wave.

"Mika, Cadence, this is Priscilla, Brayton and Clay. Clay and I found the kittens," Tom introduced.

"And they're gonna be okay because they know we're rooting for them," Clay declared.

His mom put an arm around him and pulled him close.

After murmuring greetings to the Davises, Mika looked up at Tom. "This seems like it's going to be a long haul. Can we do anything? Go out and grab some food and coffee?"

"Or bagels," Cadence piped up and looked down at Clay. "You like bagels?"

Clay put a hand to his stomach. "I don't think I could eat a bagel."

"I hear you, man," Cadence replied.

"Do you have a cat?" Mika asked Tom.

"No," he answered.

She turned to her daughter. "Then we need to go to Petco."

"Rad!" Cadence cried.

"Mi—" Tom began.

"I want mine," Clay said hurriedly. "I mean, Mr. Pierce, can I have mine? If she...well, can I?"

"Not my call on that, bud," Tom replied.

"Like at this juncture we could say no," Priscilla mumbled, but her lips were turned up.

"The dog's gonna be pissed," Brayton said.

"Basil's gonna love her!" Clay declared, brightening at thoughts of a house-full-of-pets future, some of his worry washing away.

"Mr. Pierce?"

Everyone's attention went to the voice, and Tom turned to see the vet walking their way.

He felt Clay pop out of his seat, his mom and dad following him, Mika and Cadence closing in on Tom. He also felt the tension around him.

Last, he felt relief with what he saw in the doctor's eyes.

"Three of the ones in the box have perked up nicely and I expect them to fully recover," she said when she stopped close. "The last two are taking their time, but their vitals have improved and we're hopeful. I want them here overnight. I want them settled and to keep giving them the fluids they need. They're very young, I'm not certain they've been weaned. I want to see if they can drink and eat on their own and do their business. We'll call you tomorrow with an update."

"Can we see them?" Clay asked.

The doctor looked to Clay. "Yes, it'd be good they have some love and attention from humans." She glanced at Clay's mom. "Not sure they've had much of that."

All three of the women made a noise hearing those words.

But without delay, the vet led them back and left them with the tech who was keeping an eye on the kittens.

Tom didn't even make it to the table before the ginger who'd stumbled through his tennis balls, trailing its line, tumbled over to Tom in that graceless, endearing way kittens had.

He saw immediately its eyes were brighter, less sunken, and he had more energy.

"Someone's been claimed," Mika murmured from beside him as Tom started stroking the cat's fur.

Though, stroking wasn't exactly the word for it, since it was so tiny, it was more like a full-body thumb rub.

Clay went right to his girl where she lay on her side. He bent over her and petted her with such tenderness, Tom instantly felt there was all the hope there could be for this world.

Cadence was running inventory.

"Boy, girl, boy, girl, girl," she decreed.

His ginger was a boy.

"We need a cat here in A-Z, Mom," she decided. "Or two."

"We have three at home, and Ruffles," Mika returned.

"Ruffles?" Priscilla asked, having carefully picked up one of the girls, she was snuggling her.

"Cadence's guinea pig," Mika answered, claiming the boy.

"I'd fly them all out here with us," Cadence declared, petting the last girl, then explained to the Davises, "We live in New York most the time." She returned to her original topic. "But Mom says it's too traumatic for them."

"They're at home with Teddy and their routines, their favorite places, their toys, their litter boxes. Cats and guinea pigs don't understand the concept of air travel and they don't like change."

"Says you," Cadence returned.

"Says Moon, Ringo and Grohl," Mika shot back. "Seeing as they peed all over the house when we tried bringing them with us, and Ringo threw up every day."

"It was kind of a scene," Cadence admitted in a whisper to Clay.

Clay grinned.

"And we don't have a Teddy for the house out here," Mika kept at her girl.

"We can watch them when you're in New York," Clay offered.

Brayton looked to the ceiling.

Tom was the one grinning now.

"Nala will wanna visit with her brother and sisters anyway," Clay went on.

"Lord, baby, he's already named her," Priscilla whispered to Brayton, half worried, half looking like she wanted to laugh.

Brayton didn't look like he wanted to laugh.

He looked proud of a son who gave a shit about creatures weaker than himself and in need of love and kindness.

As he should.

"Then you'll have to bring her over to my place, because the others will be with me," Tom shared.

Everyone looked at him, but it was Mika who spoke.

Cautiously.

"Four cats, Tom?"

He stroked the ginger who was lying contentedly on the edge of the table, leaning against his hip. "I have a big house. I live in it alone. I have kids who live close, or close enough, who are grown, but they love animals. Plenty of room. Plenty of attention."

He looked down at the treatment table.

His boy was the only ginger, and he had little white footies.

There was also a ginger and black tiger, a gray, white and black tiger and a buff gray. And Clay's girl was a buff-gray and black tiger.

He suspected superfecundation.

It didn't matter how many fathers, there was no mother, and these babies needed homes.

Though, he figured Chloe would make off with one, Matt would claim another, and Sasha would want her own. But until she stopped crashing at one of her parents' homes and started to grow up and take responsibility for herself and her life, she wasn't going to get one.

No one, though, was taking his ginger.

"I don't see why not," he finished.

When he looked up, he saw Cadence beaming at him, but even though it was she who asked the question, Mika was giving her attention to her cat, her hair having fallen, hiding her face from him.

"We should probably let these guys rest and recoup," Brayton suggested.

"And we should go out to brunch and pick names and stuff," Cadence added.

"Brunch with Tom Pierce and Mika Stowe?" Priscilla breathed, her eyes growing wide.

"I'm in," Tom said.

"Wow." Priscilla was still breathy.

"My treat," Brayton put in.

Not a chance.

"We'll talk about that at brunch," Tom replied.

"Oh my God, we haven't even picked a place, we've barely even agreed to all go, and the menfolk are already marking territory," Cadence lamented.

Mika chuckled.

"Dad always buys," Clay said authoritatively. "Even with Granddad and Grandpops. They get into huge fights about it. Still, even if he has to be sneaky and they get all mad, Dad buys."

"We'll talk about it at brunch," Tom repeated.

"Over Easy?" Priscilla suggested.

"We should go to Jewel's!" Cadence said excitedly.

"That's not very close, honey," Mika replied to her daughter.

"So? It's Saturday and Jewel's is the best," Cadence returned.

"These fine people might have other things to do with their day," Mika explained.

Cadence turned to Tom and the Davises. "Do you?"

"Something more important than having brunch with the best tennis player of his generation and a world-famous artist and her daughter?" Priscilla asked back but answered before Cadence could say anything. "No."

"Then Jewel's it is," Cadence decreed.

Brayton sent him an "You okay with this?" look.

Tom nodded and returned the questioning look.

Brayton nodded too.

Thus, the cats got their farewell-for-now cuddles, they left the treatment room, Tom left his contact details with the receptionist, they all climbed in their cars, and they went to Jewel's.

# CHAPTER 7

## THE SECOND CHANCE

*Mika*

"Mo—"
"Zzst!"
"Mom!"
"Zzst!"
"Stop 'zzsting' me, and lis—"
"*Zzst!*"
"But he rescued kitties!"

We were driving back from brunch, and Cadence had dropped all pretense.

As she would.

Because Tom rescued kittens.

Not only rescued them, but he was going to adopt four of them.

*Four.*

And he'd tricked Brayton into letting him pay for our brunch, doing this by giving the money to Clay, who then decreed *he* was going to pay for brunch, something Brayton couldn't find it in himself to refuse.

"You're on, man," Brayton had warned Tom, indicating the new relationship would continue, which was probably one of the reasons Tom had smiled so big at the warning.

But it was cute and sweet and funny how Tom and Clay were bonding over their traumatic morning and how Brayton and Priscilla were encouraging it.

He'd also let Clay and Cadence name his cats.

The ginger was Ace (obviously).

There was some discussion over the girls, and for a while it looked like it might be Steffi and Marti (for Martina, my suggestions). But Brayton threw in alternates which couldn't be denied, and they ended up Venus and Serena.

The final boy was Boris, after Boris Becker, Clay's third favorite player of all time (Tom held the number two spot).

It was discovered Clay was a tennis fan (Roger Federer was his number one), and plans were made for the Davises to go to Tom's house the next weekend to see how the kittens were faring (as we all hoped they'd be recovered and closer to being in their forever homes by then). After, Tom and Clay were going to go to the courts at Tom's club, since Clay'd been taking tennis lessons for a couple of years and was at the courts where Tom was that morning to volley some balls against a backstop.

Dream come true for the kid, showing up at his local courts, and finding Tom Pierce practicing his serve there and ending that morning out to brunch with him.

Watching Clay live that out was pure magic.

Tom got a call from his youngest daughter while we were waiting on the sidewalk for our table, and he left our huddle to take it, which was very polite.

He also got a call from Paloma after we were seated (he told us Sasha was calling, he didn't mention Paloma, I saw her name come up on his screen).

And he left the table to take it.

Again polite, though I wasn't a huge fan of how my heart twitched when I saw her name on his phone.

But I learned something profound in that moment.

My heart had been banged around pretty good in my life.

So I could take it.

After the drama of the morning, the brunch was an easy and fun getting-to-know-you between us all, with definite indications that those roots of friendship would take hold and dig deeper.

I'd given Priscilla my number and we made plans to go out for drinks.

Brayton and Pris had given theirs to Tom.

Cadence had given hers to Clay (and Tom...*Christ*).

Worst part?

I feared I'd let the cat out of the bag.

My daughter was astute and observant.

But even someone who was not would read correctly into a woman who one minute, was sitting outside, enjoying a cup of morning coffee in the sun in her courtyard while making a phone call. And the next she was in a flurry, looking up a veterinary hospital and preparing to haul ass into town because a man she knew sounded upset regarding some kittens.

Cadence had asked where I was going, foolishly I told her, and she jumped in my car.

So now, she wasn't beating around the bush.

She understood there was something there for me with Tom, and she wanted me to explore it.

And I needed time and space to try to understand why I'd heard Tom was in the midst of rescuing kittens, his urgent tone registering somewhere deep inside me that would not be denied, and I thought of nothing but finding him and getting to him.

As for Tom, I didn't get the chance to apologize for being a judgmental bitch. I also didn't get the opportunity to warn him that Nora was coming and find some way that didn't include telling him about Paloma and Roland to share Nora was intent on breaking him and his girlfriend up.

Tom had someplace to be, it ended our party, he'd said to me, "I'll call," and then he'd sauntered with his athlete's grace to his sleek, dark silver Jaguar SUV. A car so perfect for him, I had a physical reaction to watching him fold into it.

The result of that morning's activities?

The drive from Arcadia back home was over an hour, we were almost there, and on and off through that hour, my daughter had been pestering me about Tom Pierce.

Thus, I'd pulled out the Zzsts.

They never worked.

I never quit trying.

"He's good-looking and he's got a great voice, and did you see how Ace just curled up by his hip like Daddy just showed up and all would be well?" she demanded.

I didn't need my daughter referring to Tom as "Daddy" in any instance, because when I saw the kitten do that, I knew who *I* wanted to be *my* daddy.

Christ, what was going on with me?

"We're friends," I told her.

"I caught him staring at you eight times during brunch. *Eight times.* I counted. That does not say 'friends.'"

I'd caught a few of those as well.

And they felt good.

"He didn't try to hide it, but you did," Cadence went on. "Still, I caught you staring at him five times. I counted those too."

"Okay," I said, just to get this over with. "I'm attracted to Tom Pierce. He's attractive. That happens."

"He's dope. And you should go for it."

"Honey, I don't want to talk about this."

"Why?" she asked.

"Because I don't know how to feel about it. Things between me and Tom are complicated. They always have been. Now he's back in my sphere, I'm feeling a lot, my head's messed up with it, and if you don't mind, I'd like to have some space to sort it before I talk to my daughter about it."

"Okay," she said agreeably.

I glanced her way.

She had a slight smile on her lips as she stared out the front windshield.

She responded to honesty and openness.

But that smile wasn't about me being honest and open.

Damn.

We drove the rest of the way home, I parked in the garage, and before I hit the opener to make the door go down, Nora took up position leaning against the jamb of the doorway to the house.

She was holding a martini glass filled with clear liquid and three of my bleu cheese stuffed olives stabbed with one of my gold toothpicks.

She had called that morning to share when she'd arrive.

As she'd caught an early flight, and we'd taken off to get to Tom and would not be there for her arrival, when we were on our way to Jewel's, I'd asked Cadence to text and tell her where to find the hidden key.

Obviously, she hadn't had trouble finding the key.

"Nora, it's just past noon," Cadence greeted after she jumped out of the car.

"Why do you Merriman women persist in telling me the time?" Nora drawled. "I own no less than three Rolexes, darling. And then there's my diamond Chanel, my Van Cleef Alhambra and my Chopard."

On her last, she raised her other hand and shook it at us, her wrist adorned with a rose gold watch that was attached to a deep-blue alligator strap.

I wasn't that close to her, but I could still see the moving diamonds on the face.

"Because you're drinking a martini!" Cadence returned.

"It's just past two my time. And just past two is known in my circles as 'Martini Time.'"

"Pretty much every time is martini time, isn't it?" Cadence asked as she stopped in front of her dearest auntie of the heart, quite the position to hold, as I'd fortunately been able to give her a number of them.

"Are you going to embrace me or continue to berate me?" Nora asked.

Cadence gave her a hug.

I got mine in turn, and we headed into the kitchen.

"Are you settled?" I asked her.

"Your guest suite is sublime. But your lack of staff is alarming. I had to carry *all three* of my bags down the stairs. I was so taxed with this effort, naturally, I immediately raided your bar."

I stopped dead.

"Three suitcases?"

She gave me a look and said nothing but, "Darling."

That could mean anything from "I'm staying a month" to "You know me, I have to have choices, even if I'm only going to be here until Tuesday."

I didn't have time to pin down which one it was, Cadence led us to the family room, one of my favorites in the house.

In that room, I'd allowed the ceiling between the beams and the fireplace to be painted pink after I found the fabulous couch in pink plaid. It was busier than the living room at the front of the house, homier, with lots of plants and candles and books.

Nora gracefully sank into the cream armchair angled to face the couch. I sank onto the thick pad of the wicker armchair angled next to it. Cadence sprawled on the couch.

"So we spent our morning flying to the side of Tom Pierce as he saved a litter of kittens, did we?" Nora asked drolly, rim of her glass to her lips, dancing eyes aimed at Cadence, before she sipped.

Apparently, Cadence shared more than where the key was located.

"Mom says it's complicated and she needs space to sort her head out," Cadence offered.

Nora's eyes drifted to me. "I bet you did."

"Behave," I warned.

"Why would I do something that boring?" she asked, but she didn't give me time to answer. She asked another question, "Were the kittens saved?"

"It's hopeful."

"Were they adorable?"

"Yes."

Her mouth hitched. "Indubitably."

"He's going to adopt all four of them," Cadence put in.

"Well, I would expect nothing less," Nora purred, and gave me a glance so filled with meaning, I stood.

"You." I pointed at Nora. "Drink and try to be the least annoying you can be. I know it'll be hard. Expend that effort." I turned to my daughter. "You. Entertain your aunt and don't get your hopes up."

Cadence gave me a salute.

Nora gave me a knowing look.

I walked out of the room and up the stairs to my bedroom.

My house was square with a courtyard in the middle. The bottom floor was sunken into the earth to assist in keeping it cool and to help it not make too much of a mark on the landscape.

Cadence and my domain was the upper floor.

My master was enormous, as was the bath that went with it, and it had a seating area that had a push-out wall of glass that extended onto a balcony.

My studio also was huge and had a balcony with a set of stairs that led down to the back garden. A magnificent and expansive space filled with prickly pear, barrel, ocotillo, pinkflower hedgehog, beaver's tail and fishhook cacti, as well as multiple varieties of yucca and agave, with containers filled with aloe, bougainvillea and hibiscus. All of this was dotted with a variety of mature, desert-indigenous trees that threw beautiful shade. The garden included meandering paths of flag-stone with unexpected clearings that had seating areas.

The plants were native and needed little tending, but I had someone come out and see to it occasionally when I wasn't there.

When I was there, however, it was all mine.

Cadence's bedroom and "space" were large as well.

Completing the upstairs were two smaller guestrooms with attached baths and a large storage area.

The lower floor included kitchen, dining room, breakfast nook, living room, family room, study and the larger guest suite that had a sitting room and its own private terrace.

The house was actually massive, over six thousand square feet, ludicrous for two people who were there maybe half of their time (and for Cadence, it was less).

But that was the point. Something completely different than our brownstone in the City, which was fabulous, tall but narrow and stuffed full of our lives.

This was not that.

I owned twenty acres. There wasn't a house or any form of humanity to be seen in any direction. It took us twenty minutes to drive to the grocery store.

This was freedom. And it was quiet. And it was air and warmth and darkness at night. And it was solitude.

And fuck it all, I'd bought it because it was close to Tom Pierce.

I pulled my phone out of my back pocket, curled into the armchair in front of the fireplace, and before I continued to be a loser and found some reason to avoid it, I phoned him.

Again, since he left brunch with something he had to do, I thought he'd be busy and wouldn't pick up, so I could leave him a voicemail.

He picked up on ring two.

"Mika."

Ah, hell.

"Tom, I'm sorry. I thought I'd get voicemail. I don't want to interrupt you."

"What I had to do was meet up with my youngest and have a few words with her. That didn't last long because it didn't go well. I'm now just home from Petco but on the Internet, wondering if I should spend over five hundred dollars on an automated litterbox."

"Left to perish, now spending life relieving themselves in the Ritz of litterboxes. I'm feeling this," I encouraged.

"I am too," he muttered, distracted, and I envisioned his long body stretched in an Eames chair, laptop perched on his muscled thigh, clicking ADD TO CART.

"Your chat with Sasha didn't go well?"

The question was nosy and not my business.

But I found it easier to say than, "I'm sorry I was such a bitch." Or, "I bought my Arizona house to be closer to you because I was going to approach you because I thought you felt the same as me all those years ago, deep down, because you couldn't really feel it due to you being taken. And now you're taken again, but I've wasted years, and I can't do it any longer. I want you in my life. However, I still don't know how to be friends with you since my heart's desire at this moment is learning the noises you make when I make you come."

You could see my dilemma.

He didn't tell me Sasha was none of my business.

He said, "She has no aim in her life. She's not working. She's not studying. She's twenty-one and living off her trust fund, and she can do that easily since it's a fuck ton of money, but more, she's either at my house, or one of her mother's houses, eating our food and using our water and electricity, so she doesn't have to dive into it much, except to buy a lot of clothes, put gas into her car and eat out nearly every meal she consumes."

Whoa.

Tom continued speaking.

"I broached how I was moving from concerned about this to being annoyed by it, and she told me it was not my business. I told her, as that's the case, my guestroom soon won't be available to her anymore, and that I'd be speaking to her mother and Bowie about following suit. She said she'd live with Judge and Chloe or Matt. She said they understood she was letting life guide her to her path, and it hadn't guided her to anything yet. But she had to be open to follow wherever that led. I said it had, to being a freeloader and a bum, and I knew my daughter, she was neither, so what's up with this horseshit? She told me I was acting like a jerk and demanded I leave her mother's condo. Since it isn't her condo, but I'd paid for half of it back when we first bought it, I refused. She left. I followed and buried my sorrows in cat toys at Petco."

I was silent.

"Too much?" he asked like it was a dare.

"No, though it's a lot," I admitted.

"Not your problem," he murmured.

"How long has this been going on?"

"Years, Mika. Fucking *years*."

I knew this to be true not only because there was no reason to lie, but because my heart dragged at how weary with worry he sounded.

Without anything useful to say, I said my earlier thought out loud. "Whoa."

"That about covers it, except you left out the shit, hell and damn." I heard him take a breath. "I was not measured with her. No excuse. I lost patience and I shouldn't have."

"You had kind of a wild morning, Tom."

"Is that an excuse to call your daughter a freeloader and a bum?"

"If she's acting like a freeloader and bum, yes. It is."

This time he was silent.

"I'm sorry you're going through this," I told him.

"She has something up with her. I don't know what it is. Her mom doesn't. Her sister, brother. We've asked, she says it doesn't exist. We're being too sensitive. We don't *get* her. But she's just bouncing from place to place, lost. She seems closest to Bowie's son, Gage. But he's a year younger than her. He's protective and he loves her like a blood sister, but he's hardly the person to give her sage advice or shake her shit and get her motivated."

"I don't know what I'd do if Cadence was in this kind of way," I shared.

"There's little you can do. It's agony," he replied.

And he didn't hide it was just that, he sounded agonized.

"Christ, Tom, I'm so sorry," I said softly.

"You showed at the vet hospital."

Well, damn.

Here we were.

"Yes."

"What was that, Mika?" he inquired.

No more procrastination, he didn't deserve it and I couldn't take it.

"Okay, Tom, I acted like an entitled bitch, not a friend. You're right, I know nothing about your situation, and I rushed to judgment. I shouldn't have. I feel shit about it. And I apologize."

"Apology accepted," he stated so instantly, I felt my body jolt with surprise. "Now, do we have to meet about Winston, or can you just tell me what this is about?"

"It would seem, not including my friend, he raped four women while he was on the tour and Core Point Athletics went to great lengths, and great expense, to cover them up. And I have an abundance of evidence that, if it's real, proves that true."

Tom was quiet again, but this was loaded silence. Immensely loaded. I fancied I could feel the weight of it, not to mention the heat behind it coming through the phone.

"Tom—"

"Just a minute, honey," he said with forced gentleness.

I waited and it felt like he took the whole minute and then some.

Finally, he asked, "How did you come by this evidence?"

"I don't really know. It was couriered to me the day I phoned you."

"Are the women named?"

"Yes."

"Do you know any of them?"

"Personally? No. Though a couple ring bells."

"Do you think your friend is behind this and has taken this course because she wants something done, but her name kept out of it?"

"She could be. She has means. But if she isn't, I'm loath to call her. It's a wound I don't want to reopen."

"Understandable," he murmured. "I need to see what's in that envelope."

"I'd appreciate it. I feel very alone with this, but something has to be done."

"Agreed," he replied. "But listen, I have to call Genny. We need to discuss Sasha. I think we need a family meeting. Once I have that set, I'll text you and we can arrange another time where I can look through what you have."

"This time, I'll come to you."

I offered that because it was only fair, he'd driven all the way out only for me to act like a jerk.

I also offered it because I was hoping he'd invite me to his house. I wanted to see where he lived.

Yes.

I was up to my neck in this, damn it.

"We gonna try to be friends, honey?" he asked quietly.

Up to my neck, treading fast, going under.

And the water felt warm and inviting.

"I'd like to give it a go, Tom."

"I would too," he whispered.

Did it get dusty in my bedroom suddenly?

"I'll text you," he said.

"Perfect," I replied.

"I'll make you dinner."

Oh God.

I wanted that too.

A lot.

I cleared my throat. "Okay, that sounds great."

"I have to call Genny. I'll get in touch soon."

"Awesome, and good luck, Tom. I hope you guys figure it out. Especially for Sasha. It isn't a good feeling, being aimless."

"Have you been there?"

"Yes. My whole life growing up. But the minute I took off, the minute I hit New York City at age eighteen, I figured it out."

"I'd like to hear that story."

It was ridiculous, and terrifying, how much I wanted to tell him.

"I'll give it to you over dinner."

"Right. See you soon."

"You will. See you, Tom. And thanks for being cool about me *not* being cool."

"Thanks for giving me a second chance."

"I think that's going to be my pleasure."

"Figure that will be mutual. 'Bye, Mika."

"Later, Tom."

I hung up.

I smiled at my phone.

I jumped out of my skin when Nora drawled, "See? That wasn't so hard."

I peered around my chair to look at my friend who was leaning in another doorjamb.

Mine.

"Jesus, have you been eavesdropping?" I demanded.

She drifted a reloaded martini glass out to her side. "Of course."

"Don't do that," I ordered.

"Lord, do you *not* know me? I left my island. I'm"—she cast a glance with just a hint of a curl to her lip around my room—"*here*. Your house is lovely. I'm getting very *Star Is Born* vibes, the good version. And you know how much I love Barbra. Nevertheless, it's thousands of miles away from Bergdorfs. I nearly got cold feet and demanded the pilot turn back, but then I looked it up and they have a Neimans and Saks here, and a standalone Dior in some mall, so I decided to brave the Wild West. Nevertheless, I didn't come out here *for my health*. I have a mission. And I never fall down when there's a mission."

"Tom and I have decided we're going to try the friend thing. It's all good. You can stand down and I'll book us into a spa."

"There is the small matter of Paloma," she noted, gliding in and delicately resting her slim ass on the ottoman at my feet.

"Obviously, he likes her. Maybe she's changed."

"And maybe I'll again get into a size seven shoe, after carrying my progeny laid waste to my feet. However, a plastic surgeon can rejuvenate only so much. I've availed myself of all the magic to be had in that arena, and as for the rest, I must live with the consequences of my actions. I sense Paloma Friedrichsen is the same as my *big fat feet*."

"Nora—"

She cut me off.

"Relax. Mother knows what she's doing. I'm like a cat. My attack is soft and subtle, though the scratch is horribly painful and bloody, of course. And when I'm in stealth mode, which I am, no one will even know it was me behind it."

"Did you just say 'stealth mode'?"

She ignored that.

"I also have a variety of reports in on this situation, such is the desire for people to spill the tea on Paloma. She's a walking, breathing, venom-carrying example of why you don't shit where you live. She's hated on five continents. And the word is, Tom and she are not serious. If a label has to be slapped on them, they're fuck buddies."

I felt my heart leap.

"Seriously?"

Nora nodded. "I have it from no less than six sources. That said, Paloma wants more. Tom is one of the few men around of his looks, wealth, fame and stature who's available and who'll date an age-appropriate woman because he has scruples and honor. She's fading and fast. Apparently, before Tom she went after Ned Sharp. He took what was offered, then discarded her like the trash she is. Rumors swirling were that he fucked her once and was not moved to go for seconds. So he's out. Unless she goes after Jamie Oakley, who apparently detests her for reasons *I cannot wait* to find out, Tom's her last and only hope." She leaned toward me and there was a very serious look on her face when she finished, "And she knows it."

"That sounded sinister," I whispered.

"Did you miss the venom-carrying part of what I said?"

I was beginning to feel very not good about this.

"I found out about her and my husband," she went on. "And then Roland ended it with her. We stitched our marriage back together and part of that was practicing extreme honesty. It would later come to light our marriage counselor was a quack, but that's beside the point. Roland's extreme honesty included him griping about how difficult it was to scrape her off. Pretty tears and pouty tantrums and avowals of love, which soon became threats and attempted bribery. That in the form of outright demands for money, or she'd talk to some journalist or other and let it be known to society that he was a cheat, and I couldn't keep my man faithful. Roland eventually shared with her that half the men of his set were fucking around on their wives, and if she did that, she'd never get another Cartier bracelet again. She quieted down and went away. But one must wonder what a desperate woman could get up to."

Yes.

Sinister.

Damn.

"Tom is not having an easy time of things lately. There's something up with his daughter," I informed her.

She nodded again. "And he's chosen poorly. The best thing to do when you make a mistake, however, is cut your losses and move on as soon as you can."

"Can you let me broach this with him?" I tried.

She took a sip, eyeing me, then she said, "Oh, I see. You've refused him to be a part of your life for decades, you let him in, and then tell him, 'By the way, *friend*, your girlfriend is a conniving *witch*. You need to cut her loose.' Is that how it's going to go?"

"Well, obviously, I was going to give us some time to feel out our friendship before I shared the bad news," I retorted.

"Darling, listen to Mother. Operations such as this are best *clandestine*. Trust me."

"And that says, 'Let's be good friends'? Me a part of doing shit behind his back?"

She looked aghast and held her martini glass to her chest in lieu of clutching her pearls.

"*I'm* not going to involve *you*," she replied.

"Nora—"

"It'll *allllll* be fine."

"Nora," I snapped. "He means something to me and I'm finally going to let myself have him. Maybe it's not how I want him, but he saved then adopted four fucking cats today. No, *kittens*. For the next two years...or more...every stick of furniture in his house will be in danger of being ripped to shreds and every breakable belonging shattered. He can't travel without making certain they're cared for. He can't wake up without one of his first thoughts being his babies need feeding. This could last for the next fifteen to twenty years of his life. He made that decision without blinking and had just gotten home from Petco when I called. He was considering buying a five-hundred-dollar litterbox. He's *that* man, Nora, and I want that man in my life. So give me this without fucking it up. *Please.*"

"I won't fuck anything up, baby," she said softly.

"Well, thank you," I bit out.

"I believe you need a martini," she noted.

"I believe you're right."

"Can we still do the spa thing?" she asked as she rose, reaching out a hand to help me from my chair.

"Definitely."

"Cadence must go with us," she decreed.

"She's here but still in school. She's supposed to be studying."

Nora rolled her eyes.

"Darling, I took my girls out of class for spa days at least twice a semester," she informed me. "It's exasperating to have to go in the evenings or on weekends when all the working riffraff is in the way. And a girl has to have a facial and all her bits waxed, and she shouldn't have to wait for school breaks or mingle with the rabble to get them."

She gave a faux shiver as she preceded me down the stairs.

"I don't know if I love you because you're so horrible and someone needs to love you, or if I love you because you're so good at pretending to be horrible."

"That's me, keep them guessing," she said breezily as she swanned toward the family room, calling, "Your mother has declared it Martini Time for all!"

I heard Cadence call back.

"Dope!"

Nora had been serving my daughter alcohol since she was sixteen.

Considering the fact she was already probably sneaking it with her friends, I didn't mind. Her doing it with adult supervision and learning through example and consumption was a lot better than her getting blotto and being prey to whatever monsters were lurking out of sight of mothers.

Therefore, in that moment, I smiled.

And thought that Tom and I were going to be friends.

I kept smiling.

Because it wasn't what I wanted.

*I'm responsible for these animals now, Mika.*

But I was going to take it.

# CHAPTER 8

## THE FRIENDS

*Mika*

*I*t was Tuesday evening.

I was driving to Tom's.

He was making dinner for me.

I was going to see where he lived.

I was going to spend an entire evening, just him and me.

And something was the matter with me.

Stopped at a light, I glanced, and my nav told me I'd be at his house in seven minutes.

I instantly felt worse.

*Way* worse.

I pushed some buttons on the screen on my dash and phoned Nora.

Her voice filled my car.

"Darling, why are you calling? Is everything all right? Have you arrived? What's going on?"

"I think I have to cancel. I'm feeling weird."

"I told you not to eat that fourth crab Rangoon last night," she said.

"No. It's not my stomach. I've got this strange"—I put a hand to my sternum and rubbed—"tightness."

"Where?"

"In my chest. It's kind of hard to breathe. Do you think I should find an Urgent Care?"

Nora didn't answer.

"Nora?" I called. "I've never felt this way, and I don't like it."

"Darling, you don't need an Urgent Care. You need to come to terms with the fact you're human. You are the fabulous and fascinating Mika Stowe who owns every room she enters. But you are also Mika Stowe, female with female parts and female yearnings and female needs who's about to have dinner with a man you want to pounce on, you want him to want to pounce on you too, and you're scared he won't want that. Or maybe you're scared he will, and he'll do something about it. In other words, you're having a panic attack."

"This isn't a panic attack," I scoffed.

"It completely and totally is."

Okay, wait.

Was it?

"Every time I looked at Roland, I'd get weak in the knees. He was so handsome," she declared. "But the *sex appeal*, darling. Lord. He was *magnetic*. And he had follow-through. He was, quite simply, a superlative fuck. He was also charming. He was attentive. He was ambitious. He had his own money, and he worked hard to make more. He played hard too. He took life by the throat. And he wanted me. I was bewitched. Besotted. But I made a fatal mistake in falling in love with him."

Focusing on what she was saying rather than the feeling in my chest, I asked, "What was that?"

"I would realize far too late that I didn't like him."

We had oft discussed Roland.

But she'd never told me that.

"Wow," I replied.

The light turned green, and I moved forward with the other cars.

"Yes. We were lovers. And we were fighters. There was passion.

Emotion. Fiery. Consuming. To this day, if he came to me, apologized, and I felt the barest *hint* he was genuine in his contrition, I would take him back. Yes, I am that weak for him, which is why I still hate him so actively, because I miss how alive he made me feel, how desirable and glorious. But we were not friends. To be married, for any relationship to have any true meaning, you must be friends."

I was holding tight to the steering wheel, almost as tight as my chest was feeling.

And what Nora was saying wasn't making it any better.

Alas, she wasn't finished.

"Further, dearest. It's true. You are no longer that thirty-year-old lovely who had lived enough finally to be interesting, but still had perky tits and firm skin and no hairs growing in bizarre places. And yes, that is terrifying. You captivated Tom Pierce when you were young and both of your lives were just beginning, but it was not meant to be. Now, who are you? He's a man, of course he's still considered vital and charismatic. He has years yet to live before he'll cease to be a good match, though with his money, he'll always hold vestiges of that. You're a widowed mother, and no matter your accomplishments in your past, and the ones you'll achieve in your future, the accomplishment of having a heart-shaped ass, a wrinkle-free forehead and no baggage in tow is out of your reach. What could he possibly see in you?"

Now I was breathing heavily. My lungs felt caught in a vise. It was so bad, I was considering pulling over.

"But," she went on softly, "it's been a long time. This means you're out of practice. You don't understand it is categorically true that we, my darling, are not grape juice. We are fine wine, crafted by artisans, and we don't want a man who doesn't appreciate us. This is why good wine is so very expensive, Mika. It's a mortal sin for someone who will not understand how precious it is to be allowed to let it touch their lips. You're about to have dinner with a wine aficionado. Of course you're nervous. But you have this, Mika, because, you must never forget, you are all that's you, you are all you crafted yourself to be, and it is magnificent."

Okay, maybe I was feeling a bit better.

"Now, listen to Mother," Nora continued. "Pull over. Take three very deep, very slow breaths. Center yourself where you are, safe and sound in your car, talking to your wise and dear friend, about to have dinner with an interesting man. Then go make a new friend, my darling. I'll stick with you as you do as I say."

I made no reply, found a turnoff into a shopping center and slid into a parking spot.

Then I took in three breaths, deep and slow, and put myself where I was. Safe in my Tesla. In Phoenix. Four minutes away from Tom.

And I was me.

In my life, I had been dismissed and even scorned by people who didn't get me or my point of view or my work, or worse for them, the power I wielded by being self-contained and not giving that first fuck that they didn't understand who I was.

I had felt the jealousy of other women and other artists and people I didn't even know waft by me like a missed punch.

I had slept with who I wanted and spent time with who I liked and went where I wanted to go and followed my creative spark wherever it danced.

This had led me to Rollo.

It had given me Eleanor and Nora and Teddy, and most especially, Cadence.

It had given me my life and my work.

And now, it was giving me Tom.

"Better?" Nora asked.

"I love you," I told her.

"I know. It's one of my life's most precious gifts. Have fun, my dearest. Hugs and kisses."

And she was gone.

For good measure, I took another deep breath and slowly let it out, making sure I was good before I got on the road.

There was still a strange sensation in my chest.

But I *did* have this.

*I had this.*

I was revitalizing a friendship.

Just friends.

I suspected Tom would be a good friend.

And you could never have enough of those.

When I arrived, driving through it, I was not surprised by Tom's neighborhood. The homes were on large lots. They were sprawling and attractive. It was dark, but still, I could see there was tons of greenspace built in.

And as I pulled into his drive, I saw his house was remarkably modern with a nod to mid-century, but mostly it was contemporary. Clean lines. Beautiful stone. Interesting windows. Clever uses of wood. Nuances of Japanese stylings.

It was not a feast for the eyes. In fact, a lot of people would hate its razor-sharp edges and eschewing of adornment, focusing the attention on the architecture. The welcoming expanse of windows. The depth of the entry that gave a sense that you've arrived somewhere important. The subtle art of the Japanese box doors that covered the bays of the garage.

But what I saw was full of personality, even wit.

I loved it.

He had no grass, his yard was xeriscaped, which further made me happy.

What threatened to return that intensity of the feeling in my chest was Tom walking out the front door in casual gray pants and a navy-blue, long-sleeved T-shirt.

His feet were bare.

I did an involuntary Kegel and quickly busied myself with grabbing the handles of the jute grocery bag I'd brought. In it was a bottle of wine, the tub of snickerdoodles Cadence made for Tom that day (my little schemer) and the envelope filled with damning things. I also snatched up the handles of my handbag.

I turned back to my door just in time for Tom to open it.

The man walked out in his bare feet to open a woman's door.

Shit.

I peered up at him, did not quite manage to bury how fascinated I was with the lock of his dark hair that had fallen over his forehead, and my smile felt weird.

"Hey," I greeted.

For some reason, his lips quirked.

The Kegel that caused nearly gave me an orgasm.

Friends.

Just *friends*.

"Hey," he replied, bent, reached in, then pulled the handles of the jute bag out of my hold, dragged it across the space in front of me, threw them over his shoulder, then he took my hand and helped me out of my car.

He maneuvered me out of the swing of the door and closed it.

"Well, thank ye, kind sir," I said when he looked down at me. "That little ole bag would have veritably *crushed* me under its big ole weight."

He burst out laughing.

He then slung an arm around my shoulders and began to guide me up his walk.

I had no choice but to wrap my arm around his trim waist.

I tried not to process how it felt.

I still processed that it felt amazing.

When he quit laughing, he asked, "Is everything in this bag for me?"

"Yes," I answered. "As such. I want the bag back."

"So why the issue with me carrying it?"

"I would have liked to have given it to you."

"Sorry, honey," he murmured, though he was not sorry, I saw, since I was looking at him. I heard his lack of remorse as well, since obviously I was listening to him.

My snit was erased when we walked into his house.

General curb personality outside.

Tom Pierce personality inside.

At a glance, I loved it.

I didn't get the chance to fully admire his sunken living room, wall of windows with a view to his pool that included a seating area with firepit right outside the glass panels. It was sophisticated, but warm.

There were things about I wanted to inspect more closely. And I saw a ton of framed family pictures I wanted to inspect even closer.

However, a gaggle of fur was stumbling, bumbling and tumbling its way to me.

Tom let me go as I crouched down and endured the single most feeble feline mass attack in history.

I still couldn't stop myself from letting them win, planting my ass on Tom's tile and allowing them to crawl all over me.

"How's it going with this brood?" I asked.

"Chloe has claimed Venus, as she would. We FaceTimed, and Matt has dibs on Boris, which is no surprise. That leaves me with Ace and Serena once they're fully off the bottle and all sorted, and Nala goes home with Clay."

I tilted my head back to catch his eyes.

"They're still being bottle fed?"

"The doc thinks they're three to four weeks. Ace, Venus and Serena are at times lapping up a gruel of wet food and formula, so they're good. Boris and Nala are still on bottles, though they're drinking some formula with a spoon, and they're smart and perceptive. They're watching their brother and sisters and interested in what's going on at the bowls. I suspect they won't be far behind."

I tried to get pets on the blundering mess who were more interested in the lump of human play palace that had landed in their midst than getting love as I asked, "They're good roaming free?"

"They have separation anxiety, unsurprisingly. I created zones in the house. I heard your car come up, I moved them to their zone for the landing."

I glanced up at him and saw he was pointing at plastic coated wire barriers that were blocking the cats, and he and I, into their zone.

"When I move rooms, and I'm going to be there for a while, I move their bed and their things. As they get older, their zones will get bigger. For now, we keep it pretty tight."

"Every time you move rooms?"

He shrugged. "They're getting better. But if I'm out of sight, and they notice, they start crying."

"What do they do when you sleep?"

"We had no sleep Sunday night when they first came home. They were wretched. Scared of the dark. Scared of a new place. Light didn't help. Being in their carriers scared the shit out of them, which isn't surprising after that box. Setting them up in my room where they could see me didn't work either. Last night started much the same. So I got in their zone with an air mattress so I could sleep on the floor with them. They settled. I slept. It was a win-win."

Now my chest wasn't feeling funny.

It was just my heart.

"You slept on the floor with them?"

"I'll give them a few nights of that, then we'll be weaning them off it too. They'll get used to warmth and safety and food, and I'll probably wish I had an excuse to keep them locked in their zones again."

He'd slept on the floor with five kittens.

This man was just...

He was just a good man.

"Keep them occupied, will you?" he asked. "I'm going to check the kitchen zone and make sure it's still good."

"I...sure," I agreed.

He strolled off.

I watched with no small amount of fascination as he hitched one long leg, followed by the other over the fence that made the landing zone, rather than moving it so he could get through.

The kittens were still enthralled with the opportunity for thigh-aided somersaults and tumbles into a lap that I afforded.

For about twenty seconds.

They then noticed Tom wasn't there, and it was Ace first who broke off, trotted toward the kitchen and started keening.

Venus went next, Serena followed, Nala and Boris weren't far behind.

I got to my feet and scooped up Nala and Serena, which took their attention, but they still mewed pathetically.

Tom reappeared, things quieted a bit, and he claimed Ace, Venus and Boris.

"Follow me," he ordered, and at hearing his voice, the noise stopped altogether.

After he set aside the barrier so we could get through, I followed him.

There was a large, caged-off area in his fabulous kitchen, angled so the cats could see him if he was working behind the island, or anywhere. It was filled with a plush cat bed, a mess of a few blankets, all of this on top of something that was plugged into the wall, so one of those blankets gave off heat. Completing this were an abundance of toys, and a sturdy bowl of water kittens couldn't turn over.

Down went Ace, Venus and Boris.

I put down Nala and Serena.

They all sat on their behinds and gazed up at Tom in a way I didn't hesitate.

I pulled my phone out of my bag, quickly activated the camera, made my adjustments, shifted into position to fill the frame as I wanted it and snapped ten shots.

Tom strolled to the island while I did this.

The cats' eyes followed him.

I kept shooting.

"Wine or a cocktail?" he asked.

"What's for dinner?" I asked back.

"Spaghetti and meatballs, garlic bread and salad."

It was good I brought a red.

"Wine," I told him.

The cats were now wandering to various things of interest in their space, so I scrolled through the pictures I took.

I named the series immediately.

"Hero Worship."

"Normally, we'd eat outside. Enjoy this weather and the firepit. But for the kids, we have to eat at the counter," he told me.

*The kids.*

"That works," I replied, dumping my bag on the island.

He was pouring from a bottle already opened, and I saw he had his glass close by.

His wineglasses had a curved edge at the bottom of the full bowl, and they fit him and his aesthetic like they were purposely made for it.

When he handed my glass to me, I noted, "I like your house."

"It's getting there. I'll give you a full tour later."

"Getting there?"

He moved to the range. "Chloe, and a designer she browbeat into seeing her vision, set the stage. I thought I'd win Genny back. I didn't have interest in where I lived until that happened. It didn't happen, and I took an interest."

He pulled the lid off a pot, steam rose, the air filled with a toma-toey, garlicky, herbed scent of heaven, he picked up a spoon, stirred and kept talking.

"It's beginning to feel like mine and like a home."

I slid onto one of his white-leather-covered stools at the island.

"You thought you'd win her back?" I asked carefully.

He returned the lid to the pot and moved to another one that was steaming.

And without hesitation, answered, "Yes. Though, I didn't factor in Corey."

"Corey?"

He picked up a box of spaghetti that was sitting on the counter and turned to me.

"Corey. Thanks to Sam telling everyone, but I can confirm it's true, you probably know he broke Bowie and Genny up back in the day. And he put them back together after he killed himself."

The first part I knew.

The last part, I was astonished.

"How did he do that?"

"Forced them in a room together and admitted what he did via a letter from beyond the grave."

I was no less astonished.

"That was...that was all it took?" I stammered.

"First love," he murmured, shifting his attention to the spaghetti. "And more. History. Longing. All that shit. They were official maybe three days after they reconnected."

*Ouch.*

That had to have hurt.

"Tom," I said softly.

He twisted his neck to look at me.

"We don't have to talk about this," I told him.

"I cheated on her, Mika," he said, painfully direct, but I wasn't sure the arrow hit my heart, rather than it being embedded in his. "You guessed right. We lied to the press because it wasn't their business. She and I are good now, we've shifted to friends. I admire and respect Bowie, and it's odd, but good, that we've also become friends. It works. Am I happy with the way it turned out? In a way, no. In a way, yes. Now that I've learned to be honest with myself about it, I realize that it probably would be some form of this either way."

Some form of this?

"I don't follow," I told him.

"Our marriage was over," he shared, this news not astonishing me. No, it was downright shocking. "I was pissed why it was over, and I love her. You do horrible things to people you love. The more you love them, the more horrible it is, what you do to them when they hurt you. She left me but didn't leave the marriage. Just shut me out. Of her heart. Her thoughts. Our bed. It hurt like fuck. When nothing I did had any impact, instead of walking out on her, ending things, I struck back. It took me time, and quite a bit of uncomfortable reflection, but I recognize it for what it was."

He took a deep breath and laid it out.

"I did not stray. I did not wander onto the wrong path. I would like to think of it that way, but I'm a grown man. Anyone who does that kind of thing knows better, and they don't get those excuses. It was toxic and immature and fucked right the hell up. I'm not proud of it. But the truth of the matter was, with how impossible she found it to forgive me, and she found it completely impossible, and how quickly she reengaged with Duncan, it had been over long before it was over. That said, I fell out of love first."

As I sat there, stunned silent and processing all he said, he turned back and poured the entire box of spaghetti into the water.

He dropped the spent box on the counter, gave the pasta a whirl with a wooden spoon, stepped to the side of the range, turned again to me, and leaned back into his hips, crossing his arms on his chest.

"I love her still," he said. "That isn't it. It was that I stopped being *in* love with her. It was the Genny Show from the beginning. Even talking to her about how that was rubbing me wrong, she did not see my perspective, and it remained the Genny Show. She took me for granted. My part in that, I let her without much of a fight. And I'm not downplaying my part. I should have spoken up more, and I should have made certain she understood where I was at when it started to negatively affect me. But then she thought I'd simply hang around while she cut me out and worked through shit and didn't let me in on it. She took a break from me but did it keeping me on a string."

He shrugged.

I waited.

He continued.

"Maybe I'm too prideful. Maybe I should have tried harder to break through. But I think I was just done with my world revolving around Imogen, and because of that, because I'd given her that for so long, the wound of her finding it so easy to disconnect from me festered. In the end, we weren't meant to be. What we had, it was mostly good, a lot of the time amazing. For a long time, I was so happy it was almost unreal. There was a great deal of love and support and joy. We were meant to make Chloe and Matt and Sasha. The love we shared when it was there was beautiful, and I cherish it. But then, it was gone."

"But you thought you'd win her back," I pointed out.

"I was in denial. I am not good at failure. I failed her. My family. Our marriage. The woman I was with, the one who was not my wife, she listened, and she gave a shit, and the reason it eventually went as far as it did, I realized my wife didn't do either."

Now, that was an arrow I felt pierce my heart.

"Holy shit, Tom," I whispered.

He shook his head. "I'm not landing it on Imogen's shoulders. It sounds like it. But I'm not. There was love, and we stopped paying attention, and then it wasn't the same. One way or another, it would have ended up how it did. I wish like hell I hadn't done what I'd done to hasten that ending, but I can't change it. Part of me, honest to fuck, doesn't want to. Susie, who I met and became intimate with, gave me something I needed, and it wasn't an orgasm. I just wish I'd deducted the betrayal part from that scenario and came clean with Imogen rather than striking out at her."

"That probably would have been a better call," I said hesitantly.

He didn't respond to that.

He said, "The wildest part of all of this is that I get it now. Watching her with Bowie, I get what she needed. He's his own man, has his own thing. His business, his sons, his interests, a life he built that she fits into. But mostly, he's about her. He's that man. He's good with packing his laptop, working on the road, in his office in their house in LA, doing Zoom meetings when needed, and being at her side. And from what she's told me since, he was not that man before, which was one of the reasons Corey's bullshit worked to tear them apart. He became that man, because that was the man he wanted to be...for her. I was that man for her and didn't want to be. Was it a failing I was not that man? I don't think so. Does it make him less of a man that he is? No. It just proves my point that we weren't meant to be. We were when we were right. We weren't when it went wrong. Does that make sense?"

I nodded.

"So there it is," he concluded.

"That was all...very honest," I noted.

He tossed a hand in the direction of the range.

"It's important you have it for us to move on however that happens. This is a lot of food, but you can leave. I'll get it. I won't like it. But I'll understand," he offered.

"Tom..."

I trailed off because I didn't know what to say.

"You know, the thing I can't live with, I'll never be able to live with," he started, "is that I'm not that guy. But I allowed myself to be that guy. So now I'm that guy and I always will be. I can never change it. I can't take it back. And that's on me. I did what I did to Genny, our marriage, our family, and it doesn't matter what was happening in my relationship with my wife, that is all on me."

"How did the kids handle it?"

"They suffered. Chloe, silently, then it blew up for her. Thankfully, she'd found Judge before that happened and she had someone solid to take her back. Sasha, she and I have always been very close, so she came to terms with it quickly, though I worry what she's going through now might have something to do with it, and even she doesn't realize it. Matt was pissed. It's only recently he started to let me back in."

God, they'd been divorced for a while, separated for longer, I was sure.

Being estranged from your child that long?

It would kill.

"Christ, I'm sorry, Tom."

His brows went up in surprise at my words.

"Life is messy," I explained.

It was lame, but that didn't make it untrue.

"I may have behaved like a motherfucker, but I'm not a motherfucker, Mika."

He slept on the floor with scared kitties.

I knew that already.

"All right."

"I didn't think I was that guy, but letting myself become that guy, and watching the fallout I created, I won't do it again."

I was confused as to why he was so adamant about making that point.

I mean, *he slept on the floor with scared kitties.*

I got it.

The only response I had was to repeat more firmly, "All right, Tom."

He stood there for a moment, and all he'd been saying stopped being my focus, so it was only then I realized how tense he was.

"It's all right, Tom," I said gently.

"She's never going to know any of this, Mika. Genny. I'm the bad guy, because I *am* the bad guy. And it's going to stay that way. Yes?"

I didn't know why he was making this point either. I was hardly going to be hanging out with Imogen Swan and letting things slip.

I still said, "Yes."

"That's the consequences of letting yourself be a motherfucker," he shared.

"You made a mistake. You're not perfect. I'm switching stances and beginning to think you're being too hard on yourself."

"My son barely spoke to me for nearly two years. That's how badly I hurt him. That's how deeply I shook the foundation of the man he thought his father was. Trust me, I'm not being too hard on myself."

Another shot to the heart.

Disappointing Cadence like that?

I couldn't even think the thought, it was too unbearable.

"Okay," I said quickly.

He said nothing nor did he move.

I tipped my head to the jute bag he'd set on the island and informed him, "Cadence made you snickerdoodles. You seem to be rocking negative two percent body fat, but don't give them to your neighbors. They're worth an extra nine holes on one of the probably seven golf courses in your community."

The line of his broad shoulders relaxed.

"We only have three," he replied.

"Only three?" I asked, fake-aghast.

His lips tipped up, he shook his head, and visibly, the rest of his body relaxed.

I took a sip of my wine (excellent) and said, "I hate to be an ungracious guest, but you need to stop confessing all your crimes and feed me."

"Right," he said quietly.

"Can I help?" I hinted he let it go and get a move on with the food, but mostly our evening.

His hard part was done.

"The garlic bread's ready to be put in the oven. It's pre-heated. Can you slide that in?"

"You betcha." I came off my stool.

We worked side by side, though for mere moments, considering my one task was to slide a tray in the oven (and Tom made homemade garlic bread, it looked divine, I couldn't wait to taste it).

I got more tasks as Tom gave me a stack that included placemats, plates, napkins and silverware.

I set up our spots at the counter.

In their zone, Venus and Ace cavorted while Boris, Nala and Serena, in a kitten pile on the plush bed, napped.

Tom finished things up, we dished out, sat beside each other, and Tom told me to dig in.

I did.

It was delicious.

I was swallowing when he said, "It hurt like hell, listening to that message you left after the Elsa Cohen thing."

I suddenly found swallowing difficult, turned to him and whispered, "That was out of line and I'm so sorry."

"I wasn't fishing for an apology, Mika. I deserved it. I just want you to know how glad I am to have you back."

The tightness in my chest was long gone.

But now, it warmed.

I shunted to my left, bumping him with my shoulder.

He reached out, wrapped his long fingers around my hand and gave it a squeeze.

Too swiftly, he let go.

And we let it go and got on with eating.

---

WE WERE IN TOM'S SUNKEN LIVING ROOM.

The cats had been relocated into their local pen. Ace, Venus and Nala were napping, Serena and Boris were frolicking.

Tom was reading the contents of the envelope and freaking me out.

"Maybe you need to take a break," I suggested as his expression moved from stormy to homicidal.

He lifted his gaze (he was wearing dark-framed reading glasses, they were insanely attractive on him).

"Core Point has approached Hale and Judge. They want to discuss being major sponsors of a program that Trail Blazer is hoping to launch soon. They're talking naming opportunity. The kind of money they're considering throwing at this, their aim is to be synonymous with Hale Wheeler, who is Luke to Corey's Darth Vader, but he grew up as my son."

I knew of Hale Wheeler, most everyone did.

Hale was Corey Szabo's only child. He'd inherited his father's vast fortune upon his death. As such, Hale was now the richest man in the world, but wouldn't remain that way, considering he was redistributing massive parcels of his father's wealth. Due to these efforts, he was quickly becoming a sort of folk hero. A new-style Robin Hood with a more lawful way of obtaining the means, and a more thoughtful way of distributing it.

Because of this, he was fast rocketing beyond the richest man in the world to the most famous.

The fact he looked like a movie star didn't hurt.

Since I'd paid attention to Tom from afar, it hadn't escaped me in the years that had passed that Hale had been unofficially adopted by Imogen Swan and Tom Pierce, Tom especially.

I didn't think I'd ever seen a photo of Hale with his birth father.

But I'd seen dozens of Hale with Tom, from when he was young to recently.

There was something worth pursuing, however, at how forcefully Tom claimed Hale as his. And I sensed it didn't have to do with how Corey Szabo had interfered with his plans to reconcile with Imogen.

Though, I wouldn't be pursuing this now.

"Hale and Judge are thrilled and are considering this deal," he finished.

I said the only thing I could to this news.

"Oh shit."

Tom nodded, lifted the papers he was holding and shook them.

"We need to start with getting this authenticated. It's a very weird hoax, if it is one, and if it is, we'll have to move on to why someone would attempt to punk you in this manner. It would be beyond disturbing."

He could say that again.

"However, it looks real," he carried on, tossing the papers on his coffee table, and taking his glasses off in a manner only Daniel Craig playing James Bond could make attractive, though Tom did it with zero effort. He then dropped the glasses on the papers. "We still need to verify that. We then need to talk to an attorney. Once we assess if we have any vulnerabilities, and how we feel about those, then we'll form a game plan. But in the immediate, I must talk with Hale and Judge. I don't know how close they are to putting ink to paper with Core Point, but if this is what it looks like, they're going to have to pull back."

"Agreed."

His gaze stayed steady on mine when he requested, "Will you leave this with me?"

"To read without tearing your living room apart?" I inquired dubiously. "I don't think so. I think you need company, someone feeding you snickerdoodles and making you pay attention to your kitties, so you won't lose all faith in the world and then, perchance, hunt Andrew Winston down and string him up by his balls. Which, incidentally, was my first reaction when I read all of that."

His lips twitched but he said, "No, I mean just leave it with me. Full stop."

My chin went into my neck. "You mean, to deal with?"

"Yes."

"Take it off my hands and handle it for me," I went on.

"Yes."

That warmth in my chest was coming back.

However.

"Tom, I'm a big girl."

"I know you are."

"This isn't your problem."

"It isn't yours either."

"It was delivered to me."

"It still isn't yours."

"Well, it certainly isn't yours."

"I'm troubled this landed on your doorstep."

"I am too."

"I'd like you removed from it."

"Tom—"

"Please, Mika, leave it with me."

He'd said please, and even though the tone made it sound like an order, he was, in his macho way, actually *pleading*.

I was curled into the side of his couch.

He was in his armchair.

We both had glasses of wine. He'd opened another bottle, and I, personally, was on glass number three.

Dinner was exceptional. I ate so much, I didn't have room for a cookie.

Tom ate more spaghetti than me and had three cookies.

Men.

Conversation had been easy. Like that night at Eleanor's so many years ago, and then some.

He was an active listener. He was a very sexy-fun teaser. Mr. Eye Contact. And definitely interested in learning what I'd been up to and more about Cadence, and he laughed when I shared about Nora (they knew each other, not well, but like his relationship with Eleanor, Nora and her siblings still donated to Tom's summer tennis camp on their mother's behalf).

On the other hand, I kept us out of the heavy by letting him semi-third-degree me.

It didn't suck, bragging about my kid, or laughing at how hilarious my best friend was.

I did ask him about Sasha, and he shared that the family decision was that she either check into life in a meaningful way, or she was on her own. No free room and board from Tom or Imogen and Duncan, and Chloe jumped on board with that. Matt, who had plugged into the meeting through Skype, since he was in Indiana at vet school, wasn't sure, but no one pushed him.

If she didn't respond, the issue would then become, since Tom and Imogen still had power over her trust fund, when they'd cut that off.

That decision, if it should need to be made, was for a later family meeting.

We skirted Rollo.

And he'd said, "Your work is going to need its own dinner," which made me absurdly happy, not only knowing we'd have another dinner, but that he was interested.

Now we were with that envelope.

And he was a man who could eat more spaghetti than me, chase that with cookies, sport the lean waist and muscled flesh I felt under my fingers in the brief time I had with my arm wrapped around him.

He was also a man who felt it was his job to run interference for women so they didn't feel the unpleasantness of life.

I didn't know what to think of this.

It was kind to the point of chivalrous, which never felt bad.

However, like the kittens were his responsibility, not one he looked for, but one he assumed nevertheless...

What was in that envelope was mine.

Rollo was also a man like this. A Southern boy who could brawl like Ronnie Van Zant and cherish like Paul McCartney.

He didn't know what to do with the woman that was me. His mother was a ball buster, but she was also a wilting Southern belle, a dichotomy, it was my experience, only Southern women could pull off.

Rollo had learned early, though, that when I had something in my teeth, he didn't pull it out and cut it up into bite-size pieces for me, discarding any grizzle.

He learned to get a kick out of watching me gnaw.

Tom wasn't who Rollo was to me.

Still, if we were going to be friends, he'd have to learn.

"I can't do that, Tom."

Without hesitation, he nodded.

Then he asked, "Will you leave it with me for now? I want to read through it thoroughly. I've no idea how to set about seeing if it's authentic, but I'll give that some thought and talk to you before I call anyone in."

That I could do.

"Sure."

He sat back and took up his wine.

"I know one of the women named," he stated, and took a deep sip.

"Oh no," I replied.

He swallowed, looked at me. "Miranda Trainor. A friend. British. She was on the circuit. She was good. Not great. But she had a lot of talent. She had a career. However, she quit abruptly." He took another sip of his wine, tipped his head to the coffee table, and concluded, "Now I know why."

Goddamn.

"Dates coincide?"

"To my recollection, yes."

I studied him.

Then asked, "Are you going to throw a chair through your fabulous floor-to-ceiling window?"

"Maybe."

"Please don't. I like your window."

"I'll try to refrain."

"Are you still friends with her?"

"We lost touch around the time she retired. And, mind you, she retired when, I think, she was twenty-four. Whatever age, she was very young. In fact, it was shortly after the first time I met you. We were all in New York for a charity thing. She was at the show with Winston, Patsy, Rod and me."

"Shit," I hissed.

"Mm..." he hummed and took another sip.

I studied him again.

Then said soothingly, "Tom."

"It's unconscionable."

"Yes," I agreed softly.

"All of it. Core Point, maybe what they did was even worse. They sanctioned it. They sponsored him as an athlete, and they sponsored him as a rapist."

"That would make a catchy headline," I didn't quite joke, because it would, and such a headline would be devastating to their bottom line.

He took another sip from his wine before he said, "You're a woman. You understand in a visceral sense what a predator like that means. What a betrayal it is that any entity would move to protect someone who perpetrated such violations. Even attorneys who defend those monsters. Everyone is entitled to a defense, this is true. But unless it's a public defender who has no choice, any scum who'd stand beside a rapist and try to get him off is only slightly better than the man who committed the crime. I, thankfully, will never understand it in the way you do. But as a man, powerless against this continued plague, I can't even describe how helpless it feels that it just keeps happening with the apparatus in place to protect it. As a father of daughters, well, I think you get that part."

"I do."

He said no more, and I sensed he needed to sit with this for a while, so I didn't either.

We both drank more wine.

Eventually, Tom sighed.

Then he said, "If this is true, Andrew will never live it down. It could be he's still doing it, and someone will come forward where the deed was done within the statute, and he'll go where he belongs. But I'll not rest until Core Point Athletics is dismantled and ceases to be anything but a curdling headline buried in a newspaper's Internet archive."

"As much as it upsets me to see how much it upsets you, I think I took this to the right guy."

He was deep in thought, but with that comment, he looked right into my eyes.

"You absolutely did."

I smiled at him.

He returned it.

Neither of us really felt it, but the camaraderie was there all the same.

"Dinner at mine next time?" I offered.

"I'd love that," he said quietly.

"This weekend. It'll include Cadence and Nora."

"It's a date."

"You'll have to find cat sitters."

"Chloe and Judge will come down. She'll need bonding time. And so will Judge."

"Saturday? Six?"

"I'll be there."

"This has been a great night, Tom."

"Are we done, or do you want to watch a movie?"

I, one thousand percent, wanted to watch a movie.

"About half an hour in, I'll need a snickerdoodle," I warned as my way of accepting.

"Thanks to your girl, that can be arranged."

I smiled at him again.

And again, Tom returned it.

But this time, we both felt it.

# CHAPTER 9

## THE ENDINGS

### *Tom*

*T*om was walking to his office after leaving his final consult for the week.

They had a running back with a painful bone spur caused by early onset osteoarthritis. The patient wasn't feeling any of their treatment options, he wanted quick-fix surgery.

Tom wasn't a fan of cutting when physical therapy could alleviate the problem.

Mostly, he worried about an athlete who wasn't processing the underlying cause behind a concerning symptom that could lead to a variety of future complications, especially if he kept playing. Osteoarthritis was far from unusual for any athlete, and there were a variety of treatment options that didn't include opening up a body.

The man was in his late twenties, and Tom had seen how he'd flinched when the word "arthritis" was uttered.

In many people's minds, that was an old person's disease.

Strictly speaking, it wasn't.

Athletes, people in the military, painters, construction workers, dancers—all of them were at risk of early onset arthritis.

The patient didn't want to discuss that or his diagnosis. He wanted to discuss available surgery dates.

Cut and go was not Tom's philosophy.

His patient had lived a life of extreme physical fitness. Adding two sessions of PT a week to relieve pain and get the muscles doing what the bone shouldn't be doing was not a tough course of action.

But the season was over, the man had plenty of time to recover from a surgery before the next one, therefore, he wanted to cut.

Tom was at the time in his life where his paycheck wasn't about performing. He had a clearer picture of what the future meant when you did not need to be in peak physical condition, and if you weren't, time was of the essence to get you back to that place. He could now see the ramifications of not considering that a great expanse of your future did not include competing. He was fully aware of the fact that a career in professional athletics as a player was a blink of an eye in a lifetime. Decades would pass after you retired, and you would not want to live those with degradation of function or worse, chronic pain, and worse than that, future surgeries that might include joint replacements.

Not to mention, surgery was always a risk. Tom felt, if there were viable options, anyone should exhaust all of them before being anesthetized and cut open.

His patient wasn't interested in Tom's wisdom.

They often were not.

It was the same frustration a parent had, that frustration of a doctor when a patient wouldn't hear them, and in Tom's case, that doctor also being a retired pro.

Thus, although it was likely Tom would have made the same decision back when he was competing, he was feeling mildly impatient as he headed to his office.

Though, now that his day was effectively done, he was more than mildly impatient about something else.

When he was in town, and not somewhere calling a tournament, his clinic days were Wednesday and half day Thursday.

After he finished his notes for that day, and ran through emails, his Thursday was complete, and he was headed home.

He entered his office thinking about that.

His workweek, as it was, was over. He had Clay and his family coming on Saturday. Dinner with Mika on Saturday night.

As far as plans, there was nothing else on his schedule until he hit the clinic again next Wednesday.

He was a voracious reader, and he was into a good book.

He swam laps in his pool every morning. He played at least a round of eighteen holes once a week. He had four friends who lived close, two in his neighborhood, who were tennis partners. As such, he was able to get a match or two in every week. He also did bi-weekly weight training.

He had lunch or dinner with Chloe and/or Judge when they were in town, used to do the same with Sasha (he suspected that would be on hiatus for a while) or drove up to Prescott to see them, or Genny and Bowie, and to hike.

And there were some programs he followed on TV (though, he wasn't generally a TV person).

He liked to cook and try new recipes.

He'd hear of interesting wellness concepts, and he'd give them a shot, like hot yoga (not a fan) and meditation (he'd added this to his daily routine).

He wrote papers with his colleagues. He completed his CME credits. He had his summer camp, though other people administered it. He was a spokesperson for the Trail Blazer program. And he sat on a couple of boards.

Now, he had the cats.

Yesterday, since he was going to be at the office all day, he'd brought them in. They'd captivated the staff and weren't alone for long, but the alone times were good. They needed to be able to be without Tom, or anyone, eventually.

And that was the day's test. His neighbor had gone to his house mid-morning to check (and she reported they were fine, all were napping when she arrived—animals were survivors and perceptive to their conditions, dangerous or safe—humans could learn a lot from them).

They had to wait for him to get home.

But very soon, they wouldn't need him, and three of them would be somewhere else.

That was it.

That was his life.

Most would see that as full.

Further, he understood he was lucky and could afford to live as he did.

But Tom, who spent thirty-five years with an all-consuming singular focus, the next nineteen with a wife, a family of growing kids and two careers, now had an empty nest that felt very...

*Empty.*

He was at odds.

Restless.

And, frankly, unhappy.

He was a man who needed his time occupied, all of it, and he knew that about himself.

It wasn't that he couldn't relax. He could check into a book. Check out for meditation. Go to the driving range.

But he was goal-oriented.

Driven.

He needed a challenge.

Mika's envelope certainly filled that bill.

The problem with that was, he'd turned it around in his head, and he had no clue even where to begin.

He'd made a call to a friend to get some advice and was waiting for a callback.

The bottom line was, what was in that envelope was too important to fuck up, but he knew one thing. Whatever needed to be done, he didn't have the skills to do it.

Concerning him even further was trying to understand why it had landed on Mika's doorstep in the first place.

Something that was moving out of concerning him, and instead beginning to annoy him, was that Paloma was dodging his calls and vagueing her return texts.

She'd phoned once, when he was at brunch after he and Clay had saved the kittens, and he'd had to cut that conversation short because he didn't have time to get into what he needed to discuss with her.

Since then, he'd had no meaningful communication with her.

He sensed she knew his decision, and she was avoiding it. He'd left three phone messages since Saturday, twice as many texts.

The texts didn't go unanswered, but her responses were ambiguous and had no follow-through. She was out to dinner. A friend was in need. She was making plans to go skiing in Aspen, *You should join us, darling*, but his reply of, *I'd really like for us to sit down and talk* went unaddressed.

Anytime he made clear they needed to speak, it was either ignored or, *I'll call soon*, and then she didn't.

It was disquieting how little he cared.

He could end things now, or he could end things when she was ready. The result would not change, just the time it happened.

He still wanted it done, rather than allowing it to linger.

Because now, he had Mika, and he knew what he wanted to do with her.

And he couldn't, until things had been settled, officially, with Paloma.

He hit his office, touched his phone, and saw two messages on the screen he knew he intended to deal with immediately.

He started with the priority.

Opening the text string he'd begun with Mika.

His last was a picture of Nala from that morning's feeding. She had formula all over the fur around her mouth. It was a picture Mika had requested. Or more to the point demanded. She, and Cadence, wanted a running photographic report on how the kittens were faring, and Tom was giving it to them.

Mika's response to the latest was, *Cadence wants to learn to bottle feed. Can we come over and do that soon, before they're all fully weaned?*

*Absolutely*, he replied. *Tomorrow?*

He then went to the second text, read it, sat behind his desk and made his call.

"Hey, Tom," Jamie Oakley answered.

Jamie was Judge's dad, Tom's friend, and the person Tom had decided to reach out to try to strategize what to do about what was in Mika's envelope.

"Hey, Jamie. Thanks for finding time to talk," Tom replied.

"Always have time for you. But it must be said, your text was intriguing," Jamie noted.

Tom had been vague, but not about the urgency of needing to talk.

"It bears out, though not in a good way. I need some advice on how to proceed with something that's extremely sensitive."

"That being?"

Tom laid it out about the envelope Mika received, he did it in short, but he was nevertheless thorough.

"Well...fuck," Jamie muttered when he was done.

"That covers it," Tom agreed. "Now I need the information validated, without tipping things for Core Point or Winston, but also not triggering any of the women, if what was reported is true, or even if it's not. In other words, I think I need a talented investigator. But mostly, I'm calling to ask advice because I'm not sure what I need."

"You're right. You need an investigator. I have one in-house," Jamie replied. "She's exceptional at what she does. This isn't her normal line of inquiry, but I suspect it'll be something she'll...I can't say enjoy, but she'll definitely get something out of sinking her teeth into it."

Tom's phone notified him a text was coming through, he took it from his ear, checked the screen, and saw it was from Mika.

*Sounds perfect. Time?*

He was smiling when he put his cell back to his ear.

"Are you sure you want to be involved?" he asked Jamie.

"Can you scan and encrypt what you have so she and I can go over it?"

"I can have that to you this afternoon, or my afternoon, your evening."

"I'll give her a heads up. Let us have a look, and I'll call tomorrow. But I can say if it is what you say it is, I don't have any issues being involved."

Tom had not been expecting an offer of help, but he wasn't going to turn it down. "Great."

"You know, Core Point is interested in Trail Blazer," Jamie noted.

"Yes. I know. I spoke with Hale and Judge yesterday morning. I didn't share. If it's not true, I want the circle who knows about it to be tight. Neither of them would say anything, but both of them would want to do something. That said, I made the case for them to hold off on any final decisions, and definitely not sign anything until I feel I can have a deeper discussion with them about it."

"They were okay to hold off without knowing why?"

"Judge wasn't thrilled about it, but Hale knows me. He knows I wouldn't ask without a reason. He talked Judge around."

There was a hesitation before, "And if it is true?"

"If it's true, regarding Winston, I did a little research, and it depends on how the authorities would categorize the crimes. It might be too late to go after anything but his reputation. However, even though I don't know how I'll do it, I'll find a way to bury Core Point."

"I can help with that."

Jamie was not only a wealthy man, he was a powerful one. He could do vastly more damage than Tom.

That wasn't the reason Tom had gone to him.

But it was a bonus.

"Good to know."

Jamie let that sit before he requested, "Since I have you, can we talk about something else?"

That something else was likely Chloe and Judge's wedding, which was getting entirely out of hand, as it would since it was Chloe's. She was all about impact and drama, and apparently walls covered entirely by fresh flowers, thus it was fortunate both her parents, and Judge's dad, were all loaded.

This meant his tone held humor when he said, "Sure."

"It's also sensitive," Jamie warned.

That was confusing.

Jamie adored Chloe, and as such, indulged the drama at every turn.

In fact, he was more inclined to do that than Tom and Imogen were, he was so happy she was the one for his boy.

Then again, she proved she had the grit to stick when it was important, and she'd done that within days of meeting Jamie.

In circumstances that extreme, bonds formed quickly.

"Okay. Shoot," Tom invited.

"It's about Paloma."

Tom's head ticked with surprise. "Paloma?"

"Since you started things with her..." There was a long pause, "Shit, Tom. I've been struggling with this, not that it shouldn't be shared, it should, just how to share it. Now, too much time has passed, I'm worried I let it go too long and things between you two have gotten serious."

They hadn't.

"Jamie—" Tom started to reassure his friend of that.

"She's not worthy of you, Tom."

Stunned at that statement, Tom quietened.

"She hit on me when Rosalind was in treatment."

"Jesus Christ," Tom bit out.

Rosalind was Jamie's wife. She died of cancer. Jamie had been devoted to her, before her illness, during it, and still now, years after her being gone.

"It wasn't only inappropriate, it was repellent," Jamie continued. "You're not in the New York circle. It's known what she's like here, to the point she's shunned. When she did what she did with me, I wasn't surprised, but how it happened, it wasn't subtle, it was aggressive. And insulting. That she would think, when my wife was dying..."

He trailed off.

"Jamie—" Tom tried again.

Jamie cut him off.

"She's a leach. Fame and money. Maybe fame more than money. She had a career having her picture taken, perhaps it became an addiction. That adulation she received because she's attractive. I don't know her financial situation, but I do know she has no interest in men who are not extremely well off. She targeted Ned after me."

Tom sat straighter. "Ned Sharp?"

"Yes. Ned Sharp. Alex's dad."

Alex was engaged to Rix, Judge's best friend. She and he both worked for Trail Blazer.

This incestuousness was rubbing Tom the wrong way.

And what Paloma did was just vile.

"They had a thing," Jamie went on, sharing something Tom didn't know, that being indicative of how surface their relationship was. He hadn't asked her history; she hadn't given it to him. "But Ned's impenetrable. No woman gets too far in with him. It lasted about a nanosecond."

"We're not serious, Jamie," Tom assured him.

"Well, good," Jamie murmured, but the relief wasn't hidden.

"She asked to move in," Tom continued. "We weren't that, so I was surprised she did. Now, maybe I'm understanding. I've been trying to nail her down to end it. I'm getting the sense she suspects that's going to be my response, so she's been avoiding me."

"It seems fucked up to say I'm happy to hear it's over, but I am."

"On the other hand, I hate to hear she did that to you while things were as they were with Rosalind," Tom returned.

"She wasn't the first to give it a go, though she was the only when Rosalind got sick."

Even Tom felt nauseated at the thought of it.

And he'd taken that woman to his bed.

"That isn't right." An understatement. "But she won't be in my life, or any part of our family soon, Jamie. And that was a decision I made some time ago, it isn't about what you said, so that decision isn't on you."

"Again, fucked up, but again, glad."

"I appreciate you telling me. Though, I'm sorry you had to struggle with it."

"Sometimes, life isn't a lot of fun."

Jamie sounded weary.

And that sound dragged on something aching in Tom.

He knew both Judge and Chloe, and Judge's sister, Dru, were worried about Jamie. Worried he might not be moving on from losing Rosalind.

That said, the weariness Tom heard was indicative of something deeper.

He knew that because he felt the same weariness.

Straight into his bones.

His kids were grown, their life decisions out of his hands, but he still worried about them, Sasha especially. And even though he could change how he was responding to her behavior, and that might have some effect on her life, she was still an adult and entitled to make her own decisions about how she wanted to live it.

His wife was gone, for a different reason than how Jamie lost his, but he was alone.

And, likely the same as Jamie, he was uncomfortable connecting in any meaningful way again.

Jamie's first wife, Judge's mom, had been an addict. He'd lost her to her addiction. And many years later, both he and Judge had irrevocably lost her to it when she'd died from it.

His second wife he'd had to watch fade away.

It was understandable he'd be wary of broaching another relationship.

Tom, on the other hand, had done nothing to stop the degeneration of his marriage, and then he'd struck the fatal blow. He'd loved Genny. They'd had a good marriage and a beautiful family.

Corey's words floated up in his memory.

The last conversation he'd had with the man before he'd died.

*You need to fight for her.*

Tom hadn't fought for her.

He hadn't fought for any of it.

He'd worked and fought for every title he won, for his medical degree, to stay integrally involved in tennis. And he'd exceeded in his success in all of these arenas.

But he hadn't fought for what was most important in his life.

That aching thing inside him began to feel more painful.

Because Tom had been good to have the kind of relationship he had with Paloma. Only feeling relief that he knew his decision to end things was the right one.

Giving that space in his head, he noted it was almost inhumanly detached.

However, that wasn't him.

Just like cheating on his wife hadn't been him.

But he'd done it.

He wanted Mika.

He was looking forward to finding out if she could cook. He wanted to get to know her daughter better. He wanted to see the rest of her house. He wanted to watch another movie with her, and more beyond that. He wanted to talk books with her. He wanted to go to art museums and listen to her take on what he was experiencing. He wanted to tell her how much her poems moved him, how deeply he felt her films.

He wanted her in his bed.

And he had no business wanting any of that.

But until right then, that was where his mind was heading.

First, end things with Paloma.

Then, begin things with Mika.

He had zero emotional attachment to a woman he was fucking.

This right after emotionally devasting the woman he loved.

And using a vulnerable woman to do it.

"Tom?" Jamie called.

"Yes," Tom answered, now not mildly nauseated.

He was sick to his stomach.

"You all right?"

"Yes," Tom lied.

"I have time."

"Sorry?"

"If something is on your mind, I have time to talk," Jamie offered.

"I'm good," Tom lied again. "I'm still at the office. Need to deal with some things and then get that file to you."

"Right. Dru and I are headed out your way soon. Something about fittings or tastings or I don't know what's new with all of that. Dru stays on top of it. I just say yes."

"If you get invited to a tasting, and I don't, prepare to say yes to taking on paying for my half of this circus because I'll withhold in protest."

He heard Jamie laugh.

Then he said, "We'll talk soon."

"We will. Thanks, Jamie."

"No worries, Tom."

They rang off.

And Tom focused.

He wrote his patient's notes.

He dealt with emails.

He discussed what he needed to discuss with the assistant he shared with one of the other part-timers in their six-doctor practice.

He went home, dealt with the cats, and scanned all the documents in the envelope Mika had received, and not only encrypted them before he set up a cloud drive he shared with Jamie, but password protected them.

Only then did he text Mika to give her the timings of the first two feedings.

Given the fact they were dealing with a teenager, he wasn't surprised when she selected the one o'clock feeding time.

*See you then*, he replied.

But he felt sick about that too.

Because the minute he sent off that text, he got it.

He got where Mika was decades ago when she made the decision she couldn't be his friend. It would hurt too much, being attracted to him when he was unavailable.

He got it because that was why he felt sick.

He was attracted to her. He wanted her. Her body. Her mind. Her time.

He wanted to explore a relationship with her.

But he shouldn't.

And he couldn't.

Because she deserved better.

Now, in the short run, he was fucked. They were connected by that envelope.

But in the long run, he had to find a way to end it.

Ending other things, however, was something in his control.

It was also something he could no longer allow to be delayed.

And if Paloma wouldn't pick up, he had no choice but to circumvent her decision.

He did it by calling, and since she was still playing her game, he got her voicemail.

Therefore, he left one.

"I've phoned repeatedly, Paloma, and texted, making it clear there's something important we need to discuss. I sense you know what I wish to talk about. I hate to do it this way, but I think it may be best at this juncture to be direct. I'm afraid I feel we don't have a future. I would have liked to end things with you more thoughtfully, but this shouldn't drag out for you or for me. If you wish to talk about it, you know how to reach me. I'm sorry, Paloma, we just weren't that to each other. I thought you felt the same. But since you don't, you should feel free to find someone who gives you what you need. Take care."

He rang off and was considering taking a run to try to work through all he was feeling when his doorbell rang.

He'd lived there long enough, it had ceased being an odd sensation that there was no barrier between him and the world, something they'd had to make sure was in place when he and Genny were together, for her safety, and their kids'.

He understood after the fact that he had unconsciously, but nevertheless purposefully, selected a community that wasn't gated.

It was patrolled by security.

But it wasn't gated.

It had felt like a kind of freedom.

Now he was wishing he had a call from the gatekeeper as a heads up.

Feeling heavy, he went to the front door rather than to his room to change clothes.

The good news was, that heavy vanished when he saw who was outside.

The bad news, it was replaced by a jolt of foreboding.

He signed for the envelope, which was the same manila that Mika had received.

He inspected it.

Just his name and address on the outside, exactly like Mika's.

Nothing else.

"Do you know who sent this?" he asked.

The courier hit his machine with his stylus and answered, "Information, Limited."

Bogus.

"Thanks," he murmured.

The man jerked up his chin and moved off.

Tom opened the envelope the instant he closed the door.

There were fewer sheets of paper, and all of them were the same thing, albeit from different years.

Lists of Core Point board members during the years they sponsored Andrew Winston.

"Fucking fuck," he gritted, that jolt of foreboding becoming a shock of apprehension, as he saw, on each, one name highlighted in yellow.

AJ Oakley.

Judge's estranged grandfather.

And Jamie's estranged father.

Tom understood why he got this information.

But he didn't like the coincidence of his phone call to Jamie that day, Judge and Hale's relationship with Core Point being negotiated, and how that might factor in his nebulous-until-very-recently connection with Mika, who had incomprehensibly been recruited into this fucking mess.

He couldn't take a run because he had to call Jamie again.

He was not looking forward to it.

Though one thing was certain.

By tomorrow, Jamie's investigator would be all over it.

# CHAPTER 10

## THE CIRCLES

*Mika*

"This is proof," Nora drawled from the seat beside me in my car. "I have lived a fiendish life. As such, I have died and gone straight to hell."

"Yeah, it's pretty gross," Cadence agreed from the back seat. "But what are all those big green areas?"

"Darling, don't look," Nora said urgently. "Turn your eyes away or it might beckon you. I've heard its power is strong. If it takes you, your mother and I will be forced either to wade in and save you or wander along with you in a new circle of hell. I love you, my dearest, but if you're lost to it, I'll warn you now, I won't follow."

"Stop it, Nora," I ordered, then to my daughter, "It's a golf course."

"It's...pretty?" Cadence asked like we could answer her.

I really wanted to find them amusing.

I wasn't in the mood to feel amused.

Tom had backed out of dinner that night, and I got it.

But it didn't put me in a stellar mood.

"This is...it's..." Nora was so beside herself, she was stammering. Unsurprisingly, she got over that quickly. "Surely God, in heaven *above*, wished for us to build *up* as our way of reaching Him. Not sprawl *out*, destroying all He created," Nora noted.

"It's an affluent suburban neighborhood. It's built through the ingenuity of man, which is another of God's creations. It's one of innumerable of its kind in the world. It's hardly Dante's *Inferno*," I said.

"I fear we've hit the first level, or perhaps the third, or there's a tenth even Dante feared to explore, and this is it," Nora retorted.

She was also in a bad mood because she was a woman from the Upper West Side currently being driven through a suburb in Scottsdale, Arizona.

She was further the woman who, only under duress, would go to the Latin Quarter in Paris because, *"The farther you get from la Rue St. Honoré, darling, the more beastly things become,"* and this "farther" was pretty much just across the Seine.

I should have known Scottsdale would be too much for her.

She was also, like me, in a bad mood because Tom had begged off for dinner that night and postponed showing Cadence how to feed the kittens for today, Saturday.

He did this ostensibly so I could see Clay, Priscilla and Brayton again (though, the dinner thing he'd said had something to do with a family matter).

Upon hearing this change in plan, Nora had poured my eighteen-year-old daughter a gin and tonic, taught her how to get a perfect curl in a lemon twist, and they sat in my courtyard and dissected this dire news, probably correctly reading from it that Tom was limiting our time together.

He was, I was painfully aware (as were they), seeing another woman (Nora had shared with Cadence, they'd formed an unholy alliance—as her mother, I should have intervened, but I'd learned early intervening with Nora was nigh on impossible).

They then decided, while eating lobster mac and cheese and crab swirls (the first delivered direct from Boston, the second from Maryland, both from Goldbelly, acquisitions Nora had ordered before she'd even left New York, *"Because, dearest, you don't expect Mother to eat tacos for weeks, do you?"*—needless to say, these deliveries weren't the first or last *and* Nora had put Cadence on the case, and while I was working, they'd gone in to visit AJ's Fine Foods to "stock up" and *"Mom! It was rad! Aunt Nora spent eleven hundred dollars. I thought the cashier was going to faint!"* Needless to say, my daughter wasn't writing many papers).

I wasn't sure Phoenix was ready for Nora Eugenie Elizabeth Ellington.

Sadly, they had her.

I digress.

Over gin, lobster and crab, they decided Tom was putting obstacles in the way of us due to his extreme, almost pathological attraction to me, and his fear of commitment due to his failed marriage.

And they didn't like it.

On my part, I suspected he was in a relationship, his last ended decisively because he'd had an affair, and as such, he was not going to put another woman through what he'd put his wife through, not even a hint of it.

We were friends, it wasn't going there (ugh).

That said, not many women liked their men hanging with single women.

Tom hadn't even mentioned Paloma to me.

But Tom and I had spent precisely five and three-quarter hours together (I'd counted), and for two of those hours, we'd been watching a movie.

Maybe there wasn't time to share about his girlfriend.

Maybe it wasn't my business.

Definitely he was being ultra-cautious because he'd hurt one woman, and he was never going to do it again.

And that wasn't guesswork. He'd said it to me directly.

Much better to have me there with Cadence, Nora, Clay, Priscilla and Brayton to nurse a few kittens, and not be going back and forth between houses, sharing dinners, watching movies, getting to know daughters and tempting the fates.

I drove into Tom's drive with relief because we were there, we'd soon have company, and neither female in my car could complain anymore.

"I don't hate it," Nora decided while surveying Tom's house.

"I like it," Cadence decreed. "It seems very...him."

My girl was right about that.

I glanced at Nora as I got out, catching her now studying me with a gentle expression on her face that belied everything out of her mouth since we hit Scottsdale Road.

She knew me too well.

"We're *just friends*," I said for what felt like the millionth time.

She didn't deign to respond.

She turned away and elegantly alighted from the Tesla.

I did the same, though perhaps not as elegantly.

There was another car in the drive.

The Davises were already there.

Tom didn't come out this time to open doors and ooze sex appeal.

I was both grateful for it, and I missed it.

We made our way up the walk, Cadence going faster than Nora and me, mostly because I was dragging my feet and I'd clamped on to my friend's hand so she had no choice but to drag hers with me.

"I'd like you to be more careful with my daughter," I said under my breath. "She likes Tom. She's never been like this with a man and me. But no matter what you want, he's with Paloma. And considering history, I suspect he's going to guard that. We really are just friends, only becoming reacquainted very recently. So how about you take it down a notch?"

She turned her head to look at me through her Chanel sunglasses, retorting, "He's terrified of you. I understand this. You're terrifying."

"I'm not terrifying."

"You're all he wants in a woman. My guess, Imogen Swan was the same, and look at the mess he made of that."

"*Nora*," I snapped.

"Don't worry, darling. I'll behave."

She might.

She probably would not.

"My daughter?" I prompted.

"Hi, Tom!" Cadence cried, forcing us to stop our conversation before I got a promise from my friend to get with the program.

"Hey, Cadence," he greeted, then looked beyond her to us. "Mika. And welcome, Nora. Good to see you again."

Everything else flew out of my head when I laid eyes on him.

He was wearing dark-blue athletic joggers made of some wicking material and a white, long-sleeved shirt that fit his upper body like a second skin.

And I wanted to be on my knees in front of him in that outfit, except with the joggers down around his thighs.

"Hello, Tom," Nora called, then murmured to me, "Second circle, Mika."

"What?" I asked distractedly, tearing my eyes from Tom as we stepped into the shade of the tall overhang that jutted out at the front of his house.

She pulled her glasses from her nose, slid her gaze to me and said, "Lust, darling."

Yes, she knew me too well.

I might have growled.

She grinned and strode forward, raising her hand to take Tom's outstretched one.

"Cadence! Look how big Nala got!" I heard Clay exclaim from inside.

"So cute!" Cadence exclaimed in return and disappeared into the shadows of the house.

Thankfully, when I made it to him, Tom didn't shake my hand. He bent and kissed me on the cheek.

But when I caught the look on his face, I asked, "Everything okay?"

"Can we talk privately before I take Clay to the club?"

We hadn't been invited to the club, and as much as I wanted to watch him work with Clay, and just spend more time with him whatever we were doing, I felt there was a message behind that, so I wasn't going to insinuate myself, or my daughter and friend, into it.

"Sure," I answered, not at all sure with what I saw on his face.

He nodded, and with a hand light on the small of my back, he ushered me inside.

Greetings and introductions were made, Priscilla and I talked about how big the kittens were getting (and I'd seen them only a few days before, still, they were filling out beautifully and were forming those adorable, roly-poly kitten bellies), but Tom didn't waste time showing Cadence and Clay how to bottle feed.

I took this as a hint he wanted this done and he wanted us out, which may have been the wrong bead to take.

Perhaps it was time to feed, and he didn't want the cats to wait.

And he wasn't unfriendly to me. Still, the distance I felt between us was miles, even if he was right there.

There was making sure we didn't stray from just friends, something I understood.

There was being remote and abrupt, which he was being, something I did not understand.

And it didn't feel good.

"Not on his back, like a baby?" Cadence asked, looking confused as Tom helped her set Boris up on his belly to take his bottle.

"Think of how kittens feed from their mommas," Tom urged.

"Oh, yeah. Right. Makes sense." Cadence radiated a smile at him that punched a hole right through my heart.

I'd never seen her smile at a man that way, like a daughter pleased she made her father proud.

It was crushingly beautiful.

And I felt that.

Crushed.

She focused on what she was doing. I focused on pulling myself together. Clay focused on his kitty. Priscilla watched her son dotingly. I was doing the same with my daughter, though maybe for a different reason.

But Nora was yawning broadly (behind a hand, she wasn't a savage) when Tom's head jerked.

"You got this?" he asked Cadence.

She nodded up at him, expression serene, in kitten la-la land.

Tom glanced at me, I nodded too, in order to indicate I'd keep an eye, even though I didn't know how to feed kittens, and he headed to the door.

Since we were in his sunken living room, I stopped keeping an eye and looked to the door, fearing who was behind it.

Was it Paloma, there for a surprise visit?

Or was it Paloma, and he knew she was coming?

That would explain the remoteness, at least.

It would also be awkward, and weird, since he could just say she was coming.

However, hadn't they been together long enough she didn't knock on the front door, but rather came through some more family-like entry, or at the very least just let herself in?

I felt Nora get close and whisper in my ear, "Just friends?"

She didn't know me too well.

She knew me *too well*.

I gave her my attention. "Go away."

She smiled wryly and did not go away.

I heard Tom speak and again looked to the door.

"Jamie, Dru, this is a surprise."

"It is?" Jamie Oakley asked, his handsome face confused.

Well, good.

Not Paloma.

Family.

Or at least future family.

I had been to a number of parties and events Jamie Oakley had also attended. We'd met. We'd carried on a conversation or two. I'd known his wife slightly better. She was a lovely woman, and her loss was deeply felt in that circle.

Watching Tom invite Jamie and his stepdaughter Dru into his house, I saw that Tom was rugged athlete to Jamie's chiseled industrialist. They were both immensely good-looking. They were both urbane. But there was something underscoring that, perhaps it was ferocious ambition or a wicked competitive streak that was so ingrained, it was almost a physical feature, and that was what made them so alluring.

Although it was impossible not to notice his good looks, I'd never thought in that way of Jamie. He was always Rosalind's.

But she'd been gone for some time now, and he was adrift.

And available.

So that thought sprang directly to mind.

"Was I supposed to know you were coming?" Tom asked, closing the door behind him. "I thought we were meeting up in Prescott later this evening?"

And there were the family plans.

"Chloe told us to come here, not head up north," Jamie replied. "We assumed you were in on whatever reasoning was behind that"— his gaze took in the room, startling when it fell on Nora and me —"and you have company."

"Let me introduce you," Tom said, bringing them into the sunken area where we were with the kittens, who, with all this company to help keep them contained, were not in one of their zones.

"Oh my God, Dad, look at all the kitties!" Dru exclaimed, rushing forward.

On the other hand, I'd never met Drusilla Lynch.

She had her mother's flame-red hair, and she was stunning.

I didn't know the story of her birth father.

I did know her stepfather protected her like she was royalty, thus, me never having met her.

Drusilla caught up Serena and was cuddling her while she was introduced to us.

Jamie did cheek touches with me and Nora, but Tom stepped away and pulled out his phone.

"Oh yes, of course, his daughter is marrying your son," Nora declared after Jamie finished greeting her. "However did I forget that?" She turned to Priscilla and Clay. "As ever, it's like the beautiful people have magnets under their skin, they're so inclined to be drawn together." She dipped her chin regally to them. "You two know all about this, obviously."

Priscilla smiled.

"Don't know about me," Brayton said. "Live my life worried she'll get an eye exam and leave me in the dust."

"Oh, Bray"—Priscilla rolled her eyes—"*please.*" She refocused on Nora. "That's your cue to keep telling him how hot he is."

"I could spend all afternoon doing that." Nora placed her hand on her chest and assured, "But only as a connoisseur, of course."

"Please don't, his head barely fits through the door as it is," Priscilla replied.

"I'll just go over there while y'all talk about me, that good for you?" Brayton asked his wife.

"Perfect," she answered.

Nora chuckled.

Brayton caught Venus before she fell off the step she'd managed to climb.

"Chloe isn't picking up," Tom shared.

Jamie took out his phone. "I'll call Judge."

The front door flew open.

We all jumped.

"*Where's my baby?*" a beautiful woman who happened to be Tom's eldest child exclaimed dramatically as she strutted cross Tom's floor with a rat-a-tat-tat of her high heels and more swagger than Naomi Campbell on a catwalk.

Behind her walked a handsome man who, even though their coloring was different, bore more than a striking resemblance to Jamie Oakley.

This was because it was his son, Judge.

"There she is," Chloe said, making a beeline to Brayton. She held out her hands when she arrived, saying, "Hello, handsome stranger. Please give me my precious."

Lips twitching, Brayton handed over the cat.

Chloe held Venus out on front of her, inspected her like a jeweler would a diamond before they picked up their eye loupe, then she snuggled the kitten to her neck, cooing, "Don't worry, Mummy's finally here."

"Did I have a fourth child whilst in a coma and she was whisked away from me?" Nora asked, eyeing Chloe.

"Oh. Em. Gee. She's, like, so totally you, Aunt Nora, but not blonde," Cadence proclaimed.

"Rich brown to caramel balayage, my love," Nora good-naturedly drawled her correction which made Cadence scrunch her nose and smile at the same time.

Chloe took in the room, and the instant she caught sight of Nora, she declared, *"Mon dieu!* I'm in the presence of greatness."

"Of course you are, darling," Nora purred.

Chloe then looked at me and registered zero surprise I was there. None.

Did her father tell her about me?

"And Mika Stowe, my high school hero," she said, her tone now oddly subdued.

Not knowing what to do, I executed a little bow.

"You've got company."

This was a new voice, male, and it sounded more than mildly annoyed.

I shifted my attention to Judge Oakley and saw he appeared as he sounded, and his eyes were not on Tom's company.

They were on his fiancée.

"Yes, *mon beau.* Didn't I tell you Dad was playing tennis with his new partner today?" She indicated Clay.

"No, you didn't tell me that," Judge returned.

"It must have slipped my mind," she murmured, so openly lying, I nearly laughed. "But now, we can all go to the club!" she stated brightly. She beamed at Brayton, and still snuggling Venus, she held out a hand. "Hello, I'm Chloe Pierce, Tom's daughter, and his favorite, no matter what he says. Especially right about now."

I watched Brayton smile at her and take her hand, then I looked to Judge, but caught Tom and Jamie exchanging a glance.

I then felt something.

I turned my head the other way and caught the glance Nora wished to exchange with me.

I'd only just managed that when Chloe called, "Mika, Nora, of course you're coming to the club with us, yes?"

I opened my mouth.

I heard Tom make a noise like a grunt.

But Nora got there first.

"But of course we are. Wouldn't miss it for the world."

---

I WASN'T CERTAIN WHAT WAS GOING ON.

I was certain it was making me nervous.

I didn't often get nervous.

But now, the Davises had left to go home.

Tom had left Nora with a martini, Dru with a margarita, and Cadence with a La Croix in his living room with the cats in their zone.

And for some reason (this reason being Chloe asking me to join them), I found myself in his study with him, Jamie, Chloe and Judge.

At the club, I watched with a melting heart as Clay started out visibly—and clearly painfully—nervous to be playing with one of his heroes.

But Tom, an old hand at this, effortlessly made him comfortable to the point Clay was loose, laughing and joking. In the end, he and Tom beat Bray and Judge in the quick match they played, and when they did, Clay's smile could have lit up an entire stadium.

It was one of the most beautiful things I'd ever seen. I wished I'd had my camera to capture it.

I also spent that time drinking sparkling rosé and listening to Nora and Chloe riff off each other while Priscilla laughed and Dru giggled as all five of the men were on the court, doing things with rackets.

But now we were back, late afternoon had melted into early evening, I was hungry, had too much wine, so was also feeling sluggish, but all the other things I was feeling were freaking me out.

Judge was still peeved at his woman.

Tom and Jamie seemed half-perplexed, half-irritated.

I was just perplexed.

And nervous.

"Have I said how much of a thrill it is to meet you, Mika?" Chloe asked me.

She had, over sparkling rosé.

She was of the generation that was one of the first to "discover" me.

She'd read everything I'd written, read about everything I'd done, and watched all my films.

Chloe Pierce was a huge fan.

This was lovely, obviously.

However.

I opened my mouth.

Judge spoke.

"Stop procrastinating," he ordered his woman.

"Judge," she retorted.

"Chloe," he said.

"*Judge*," she snapped.

"*Chloe*," he bit out. "Spill it." Hesitation, then a growled, "*Now*."

Her eyes grew wide and angry color hit her cheeks.

"If you don't, I will," Judge threatened.

At that, she rolled her eyes to the ceiling before rolling them back and biting out, "Fine."

With that, she turned to her father.

I saw he was braced.

Because he was, I did the same.

"Right, Uncle Corey left me something," she declared.

What?

Why did I need to be in the room when they discussed family business?

Tom was now so braced, he looked carved from stone.

"What did he leave you?" he forced out.

"Not exactly some*thing*, more like some*one*," Chloe said slowly, obviously buying time.

"Baby," Judge warned.

"Ugh! Fine!" she cried. "He left me a secret operative."

Tom's head ticked.

So did mine.

Jamie's brows snapped together.

"He left you a what?" Tom asked.

"His name is Rhys Vaughan, and he…."—she turned my way, her gaze pinged off me in a manner that was, from my short acquaintance with her, entirely not her, and she turned back to her dad—"I'm afraid he's gone rogue."

"Chloe," Tom gritted. "Spit it out."

She twisted fully to me.

"I was the reason you got that envelope," she confessed.

I was already completely still, but I grew more so.

I stopped being that when I felt what was bearing down on us from her father.

I sat forward on the couch, holding a hand up Tom's way.

"Tom—" I started.

He didn't even look at me.

He didn't look at his daughter.

"Judge, explain," he demanded.

"It's what she said," Judge told him. "Corey left her some guy who is…."—he shook his head—"I don't know exactly what he is. Private investigator. Industrial spy. Whatever he is, he's good at it, very good, and he's at Chloe's command."

Tom turned back to his daughter. "And you commanded him to send an envelope of incriminating evidence to a friend of mine?"

"Well—" she began.

"Why the hell would you do that?" Tom asked irately.

Chloe was losing patience.

She proved this by returning, "So you'd ride to the rescue, *Dad.*"

"Shit," Jamie said under his breath, but he sounded amused.

I wasn't.

I was now not freaking out.

I was just freaking confused.

Chloe threw up both hands. "And you rode to the rescue, didn't you?"

Tom was shaking his head, his mouth attempting to form words, but apparently, he could get none out.

"Here it is, I don't like Paloma," Chloe announced.

I made an actual peep and slid to the edge of my seat because this was now family business, for certain, and I needed to make my escape.

Chloe turned back to me. "Please don't leave. Obviously, I like *you*."

"I think—" I tried.

"Really, please stay," Chloe urged.

I looked to Tom.

He was staring at his daughter and had rediscovered his voice.

"You sent sad and tragic information to a friend of mine to try to fix her up with me?" Tom asked incredulously, probably hoping she'd say it was all a joke and surprise! You're on candid camera.

"I was unaware what the information was," Chloe said. "Rhys simply told me he'd 'handle things.'"

"And she wasn't aware that Granddad was a part of it," Judge added. "Now, it's more. Now it isn't about Chloe playing at making a match. Now, it's clear Vaughan has a message to send. This isn't about Chloe asking him to do her bidding. This is about Vaughan seeing to a different directive. One, if I had to guess, that was given to him by Corey Szabo."

"Fucking *fuck*!" Tom exploded, making me jump by the violence behind it, and he stood.

He then cleared the seating area where we were all sitting around the low, glass coffee table that was covered in precise stacks of hardback books, from fiction to biographies to coffee table tomes, and he started pacing in front of the desk at the end of the room.

I stood too.

"Tom, maybe I should—" I tried again.

That was as far as I got.

Chloe stood as well. "Mika, truly, you—"

Tom stopped pacing and announced, "Chloe, Paloma is out."

I went stock still.

Though my heart took a giant leap.

"I ended things with her," Tom continued. "I didn't tell you because my love life really isn't your concern."

"*Mon père*—" she started.

Tom cut her off.

"Don't be cute. Don't be clever. Don't be glib." He raked his hand through his hair, and said gently but exasperatedly, "You fucked up this time, honey."

His daughter stubbornly crossed her arms on her chest.

"You set this in motion," Tom reminded her. "Now, we have that information, and we have to do something about it. And that something implicates your future husband's grandfather."

"I think I might be missing something," I noted.

Tom looked to me. "I was going to speak to you about it before we went to the club. On Thursday, I got another envelope. I'd already asked for Jamie's help. When I saw this new information, I had to go to him again. We also had to share fully with Judge and Hale. Jamie got his investigator on it, and she discovered a few things. The information in the second envelope I received was that AJ Oakley, Jamie's father, Judge's grandfather, sat on the board of Core Point Athletics during the years they were sponsoring Andrew Winston."

"Oh shit," I muttered.

"Yes," Tom agreed. "Worse, from some of the shorthand on the notes in the envelope you received, we think it was at AJ's instigation, and through his direct machinations, Core Point moved to quiet those women by paying them off."

"Well, hell," I whispered.

"Yes," Tom repeated. "And AJ did something to hurt somebody Chloe loves." He jerked his head to Chloe then threw his hand out to indicate the room, primarily Judge as well as Jamie. "Several somebodies in this case." Tom drew in a big breath. "And Corey Szabo did not stand idly by and allow people he loved to be hurt."

I sucked my lips in between my teeth.

I did this mostly because I was impressed Corey Szabo felt so deeply, and he made that clear even after he was gone, and further did it in such a badass manner, leaving some talented operative at the beck and call of his loved ones.

I partly did this because I wanted badly to burst out laughing, but I didn't think that would go over very well at that juncture.

Sadly, Tom read it for what it was.

"You think this is funny?" he asked.

I let my lips go and said, "I'm sorry, Tom. I don't think it's funny... as such."

I totally did.

I knew AJ Oakley.

He'd hit on me, twice.

He was old enough to be my father.

He was putrescent.

He was everything wrong with masculinity, rolled up in a stubby, beer-bellied body and shoved under a cowboy hat.

I despised him.

Not just because he hit on me, but because he was a revolting individual who said monstrous things, did heinous deeds, hurt shocking amounts of people, and got away with it because he was rich and white and male.

It did not surprise me in the slightest that he was behind Core Point silencing those women.

In fact, knowing he was in on it, the aggression of those endeavors came even more clear.

I did not know Jamie well, but what I knew of him, I liked. And although Judge was understandably perturbed with his fiancée, he seemed a good guy too. I would not want them to feel any pain through this.

But if AJ was one of the many bad actors who was brought low when the Winston/Core Point situations saw the light of day, I would buy an expensive bottle of champagne and toast the fuck out of it.

"I'm not close with my father, Mika."

That was Jamie.

I looked down to see him sprawled at an angle in one of Tom's armchairs that sat opposite the couch Chloe and I were no longer sitting on. One of Jamie's legs was crossed over the other, and if I didn't know better, I'd think he owned the house in which he sat.

Now *that* was attractive.

It was fixed, natural, part of his personality to be at one with his surroundings and confident in them.

His father would probably have pissed in the corners before he took his seat, then when you protested, he told you to like it, or he'd rub your nose in it.

"In fact, I'm very close to impoverishing him," Jamie went on.

I sat with a plop.

"Whoa," I said once I was down.

"This..." he paused, "*information* isn't another nail in his casket. It's a stake through his heart." He held my gaze. "And if I can manage to do it without harm to the women involved, I will drive it home."

Whoa wasn't the word for it.

Hot damn was.

Remind me not to get on Jamie Oakley's bad side.

Or Corey Szabo's, even if the man was dead.

"Are you all like that show *Yellowstone*, but without the cattle?" I asked after a show I'd never watched, but Nora waxed poetic about it at length.

She watched every episode the instant it aired.

And then she watched it again.

After that, she called me and cackled about it.

"I get to be Beth Dutton," Chloe called.

Tom let out a very loud, very long, very beleaguered fatherly breath, then leaned back against one of the chairs that sat in front of his desk, crossed his arms on his chest, and assumed a pose of defeat, staring down at his tennis shoes.

I understood why.

Beth Dutton was Nora's favorite character.

Enough said.

"I'm veritably *starved*," Chloe proclaimed. "Are you starved, Mika?"

"Um—" I didn't quite begin.

"Of course you are. Dad always has a full larder. Let's let these boys struggle with weighty things, and we'll go make something delicious."

She took my hand and started dragging me around the coffee table.

Tom lifted his head and caught my eyes as I went.

*Okay?* I mouthed.

He nodded.

I bit my lip.

Chloe pulled me from the room.

A lot had happened in there. I was a touch worried that Chloe called the character she did, considering Nora's devotion, and her father's reaction.

Mostly, though, I was ridiculously elated that Tom had broken up with Paloma.

I shouldn't be.

It really had nothing to do with me.

Tom and I were just friends.

But...

I *totally* was.

# CHAPTER 11

## THE BLEEDING

*Mika*

The bed in my room was a mattress set on a platform that was in an alcove that had a large, arched opening and step to get to it.

It had a ceiling fan for cooling hot nights and white noise for helping me sleep, and it didn't need nightstands. I could put my books and drinks and pots and bottles on the platform beside the mattress.

I loved the simplicity of that area crafted of white adobe. So much, my sheets, shams and bedspread were all white, as were the shades of the two sconces on the wall at the head of the bed that offered light for reading.

I couldn't speak for the woman, never met her, but knowing her affinity for black and white, I had a feeling Yoko Ono would love it.

In the present, however, with jacket on, purse strap still over my shoulder, I stepped up to the platform and face planted on that bed.

Face still in the bedspread, I felt the mattress move when one body joined me, then again when the other one did.

"Is she broken?" Cadence asked.

"No, she's working *perfectly fine,*" Nora answered.

At Nora's answer, I rolled to my back, glared at the ceiling and announced, "I totally blew it."

"You did nothing of the sort," Nora replied.

I didn't move an inch, just shifted my eyes to look at her leaning into a hand and looming over me as I retorted, "I spent all night flirting with Jamie Oakley."

"Light, harmless flirting." Nora put descriptors on it.

"I'm uncertain Tom found it harmless," I returned.

In fact, I was certain he found it harm*ful*.

I was certain of this considering his mood was so thick by the time we bid adieu, I had to fight back the urge to request a machete to cut through it as we made our way to the door.

"Then he should have staked his claim," Nora stated breezily.

"Euw. Mom's not a 'claim,' Auntie Nora," Cadence cut in. "She's a woman."

"She's both, darling," Nora replied to my girl. "And when you find the man, or woman, or whatever, who you want to make yours, you best be staking your claim too."

"No one is a belonging," Cadence educated.

"Indeed," Nora retorted. "We nevertheless give ourselves. Our love. Our attention. Our time. Our devotion. Our thoughts. Our promise of fidelity. Our care. Are those not every important thing we possess?"

"Yes, but those are *given*," Cadence pointed out.

"Consider this," Nora returned. "They are given when they are *won*. To *win* them you must earn trust. Prove loyalty. Offer support. Validation. Protection. Love. And you must give large pieces of yourself in return, all those parts I mentioned before. And one of the ways to start doing that is by *flirting*. Another way to do it is to make sure the person you wish to win knows you wish to win them, and you do that by *staking your claim*."

Stymied, Cadence had no rejoinder.

Although this life lesson for my beautiful girl was fascinating, and I had a few caveats I wanted to add, I was too bogged down by the fact that, evidently, even though Tom had ended things with Paloma, and even with how matters had taken an unexpected course with that envelope, and that was explained to me, Tom's distance *from* me was not erased.

We'd had hamburgers flavored by dollops of spaghetti sauce and stuffed with mozzarella (no, Tom did not have enough of any of this in his "larder," at least not enough to feed eight people, Dru and Cadence had taken my Tesla to procure it, and Tom had been pressed into service to grill the burgers, something he did expertly, because… of course he would).

Chloe, by the way, made tater tots from scratch.

They were divine.

I'd formed the burgers and thrown together a salad.

We'd worked together in Tom's kitchen like we'd been doing it for years.

It was unnerving.

And awesome.

Through this, and beyond, Tom was cordial, but distant from me, and this became more obvious with no Davises around, no tennis to be played and no one showing up unexpectedly at the door.

He was great with Cadence and Dru.

It warmed the heart to see how loving he was with Chloe. How respectful and friendly he was to Judge and Jamie.

Though he was gracious yet wary around Nora, but most everyone was.

Nope.

It was just me.

So, when Jamie lightheartedly started flirting with me—me, a woman who prided herself in never, *ever* playing games—hurt and confused (and let's face it, we're talking Jamie Oakley here, so perhaps a little flattered), I flirted back.

It was fun.

It was still pointed (on my part).

And I sensed Jamie had ulterior motives too, and they didn't include being serious about me.

The longer it went on, the more audacious Jamie became (and we'll just say, he was an excellent flirt), the more I joined in, the darker Tom's mood.

Nora and Chloe watched this, practically purring.

Cadence and Dru seemed to miss it, but they were fast becoming best buds and already had a coffee date at Wild Iris up in Prescott (my daughter was never going to get her papers written).

Judge, I felt badly to note, spent a lot of time trying to run interference by attempting to divert Tom's attention.

The attempt was valiant, but alas, this didn't work all that well.

And when we left, Tom practically slammed the door behind us.

I transferred my attention back to my ceiling and whispered, "God, I fucked things up."

"You know who's thinking that same thing?" Nora asked.

I didn't answer.

She did.

"Tom Pierce."

"I think I need sleep," I muttered.

Nora came right in and gave me a peck on the cheek.

Staying close, she ordered, "Don't miss a wink. You were perfect. I was so proud of you, I almost burst."

Ugh.

She scooted off the bed.

Cadence came close.

"It's messed up, but I think Aunt Nora's right."

"Playing games is not as fun as people make it out to be," I told her. "And if you do it too much, it can begin to define you."

She scrunched one side of her mouth up so much, her cheek scrunched with it and one eye winked, doing this along with giving a one-shouldered shrug, before she said, "But I guess if the guy you like, who also likes you, isn't doing his part, you have to do something to wake him up. Am I right?"

"I don't know," I answered honestly. "Thus, my dilemma."

"He likes you," she said softly. "It'll be okay."

"Don't put too much stock into that, kid. A lot of the time with things like this, it isn't okay."

"I won't," she promised, bent, kissed my forehead, and also scooted off the bed. "'Night, Mom," she called from the door.

"Sleep tight, baby," I called back.

"I will. You too."

And the door closed.

Shit.

Damn.

And hell.

I got up on an elbow, pulled my bag to me and yanked my phone out of it.

I then opened my text string with Tom.

And I came back to me.

Direct.

Honest.

No game playing.

*I fucked up tonight. Can we get together and talk?* I texted Tom.

It was late, nearly midnight. I expected his phone to be on a charge somewhere in his big house, and he was sleeping.

As usual with Tom and his mobile, I was wrong.

It was not.

And he was not.

I was barely at the edge of the bed pulling off my booties before my phone chimed with a text.

*Yes, you fucked up. No, we don't need to talk.*

I stared at the phone, waiting for those three dots to come up to tell me he was going to say more.

They didn't come up.

So mine came up for him.

*I'm not a game player.*

I sent that and was typing more when I got, *Really?*

I deleted what I'd been typing and shot back, *That would be the fucking up part.*

*We aren't that. It doesn't matter,* he returned.

Oh, God.

*I'd really like to talk.*

*Okay. We'll meet. But I'm going up to Prescott tomorrow. I won't be back until Wednesday.*

*Dinner Wednesday night?*

*We'll see.*

Shit.

Damn.

And hell.

*Are you pissed at me?*

I waited.

But not for long.

*We're not that, Mika. As I said, it doesn't matter.*

*That wasn't what I asked.*

I waited a long time after that.

And then I got, *You can flirt with and fuck whoever you want. It has shit to do with me. As I've said, WE ARE NOT THAT.*

It was the "and fuck whoever" and the capitalization that got me.

Not to mention him lying, because he was pissed, he just wouldn't admit it.

Oh, and I shouldn't leave out him being all about how he was glad to have me back in his life, then turning around and acting like I didn't matter to him.

He was pissed.

But now, I was angry.

*Message received*, I sent.

I then turned on do not disturb, walked my phone down to the charge in the goddamn kitchen, walked back up, got ready, crawled into bed...

And did not sleep one wink.

---

IT WAS WEDNESDAY.

I was standing at my workbench, staring at the pieces I put together.

I wanted to rip them all up and scream.

Nora walked in.

I stifled the urge to gather everything together and hide it away.

Precisely what I'd been doing whenever my daughter got anywhere near my studio.

Instead, I stayed still, hands on my hips, looking down at all of me bleeding across a workbench, raw and exposed.

"Lord, God," Nora whispered.

See?

Bleeding.

"What is this, darling?" she asked softly.

"I don't know," I bit off.

"Mika."

I stared at the bench.

"Mika."

I didn't move or speak.

"Michelle."

I turned my head to her.

"Can I hold you?" she asked.

"No." I shook my head stiffly. "I'll lose it."

"Is this...is it..." She flung a hand to indicate the bench. "Is this for public consumption?"

"I haven't decided."

"Is it for Cadence?"

"Definitely."

A pause then, so soft, they were almost not words. "Are you letting him go?"

"No. I'm giving him to our daughter."

She looked down at the bench.

And then she read, "*Two. That's what it took. To take you from me. And her. Cleaving you in two. Nothing else would have done it. I had to leak out. Across the asphalt. She had to spread. Along the earth. You had to fade. Into nothing. It was the only way. We would lose you. And we lost you. When you became two.*"

My vision turned watery.

Another poem sprang instantly to mind.

That's how it happened. It poured out of me when I opened the tap to losing Rollo.

"Call him," she urged. "It's Wednesday. He'll be back."

I turned to her. "Fuck him, Nora. He hasn't texted once since he acted like a massive dick."

"He's dealing with a breakup. He's dealing with what was in that envelope. He's dealing with his feelings for you."

"I don't let men shit on me. You didn't know me back then. Before Rollo. That kind of thing is a hard pass. One and done."

"Right, then, even though I think you're making a huge mistake, at the very least, you have to know what he's doing about what's in that envelope."

"I'll contact him when I'm not as pissed as I am now."

"And I will not hesitate to remind you, you're as pissed as you are because he means something to you."

"We barely know each other."

"Stop it."

"Stop what?"

Suddenly, she rapped her knuckles on the workbench, and I almost snarled that she'd dare touch it.

"When did this begin?" she demanded.

"I don't talk about my work when it's in progress."

"Hogwash," she fired back. "You talk about it all the time. When did this begin?"

"Nora—"

"I know when it began."

She probably did.

"Rollo would be devasted," she announced.

My skin caught fire.

"Don't you even—" I gritted.

"He'd be torn apart."

"You have no—"

She leaned in and hissed, "And he'd be pissed *as fuck*. Live your goddamn life, Mika. Stop hiding behind your love for him. Stop quivering in fear behind his loss. That wasn't the woman he married. It isn't *you*."

My words were a blaze of fire when I spat, "I'm not doing that. I live my life, Nora. Don't pretend you don't know that."

"I *do* know that. I do. And you aren't lying. You have. But now that life could include something more, so *now* you're doing it. And you know I don't lie. You not going after what you want because you're scared would tear Rollo apart, and you using him as a shield, he'd be furious."

With that, she stalked out.

And I reached out, sweeping an arm along the workbench, all the photos and papers shuffling together, some falling on the floor.

I gathered them up, stacked them, shoved them in their folder, tucked it out of sight.

Then I went out on my balcony. I jogged down the stairs. I kicked off my shoes. And I walked through my garden, into the desert.

And I kept walking until I pulled it together.

Only then did I head home.

---

I LASTED UNTIL SATURDAY.

After that, no word, no update, the anger I'd let flow through the soles of my bare feet into the healing earth started building again.

I chose another path to release it this time and grabbed my phone.

*I'd like an update on what's happening with the Winston situation,* I texted.

Tom, the jerk, made me wait.

It took him two fucking hours to reply.

*We have it in hand. You don't need to worry about it.*

They had it *in hand?*

*They* did?

Was he fucking serious?

*It's mine, Tom,* I reminded him.

Now who was playing games?

He was.

Nearly forty-five minutes passed before he texted, *It's a family thing, Mika. You know that.*

*It's not a family thing. It was sent to me.*

I could tell he was getting hot because he didn't make me wait this time.

He returned, *By family.*

*Not by family. By some PI.*

*Who was retained by family.*

*I have a right to know,* I shot back.

*Be glad you're out of it.*

*I'm not glad. I deserve to know what's going on.*

*Mika, you're out of it. It's what's best for you.*

*Says who?*

*Obviously...me.*

*You don't get to make decisions for me, Mr. Pierce.*

*You're wrong, baby. I do.*

It was the "baby."

It was totally the "baby."

Use the word "baby" wrong, and a woman will fuck your shit up.

I did not reply.

I was suddenly on a mission to fuck a man's shit up.

I stomped to my room. I put on footies. I put on booties. I grabbed my jacket and purse.

And I found my daughter and best friend watching television in the family room.

"God, I hate Carrie," Cadence was saying.

"Don't we all, darling. Don't we all," Nora replied.

"I'm going into town," I announced.

Both of them twisted to me.

"To do what?" Cadence asked.

I didn't quite meet her eyes when I answered, "Tom and I need to have words."

I might not have met eyes, that didn't mean I missed their slow smiles.

Whatever.

"I'll be back soon," I declared, turned and marched toward the garage.

I still heard Nora's, "I wouldn't hold your breath, honey" and Cadence's giggle.

Argh!

*Whatever.*

I was out of there.

# CHAPTER 12

## THE CONFRONTATION

*Tom*

$\mathcal{H}$e was sitting out by his pool. The color he'd selected to light it tingeing the night a deep blue. The firepit was crackling. A whisky was in his hand.

And Tom was brooding.

Brooding.

With whisky.

Jesus Christ, when had he allowed himself to become cast as the lonesome lost?

He threw back some liquor, felt the burn, and his phone went.

That was when he felt his pulse spike, and he liked it.

Even though it'd been nearly an hour since his last text to Mika, he thought the call was her.

He looked at his phone.

It wasn't.

It was Genny.

Tremendous.

However, she was the mother of his children, she was also his friend, and as such, he always took her call.

"Genny," he answered.

"Tom, do you have a second?"

He had a fucking million of them.

"What do you need?"

"I just…well, I don't know how to begin."

Tom sighed.

He loved her. Would die loving her.

But he was in no mood.

"Begin at the beginning, Gen," he invited. "I think we're well past not being able to say things to each other."

"Okay then," she began. "Chloe and Judge just left, and she was in a state, because apparently she pulled some shenanigans to hook you up with Mika Stowe, they didn't work, and you know how she gets when her shenanigans don't work."

"Yes. Exactly how your mother got," he replied, though it wasn't with irritation. It was with fondness, because no matter how irritating the woman could be, Tom had never known Marilyn Swan to do a thing in the entire time he knew her that wasn't steeped in love.

And the same thing could be said about their daughter.

"Exactly that."

"It'll blow over, Genny."

"Tom, why aren't you seeing Mika?"

He felt his spine straighten at her unexpected question.

"Sorry?"

"I don't…just to say, she's kind of perfect for you. You should give it a shot."

He set his glass aside, bent forward, resting an elbow in his knee, and started, "Genny—"

"She's got her own thing, so you can do your own thing. She's smart and creative and talented. She's attractive. She hates the limelight, just like you. Chloe says she's a fabulous mom and her daughter is quick as a whip and very sweet. She created that. All alone. You've always admired her."

"Maybe we shouldn't talk about these things."

"We're friends, right?" she asked. "Friends who have shared a lot together. Children. Love. Our bodies. Years of our time. I know you. I *know you*, Tom. And it's like Mika Stowe was made for you."

"All right, maybe I don't *want* to talk about it."

She stopped fucking around and got down to it.

"You can be happy again."

"Gen—"

"Do you need my permission? Because you have it. You've had it for a long—"

Goddamn it.

He was not doing this.

"*Imogen*," he bit.

"You're not going to gag me with your guilt, Tom," she bit back. "Enough. It's done and gone. It's over. We all love you. We want you to be happy."

"Would you like to know what I want?" he retorted.

"Of course I would."

"I want to be happy, but more, I want to make sure the ones I care about are."

"And?"

It was incredulous when he parroted, "*And?*"

"You're very adept at that, Tom. I should know. You made me that way for decades."

"And then I stopped."

He felt the air move out of her, and she was a hundred miles away.

"You see my concern," he stated drily.

"Tommy, honey," she whispered.

"Can I ask a favor and we not—?"

He was cut off, not by Genny, but by his doorbell ringing.

Excellent.

Whoever it was, it was an excuse to end this call.

"Someone is at the door. I have to go."

"We need to talk about this more," she said quickly.

That was not going to happen.

"Fine. But later. Tell Bowie I said hello and have a great night."

"Like that's going to happen now," she mumbled.

"Don't worry about me," he ordered, hesitating as he walked to the door because it was made of glass, and he could see Mika on the other side of it.

What the fuck?

And…

Shit.

"I'm fine," he finished.

"Right," she continued to mumble.

"Must go. Love you, Genny."

"And I love you, Tom," she replied.

That used to cut him up, the times she'd say it close to when they split, and later, close to when she reunited with Duncan.

Now, he barely heard it as he disconnected and prowled to the door.

He pulled it open and shared, "We're not going to do this, Mika."

He found he was wrong about that because she pushed right in.

The kittens, now big enough to be cordoned off to entire rooms, tumbled her way.

She ignored them and rounded on Tom.

"*Baby?*" she snapped.

That wasn't what he was expecting.

"What?" he asked.

"You can call me 'baby' when you're fucking me, Tom. Until that time, *refrain*."

He grew perfectly still.

She kept ranting.

"Even *if* you *were* fucking me, you don't get to decide for me. And under no circumstances do you get to ghost me, avoid me, talk shit to me, distance yourself from me."

She took a step with her long legs his way and got up on her toes to get into his face.

So close, he could swear he felt her breasts whisper across his chest.

And she kept at him.

"And those are all big, so I hope you're taking mental notes. But most of all, you don't get to come back in my life, pretend you want to be there, then step out *whenever the fuck you want.*"

"You need to step back," he said quietly.

"I'm not going to step fucking back," she returned heatedly. "We're doing this. *Now.*"

"Mika, honey, please, step back."

The flames of fury danced in her eyes for a second. They sputtered. They died. Her expression went slack.

And her lips whispered, "Oh."

But she did not step back.

"Hon—" he began.

He didn't finish because her breasts were no longer whispering against his chest. They were plastered there. She was pressed to him from belly to chest. Her long, slender fingers were in his hair, pulling his head down to hers.

And she crushed her lips against his.

She opened her mouth, made a noise low in her throat that seared through his cock, but she didn't get her tongue in his mouth.

He pushed it back and took hers.

She melted into him.

He wrapped his arms around her.

Christ.

He was finally tasting her.

Shit.

Fuck.

Christ.

Better than a million dreams.

*Christ.*

He broke the kiss and took a wide step to the side.

"Mika, this can't happen," he said, his voice firm, but gruff.

She reached out, fisted her fingers in his shirt, and didn't pull him to her. Her hand was the hook on her line to come back to him.

And she did.

"Yes, it can."

He wrapped his hand around hers at his chest, leaned away when she leaned in, and said, "Honey, trust me. You don't want to get involved with me."

The heat faltered in her eyes as bewilderment fought it.

"Pardon?"

"You don't want to get involved with me," he repeated.

"Why?" she asked.

To get them beyond this, especially for her, Tom gave it to her plain.

"I'm no good for you."

Her head quirked, the heat gone, she was now completely bewildered.

"Come again?"

"You deserve better."

"Better than what?"

"Me."

Now openly dumbfounded.

"Better than you?"

He tried to pull away.

She followed him.

"Honey," he whispered.

He watched her get serious, studying him to the point it felt like she was examining him.

Then she said softly, "Oh my God, you believe that crap."

Tom started to get pissed.

She let his shirt go and caught his head with both hands.

"Tom, you slept with kittens."

"You're reminding me of that because…" he prompted.

"Because that's you. Because you…you…" She shook her head. "Because you're you."

"I care about you."

"I know."

"I'm attracted to you."

She shot him a smile he also felt sear through his cock.

"I know," she repeated.

"I don't want to hurt you."

"Well, Mr. Pierce, I don't want you to hurt me either. And guess what, big man, I know your history. You laid it out all over the kitchen, and it seemed to me you were pretty damned thorough. I'm also a big girl. So here's something for you to take in right fucking now. This is my decision. And in all that shit I was listing earlier, I'll reiterate a big one. You don't get to make my decisions for me. I know what I'm getting into, and if you hurt me, I made myself a fool. But you're not going to hurt me, are you, Tom?"

He stared down at her.

"Are you?" she pushed.

He looked into her blue-blue eyes, open, intense, honest, expectant.

Hopeful.

And then he said, "It's Dr. Pierce."

"What?"

He put his hands to her hips.

"It's *Dr.* Pierce, baby."

He felt her frame twitch under his hands.

She smiled.

Then she pounced.

Tom met her midway.

He wasn't going to fuck her for the first time on his landing, and she kissed like she wanted to devour him.

He wanted her to do that.

Just not on the landing.

This meant he had no choice but to break the kiss again.

She made another noise.

It was time to get where they needed to go.

He caught her hand and pulled her to the baby gate that guarded the hall to his room.

She gasped as he lifted her and dropped her over the other side. Without delay, he swung over it, leg after leg.

He then grabbed her hand again and dragged her to his bedroom.

He flipped on the lights and got her to the side of the bed where they stopped.

He meant to go on, but she said, her eyes moving around the space, "Okay, this room is the fuckin' shit."

"I'll give you a full tour later," he offered.

Her gaze came to his. "The shower?"

He grinned at her. "That'll be first."

He didn't know if it was what he said, or her watching his grin.

On the landing, she'd pounced.

Now, she attacked.

There was no way in fuck she was taking this over.

He'd waited too long for her.

She was his.

But she was like wrestling a lioness. She was gangly limbs and power and cunning.

She was about touch and exposure, and she didn't give a fuck about clothes tearing.

She was mouth and those tapered nails of hers and lots and lots of hair all over his skin.

She was lips and teeth and eventually, there was nothing for it.

He had to maneuver her to her back, spread her legs, go down and *latch on.*

There they were.

She settled like a contented kitten and opened to him.

He hummed his victory into her cunt.

She moaned and swung a leg over his shoulders.

Her mouth was a dream, but her pussy was heaven, musky and sharp and tart and so goddamned wet.

Fucking fuck.

Perfect.

Mika writhed and she made noise, Christ, abandoned. It slithered across his skin. Drove up his ass. Slid along his cock. Hardened his nipples.

He heard it shift, sensed her tense, and lifted his head to demand, "Don't come."

She lifted her head as well, eyes and expression dazed and gorgeous, "Baby, don't stop."

"You come when I'm in you."

She readily agreed. "Okay, then get in me."

"I'm not done."

"Tom."

He licked her while she watched.

Her eyes rolled back, and her head dropped.

He grinned and went after her again.

And kept at her.

And more.

Until she had his hair in a fist, and she was chanting, "Tom, Tom, Tommy, sweetheart, baby. Need you."

It was time.

He moved away, reaching to the drawer under the bed for a condom.

She molded herself to his back while he did, kissing his shoulder, neck, running her tongue along the line of his hair there.

But she sat back and watched with greedy eyes as he rolled on the prophylactic.

"Why, Dr. Pierce, you have a very big, very pretty dick," she teased.

She tore her gaze away to catch his smile, then he caught her behind her neck and got off on her shocked, excited gasp as he yanked her to him, moving into her.

She was on her back, and he was between her legs.

And then he was inside.

She closed around him, warm and tight.

He closed his eyes and dropped his forehead to hers.

She wrapped him in all her limbs.

Neither of them moved or spoke.

It took long moments before Mika broke the silence.

"In case you're wondering…"

He opened his eyes and looked down at her, hair all over his sheets, eyes staring right into his.

God, so Mika.

All of it.

Her.

Here.

His.

"Yes," she went on softly. "We fit *perfect*."

"Honey," he whispered, feeling that, knowing he would before he did, loving that she did too. Both.

It was almost too much.

But he was anchored to her. Steadied.

Strong.

He hadn't felt that way in years.

She shifted a hand so she could cup his jaw.

"Fuck me, Tommy," she urged, lifted her head, touched her mouth to his, and dropped back to his bed. "Make me yours."

Tom had no choice but to do what he'd wished he could do since he met her.

He gave her exactly what she wanted.

---

SHE MOVED ON HIM, HER BODY RIPPLING AND ROLLING, HER CUNT clutching and releasing, her hands up in her hair, fat tendrils having escaped, floating down her chest, teasing her nipples.

He held on to her hips, watching her ride, watching her expression warm, then heat, then she lost herself to it, and he watched her come.

Rolling and rippling, clutching and releasing, she made him come too.

---

ON HER KNEES BEFORE HIM, MIKA HAD A HAND PRESSED TO THE GLASS of the shower that was situated exposed to the room on a platform above the bed, her head turned his way, her face nearly hidden by the mass of her hair.

He powered inside her.

She gasped. She mewed. She moaned.

She begged.

"Tommy, please."

"What?" he growled.

Her head lolled back. "God, yes. Please. Damn."

He fucked her, pinched the nipple of the breast he was holding.

Her body jolted.

"Harder?" he asked.

Her head lifted slightly, her eyes round.

"Can you go harder?"

"Yes."

Her lips parted in awe.

He fucked her harder.

She bounded on his cock while he did it, arching into him.

Mika dropped her head forward.

Tom threaded his fingers in her hair, closed them, pulled her head gently back and watched her tits bounce in the reflection of the glass as he took her.

"You were right," he gritted.

"What?" she gasped.

"We"—he drove in—"fit"—he drove in again—"perfect."

He moved his other hand to her clit and pinched it.

She bucked on his dick as she came.

He shifted them back, bent her over into the bed, and let her spasming pussy milk him dry.

When he finished climaxing, Tom folded over her, and between labored breaths, he kissed her shoulder blade.

"All that gentleman shit is a ruse. You fuck like a goddamned monster," she breathed into the bed.

He lifted just enough to be able to move her hair away from her face, sliding it over her shoulder.

She slanted her eyes his way.

"No, baby," Tom contradicted. "I fuck like a champion."

She huffed out a laugh.

Tom buried his face in her hair and laughed with her.

"BABY?" TOM ASKED.

Languidly, Mika raised her head from his chest and looked down at him.

"What?"

"It was a question," he told her.

"What was a question?"

"The word 'baby'? Really? That drove you in a snit to my door?"

Her brows drew together.

"Are you seriously giving me shit right now when you've fucked me useless?"

His lips twitched.

"Yes. I seriously am."

She let her face collapse into his chest.

He started chuckling.

"It wasn't a snit," she grumbled.

"Oh, it was a snit," he challenged.

"Another thing to take note of, I don't do snits. If I'm pissed, watch out."

"Yeah. You'll lecture me for thirty seconds then pounce and you won't settle down until you have my mouth between your legs."

"Oh my God," she groused, though there was nothing behind it.

She sounded half asleep.

Tom smiled at the ceiling.

"Don't annoy me. I can't fight back. I'm fucked out. But I have the memory of an elephant," she warned.

He said nothing and slid his hand over her ass before he clamped on.

"You can't be ready for more," she muttered.

"I can't?"

"Christ, you're a machine. Don't you need to go hydrate at least?"

He glided his hand to the small of her back. "Don't worry, honey, I'll let you rest."

"You're not human," she mumbled.

Tom wrapped both arms around her and whispered, "I'm very human, Mika."

That made her shift her head.

She kissed the base of his throat, and said, "I know. Lucky me."

Tom closed his eyes and urged, "Sleep."

"Okay," she murmured.

He felt her weight settle into him almost immediately.

Tom didn't move his arms.

Not even after he followed her.

---

"SHUT UP." PAUSE THEN, "I DON'T KNOW." ANOTHER PAUSE. "I SAID shut up."

Tom opened his eyes.

Mika was draped over his torso. The sun was shining in his windows. She had her head raised, her elbows in the mattress, and her phone to her ear.

"Maybe Chloe's secret operative is also an assassin, and I can talk him into doing a hit on you," she stated. "No. And we're done. Say goodbye, Nora." After that, she let out an, "Ugh," he heard her phone drop to the floor, then she slithered back over his chest.

She caught his gaze and stopped.

"Please, don't use my daughter's human meddling tool to kill your best friend," he requested.

"You're awake."

"And she's acutely perceptive first thing in the morning," he teased.

She halfheartedly slapped his chest.

He kept teasing. "I could hardly remain asleep with you lying on top of me and yapping on the phone."

She arched her brows. "Yapping?"

He folded his arms around her and pulled her up his chest so they were face to face.

"Yapping," he whispered, and she watched his mouth do it.

He let her kiss him.

When he was done doing that, he rolled so he was on top and kissed her.

He stopped when something wet registered against his hip.

When he pulled away, though not far, she shared, "I think one of the condoms got lost in the sheets."

"Great," he murmured, moving them out of the wet spot.

"Do you want me to make you breakfast?" she asked.

"No, I want to make you breakfast."

Her mouth turned down. "You've already cooked for me."

His brows went up. "Is this a one-night stand?"

"No," she stated firmly.

No.

It was not.

"I'm making you breakfast," he decreed.

"Whatever," she said to his ear.

"Mika?"

Her gaze came to his.

He drew in a breath.

And then he asked an important question.

"Do you know what you're doing?"

Her expression grew soft, sheer beauty in his bed, and she pressed deep into him before she replied.

"Yes, Dr. Pierce. I know *exactly* what I'm doing."

# CHAPTER 13

## THE PANCAKES

*Mika*

The good news, the kittens were no worse for our abandonment during the fuckathon.

All five of them were now hale and hearty, weaned from the bottle and litter trained (or, for that last part, it was, according to Tom, "mostly").

Once we made it to the kitchen, and ushered them in with us, we were gated.

They then happily frolicked across Tom's tiles with their plethora of toys, access to the boxes in Tom's utility room, with bellies full from stuffing their little kitten faces from a line of kitty dishes at the floor-to-ceiling windows that Tom forked kitten food into before he even made coffee.

So, obviously, I started the coffee.

The other good news?

There was no bad news.

Tom let me help cook, and I was on bacon duty while he made fluffy blueberry pancakes.

We sat at his island to eat.

He made great spaghetti.

But his blueberry pancakes were *insane*.

"Okay, now I'm glad you didn't let me cook," I said with mouth full.

"Not good at pancakes?" he asked.

I lifted a loaded, dripping fork. "Not this good."

He smiled and took his own bite.

"Should we get through the tough stuff, or should we wallow in a haze of fantastic sex and mind-blowing blueberry pancakes?" I queried half-jokingly.

His gaze slid to me.

And it was all serious.

"I don't want Winston in this, honey."

Having a moment to consider it, I realized I was *way* down with that.

Thus, I nodded. "Okay."

"And my guess is, you're not ever going to flirt with another man in front of me, yes?"

Well, there you go.

He went right after that one.

I pressed my lips together and nodded again.

"How about that be all the tough stuff we cover for now?" he suggested.

"So you *were* pissed about the flirting," I noted.

"Livid."

He crunched into some bacon.

I felt my eyes crinkle.

"You're *sooo* into me," I teased.

"Yes," he said simply.

The crinkles disappeared and a lump formed in my throat.

And that was it. No fanfare. No prevarication. No games.

But that was all there needed to be.

This man.

I had him.

Finally, he was mine.

*Yes.*

"I can't say I'm the jealous type, though I prefer not to be given any reason to be," he continued. "Obviously, we need to put time into feeling this out. You don't live in Arizona. I do. You have your daughter still at home with you. I have commitments that mean travel. But I hope, after exploring and time spent together, we can come to the point where we feel solid. That said, what you did with Jamie wasn't okay. I was married for a long time. I was out of the game. When I was back in it, I realized I'm not a player either."

I did not doubt this.

What had been going on with him when he was being distant with me (also, lest we forget, a dick) was something else.

Something I'd allow to get lost in the haze of sex and pancakes.

But after that lifted, we needed to talk.

However...

"I was hurting because you were ghosting me, yet I was right here, in your kitchen, cooking with your daughter," I explained.

"I was working through some things which evidently needed you jumping my bones to shake loose."

I rolled my eyes.

When I rolled them back, he was smiling.

It faded when he said, "I hate I hurt you. And I'm sorry I did. But I'm glad you called my ass on it, and we worked it out."

"How about we continue to work through those things a bit more, though we can start doing that after the haze fully lifts, and maybe after we've had tons more sex?"

He didn't evade.

Not even for a second.

He said, "That's a plan."

Okay.

Good.

And God, nothing better than a man who was willing to be real and put in the work.

I forked into my pancakes. "So...travel?"

"Melbourne, January. France, end of May. London, end of June. New York, September. I've got three years left on my contract. But I'd still want to do it after that, so I hope to negotiate another five years. Most times, I'll do the Davis Cup, but those events are negotiated separately, due to commitments to my medical practice and my family."

He then forked into his pancakes while I noted, "I like Melbourne, Paris, London and obviously, New York."

His fork was arrested halfway to his lips, and it wasn't moving.

"Tom?" I called.

He turned his head my way, his fork still unmoving.

"What'd you just say?" he asked.

"Well, we're new, but I'm a pretty solid person, and my take on you is that you are too. In other words, as noted earlier, this isn't a one-night stand. I hope we figure things out. But I've got a good feeling."

I shot him a cheeky grin.

He just stared at me.

That was concerning, which made me keep talking, though it was more like blathering.

"So, you know, not to invite myself along, but if we figure things out, and you can have company while you work, and more importantly, you want it, it would be no hardship to go to any of those places with you. I mean, I might watch a few matches, if you can get tickets. But mostly, I'd be cool to tool around while you worked. Then we could do dinner, or I could go with you if you have some company stuff you have to do, and they allow a plus one. And, of course, we could fuck around the world, which obviously, we've proved in a short period of time will be all kinds of fun."

He put his fork down.

He reached out.

He wrapped his hand around my jaw.

He then slid his thumb across my cheek.

And without a word, he let me go and turned back to his plate.

Although it felt lovely, I didn't know what it was.

And then I did.

*The Genny Show.*

"You can absolutely come with me," he said to his plate, his deep voice deeper, the timbre resonating all through me, then he took another bite of pancakes.

I was going to reply, but abruptly, his head whipped around.

In the next second, he looked to the ceiling, pleaded, "Deliver me," and a voice was heard from the other room.

"Dad!"

"Oh fuck," I whispered.

"In the kitchen!" he called.

Oh fuck!

"Tom!" I snapped low, "I'm only wearing your shirt."

As for Tom, he was in nothing but a pair of fleece joggers.

"Good. Maybe she'll take a hint and leave her father alone for once."

"Well, well, well," Chloe drawled.

I twisted toward the doorway to the living room.

And froze stiff.

Because outside the kitten gate, Chloe was there.

And Judge.

And Imogen Swan and Duncan Holloway.

She was even more beautiful in person, and that was saying something.

Lord have mercy on us all.

"Hey there," I called stiltedly.

Chloe grinned.

Judge looked to the ceiling.

Holloway looked to his boots.

Imogen, her face running pale as a sheet, murmured, "Apologies," and she dashed away.

A stunned Chloe's eyes followed her.

Holloway went after her.

"Oh dear," I whispered.

"Fuck," Tom clipped, slid from his stool, kissed my temple and said, "Be back."

He moved toward the gate.

"We'll just..." Judge trailed off.

Then he nabbed Chloe's hand, and they disappeared from sight.

Tom did too.

I dropped my fork and raced to Tom's bedroom.

Tom's master wasn't just a master.

It was a master plus the bath in a way I'd never seen before.

It, too, had a sunken area that included a bed that was a mattress set into a platform (he also didn't need nightstands). This was built against the area up top which was the bathroom exposed entirely to the bedroom, including the huge, double-wide, all-glass shower that was situated above the bed platform.

There was a large seating area jutting out from the house to the side. It had two-hundred-and-seventy-degree views of his gardens, with a walkout off to the front of the house that was a fenced-in terrace.

The colors were stone, white and exposed wood.

It was magnificent.

At that juncture, I didn't see it.

I had on panties and bra and was pulling up my jeans when Tom stalked in.

Oh dear times a thousand.

I asked a stupid question considering the look on his face.

"Is she okay?"

His response was not delayed.

"Suffice it to say, she's happy. She loves her new husband. She loves her new television show and revitalized career. She loves living between LA, Phoenix and Prescott. She loves Duncan's boys. She loves our big family staying together in its way and getting bigger with what Duncan brings to it. But she was not prepared to see her husband of twenty years bare chested on a stool at his island sitting next to a woman wearing his shirt and having sex hair."

He said all this while walking to his closet, and into his closet, and while in said closet.

However...

*Her husband?*

*A woman?*

I quickly grabbed my shirt and yanked it on.

It had gotten ripped in the sex frenzy.

Fabulous.

He came out of the closet tugging on a long-sleeved tee and still sporting a face filled with thunder.

"I'll just take off and call you later," I said.

He stopped dead and scorched me with his angry stare.

"Sorry?" he asked.

"I'll get out of your hair. This is a family thing."

"I don't want you out of my hair."

Now it was me who was staring, but it wasn't scorching. It was surprised.

He kept speaking.

"I want you here. I want time with you. We've fucked around too long. Now we've stopped fucking around in the shit way and started doing it in the right way. I want you to spend the day with me. I want you to spend the night again. Do you need to get home to Cadence?"

I thought about my conversation with Nora that morning which included her telling me to take all the time I needed, even if I needed six months. She'd fly Cadence home after spring break and would send shipments from Goldbelly so we could have sustenance and barely leave the bedroom.

"Not particularly," I said slowly.

"Then why are you saying you're leaving?"

I tossed a hand to the door. "Is Imogen still here?"

"No. She and Duncan left. But Chloe and Judge are still here because I told her to stay because I have a few things to say to her."

"Maybe you should say them without me."

His head ticked before he asked, "What's going on here?"

I opened my mouth to answer, but he carried on before I could get a word out.

"I'll tell you where I'm at, Mika. I'm not a twenty-five-year-old guy, figuring shit out. I'm a grown man who knows what he wants. That being you. So to finish our earlier discussion, as far as I'm concerned, we don't have anything to figure out. We're there. Would I have liked us to have a lazy day getting to know each other better in a variety of pleasurable ways? Yes. Did I want that interrupted by my well-meaning, but meddling-and-nosy-as-fuck daughter? No. That happened. Chloe will be Chloe, and she'll aways be Chloe, as she's been from the moment she left her mother's womb. If you want me, she comes with me, and like me, you're going to have to deal with it."

I didn't take even a millisecond to think about it.

"I'm totally in," I replied.

"Then stop talking about leaving."

I beat back saluting.

But that motion was in my, "I have my orders, Dr. Pierce."

"I'm totally getting you a nurse's outfit," he muttered.

"I'm totally fucking you in it."

The scorch was back in his gaze, but I liked this one.

"Come here," he ordered.

Damn, he was bossy.

I loved it.

I went there.

He hooked me with an arm, pulled me close, kissed me hard but closed-mouthed, then he let me go, took my hand and led me out to the living room.

Chloe was snuggling Venus like nothing was amiss.

Judge was on a couch and Boris and Serena were crawling all over him.

It was naptime for Ace and Nala.

Chloe practically preened when she caught sight of us.

I felt Tom's heat come back (not the good kind this time), and I knew he saw his daughter's expression too.

Chloe didn't miss her father's reaction.

"It was Mom's idea, Dad," she said quickly. "You had some conversation with her last night, and it upset her. She was worried about you."

"Because you told her about Mika. She confronted me about Mika. I was in a bad mood. Then Mika came over, and my mood lifted significantly."

"I can see that," she replied gleefully.

"Chloe, for God's sakes," Tom retorted with exasperation. "You have to learn to keep your nose out of other people's business."

"Are you honestly saying that to me right now?" she demanded.

"I'm honestly saying that to you right now," he returned. "And it's not about me and Mika. It's about wrangling your mother into your plots, which made her phone me last night, as you intended, and went on to make her feel what she felt fifteen minutes ago."

A shadow moved over Chloe's face.

"Exactly," he bit off.

"How could I know—?" she began.

"Your mom and I are done," Tom declared. "It's over. That doesn't mean we didn't have a life together. We didn't love each other. And there's a big difference between her ex-husband having a woman in his life and seeing what she saw when you walked in on us. She's been with Bowie for a long time. If I walked in on them as she walked in on us, it would hurt. It's reflexive. Love is the heart. The heart is a muscle. And muscle has memory that doesn't die."

That was tragic and romantic and amazing and beautiful and so very, perfectly, profoundly correct.

And I was so delighted he understood it the way he did, I wanted to suck face with him right on the spot for knowing it and being able to state it so concisely and eloquently.

Obviously, I refrained.

"I'm sorry, *mon père bien-aimé*," she murmured, and although quiet, I could see it was genuine.

"Mika and I are together," Tom stated.

Now *I* felt like preening.

"We're going to explore this," he went on. "So now, what are you going to do?"

Chloe looked befuddled.

I nearly burst out laughing.

I refrained from that too.

Judge finally entered the conversation.

And he sounded more exasperated than Chloe's father.

"For fuck's sake, baby, you're gonna *butt out.*"

"Oh, right. *Bien sûr,*" she said.

She so totally wasn't going to butt out.

"Can I take Venus with me when we go home?" she asked.

"No," Tom denied. "She needs two more months with me and her litter before she's separated."

His daughter gasped in horror.

"*Two months?*"

"They're developing in a lot of ways, not just physically, also socially. They've imprinted on me for the time being. They need me and their siblings. People remove kittens far too quickly from their litters."

"Okay then, maybe they'll imprint on me, and we'll take all five of them home and keep them until they're ready to leave the nest," she haggled.

"Jesus Christ," Judge hissed.

She looked to him. "Please don't sit there playing with two of them and pretending you don't want all five."

He was in a tough position, since that was exactly what he was doing, with one clawing its way up his chest and the other one chasing the finger he was darting about for her.

"You're not taking the cats," Tom said.

"Father."

"No. Nala is Clay's. He comes over to play with her so she'll get used to him. And I don't think Bray and Pris will be thrilled to drive him to Prescott three times a week."

Clay was coming over that often?

How cute.

"Can we have blueberry pancakes?" Chloe asked.

"No," Tom answered.

"Fine," she snapped. "Then maybe you and Judge can play a game of tennis while Mika and I drink mimosas."

Tom looked down at me. "Either she wants a chance to get to know you better, or she has another scheme. It could be Sully, Bowie's oldest. It could be Matt. It could be Jamie. It could be Dru. It could be that fucking Rhys guy for all I know. But she wants you embroiled in it. My advice, steer well clear."

I totally was not going to do that.

Next match made, I was all in.

"All right, sweetheart," I said quietly.

"For fucks sake," he muttered.

He knew I was fibbing.

How did that happen?

Oh well.

Whatever.

When I looked her way, Chloe was preening again.

I understood that feeling.

Which was why I smiled broadly at her.

---

He had soft skin.

He had hard muscle.

He was rough and hairy in all the right places, his legs, his chest, the thatch around his pretty cock.

We were under his sheet in his bed like we were in a Rom Com, Tom on his back, me up on a forearm, pressed against his side. The sheet was tented by my head and a stack of pillows.

And Tom was allowing me to trail my fingers all over him.

As for me, I wasn't wasting the opportunity.

I was glorying in it.

The man was take charge during sex. Like, completely. You went with his flow, or he made you do it.

I'd learned that quickly. In fact, after our first go. I knew it wasn't about selfishness. He had the goods to take us both there, he got off on doing that aggressively and in absolute control, and I got off on trusting him with me.

With us.

There was more to it, of course.

Rollo left me with his share of three platinum-selling albums, the residuals that would come from that and any merchandising in place from when he was alive.

This was millions, and it was far from stagnant.

I didn't do too badly for myself, but the resurgence of interest in my work added significantly to those coffers.

But I had a daughter. She might go to college. She might have a wedding. She might need help with a down payment for a house. And I needed to be prepared.

I was self-employed, we both needed insurance, and life had a way of fucking with you, so I also had to be prepared in case one of us got hurt or sick.

We needed a roof over our head.

Food.

Clothes.

She needed a good education.

And no matter what she said, I planned for her future so she'd never truly feel need, and neither would her children.

But it went on and on.

And on.

All on me (and my PA, Teddy).

But it was all on me.

Making decisions about her schooling. Making decisions about her curfew. Making decisions about whether or not to buy her a car (here in Arizona, she didn't need one in the city—by the way, I bought her a car).

It was—

Tom's hand enclosed mine at his chest.

I focused on him.

"Glad to have you back," he whispered.

I smiled, bent, touched my nose to his and pulled away again.

When I did, he lifted my hand to his lips and kissed it before tucking it back to his chest.

"Feel like sharing?" he invited.

"I like how you fuck me."

For a second, he lay still.

Then he busted out laughing, surged up, and then he was holding up the sheet with his entire body, because that body was stretched out on top of mine.

We were grinning at each other, and he said through his, "Nice to have the confirmation, but you weren't keeping it a secret."

I ran my fingers across his stubbled jaw, up his smiling cheek, and said, "I meant it like that, but it's deeper."

"Yeah?" he prompted quietly, following my mood.

And it was nice, how he did that.

I was noticing he did it a lot.

"Being a single parent kind of sucks," I admitted.

His brows knit.

I gave him a gentle smile. "I'll rephrase. Being a parent rocks. Cadence rocks. Life with her rocks. What I'm saying is, it's a lot of responsibility. There are a ton of decisions to make on your own. And a fuckup with a kid is a huge fuckup."

"Mm," he hummed his agreement.

"And it's just...folks think that creative people are free and breezy. It's all about smoking pot or following our muse or tinkering in a studio or tapping lazily on a keyboard between facials. It isn't. It's demanding. When an idea has you in its grip, it doesn't let go until it wrings every last drop of emotion from you. You release it like it's a child. After you've nurtured it with your body. After you've worried over it with your mind. After you've labored with it and birthed it. And then people pick it apart like you shat it out, rather than painstakingly sculpted it. My work and my reputation and my life is a huge part of who I am. But it became not entirely about me when Cadence came into the world. It became my legacy for her. She already had Rollo's, and it felt like his was a yoke around her neck, one I was helping her carry. And it's just…it's…"

Tom was quiet, his eyes to mine, active and processing, and unequivocally with me.

Unequivocally.

So I finished.

"It's just nice to have someone take over in something so personal. So important. In a connection like that which is so meaningful. To be able to just let everything go for once and…"—my voice dropped to a whisper under the blanket of his body, his gaze—"fade into you."

I was worried that was too much.

I didn't worry long.

Tom framed my face with his hands, the pads of both his thumbs pressing on my lips like he didn't want me to say further words.

I lay underneath him.

And I got it.

His art.

This tennis guy.

This sports commentator.

This doctor.

This father.

This ex.

This lover.

This betrayer.

*This man.*

Being in his bed was being in his cage.

But it wasn't captivity.

Here, with him, I was no longer in the wild.

Here, with him, I didn't have to fight to survive.

Here, with him, I didn't have to find a way to feed myself, my daughter, provide a roof, warmth, care.

Here, with him, I didn't have to create. I didn't have to produce. I didn't have to earn. I didn't have to nurture or decide.

I didn't even have to speak.

I started trembling with the depth of what he was giving me.

I started weeping.

Tom watched a tear fall and groaned.

And then he kissed me.

And then he dominated me.

He made me suck him.

He made me open to him.

He made me expose myself.

He made me take his fucking.

He owned my orgasm.

He allowed me to have his.

And then he cocooned me in his warmth and strength.

Until it was time for him to take more.

---

IN HIS BED, I WAS CONFINED.

*In his bed, I was owned.*

*In his bed, I never felt more free.*

I sat back from my desk, took in a breath, reread what I'd just written, then looked out the windows at the purple sky.

It was Monday evening.

I'd finally left Tom and arrived home three hours ago.

I felt loose.

Light.

Alive.

Vibrant.

I drew in another breath and got up from my desk. I went to the workbench. I pulled out the expanding folder I kept my latest project in.

Making stacks on the bench, without hesitation, without indecision, I laid them out, page by what would eventually be page.

Once I went through it all, meticulously, I put it back, pouch by pouch. Sometimes a pouch would have only a photo. Sometimes, it'd be stuffed with ten pieces.

I had to go to my cupboard and get more folders.

And when I was done, there were plenty of pouches left after I tucked in the poem I just wrote.

I carefully stowed the project, went back to my desk and saw my teacup was empty.

I didn't pick up the cup and saucer.

I sat in my chair.

Grabbed my cell.

And with my lips tipped up...

I phoned Tom.

# CHAPTER 14

## THE DINNER

*Tom*

Tom was heading to Mika's.

It was the first time he'd been there since they began, even if it'd been nearly two weeks since that happened.

Mika came to him when she felt like coming to him, which was daily. But she was in the middle of a project, and she didn't work nine to five.

This meant she already had his key, plus his garage door opener, and twice since they started, she slid into bed with him in the middle of the night, waking him.

He made love to her.

Then they slept.

She didn't race out the door in the mornings.

Twice, she'd come into town with Cadence and Nora to meet him for lunch. Another evening, it had only been her and Cadence. They went to dinner and a movie and Cadence drove home. Mika came home with him and Lyfted back to her house the next day because Tom had clinic.

Most of the time, it was just Mika.

They'd go out to dinner, but usually they cooked together if she was there in time to eat.

And once, she'd shown in a shitty mood, closed off and surly.

The longer this lasted, Tom started getting flashbacks of Imogen, and he didn't like it.

He was stunned, and relieved to find that he hadn't had to mention it.

Mika was sensitive to his response.

When she'd noted it, she'd cuddled up to him and shared, "I can get in mental zones when I'm working. And what I'm working on now is uber personal. All my work is, but this is off the charts. It got to me today." She'd kissed his cheek and promised, "I'll shake it off and stop being such a bitch."

She'd done just that, but what she said about what she was working on made him curious.

He broached it.

And with zero reluctance, she said, "I'll show you. It's not ready now, but I'd like you to see it." There was a weighty pause that coated his enthusiasm before she concluded, "Truth, I think you need to see it."

He didn't know what that meant, but he didn't press because he knew he'd find out.

That night, she and Cadence were cooking for him, and Nora was still in town, "And she'll be here until she isn't," Mika had explained the ongoing presence of her friend. "I don't have any siblings, or I didn't, until I met Nora when I was thirty."

And that was Tom's blaring clue that Nora Ellington was a fixture in their lives, not that he hadn't noted it with the way they all behaved during their lunches.

Tom was keen to spend time with Mika and Cadence, and even Nora, who was a more mature, more acerbic version of Chloe, and therefore he liked her. He was keen to see what mother and daughter would cook for him. He was keen to get a tour of their home. He was keen to spend time in Mika's space.

And he was spending the night.

"It's not like she doesn't know where Mom is at night, sweetheart," she'd said when he'd asked after how Cadence would react to that. "She likes you. She likes that I'm with you. She knows what we're exploring is important, it's meaningful, you're not just some guy in our space. I also don't want her to have hang-ups about sexuality and intimacy. A romantic relationship includes sex and sleeping in the same bed and spending the night. It's more than okay. It's good. It's healthy. And you're going to be around for a while and not only should she get used to you, there's no reason to have barriers between us that don't need to be there."

He couldn't fight that logic, and it wasn't his daughter.

They'd spent one night apart since they got together, the Monday after they first got together. It was now the second Friday later.

So there was also the fact he didn't want to sleep without Mika.

She'd been leaving her girl and her friend to be with him, it was time for Tom to pony up.

He'd been correct that Sunday morning.

They were both old enough to figure it out and do that fast.

They got the basics down.

History: she was born in Philly and made her way from an unhappy childhood (due to her father) and adolescence (due to what she called her "itchy feet") to New York. He was born in Connecticut and spent a lot of time when he was growing up in New York.

Parents: both of his deceased, her beloved mother dead, her estranged father alive.

Siblings: Mika none, Tom a younger sister he was not close to due to sibling rivalry issues.

Location: Mika was good with spending more time in Arizona, but she was never giving up her brownstone. Tom had frequently tried to talk Genny into buying a place in New York because he vastly preferred it there to LA or anywhere. He'd made happy memories in New York and was a city boy at heart. He liked the vibe, the restaurants, the theater, concerts, museums, parks and shorter travel to places he frequented, like Europe. Genny had no interest and only went to New York to do the Letterman Show or if work sent her there. Though once Chloe got older, she went more frequently for mother-daughter shopping trips, but that was more about Chloe than Imogen. So they didn't buy a place.

Work: Mika's work was about inspiration, not location. She told him she could work anywhere. Unless it was the end game, then she needed to be in either her East Coast or West Coast studio. Tom was not giving up his practice, so that was an issue they needed to resolve.

Religion: Mika's mother was Jewish, her father Catholic. Mika was free-spirited with that, but leaned Jewish and was careful to raise Cadence in the Jewish faith in respect to her mother. Tom was non-denominational Christian.

Exes: Mika'd had no relationships since Rollo, but that didn't mean she didn't have what she described as "fun." Tom shared the fullness of his relationship-non-relationship with Paloma. And other than Paloma, since Genny, none.

He was concerned there was no one serious for her since Rollo. It had been nineteen years.

He resolved to discuss that later.

Day to day: she took cream in her coffee, he did too. She liked her steak rare, as did he. She liked spicy and didn't mind reaching for an antacid before bed to get her hit. Tom, the same. She had no issues with nudity, and he could smell her excitement ratchet up when he ordered her to suck his cock. He liked both of those traits tremendously.

In other words, they got on spectacularly.

Now, they were getting to the even better stuff.

He got to watch her with her daughter in her space.

He and Mika had begun.

Now it was about seeing if they could blend together a family.

It had been so long, Tom almost didn't recognize the feeling he was experiencing.

But he did.

He was happy.

The only pall on this was that Genny was avoiding him. He hadn't spoken with her since the Sunday she ran out of his place (Bowie either). And his texts to her went completely unanswered. The only time he heard from her was in group family texts, where she'd reply to Chloe, Matt, Sasha and in a general way, him.

Nothing direct.

Tom was friends with Bowie, and against the odds, they'd gotten close. But no two men in their positions could be that good of friends. Therefore, in no way could he phone Bowie and make sure everything was all right with Bowie's wife, and Tom's ex.

And he wasn't asking Chloe. Teaching her to keep her nose out of things didn't include giving her a reason to stick it in.

Since Sasha was nursing a snit against him too, she was out. And Tom treated his recovering relationship with Matt with the utmost care. No way in hell he was going to mention to his son that he was having issues with his mother.

He wasn't angry, but he was concerned.

He'd caught up with Genny and Bowie outside his house after she'd seen him with Mika. She'd assured him she was okay, she just felt embarrassed they'd walked in on Tom and Mika that way.

She was a shit liar.

She'd then apologized profusely that they'd let themselves into his place without knocking.

That was an issue. He was Chloe's father, but they were both adults. It wasn't okay for her to invade his space at her whim.

And straight up, that wasn't Genny's anymore.

He'd forgiven her, but he could tell it wasn't about that.

It was about Mika.

Right then, however, it wasn't about Genny, and he wasn't going to regress to a state where it was.

It was about Tom. And Mika.

And getting to the even better stuff.

He parked at the front of Mika's house, and she was coming out the door as he was walking toward it.

She closed the door behind her but didn't approach.

When he got close, she jumped him and went at him so hard, he had to drop his overnight bag to hold her more fully in his arms.

He was making out with her the same time he was laughing.

She broke the kiss, smiling.

"Hey," she greeted.

"Hey," he replied.

"Are you ready to be wowed by our culinary repertoire?"

"Absolutely."

She grinned, let him go and bent to pick up his bag.

"Hup," he grunted.

Her beautiful hair flew as she turned her head to him.

He reached into her and took the bag.

"Such a throwback," she mumbled, going for the door.

"She likes a caveman in bed but bitches about him out of it."

"True, true," she agreed, shooting him a grin and leading the way. "Toss it at the foot of the stairs, we'll take it up later."

He did that.

She nabbed his hand and led him into a room that was pinks and wicker and books and candles (now lit) and leafy plants. It was inviting and there was a fire crackling and both Nora and Cadence were there, each with their own martini glass filled with a liquid that was something vaguely yellowish green.

"Don't judge," Nora ordered, lifting her glass to him. "I got inspired with some pear juice. The color leaves a lot to be desired, but what it lacks in aesthetic, it makes up with flavor."

"Hey, Tom!" Cadence greeted, setting her drink aside and jumping out of the couch to come to him.

She hugged him without reservation and popped back.

"Do you want a cocktail?" she offered.

"Sure," he agreed.

"Nora's Pear Surprise?"

"Lord, don't call it that," Nora demanded. "Call it *La Poire Surprise de Nora*."

"Oh my God, that's *so much better*," Cadence exclaimed.

Nora flitted out her cocktail hand. "I know, darling. It's what I do. My gift."

Cadence turned back to him and lifted her brows.

"I'll give it a go," he said.

"Rad!" she cried, then she dashed off.

Nora's eyes traveled the length of him as she sat insouciantly, one leg crossed over the other in the only cushioned armchair in the room.

Nora was wearing Louboutin heels.

Mika and Cadence were barefoot.

He was beginning to love this crew.

Mika led him to the couch.

"You look fighting fit," she observed after Mika pulled him down beside her.

"Arizona agrees with you," Tom returned. "You've shaken off the pallor of the city. Soon, you'll be dripping in silver and turquoise."

She made a genteel gagging face.

Tom started chuckling.

Mika slouched back, lifting a bent leg to the couch, her knee resting on his thigh. The other leg, she rested its foot on the edge of the coffee table. She then leaned into him.

Tom relaxed into the couch but sat strong for her.

"My God." Nora raised her empty hand, palm their way, fingers curled like she was holding a ball, and she drew circles in the air. "You're already a couple. I don't know whether to start plotting my jealous revenge or order a bottle of Dom delivered."

"Door number two, but no delivery needed considering you bought two at Total Wine the other day," Mika replied.

This perked Nora up, and she sat minutely straighter in her chair, asking Tom, "Have you been to this paradise they call Total Wine?"

He was smiling when he answered, "Yes."

"I could spend a year in there," she shared.

"Is this the source of the pear juice?" he guessed.

"That, and twelve hundred dollars' worth of more shit," Mika told him.

Tom blinked. "Twelve hundred dollars?"

"Dearest," Nora said slowly. "Two bottles of Dom simply because no home should be without them. So, *obviously*. However, I, like all civilized people, normally use Veuve for my everyday champagne needs. And we bought some of that as well."

"And here's me drinking Freixenet," Tom replied.

"Good Lord," Nora snapped.

Mika laughed and said, "Relax, Nora. Tom has a walk-in wine closet. He says he doesn't know much, but I've done an inventory, and he's a connoisseur."

They shared an odd knowing glance before Nora purred, "Oo...do tell. Then do tell me why I haven't been invited for drinks."

He began to do that, but was cut off when Cadence shouted, "*Mom!*"

He didn't know Mika's daughter well, but he had two of his own, and that didn't sound like an I-need-help-mixing-the-cocktails-I'm-too-young-to-drink shout.

It sounded alarmed.

He felt that same coming from Mika and Nora as Mika instantly took her feet.

"I'll be back," she murmured as she hurried out.

When he returned his gaze to her, he saw Nora was staring at the door Mika disappeared through.

"Am I wrong? Did that sound not right?" he asked.

Nora turned to him. "She's her mother with Rollo's looks and her youth returned. God isn't supposed to work that way, giving you a child you're completely simpatico with. I know. All three of my children are friendly and sociable and constantly telling me to stop acting so privileged, insular and effete, as if I'm *acting* in *any* manner. I *am* privileged, people annoy me greatly, so I'm purposefully insular, but I have a black belt in effete. Those two are two peas in a pod. Not much riles either of them. Not much throws them either. So, no. You are not wrong. That didn't sound right."

He was pushing up to standing when both mother and daughter came into the room.

They each carried a martini glass and an expression he couldn't read.

He finished standing. "What's happening?"

"I think you should sit back down," Mika suggested.

"Why?" he asked.

Cadence offered him the glass she was carrying. Automatically, he took it.

It was harder for Mika to tug him back down to the couch that time, but she curled into him at once when he was seated, still holding her glass, her eyes to her daughter.

"You show Nora, honey, I'll show Tom."

With that, she leaned even further into him and pulled her phone out of her back jeans pocket as he heard Cadence say to Nora, "One of my friends just sent it to me."

He watched as she brought up her texts. He saw Cadence's name at the top of the string. A video share on the screen.

She hit go.

The screen shifted to YouTube, it took a moment, then the unmistakable set of Elsa Cohen's gossip show came on.

"Oh fuck," he muttered.

"Mm-hmm," Mika agreed.

He watched Elsa clap, jumping happily in her seat.

She then launched in.

*"My wonderful watchers, do I have news for you! The match of the century! I would have never dreamt it in all my wildest imaginings, and my imaginings can veer to the wild. I'll be quiet for once and just show you this majesty."*

A picture came onscreen of Tom and Mika standing outside the Hermosa Inn after they'd had dinner at Lon's.

She was wearing an edgy black top with one shoulder covered, a sharp angle cut along her left collarbone so the other shoulder was bare. She'd paired this with army pants that she'd rolled the hem into a high cuff. On her feet were Sophia Webster four-inch stiletto sandals, replete with a butterfly at the back of the heel, a thin ankle strap, and a black butterfly vein pattern, filled with soft pastel colors from blue to green to pink to yellow.

Tom was in dark jeans, a white shirt, a linen blazer and fawn suede loafers.

She was leaning her front into his side, both her hands clasping one of his, her head tipped back, her glorious hair tumbling down almost to her waist.

He was, probably, watching the valet pull up his car, but he had a small smile on his face at whatever she'd said.

Mika had eyes to his profile and was smiling radiantly, lots of teeth.

The screen returned to Elsa.

*"Oh my God, wonderful watchers! Do we love beautiful couples coming together beautifully, or what? Don't answer that. We do!"*

She leaned toward the camera.

*"I can't even begin to tell you how beside myself I am at this pairing. We have been waiting with bated breath for what has felt like forever for the fantabulous Mika Stowe to finally find a man worthy of her, and here we are! None other than the handsome, talented champion, Dr. Tom Pierce. Oh, this is such fabulous news. I cannot wait to see what happens next!"*

Mika touched the screen and said, "She goes on to gab about someone else."

Tom sat back and took a drink.

Yes, the color left a lot to be desired, but it was damned tasty.

That wasn't the only reason he took another healthy sip.

"You're hardly a stranger to attention, Tom," Nora drawled, watching him closely over the top of her glass.

"It's still annoying," he replied.

"Utterly," Mika grumbled.

He turned to her.

She did not look happy.

"It'll be a story for a while, honey. And then she'll be on to someone new," he assured.

"Uh, not to be a downer, or to contradict you, Tom," Cadence said carefully, and he shifted his attention to her to see she was scrolling on her phone. "But it looks like Elsa has a fascination with your family. Your names are in like, *a lot* of the titles of her episodes."

"I'm a minor player," he shared.

"Mika isn't," Nora informed him, and he saw she again had her eyes pinned to him.

"I can assure you I'm used to being with a woman far more famous than me," he reminded her. "And it isn't an issue in the slightest."

She lifted her eyebrows and tipped her head to the side, nonverbally conceding the point.

Mika's question brought his attention to her.

"Are you okay with this?" she asked.

She looked worried.

"Am I having dinner with you and your daughter and your best friend?" he asked in return.

Her face cracked with the start of a smile. "Yes."

"Then...yes."

She pushed into him and touched his lips with hers.

When she settled again into the couch, he did too, and looked to Nora.

"You do know after this"—he raised his drink to her—"that you're on cocktail duty any time we're together."

"I will accept that appointment with alacrity, sir," she replied.

Tom grinned.

"We made chicken mole, Tom. Do you like Mexican food?" Cadence asked.

He stared at her. "You made mole?"

She nodded.

"From scratch?"

She nodded more enthusiastically.

"Can't wait, honey," he said.

She beamed.

Christ, what a great kid.

She then jumped up, sloshing her cocktail in its glass. "Oh no! We forgot the guac appetizer. I'll go get it."

With that, she put down her glass and raced from the room.

"You got a great kid, baby," he murmured his earlier thought to Mika.

"Totally know that, my handsome man," Mika replied.

"I've decided to plot my jealous revenge," Nora shared.

Mika and Tom laughed.

Cadence came back with the guacamole and chips.

They munched, talked, drank, with Mika and Cadence infrequently heading to the kitchen to check on things.

The Winston/Core Point situation came up, and as Mika knew, but Tom briefed Cadence and Nora, Jamie's investigator was digging into it. She liked to be thorough but doing that took time.

So they were in a holding pattern.

They were getting ready to move to the dining room when his phone vibrated against his ass.

He pulled it out, looked at it, and the screen told him Paloma was calling.

Not a word from her since he ended it via voicemail. It had been weeks.

His guess, she'd seen the Elsa thing.

He ignored the call and did as he was told, that being to stay put while Mika and Cadence made the finishing touches on dinner and opened wine.

His phone vibrated again before they were called into the dining room.

He pulled it out to turn it off as Nora said, "You should take it. She won't leave you alone."

He lifted his eyes to hers. "Sorry?"

"Paloma," she stated. "My ex was involved with her, before we were exes."

Another indication he chose very poorly with Paloma.

Tom sat still and stared.

"She's difficult."

"We're no longer together," he reminded her.

"Difficult, sadly, does not have an expiration date, nor, as my ex-husband discovered, boundaries." She rose. "I'll make sure the appropriate amount of wine is poured. Sally in whenever you're finished dealing with her."

"I'm sorry about"—she stopped moving when he started talking—"your ex."

"I see you're concerned about your choice. Don't be. Men, as well as women, feel fools when they're defrauded. It's one of the things grifters count on when they're grifting people, hoping your embarrassment will keep you silent. But you did nothing any normal person wouldn't do. You had a relationship with an attractive woman you were attracted to. It was *she* who lied and deceived. The world would be a much more just place if victims got beyond being victimized and put the onus of guilt on the ones who actually committed the crimes."

Delivering that, she swanned off.

His phone had gone silent, but it rang again.

He'd tried to get hold of her for weeks, she'd avoided him.

She wanted him, she called three times in a row.

Jaw set, he answered it.

"Paloma."

"You *fucking dick.*"

Tom said nothing, and not because he'd never heard her sound like that, or what she said.

Simply, he had nothing to say.

"Are you fucking kidding me, replacing me with Mika Stowe?"

He did not explain how he felt about the word "replacing."

He pointed out, "We're no longer together."

"Because you broke up with me on a *fucking* voicemail."

"I asked you to talk, and I didn't do that just once, Paloma."

Considering she had no worthwhile reply, she went with, "You fucking *asshole.*"

"I think we're done," he said.

He didn't request she not call again because he intended to block her the instant he disconnected the call.

"Oh no you don't, motherfucker. And we're not done. Not by a long fucking shot."

He wasn't sure he'd heard her say fuck once the entire time they were together.

A grift.

He'd been grifted.

It didn't feel good.

But it was over, so he didn't allow it to feel much of anything.

She hung up.

Tom blocked her.

He did not like her parting message.

However, he had chicken mole to eat in good company.

So he didn't give it much thought.

---

"WELL, SHIT."

They were in bed.

He very much liked Mika's bed.

In fact, Cadence had given him a tour while Nora and Mika sat outside under the stars drinking more wine, so he knew now he liked the whole house.

Mika was wearing a matching cami and some loose sleep shorts, her hair pulled up in a big pony at the top of her head.

He was in pajama bottoms.

He was also stretched out, head to a tall stack of her pillows, arms crossed behind his head.

She was cross-legged beside him.

And he'd just told her about Paloma.

"What can she do?" he asked in an effort to reassure her, because Paloma couldn't do much.

She lived thousands of miles away from him.

They had some acquaintances but didn't really run in the same circles.

He had never become close enough to share anything deep with her.

And according to Jamie, she didn't have a lot of friends.

He'd belatedly noticed that about her.

There was no Nora for her. Nor anyone like Mika's Teddy, who was Mika's PA, but more, Teddy was her friend.

Mika talked fondly, even lovingly, about others in her life. Those she'd lost, like Eleanor. And those she still had, like Lyra Upton, the lead guitar and singer of Rollo's band, the Pissed-Off Hippies. Then there was Stella Gunn of the Blue Moon Gypsies, Henry Gagnon, the famous photographer, and Pearl Bazer, fashion icon.

Her life was full, including full of people.

Paloma had talked a good game, but she'd never asked him to a party with her friends, or out to dinner...with her friends. People were polite to her face, but he'd never seen anyone react to her with any real warmth.

Of course, it was all clear now.

Then, it wasn't that he didn't notice.

It was that he didn't care.

"I don't know, but I've...heard things."

Mika didn't elaborate because she was trying to protect him.

"Nora told me about Paloma and her ex."

She looked surprised. "Really?"

"She didn't go into detail. But Jamie had a few things to share about her too. We weren't that close. We weren't anything, but..." He trailed off.

She grinned. "Fuck buddies."

He grinned back. "Yes." He took a hand from behind his head and squeezed her knee. "Are you okay with that?"

"With what?"

"That I had a relatively lengthy relationship with a woman that was surface and existed mainly to provide company on occasion, but for the most part was about sexual release," Tom elaborated.

"Well, considering that's all I've had since Rollo died, I'd be a hypocrite if I was."

They were there.

And they were who they were.

Thus, Tom went for it.

"Is there a reason nothing got serious for you?" he asked.

She shrugged. "You have the spark I had with Rollo, nothing else will do."

Well...

Fuck.

That stung, even if it shouldn't. It was base to be jealous of a dead man.

That didn't negate the fact he was.

But he'd asked.

"I also felt it when I met this married man before Rollo," she said quietly.

His gaze riveted on her.

"But he was devoted to his wife and family, so that couldn't be. Still, it was so strong, I couldn't even be his friend, because I knew it'd hurt too much to endure, to feel it and not consummate it. Now, as life gives gifts even as it wrests others away, I see the wisdom of my decision because having him exceeded all expectations."

What she said meant so much, it warmed his chest, particularly the left side of it.

Which was probably why he teased, "Exceeded expectations?"

"He's a monster in bed, and I *waaaaaaaaaay* get off on it," she amended.

Tom chuckled.

She smiled as he did, but her smile died.

"I don't have good thoughts about Paloma, Tom."

He pushed up and wrapped a hand around her neck. "She'd probably just seen it. She was angry. She called. Let off steam. It'll likely end there."

"Right," she said dubiously.

"Right." He was not dubious.

She didn't say anything more, just studied him.

"I'm okay," he told her.

"I'm glad, baby. But are we gonna fuck?"

His brows rose slowly. "Your daughter is—"

"Across the courtyard and the walls are thick." She paused. "*Very* thick."

He grinned at her again.

Mika grinned back.

Then he pulled her over him.

And they commenced fucking.

# CHAPTER 15

## THE BROWNSTONE

*Tom*

Tom watched as Nora, Cadence and Mika wandered across the tarmac with Chloe and Judge.

And even though Hale was alighting from the jet, Tom took that opportunity to pull out his phone and deal with one last thing before he went away for the weekend.

He called Genny.

He got voicemail again.

As such, his voice was tight when he left her a message.

"This is the fifth voicemail I've left, and I lost count of the texts. However, I'm aware that none of our children have sensed anything amiss with you. That said, clearly, something is the matter, your problem is with me, and you aren't sharing it. This is familiar territory, Imogen, and like before, I'm not a fan. If you have an issue, call me and we'll talk it out. I won't phone again," he warned. "But I'll remind you, we share history, and we share children, and we made a commitment to keep our relationship strong for those children. Don't fall down on your side of that."

He disconnected, shoved the phone into the inside pocket of his sports jacket and moved to catch up with the rest of the clan.

Hale was there from California, dropping in to pick them up in his private jet and take them to New York so they could meet with Jamie and his investigator.

Nora, however, was catching a ride home.

Cadence was coming along in order to meet with her teachers and turn in the several papers her mother went into hilarious fits of astonishment about that she'd managed to complete.

It was Thursday afternoon, almost a week after chicken mole night, and Tom, Mika, Cadence, Judge and Chloe were going to spend a long weekend away, returning the next Tuesday.

He was looking forward to experiencing Mika's New York life. He was looking forward to a change of scenery.

And he was pleased there might be some movement in the Winston/Core Point situation because it hung like a dark cloud over all their heads, and he wanted to see the back of it, with all the guilty getting their just desserts.

By the time he got there, Hale had greeted everyone else and came in for a hug from Tom.

They held firm, clapping backs, and Tom asked, "How's things?"

"Busy," Hale replied, pulling away.

He inspected Tom.

Tom let him as this was not unusual.

Even with what he'd done, something that ended his marriage, a marriage that was to a woman who Hale was closer to than his own mother, Tom had not lost Hale.

Matt had been understandably furious.

Hale had closed ranks around Tom and made sure at every opportunity Tom knew he was loved, and nothing he could do would change that.

There were times in the beginning, losing Genny, Matt closing down on him, the girls hurt, his family in tatters because of what he'd done, Hale doing this had been the only thing that held Tom together.

He and Hale had always been close. It was an uncomfortable

admission that he'd make only to himself (and perhaps, if they ever went there, he would tell Mika). But he had always felt closer to Hale than he did to Matt.

This was because Hale was like Tom.

And Matt was like Hale's father, Corey.

It wasn't just fatherly pride when he said Matt was a genius. They'd had him tested. He simply was a genius. And Tom had always wanted something deeper with his son.

There was just an unknown barrier against it, Tom sensed for them both even before the breakup.

It was bottom line truth that Tom loved his son so much, he'd take a bullet for him.

But Hale had done what fathers wished for eventually from their sons.

As he grew into an adult, he'd adapted into a friend.

Tom didn't have that with Matt, even if he'd tried.

Again, Matt was like Corey.

Enigmatic.

"I'm good," he quietly answered Hale's unspoken question. "Did you meet Mika?"

"She's pretty. Great nose."

Christ, only Hale would appreciate Mika's distinctive nose enough to mention it right off the bat.

Hale…and Tom.

He gave his boy another clap, this one on the arm.

"Cute daughter," Hale went on.

Tom's attention intensified on Hale.

He was twenty-seven, far too old for Cadence.

But Hale wasn't checking out an eighteen-year-old.

He was jerking his chin up at Chloe while a playful grin spread on his face.

"Tom just asked for half of my fortune to pay for your wedding. Sister, you gotta scale back," he called to her.

"That is the first, and the last joke you're allowed to make of my wedding," Chloe sniffed.

"What are the colors? Blush and bashful?" he asked, even as he extended his arm to invite them to start ascending the steps to the jet.

"Are you honestly invoking *Steel Magnolias*?" Chloe demanded.

"I've not had a single girlfriend who hasn't forced me to endure that film," Hale returned.

"As usual, you're dating the *wrong* women," Chloe retorted, turning to the steps.

Hale looked down at Tom and joked, "I think she's right."

Hale was carefully, with intent, purpose, and reasoning, giving away much of his father's fortune.

But from what Tom could tell so far, he had shit taste in women, which he used as an excuse not to be with one of them for very long.

This could be a byproduct of the fact that his mother had turned bitter after her divorce from his father, and she took zero pains to hide it, so Hale had developed a phobia to commitment in order not to make the same mistake.

Or he could be holding out for his Genny.

Or Mika.

The men waited until all the women hit the stairs.

Then, Tom first, Judge next and Hale last, they all boarded the plane.

---

It was in the back of the limo when he listened to it.

Two limos had met their plane, one sent by Jamie to pick up Chloe and Judge, and they dropped Nora home.

The other was there to take Hale to his father's penthouse, a property he was considering selling because he'd never liked it.

And Hale was dropping Mika, Cadence and Tom at Mika's.

The other three loved ones in his limo were talking, and Tom was sitting back and enjoying it.

On the plane ride, Hale had adopted his brotherly ways with Cadence. She'd been a little starstruck at first, and he'd taken pains to be approachable and that quickly grew to teasing.

But Mika and Hale hit it off straightaway.

He was sensing this was a skill of Mika's. She was cool and confident, so much, he suspected to many she was intimidating. There was also a reserve to her that, out in public, as well as times like at the start with Bray and Pris, he noticed she erected.

But it wasn't a shield.

It was just that, for Mika, not everyone was invited in. Only when she felt sure about you did the aloofness melt away and the warmth surge in.

But to anyone in Tom's life, she opened up immediately.

While they were talking, he checked his phone and saw he had two voicemails and two texts that had come in during the flight.

One voicemail from the office, one from a number he didn't know.

One text was from Sasha, asking, since he was out of town, if she could stay at his place.

He ignored that and the spike in his blood pressure it gave him.

The other text was from Matt, and it was so much better than the one he got from his youngest, it gave him a sense of emotional whiplash.

Matt's noted that his spring break was coming up, and he wanted to know if he could come out to Arizona and stay with Tom.

Tom's chest felt like it had caved in, he was so fucking thrilled to get that request.

He bypassed Sasha's and sent a one-word reply to his son.

*Absolutely.*

None of these communications, obviously, were from Genny.

He moved on to the voicemails.

The office was first, and it wasn't an emergency, so he went to the next voicemail.

And he took pains to appear calm as he listened.

Paloma, from a new number, sniping at him.

"You blocked me? Are you serious? *You blocked me?* Fuck you, Tom Pierce. *Fuck you.*"

That was it.

When he finished listening, he deleted it and blocked the new number.

But he was unsettled.

There was no reason for her to call him. And there was no reason for her to be as angry as she sounded.

He'd give her a pass after she first saw him with a new woman.

Now?

No.

When he came back into the limo, Cadence was talking, and both Mika and Hale were regarding him.

It seemed he failed at appearing calm.

He gave them both a slight shake of his head to indicate he was all right, even though he wasn't.

Hale didn't need to know anything about this.

Tom would share with Mika later.

Neither Hale nor Mika made a thing of it, and not too long later, they pulled up outside Mika's brownstone.

Tom glanced out the window.

It was on a tree-lined street in Chelsea. Four story walk-up. Narrow. Wrought iron fencing around the front. Five steps up to the front door. The façade was red-and-brownstone.

Mika was asking Hale if he wanted to come in and have a drink or join them for dinner as Cadence clambered out and the chauffeur exited the vehicle to get their luggage.

"I have a dinner meeting tonight," Hale replied. "But if the invitation extends while you're in town, I'd love to come another night."

"Tomorrow?" Mika asked.

"Perfect," Hale said.

Hale got out with them, touched Cadence's arm, kissed Mika's cheek and gave a one-armed hug and slap on the back to Tom, which he returned.

"Swing by at ten-thirty to take you to Jamie's office?" he asked when he caught Tom's eyes.

Tom nodded. "Perfect, son. Thanks."

With a wave, Hale got back into his limo.

Mika took Tom's hand.

Cadence was already climbing the steps.

The front door was open, their bags nowhere to be seen, so they'd probably been set inside.

And a man of average height but rather fit build with a massive swoop of thick blond hair rising from his forehead stood there.

He was wearing a pair of perfectly tailored black trousers and a slender wine-colored cashmere sweater. At his throat, the collar of a pale pink button-up could be seen. It had long ends that were tied over-and-under, like a short scarf.

The man's large, tortoiseshell-framed glasses were such size and shape, they were immediately iconic. And his very thick russet beard was so perfectly clipped, Tom knew he had a barber do it for him.

Tom guessed this was Teddy.

Cadence was now facing him, and they did the double-cheek kiss while he murmured, "Darling."

Teddy didn't budge an inch as Cadence slid past him to get inside.

Mika and Tom approached, and Tom withstood a top to toe to top, back to toe to eyes before Teddy dismissed him entirely, looked to Mika and coolly offered a cheek, repeating his murmur of "Darling."

She kissed his cheek, went after the other one, then she stepped to the side at the top of the stoop as Teddy continued to bar the door.

"Teddy, this is Tom Pierce. Tom, this is my dearest, darling Teddy," she introduced, as if she wasn't standing on her own stoop and this introduction wasn't better done when they were at the very least inside the door.

This annoyed Tom.

However, that, he managed not to let show, and Tom offered a hand. "Teddy."

Teddy stared at it a moment as if he was going to decline a handshake or maybe offer him some antibacterial gel before he deigned to touch Tom, then he shook as a supercilious curl took hold on his upper lip.

At once, after he released Tom's hand, he melted into the shadows of Mika's house without another word.

"I told you he's protective," Mika reminded him as Tom remained where he was so she could precede him.

Protective was not the word he'd use.

"Mm," was Tom's reply.

She ducked her head but failed to hide her smile as she stepped inside.

Tom moved in behind her, taking the last step up into a vestibule with a spectacular mosaic tiled floor. Then through a second set of doors into a short, narrow hallway with a beautifully laid parquet floor.

He followed Mika as she moved into a room to the right.

And he entered Wonderland.

At what he saw, and the amount of it, he was struck mute and motionless.

All he could do was stare.

Walls of shelves filled with books. Curios. Pictures. Sculpture. A puffy, cream damask couch at the back of the room. A robin's-egg-blue amoeba chair at the front window. A beat-up leather wingchair and ottoman. A straight-backed tapestry armchair with carved-wood arms. More couches. More chairs. Tables filled with framed photos. Pedestals topped with massive bouquets of what looked like fresh flowers.

Tom wandered in further.

The space was dark. Overfilled.

There was lots of wood.

The rugs on the floors were thick, crafted of rich colors.

The famous photograph Mika took of Stella Gunn that featured on the cover of her photojournalistic book *Women and Guitars* was above the fireplace in the front half of the room.

Gunn, the frontwoman of the Blue Moon Gypsies, was a step away from her microphone. She'd flipped her head back, and all you could see of her face was part of her profile and the bottom of her jaw. Her long, dark hair was flying all around her head in fat tendrils that looked like snakes, as if she was a gorgeous Medusa and you didn't mind being turned to stone. The photo was taken feet up, this having the effect of making Gunn appear as tall and potent as a skyscraper. The way she held her guitar made it seem like it was another appendage, not hanging on her from a strap.

But the strap had rivets in it that said KAI+TALLULAH=LIFE.

As Tom continued through the room, he saw the microscope which was the first part of Mika he'd ever experienced. It was on a long, thin table behind a couch that separated the front area from the space at the back.

The microscope and its slides were the only things on the table, save for a wide, squat glass vase filled with powdery poofs of white peonies (which Mika would later tell him was another homage to Yoko Ono, as she had a predilection for black and white, so fresh white, or black flowers were always on that table when Mika was home).

He wanted to touch the microscope.

He didn't.

He was too fascinated by this space that was a cocoon of life and living. Art and study. Wonder and learning. Nostalgia and presence. Being and doing. Joy and reflection. Friends and family.

All his adult life, this was what he wanted to build.

A family home filled with all of those things.

Like his father's study had been in the house where he grew up.

And his mother's sewing room.

Tom hadn't wept when he lost his father. He'd kept it together. His dad had died in his early sixties, relatively young, and it had been an unexpected blow. It was the first loss the kids had experienced, and all three of them were undone. Even in private or alone with Genny, Tom knew he couldn't let go of the emotion or it'd consume him.

But when he walked into his mother's sewing room after she'd passed five years later, he lost it. Genny had to force him into a chair and curl into his lap and hold him for what felt like hours as the grief for both of them came unleashed.

It had been another kind of death, working with his sister Teresa to dismantle their childhood home. And that had nothing to do with

Teri acting like a pain in the ass throughout the whole melancholy exercise.

But her behaving like that didn't help.

It was on this thought that Tom stopped dead in front of the fireplace at the back of the long room that ran the length of the house.

It was a cozier area. Closer. Darker.

Over the fire was another massive photograph that he'd never seen, but it had Mika's signature.

Rollo, behind his drumkit.

Black and white. Definitely taken during a concert. His dark hair was soaked with sweat. His T-shirt plastered to his chest. The lighting of the stage illuminated him almost ethereally. The dust motes dancing around him seemed magical.

His left hand was hitting a drum off to his side.

But his right was extended, drumstick pointing toward the camera.

He had a massive, joyous smile on his face.

And he had this because he was looking at the woman he loved.

"I might soon let the world have that," she whispered in his ear.

He tore his eyes off the picture and looked down at her.

"As the cover of the project I'm putting together," she finished.

That explained her mood of a couple of weeks ago.

"I'll show you when we get back," she offered.

He wanted to see it and he didn't.

What he knew for certain was, that picture should be hers and Cadence's alone.

Which was why he asked, "Are you sure about that picture on the cover?"

She smiled, something evocative running through her eyes, before she answered, "With what I'm working on, I'm not sure of anything."

He was coming to understand why she wouldn't be.

"Indian tonight?" he heard asked crisply, their intimate tête-à-tête interrupted.

She pursed her lips at the intrusion, then cleared her expression and turned to Teddy, who was standing with his arms crossed on his chest in front of the microscope, appearing peeved.

"I'll order it before I go," he went on.

*That'd be good,* Tom thought, *Considering Mika texted you before we left Phoenix, sharing our choices and letting you know she'd text again when we landed in order that you could have it waiting for us when we arrived. Because, as you know, it's nine at night here, but even our time, it's dinnertime.*

"We'd appreciate it, honey," she said.

Teddy glared at Tom. He glared at Mika.

Then he stated, "I don't do luggage, *as you know,*" before he stormed off.

When he disappeared, Mika turned right to Tom.

"I'm on the third floor. Cadence is on the fourth. It's a lot of stairs, but the kitchen, dining and family rooms are on the second floor."

"I won two consecutive grand slams, an additional three career grand slams, and I played senior tennis competitively until I hit age fifty. I haven't quit playing, I just quit competing. I can carry some bags up a couple of flights of stairs."

His tone was light, but not light enough.

He knew this when she asked, "Are you annoyed?"

"Your PA doesn't like me."

"My PA likes one person on this earth. Cadence. He likes me sometimes, most of the time he tolerates me. He's married, and sometimes he behaves like he doesn't even like his husband."

Tom just stared at her.

"In other words, he's a New Yorker," she concluded.

"Right," Tom replied.

"He's very good at his job. I practically never have to deal with the outside world unless I want to, he's that good at it. And that job for him includes hiding that he'd throw himself in front of a train if that meant pushing me out of the path of it."

Tom relaxed. "Right."

"And this mood you're in isn't about the voicemail you listened to in the car?" She took a breath before she added, "Or the picture?"

He forced himself to relax further. "You were married and very much in love at one point in your life. You lost him. If I had difficulty dealing with that fact, I'd be an ass, considering I had the same before you, and she walked in on us eating blueberry pancakes after a night of sex."

Her lips quirked.

"So it's about the voicemail," she noted.

"The voicemail was Paloma sharing she was more than mildly unhappy I blocked her. And she used a different number to leave it."

No lip quirk, Mika now appeared concerned. "Okay, she's toeing the line of stalker territory with that."

This seemed to be a leap.

"How so?" he asked.

"She used a different number because she thought you might pick up. Blocked callers can leave voicemails. It'll just note it's from a blocked number. If she was okay leaving a voicemail, she could use her own phone."

"Since she left a message, it's obvious she wanted me to hear what she had to say."

"Tom, she threatened Roland with exposing his infidelity to a journalist."

"Okay. But she'd say what about me?"

"Whatever she wanted to say."

"And that journalist wouldn't print it unless they could verify it."

"It depends on what journalist you're talking about."

Tom shook his head. "Honey, if you think I give that first fuck what some woman in middle America who buys gossip rags thinks of me, I need to do a much better job of letting you get to know me."

That made her out-and-out smile.

He wasn't finished.

"Genny and I broke up or had huge troubles in our marriage multiple times before it actually happened. She slept with her co-stars. I slept with her co-stars. Sasha is Corey's love child. You name it, it's been said, all of it lies, all of it someone out there believes. When your life isn't fascinating enough, you seek something fascinating. And it doesn't matter if it's true or not. You need for it to be true, so you make it true in your head. If I gave even that first shit, I'd have been a broken man a long time ago."

"As you know," she began, "I've become an object of fascination of late, and I'm not even close to being done saying what I have to say or expressing what I need to express. The way it's jumbled up in my head, demanding to be released, I won't stop until I'm eighty."

"Georgia O'Keeffe had to quit painting on her own due to macular degeneration when she was eighty-four and wrote her autobiography after that. When you have something to say, and you have talent, you should say it, I don't give a fuck what your age. And if you get attention because of it, in your case, good. Because it's deserved."

Her head ticked.

But her mouth declared, "I really like you a whole lot, Dr. Thomas Pierce."

Tom stood with this beautiful woman who was in his life, in this beautiful room she'd built over the decades, and he was not talking shit when he said, "I can guarantee you I like you a whole lot more."

"Impossible," she whispered.

"Care to wager?" he offered.

She didn't, he knew.

Because instead, she kissed him.

# CHAPTER 16

## THE INVESTIGATOR AND THE JOURNALIST

### Tom

Tom opened his eyes, saw Mika's hair and felt suffocated.

He lifted a hand and pushed aside the thick cat tail that was lying across his lips and interfering with his nostrils.

It flicked back into place.

He was afraid to turn his head because he knew he'd have a cat's ass in his face if he did.

Instead, he felt his way.

His fingers encountered warm, thick fur, proving him correct, and he got an angry "*Mwrr,*" as he shifted the feline bulk off his pillow.

Mika lifted her head from his chest, blinked sleepily at Tom, then looked beyond him.

"Moon, stop being a pain in Mommy's ass," she ordered the cat in a husky voice that had a physical effect on Tom's anatomy.

Moon stepped on Tom's chest to butt Mika's face with his own, doing this purring.

White lower carriage, gray around his ears, eyes and sides of his face with more splotches down his back, full gray tail.

All the rest of the animals were Cadence's.

Moon was Mika's.

And Moon, along with Teddy, was not a fan of Tom.

He'd learned this before he woke with the cat's ass in his face. He had scratches on his hip that Moon delivered while he was moving inside Mika last night.

The cat had drawn blood.

They'd had to stop what they were doing so Mika could shut him out of the room.

Tom understood why the cat was hers when she got up after they were done and opened the door to let him back in.

It was good to know Tom was her favorite guy.

But Moon came in at a close second.

"You'll win him over," Mika was saying.

"I don't think so," Tom replied.

She got out of bed and took hold of her cat.

She then walked to the door wearing a little, stretchy nighty in a dusky plum color that covered her to mid-thigh, was high up front and back, but dipped very low under her arms, exposing side breast and lots of skin almost to her waist.

It and her sex hair and her long legs and her entire affect was perfect in her surroundings.

Her main floor was brimming with life, memories and personality.

Her bedroom took that maximalist into overdrive.

The wall behind the bed was painted in a massive mural of gigantic flowers in pinks, purples and reds.

There were big plants. A leopard print chair matched with a gold and black zebra print ottoman. There was fringe. Brass. Different-shaped mirrors and art practically coating the fuchsia pink walls. There were stacks of books on the floor that rose to Tom's hip. Gold-lacquered bamboo tables with glass tops. Floral lampshades. Ornaments that ranged from Chinese dogs to subversive Barbie doll art.

The bedclothes and the upholstery of the couch were heavy silk in bright, rich, warm shades of a pink that was almost red (couch) and purple that was almost blue (bed) with an overabundance of velvet, fake fur and animal print toss pillows.

Tom would never consider decorating a room like this or think he could abide spending time in one.

But when he'd walked in last night holding Mika's hand, it felt like a seductress had led him to her secret den, and she intended to hold him captive until he was addicted to her—body and soul.

That job for Mika, however, was already accomplished.

The result was that Tom loved being in her room, and he would with or without her.

Because every inch was so *her*.

He didn't tend to be a fantasist, but Mika also had that quality. Making her surroundings adventures, interesting ones you wanted to experience to their fullest.

His home looked and felt like a hotel. A nice one, but although he was managing to inject some personality into it the longer he lived there, it still had that clinical feel that said, "You're welcome here, but stay tidy, and then you must go."

There were times he thought he'd overstayed his welcome, and he lived there.

And when the kids were growing up, their home felt much the same way. Genny and Tom were too busy to think about it, so they hired a designer who gave them a Malibu Family Beach House Where Rich and Famous People Live! They had a housekeeper that kept it neat, so Tom wasn't sure he'd ever stepped on one of their toys.

He didn't hate it. He liked the sun and the beach, his children and wife made any space home, and Genny loved it.

Was it anything close to this?

Not by a long shot.

Tom found this wasn't a fantasy, even if it was fantastical.

It was a dream.

He heard the door close and came back to the room.

As such, he saw the look on Mika's face, and he knew Moon was now on the other side of the door for a reason.

He started to get hard.

"What if Cadence is awake?" he murmured as she put a knee to the bed by his hip.

"She isn't, but if she is"—she pulled the covers down—"you need to be quiet."

*He* did?

It was Mika who was abandoned in making—

The thought exited his head as his pajama bottoms were tugged down his hips.

He smiled.

She cleared the material from his feet.

He opened his legs for her.

She positioned between them.

He bent his knees and put his hands behind his head.

With soft licks of her tongue, she wetted him.

She took her time doing this.

Tom liked it, and let it go on.

But then, enough was enough.

"Take me," he ordered.

Her extraordinary eyes lifted to him, heat behind them.

Then she bore down.

Tom's smile got lazy.

And he managed the feat of being quiet as she sucked him off and swallowed the load.

---

"Okay, now that I have you in my thrall, Dr. Pierce, tell me what was on your mind before I sucked you off."

Of course she hadn't missed thoughts were weighing on him.

Tom grinned up at Mika, the urge to pull her hair away from her face, to feel its silk against his skin, was twitching his fingers, but he thought better of it.

It was curtaining them in her bed.

All he could see was her face, those startling eyes looking into his.

All she could see was his.

He needed that in that moment. The world shut out. Only the two of them in it.

"It's going to be a lot," he warned.

"I'm fucking up royally if I haven't demonstrated yet that I like a lot from you," she replied.

Even if he was about to bring heavy to her bed, that made his lips quirk.

Then he gave her the heavy. "I was realizing how much more of me I set aside to make the ones I love happy."

"Tommy," she whispered.

"It's on me. If I'd shared, they loved me too. They'd have wanted me to have it."

Mika, as ever, went right to the meat of the matter.

"By you referencing 'they,' are we talking Imogen?"

"I eventually want us to become a family again," he cautioned. "In other words, I don't want you to develop resentment toward her."

"That means yes," she noted.

"Honey—"

"You take responsibility for yourself, Tommy. Do you know that? Recognize it? No, you aren't perfect. Yes, you made mistakes. One of them, particularly, was huge. But you take responsibility for it." She took a breath, cupped his jaw and carried on, "Please know, I'm not that person. I know there are two sides to every story, and I've never met Imogen. But she's not my priority. You are. You always will be. Still, I won't jump to judgment. When I meet her, I'll let her form my opinion of her. That doesn't mean I can't have an opinion. And I hope she, too, can take responsibility for herself."

"She's a very good woman," Tom said.

"I have no doubt," Mika replied. "You married her. You loved her. And you have great taste."

That made Tom's lips quirk again.

Mika's did the same before she went on, "But you were up in your head, putting distance between us, because you couldn't forgive yourself. That worries me."

"She's forgiven me."

Quietly, Mika suggested, "I think the closure you need to have, baby, is she needs forgiveness too."

Tom couldn't go there.

"And you need to forgive yourself," Mika whispered.

"I'm not sure that will ever happen," he warned.

She gave a single nod of understanding.

"Part of me thinks that's okay because you're mine now, and it means you'll never do anything like that to me. But Tom"—she drew closer—"part of me finds that unsettling, because I already know you won't do anything like that to me. It's just not the man you are."

"It was the man I became."

She shifted with agitation and declared, "I'll tell you what, if Rollo turned away from me in bed, that was such a huge part of our life, our relationship, who we were, our sexuality, the depth and trust in our intimacy, I honestly don't know what I'd do. I'm a pretty confident chick, but that would be a blow. This man I loved and committed to indicating he didn't find me attractive anymore?" She shook her head. "Devastating."

At the effect her words were having, in order to keep his throat from collapsing, Tom concentrated on that, and not replying.

"With you and Imogen," she continued, "it was more than that. It was *every* intimacy you two shared. I'm not absolving where you went with that. I'm pointing out you're being very hard on yourself."

When Tom remained silent, Mika kept speaking.

"Women bear the brunt of this too, and they do it silently. Stereotypically, men wander. I'm not going to get into that now. But it happens a lot. It might not lead them to another woman, but it happens often, and it's expected. Also expected, a woman sucking it up and staying loyal, *unless* he strays, giving her a reason to leave. The thing people don't talk about is, women do it too. They wander, mentally, emotionally and physically. I've never been in a relationship long enough to have personal knowledge of this, but I have a ton of friends. There are peaks and valleys and sometimes those valleys are low and wide. You're a handsome, accomplished man expected to be confident in your vitality and sexuality. Your wife shook that. It's not a minor blow, it's a colossal one. As such, it is not a small deal, for women *or* for men. To end, you need to cut yourself some slack. You didn't do right. But you're not Roland, fucking everything that moves just because you can."

"You're worried I'll shut you out again," he deduced.

"Of course I am. I've wanted you for years. I have you. I had a day of that, and it hurt."

Christ, he did to her what Genny did to him.

Tom tightened his arms around her.

"I won't shut you out again," he promised.

"I know, because I won't let you," she replied.

He stared at her.

*I know, because I won't let you.*

Simple.

Perfect.

Precisely what he needed.

Finally, Tom allowed his hand to move. He tucked her hair behind her ear so he could cup the side of her head, open them up to the world.

He did that because with what she said, he knew they'd be safe in it.

Or at least he felt safe there.

"You're magnificent," he whispered.

"Thanks," she whispered back. "You're pretty awesome too."

"If we didn't have to get ready to go to this meeting, I'd demonstrate some more pretty awesome."

"Baby, when you come when your dick is in my mouth." She shook her head as she rolled her eyes. "Glorious. There is no better show on this planet. I don't know if I can take any more awesome this morning."

He chuckled and through it said, "Bullshit."

She grinned widely at him and replied, "Totally."

That was when he kissed her.

He did it a long time.

And after, they got out of bed to get ready for their meeting.

But Tom did it feeling lighter than he had in years.

He also did it thinking his Mika wasn't only magnificent.

She was a miracle worker.

———————

TOM WAS UNCOMFORTABLE, SITTING IN JAMIE'S LARGE OFFICE AT HIS personal conference table.

He was this because he was watching Hale, and he saw Hale was not the same.

He was comfortable.

Completely.

All his life, Hale had been active.

He was an athlete, and a good one, specifically baseball, but he didn't have much interest.

Skateboarding was more his thing. Being out with his buds at skate parks, taking risks, doing tricks.

This, however, was mostly about being away from the adults in his life.

His father never had much interest.

His mother was a piece of work.

So it was skateboarding, to the point when he was fifteen, Hale quit playing baseball altogether and spent most of his free time when he wasn't with Tom and Genny with his friends and his board.

Furthermore, anytime he could, and this accelerated when he was able to drive, he was at the beach, surfing. Or he was in the hills, hiking. He begged to go to summer camp. Then, when he got old enough, he begged to be a counselor at that camp.

In the end, he made a career out of working with troubled kids in the out of doors before he inherited billions.

Now he was wearing a custom-fitted, gray Prada suit, and he looked like he grew up at Corey's knee, making deals to take over the world.

This didn't sit well with Tom, partly because he feared this type of life would lure Hale when it was not who he was, partly because he feared Hale hated it, but was burying that to get the job done, but bottom line, he was unhappy.

They each had individual bottles of Perrier, glasses of ice and lemon and lime slices in a small China bowl, as well coffee cups filled with an excellent Ethiopian blend, and there were two silver trays on the table. One covered with slices of rustic bread topped with a crumbly cheese and fruit, with an alternate of thin toast covered in slices of avocado. The other held miniature Danish.

Tom didn't partake.

He'd had a breakfast of French toast fingers Mika made him that he ate under the baleful glare of Teddy, who was wearing another stylish outfit, perfectly turned out at nine a.m., prepared to and giving Mika a full briefing of everything he'd been doing since she'd been gone, everything she might need to know for the now...and beyond.

Through this, Teddy made no bones about showing his disapproval that Tom was in pajama bottoms and a tee and looked as brilliantly sucked off as he was.

Mika, he could tell, thought this was hilarious.

Tom did his best to ignore it, a task which wasn't that hard, considering her French toast fingers were superb, and he was still recovering from the spectacular orgasm she'd given him, and the even better talk they'd had after.

"Enjoy the food made by the groceries *I* had brought in," was Teddy's farewell, uttered like he'd personally scoured the length and breadth of New York City to make sure they had milk, bread and eggs.

Tom lifted a French toast finger in salute. "Your toil is very appreciated."

Mika snorted as she swallowed her laugh.

Teddy's eyes bulged.

Mika waited until she was back in the kitchen after walking him to the front door before she burst out laughing.

Cadence was, by this time, at school.

Now, they were being shown Jamie's generosity as they waited for Jamie's investigator to arrive.

"You okay?" Mika asked him quietly.

He looked to her and didn't lie. He also didn't share about Hale. He'd do that later.

"Just want this done."

"I hear that," she agreed.

There was a knock, and before Jamie could call out, it was opened.

Two women entered.

One was Native American. She looked taller than she was because of her presence and her shoes. And if for some reason in her profession she needed to hide how smart she was, she'd likely find that impossible.

Last, she was stunning.

The other was younger, curvy, dark hair, bombshell features.

The Native American was in a stylish power pantsuit with slim trousers and some of the highest heels he'd ever seen a woman wear.

She navigated them like she was in bare feet.

The other woman was wearing black jeans, a gray T-shirt, black leather jacket and streamlined, feminine black biker boots.

The first woman was probably in her mid- to late-thirties.

The second, Tom thought, early thirties.

"She was able to come," the Native American said to Jamie as both women made it to the table.

All the men stood.

"Welcome," Jamie said, extending his hand to the woman in the leather jacket.

They shook, and Jamie turned to the table.

"This is my investigator, Kateri True Arrow," he introduced. "And this is Georgiana Black. A journalist at *The Worldist.*"

A journalist?

Tom didn't like that jump. It was too soon.

"Jamie—" he began.

"We're there," Kateri cut him off.

"We are?" he asked sharply in return.

"All the women are on record. And the whistleblower wants to remain anonymous, but he's on record too," Kateri returned. "We need Georgiana, not only to blow this open, but also, when Core Point is involved, they'll play hardball. I could be legally obligated to divulge my sources. Jamie could. You could. We all could. Georgiana breaks this story, the whistleblower will be protected."

Whistleblower?

Fuck, that was how they had all the documents and emails.

There was a whistleblower inside Core Point.

"You have the women on record?" Mika asked.

Kateri turned her attention to Mika. "Yes."

"You approached them?" she demanded, her voice brisk.

In other words, she was pissed.

Before Kateri could reply, Georgiana butted in.

"Maybe it's better if we sit down and share with you what we've been doing."

"Good idea," Judge said.

They all settled.

Georgiana accepted the coffee pot from Jamie and poured herself some.

Kateri didn't even glance at her cup or the little Perrier bottle on its perfectly-sized silver coaster.

"Considering you all need no introduction," Georgie began, "let's dig in."

Kateri was the one who spoke the most, as she'd done most of the work.

She'd started with uncovering who the whistleblower was. Once she had him, he was her gateway to everything else, including the survivors. He ran interference for her.

They didn't quite trust him, but they did trust his motives as apparently, in all the collusions, he was the one who seemed to have the women's interests at heart.

"His daughter was raped about a year ago and boom," Kateri said coldly. "The man grew a conscience, and instead of making sure they got a couple hundred thousand more than was offered while they were being gagged, he was vulnerable to Vaughan and now he wants to 'do something.'"

Both Tom and Judge perked at that.

And Judge went for it.

"Do you know Rhys Vaughan?" Judge asked.

"Yes." She nodded. "He's a legend in the business. Almost synonymous with Nightingale, except murkier."

"Murkier?" Tom asked, not knowing who she meant by Nightingale, but since they could learn more about Chloe's inheritance of a henchman, he wanted to know more about that.

Kateri turned to him. "Vaughan is young. He's talented. He got cherry-picked by Corey Szabo early. He used to be freelance. Szabo, because he could"—her eyes coasted through Hale—"made him exclusive. He did everything for the guy. And by that I mean *anything* and everything. And when I say 'the guy,' that's what I mean. He was attached solely to Szabo. At first, it was a job. He grew so loyal, there has to be something else there, and it wasn't just money. Not even a serious amount of money. Vaughan is a closed book, so nobody knows what that is. But his work is signature. I knew when I first looked at the file it was him. When he's working, he's deft. He's invisible. And he's meticulously thorough."

Tom and Judge exchanged a glance.

Tom then looked to Hale who was regarding his bubbling Perrier glass with an enigmatic expression on his face.

But he had to feel that. A man close to Corey, loyal to him, so loyal he carried out his wishes after his death.

Hale didn't have that with his father.

Not even close.

"As he was with this," Kateri continued. "The mole, and mind, this man is still working for Core Point, was in his grip, but Vaughan went deeper. We have everything. It's not all substantiated, but enough of it is that I brought in Georgiana. She's working the story, and *The Worldist* is keeping it under lock and key. Legal is side by side with her on it. Soon, though, she's going to need to contact Winston, Cyrus Martin and AJ Oakley to give them the chance to tell their side of the story. That's when we have to brace. It isn't when the story breaks it gets ugly. It's before. When they try to break the story before it's told."

Cyrus Martin was the CEO of Core Point.

"I appreciate the aggressiveness you've shown in validating what was sent to me," Mika said. "Nevertheless, I wish you would have consulted us before taking it this far. Tom knows one of the survivors."

"Yes, but his name, and all of your names have been kept out of this thus far," Kateri replied.

"There will likely come a time when she'll know of my involvement," Tom put in.

"I understand. And we can handle that how you wish," Kateri told him. "But that particular offense occurred in England. The other three...that we know of...happened here, in New York, and would most likely be considered second- or even third-degree rape, both having statutes of limitations. And the crimes were committed outside those limits. There are no limits on any criminal offenses in Britain. Which means he could be extradited and tried in England for raping Ms. Trainor who has dual citizenship, American and British. But she's lived in England since she was fifteen, and she always competed as a British competitor. They will consider her theirs. Because of that, the British press will eviscerate him."

Everyone at the table was quiet.

"She hasn't decided that this will be her course of action," Kateri continued. "But all four of the survivors have agreed to be named."

"Brave," Judge murmured.

"Yes," Georgiana agreed. "Because they're breaking thirty-page NDAs that, if Core Point decides to go that route, which we feel is unlikely, considering they'll already be dealing with a raging public relations fiasco, and they won't want to add more fuel to that fire, things could get very tricky for all four of them."

Kateri looked at Tom. "You're going to need to create a strategy to talk to the athletes and the organizations. Anyone who wears the CP circles while they compete is going to need to dump them, and anyone who doesn't will need to be pressured to do so or ostracized. The professional organizations are going to have to penalize them or ban them. This isn't a coverup for a talented player so he'd be free to keep winning matches wearing their gear and encouraging people to buy it. This is a corporate philosophy. They have only one female executive in a multi-national corporation that employs seventy thousand people. Murmurs of sexual harassment payoffs are rampant. And according to the mole, they've covered up similar situations in the last twenty-five years with a boxer, a quarterback and a snowboarder. Georgiana is working those, and we hope to lessen the scrutiny on the First Four by adding more to their number. Although one voice should be heard, that isn't the world we live in. There's strength in numbers. As the Nassar case proved."

Learning this was bigger than just Andrew Winston, Tom's voice was a rough, infuriated rumble, when he replied, "Although I'm sadly unsurprised Winston isn't isolated in these incidents with them, I don't have ubiquity with every sport and I'm not omnipotent. And Core Point is the former, and close to the latter."

Kateri lifted a hand and pointed a black-lacquered finger at Hale and said, "That's where you come in."

Hale didn't hesitate.

He turned to Jamie and asked, "You in?"

Jamie answered, "Definitely."

Tom knew what that meant.

This story was going to make Core Point vulnerable.

When it did, and probably before, Jamie was going to do his voodoo to make it even more vulnerable on Wall Street.

Then one, or the other, or both of them would buy it and scuttle it.

"And the reason my father was highlighted in this mess?" Jamie queried.

"Because he and the senior Martin, Doyle, who started the company, were tight," Kateri informed him. "They were then. They were until Doyle died two years ago. The whistleblower says, in the beginning, AJ Oakley crafted their response to issues like this. It was then adopted by Cyrus when he came in. AJ being the author of this, considering the number of boards he's sat on, not to mention the running of his own companies, who knows how far he's sown the seeds of his philosophy."

"We think there's a good possibility this isn't a story," Georgiana said, her tone cautious. "It'll be the first domino falling. Strong women embolden women to be strong. The First Four come out, considering the reach of all of the key players involved, Cyrus and Doyle Martin and AJ Oakley, we have no idea where this will end."

Again, taking that in, everyone at the table was quiet.

Mika broke it.

"I'd like to go back to the women," she put in.

"We'll take care of them, Ms. Stowe, you have my promise on that," Georgiana said.

"Please, call me Mika, and please take no offense when I remind you, I barely know you," Mika replied.

"Do you know the work of *The Worldist?*" Georgiana asked.

Tom did.

It was a web news site that started only a few years ago. Their remit was touted as bare bones, objective journalism. They not only published articles, they also had "on-air" personalities that appeared live on their site for morning and evening slots to share encapsulated reports of recent news.

They weren't about big graphics, streamlined dresses and lots of makeup for the women, and thick mustaches and that I'm-like-you middle-aged paunch for the men. And they had no commentary shows, also no guests.

It was simply news and professional journalism that didn't take sides.

Tom frequented the site because he was a fiscal conservative with liberal tendencies on social issues, and *The Worldist* seemed to be that. But he had many friends who were liberals, or even progressives, and they felt *The Worldist* shared their point of view.

The alt-right was the only perspective that got little screen space on *The Worldist.* However, that was mostly due to the fact that most of the "news" from that side of the spectrum wasn't factual and therefore wasn't news.

In other words, more and more, especially in the past few years, people were turning to that site for bottom-line, no-nonsense, accurate reporting.

Which was what news should be.

If there was a news organization he'd want breaking that story, it would be *The Worldist*.

"Yes," Mika answered.

"We're going to see to those women," Georgiana replied. "As a woman, this is about justice for me. However, I have to set that aside because that's not my role. As a journalist, this is an important story. Parents who buy their kids Core Point gear need to know the practices of the company behind the logo. Athletes who wear it should know. And other organizations who adopt these policies need to be put on notice. Most importantly, these women should be free to speak and be heard. And to do that, they need to feel safe. That's my primary objective with this story, Mika. And it's not to make those women feel safe. It's to make them *genuinely* safe."

He felt Mika relax after Georgiana said her piece.

"Hale and I target CP. You and Judge create a strategy around professional organizations and players. Kateri will dig up dirt. And Georgiana will write the story," Jamie broke it down.

Tom looked to Judge. "I think I know one big-name player in most high-profile sports who I can trust to take this ball and run with it."

"That would have been my call," Judge said.

"We'll need to sit down with them. This should be face to face. We'll talk more," Tom replied.

Judge nodded.

"And I shall…what?" Mika asked.

"Be the first to validate them when they come out," Kateri told her. "Your word holds weight. You've been no bullshit from the beginning. If Mika Stowe adds her voice behind them, the liberal feminists of three generations will lose their minds and start waving their banners before the ink's dry."

"How would I do that?" Mika inquired.

"Come out on social media in support of them," Kateri said patiently.

"I'm not on social media," Mika shared.

Georgiana blinked.

It was the first time Kateri smiled. It was small, but it was there.

"Smart," she murmured.

"I know," Mika replied.

Kateri's smile was bigger that time.

"TikTok is life," Georgiana muttered.

Kateri ignored her and said, "If that's the case, there's really nothing you can do. At this juncture, it's up to Georgiana, the survivors, and the lawyers. Even the things Jamie and Tom will be doing are incidental. This isn't about them. Or you. Or me. It's about these women having the opportunity to speak their truth. The rest is just consequences."

Now Mika was smiling. "On that we can agree."

Kateri abruptly stood. "I have things to do. Jamie." She nodded to him. "Gentleman." She nodded to the table at large. "Mika," she finished.

Georgiana had gotten up with her, but she put several business cards on the table, and said, "If you need anything," before she smiled then said her farewell, "Nice to meet you."

The men stood again as she and Kateri left the room.

They sat when the door closed.

Mika reached for a Danish, noting, "Well, one can say that's well in hand."

"Jesus, those women could run the world," Hale noted.

Tom saw Mika munching her Danish through a massive grin.

"Don't give that idea to Kateri, she'll go for it." Jamie shook his head. "Scratch that, she already has that idea. So just wait for it."

Tom touched Mika's leg.

She turned to him.

"You sure you're good?"

"I want to live in a world Kateri True Arrow runs. I think that's a world I'd like to see."

Tom sat back.

Because he was good.

Since she was.

# CHAPTER 17

## THE HONESTY

*Tom*

$\mathcal{M}$ika invited Chloe and Judge, Jamie and Dru, and Nora as well as Hale to dinner that night.

But it was Cadence who was holding court.

And Tom loved how Mika sat back and let her daughter's bubbly personality lift up the room, giving her space to shine.

Mika had a round dining table (because, of course she would, it was easier to have more inclusive conversation). She'd painted another mural in there (and the murals were all her work, he'd learned). The one in the dining room was situated above green wainscotting, and it was a surfeit of leaves and branches, giving the impression they were eating in a treehouse.

There wasn't time to cook, so she'd phoned her favorite Spanish tapas place and there were croquettes, fried baby squid, garlic shrimp, *tortilla de patatas*, stuffed mushrooms, olives chorizo, Manchego and tortillas covering the table. She also ordered a whole *tarta de Santiago* and an entire case of different riojas.

Though, they started their night with Spanish gin and tonics that had dried juniper berries and a spritz of lime.

The food was plentiful. They were well into their ninth bottle of wine. Everyone was loose on booze and food. It was getting loud, people talking to be heard over laughter or side conversations. And Mika went for it with the theme for the night, setting Vincente Amigo playing in the background.

Tom sat back in his chair, quiet, his wineglass in his hand, listening and watching.

Hale and Judge teasing Cadence, Chloe and Dru taking her back. Jamie and Nora talking about some restaurant they discovered that they both enjoyed. Cadence telling Dru she'd teach her how to play the drums. Chloe, Cadence, Dru and Nora talking about the wedding. Judge, Jamie and Hale discussing Trail Blazer and sharing it with Mika. Cadence being exuberant, thriving in this atmosphere, her home full of people, something she clearly enjoyed. Nora being droll and forever gaining an acolyte in Chloe.

They broached movies. And TV. And discussed at length a great book many of them had read.

It felt like family, even if some of them barely knew each other.

Mika's fingers curled around his thigh, and he turned to her, seated at his side.

"You all right?" she asked quietly.

"I wish Matt and Sasha were here," he answered.

Her face grew soft. "I do too."

Tom had eventually texted his younger daughter, denying her his house as a crash pad.

Like her mother, she had not replied.

It concerned him.

But not tonight.

Nothing could hack through the thick coating of goodness that was surrounding him that night.

"We'll have a big get-together when Matt's out for spring break," Mika said, regaining his attention. "I'm looking forward to meeting them."

He nodded, and said, "And Genny."

Her head ticked. "Sorry?"

"I wish Genny and Duncan were here."

Her fingers curled tighter into his thigh.

He was disturbed by that reaction.

She knew how he and Genny wanted their family to remain close. It wasn't starting out very well. Nevertheless, on Tom's part, he wanted that back, with Mika and Cadence added to it.

"Does that concern you?" he asked.

Her brows came down over her eyes. "The fact that you're emotionally mature enough to understand the importance of history and feelings you share with the woman you were married to for decades, and you wish to have her continue to be part of your life? No."

So, he'd read her reaction wrong.

Tom smiled.

"She'll get in touch," Mika said quietly.

He did not hold out hope for that.

It could be years before she figured it out, whatever it was.

He knew that painfully well.

But now, it didn't matter.

Nothing mattered.

Except what was happening at that table.

"This is the best night I've had in maybe five years," he told her.

Her eyes rounded before the tenderness went into overdrive.

He moved toward her, kissed her cheek then slid his lips to her ear.

"You make me happy," he whispered there. "This makes me happy."

When he pulled away, her eyes were bright with unshed tears, and she leaned in and touched her mouth to his before moving infinitesimally away and saying, "Me too."

They came out of their small huddle, and Chloe immediately said, "I'll try not to gloat."

"Gloat away, darling," Nora drawled. "If you don't remind them how fabulous you are, they might forget. I gloat all the time. For instance now—" she leaned forward and grabbed a shrimp, and before she popped it into her mouth, she finished, "since I'm the one who introduced Mika to this tapas bar."

Everyone laughed.

Tom did too.

But he did it while he got up to open another bottle of wine.

---

TOM MOVED FROM HAVING HIS MOUTH BETWEEN MIKA'S LEGS AND HE did it taking his time, with his mouth and hands, exploring her skin on the way up...

And in.

He loved the little gasp she gave when she took his cock.

He loved the taste of her, the feel of her, the noises she made, the dark shadow of her hair all over her pillow, the scent of her sex and her perfume and her skin mingled with his.

She made a move with her hips and Tom stopped slowly stroking and let her roll him to his back.

She didn't rise up and ride him.

Her lips at his neck, his jaw, his mouth, his cheekbone, her hands roaming his ribs, his biceps, shoulders, her nails scratching through his chest hair, over his nipples, she glided up and down on his dick while pressed to him.

Until he'd had enough.

When he did, he sat up, and with the curtain of her hair all around them, their lips touching, their breath mingling, he dug the pads of his fingers into her hips, a silent order to go faster.

She did.

He slid a hand in between them, his thumb moving in deeper.

She moaned against his mouth.

He urged her to ride harder.

She did.

Tom didn't want to lose her, their intimacy, their closeness, and thus he caught her head just before it would fly back with her orgasm.

He then shoved his face in her neck and couldn't stop himself from sinking his teeth into the flesh there when she gave him his own.

They didn't move an inch through their recovery, Mika in his lap, both of them breathing in each other's skin.

Eventually, she slid off, and they rolled out of bed to go to her bathroom.

This was another room in her house Tom loved. The walls were coated with a collage of colorful pictures, the cabinets were lavender, and the counters and fixtures were ostentatiously opulent.

It was vibrant. It was interesting. And it was entirely unique.

Again, it was Mika.

They cleaned up.

Tom went to the door to let Moon in as Mika went back to bed.

He and Moon joined her there.

Front to front, Tom pulled her in his arms and tangled their legs under the covers while Moon walked over their bodies to find his spot.

"I can't decide which room of your house I like the best," he told her.

She let out a surprised laugh and asked, "Seriously?"

"You're everywhere, Mika," he replied. "You're in every inch."

He felt her still at his words.

Then he felt her melt into him.

He drew her even closer.

"Cadence had a good time tonight," she murmured.

"The more people around she has to love, the brighter she seems to shine," he noted.

"Like Rollo."

Tom took pains not to react to that.

She didn't bring up Rollo often, but whenever she did, melancholy limned her words.

This had the effect of making him want to comfort her and giving him absurd feelings of jealousy.

"I'm not an introvert, I'm not an extrovert either," she went on. "I like to be around people, but it's mostly to observe. I don't like giving too much of myself. I think, in the beginning, people were so harsh about what I did and who they thought I was, I built a shell around me. The thing is, I found I was comfortable in it. I liked it. So I kept it. My circle, my found family, is very tight."

"I've been noticing that," he replied. "Mine is too."

"I've been noticing that," she repeated.

They grinned at each other through the shadows.

And then Mika dropped her head forward, her forehead hitting his chin, and she whispered, "She's musical, like him. She's an incredibly good drummer. She lights up a room like he did. Everyone wants to know her, like him. She just has that energy. She's just...*electric.*"

"Chloe is just like her grandmother, and if she wasn't, I don't know to this day if Genny would be able to cope with her mother's death. Matt is like Genny in many ways. He's bright. He's talented. But he gets stuck in his head. I liked to think Sasha is like me. She used to be athletic, competitive, driven. Part of my concern about her is that she's so different than she used to be. Though, I'll admit that there is definitely a nuance of me missing my buddy. We shared a lot of the same interests. They're all my legacy, but there was a part of her that made me feel like I was going to live on in her. That was special to me. It's selfish, but it's true."

She tipped her head back.

And he continued, "What I'm saying is, Cadence is his legacy. Not just that he's part of her, he helped make her. I'm saying that he lives on in her."

"It's gutting," she said.

Tom tightened his arms as he felt that with her and for her.

"It's also wonderful," she continued. "But I worry that it'll be...I mean, you and me, we seem to be working."

He wanted to laugh.

Her tone was serious, so he did not laugh.

Though he felt it necessary to respond with an understatement, "Yes, honey, we're working."

"Okay, then what I'm saying without coming right out and saying it is that I don't want that to be too much for you."

He was confused. "That Cadence has so much of her dad in her?"

"Is that...do you think that's going to be an issue?"

"Fuck no," he replied firmly.

"You seem...you sometimes get..."

She was stammering, and that was not her style.

He pulled her on top of him and sifted his fingers into one side of her hair to hold it back.

"We're working," he said.

He saw and felt her nod.

"Can I tell you there's not a twinge of jealousy?" he asked. "No. You loved him, and my feelings are growing for you. It's irrational, but I can't deny that it's there. I'm hoping it's a reflex action and not toxic masculinity pumping through my veins."

Her body softened on his and she said, "It's not. I don't want to sound like a bitch, but after it all happened, and once I had a second to think about it, Imogen walking in on us and then throwing a drama, I mean, part of me gets it. Part of me thinks she's married to another guy, he's supposedly her long lost love reunited, it's a huge deal and everyone's in fits of happiness for them, including her, and so...what the fuck?"

Christ, he loved how honest she could be.

Right here.

Open.

Giving it all to him.

"I also think that's partially territorial," she went on. "That was the beginning. You've been mine for a while and the longer she extends the drama, the more pissed I am."

"Mm," he murmured.

"I know it's not mine to be pissed about," she noted.

"I'm sorry? I'm still stuck on the 'you've been mine for a while.'"

This time, her body twitched on his.

She then dropped her head and gave him a deep, wet kiss.

When they came up for air, she was no longer on top of him. He'd rolled her to her back and had his chest resting on hers.

KRISTEN ASHLEY

Through their kiss, Moon had been dislodged from their feet, and now he was again walking on them to find a new spot.

"To end," he said, his voice gruff, "I care about you. You care about me. It's territorial for the both of us. However, I'm also protective of you. You miss him and I sense that. So you're feeling my concern more than anything."

"It was a long time ago, Tommy. I can't say Rollo doesn't have my undying love, but I'm not harboring that in a way that will inhibit me from moving on."

"I didn't think that was the case. Though, good to know."

Mika released a soft laugh.

But her tone was not amused when she said, "Cadence is many beautiful things, and for me, one of those is that she's a memory of her father. I just wanted to make sure, since she'll be that for you too, it's okay."

"You okay with Chloe?"

"Of course."

"Honey, it's the same thing."

She relaxed under him. "Okay."

"We're good," he told her. "More than good."

"We are definitely that. More than good."

That was when Tom relaxed.

He kissed her.

Mika kissed him back.

They murmured to each other in the dark for a while longer, nothing serious, just digging deeper into each other, so all of it was important.

And then, still wound together, Moon selecting his place, draped across their feet, they fell asleep.

---

"I'm out," Judge declared.

"Thank God I have to go into the office and get some work done," Jamie muttered.

"Thank God I have to leave," Hale replied, also in a mutter.

"I'm sorry, honey." Tom turned to Mika. "But I'm doing whatever Judge is doing, and I don't really care what that is."

Mika burst out laughing.

They were at lunch the next day.

Another big party.

But they'd finished eating, and Judge had snuck the server his credit card so the bill had been paid.

And the women had decided the next thing on the agenda was to go to Saks Fifth Avenue's shoe floor.

"You'll only be annoying and put a damper on the proceedings," Chloe declared in Judge's direction. "So with our blessings, go do your thing."

"We're meeting at Dad and my place for dinner?" Dru asked.

Before anyone could confirm, Jamie turned to Chloe and Judge.

"Are you sure you two want another family dinner? You don't want to go out in the city for a couple's night?"

Chloe's quick glance to Mika was barely discernable.

Except to a father's practiced eye.

She wanted the new growth of the family roots digging deeper, just like Tom did.

Which was why she answered, "Judge and I are doing that Sunday night. We're not missing Dru's cooking."

"I'll have to nip out of the shopping early to get started on that," Dru replied.

"Do you need help?" Mika asked.

"You'll sacrifice time from Saks' shoes?" Dru asked in return.

"I love a beautiful shoe, but I also love to be elbow deep in chopping," Mika shared.

"That's good, since one of the things I'm making is maque choux and lots of chopping is involved," Dru returned.

"Don't look at me, darling," Nora put in when Mika glanced her way. "When it comes to cooking, I'm that grandmother in *Sixteen Candles* who opened the donut box and declared breakfast was served.

Without the godawful cigarette, of course. And no way in hell I'm cutting shoe shopping short."

Everyone laughed.

A member of staff who looked like the manager approached, appearing uncertain, his eyes darting between Jamie, Hale and Tom.

"Is everything okay?" Tom asked.

The man's shoulders slumped in relief that his decision had been made for him, and he took a step forward to Tom, leaned deep at the waist, and said in a low voice in Tom's ear, "I'm sorry, sir. But we thought you should know. Word has gotten out you're all here and there is a...well, no way to describe it except that there's a very large group of paparazzi outside."

"Goddamn it," Tom bit off, then to the server, "My apologies for the language."

"No worries. Understandable," he replied. "We'd like to invite you to leave through the kitchens, there's a small alley out back. Though, it's not large enough for your cars to get back there."

"What's going on?" Jamie asked.

"Paparazzi outside," Tom told him.

Nora craned her neck to look to the front. "Really? How fabulous."

Only Nora would think that.

"This is why I always dress to impress," Chloe declared.

Nora gave her an approving nod.

"It is not. You look like a model when you change clothes after work to park it in front of the TV," Judge retorted.

For a second, Chloe's face froze, then warmth infused it, and she announced, "God, I love you."

One side of Judge's lips tipped up.

"Our cars are at the front," Hale reminded Jamie.

"And I, personally, am not walking through an alley," Nora declared with a scrunch in her nose.

"I'm not either," Mika agreed. "We can go out front. It isn't a big deal. Unless anyone else is concerned about it."

"You and Tom *are* out, darling." Nora waved her hand between Tom and Mika. "No use hiding this light under a bushel."

"The women will all go in Dru's car," Jamie decreed. "Hale, you can go straight to the airport. I'll drop Judge and Tom where they want to go."

"It's a plan," Hale agreed.

While Jamie and Hale strategized, Tom had pulled out his wallet and he discreetly passed a fifty to him when he turned to the manager and said, "Thank you for the heads up."

The man nodded, smiled and stepped away.

They finished what was left to be finished and headed out.

But even with the warning, they were ill-prepared.

The manager had said a large group.

However, although Tom was experienced with paparazzi, even rabid paparazzi from the time he and Genny first started to date, he'd never seen anything like this.

And it wasn't just paparazzi.

It was fans.

As such, the plan changed.

Because the minute they started out of the restaurant, there was a surge toward them. The feeling was excitement. Names were shouted, questions hurled.

It didn't feel malicious.

However, it did feel dangerous, and as such, it caused a spike of adrenaline for Tom, and his first response was fight *and* flight.

Fortunately, the drivers of Hale's and Jamie's cars had seen what was brewing, and they were out, helping to push back the throng and form a path to the cars.

Jamie took hold of Dru and Nora and shoved them into one of the three vehicles, folding in with them and shutting the door.

Judge grabbed Chloe and strong-armed his way to another car.

Tom took hold of Mika, and reached for Cadence, but Hale already had her, and they struggled into the last limo.

Once safely closed in, the drivers pushed their way through the crowd who were taking pictures through the windows or pressing their hands and faces there.

Jesus.

Genny could cause a stir, but this was insane.

The driver got in their limo and didn't hesitate in setting them to moving.

At first, the crowd moved with them.

Fortunately, the light at the cross street was on their side, they got into a free flow of traffic and lost them.

"You good?" he asked Cadence.

She was wide-eyed and obviously shaken.

Tom's adrenaline spiked again.

Hale threw an arm around her and tucked her in his side.

"We're safe now, sweetheart. Yeah?" he assured her.

"It's never been that bad," she whispered and looked to her mom. "Has it ever been that bad?"

Tom had Mika's hand tight in his, and her hold was just as strong.

"No, honey. It hasn't," she replied. "But we're safe now. Do you feel it? We're safe."

She gave a slight nod.

Tom shook Mika's hand in his, and she turned to him.

"Okay?" he mouthed.

She nodded too.

Their phones chimed with texts.

Tom pulled his out.

It was Jamie.

*Contacting my security team. We'll have coverage at both houses. And two men will be sent to Saks. Security will also contact the store and warn them the women are on the way and share what just happened.*

*Good,* Tom texted in reply.

He then turned his attention to Hale. "Is this you? Are you dealing with this escalation when you're out?"

"I have attention, it's not that bad," Hale replied.

"You don't have a bodyguard," Tom pointed out.

A moment of hesitation before Hale said, "Sometimes I do, if there's a threat."

Mika pulled his hand to her thigh, her hold intensifying, as Tom clipped, "A threat?"

"People are strange, Tom," Hale said.

"You need security," Tom retorted sharply.

Before Hale could reply, Cadence butted in.

"It's not just him. It's, well...you and Mom."

She had her phone up and turned to them.

"You have a hashtag," she said. "Tomikaperfection."

Tom dropped his eyes to the phone.

Cadence was scrolling the hashtag.

It wasn't just about today.

There were mashup graphics with text created from older photos of Tom and Mika. There were a lot of riffs on the pictures of them at the Hermosa Inn.

And there were shots of them entering the restaurant they just left and more of them talking and eating inside it.

"Word moves fast on social media," Cadence shared.

She was dropping her hand that held her phone, but Tom reached out and asked, "May I?"

"Sure," she said, giving it to him.

He let Mika go, scrolled up with Mika leaned into him to see the screen, and he heard her sharp intake when he stopped at what he'd seen as Cadence was scrolling.

*Imogen Who?* The text said on a photo of Genny looking upset, walking through the Biltmore mall in Phoenix, hands in the pockets of some cream joggers, a matching hoodie up top, the hood pulled over her hair. She had big shades cover her eyes, her head was cast down.

It was obviously a recent picture.

What was further concerning was that Bowie was not with her.

This was slapped on the bottom corner over another picture taken of Tom and Mika outside the Hermosa. However, in this shot, Tom had turned and tipped his head down to Mika, and they appeared like they were close to kissing.

The text above their heads said, *Trading Up.*

Fuck, shit.

He flicked his finger on the screen so it would scroll away and handed the phone back to Cadence.

He tried to catch Hale's eye, but his attention was on his own phone, and considering his mouth was tight, Tom knew what he was seeing.

"We'll stop being the couple *du jour* in a few *jours*," Mika joked.

He took her hand again and said nothing, because after what had just happened, he didn't think that would be true.

Another text came through from Jamie.

*Security in motion. We're all heading to Saks. We'll wait until the men connect with staff and then the women can go in under escort. The team are closer, they should be there when we arrive.*

*Perfect,* Tom replied.

The atmosphere was heavy as they rode the stop and start of any car journey in the city.

"Is she sensitive to those things?" Mika asked quietly.

She meant Genny.

"Her skin is pretty tough. But you never develop complete immunity to that kind of thing," Tom answered. "She's adopted a habit of avoiding it and probably hasn't seen it."

Or, he hoped she hadn't.

But, as he spoke, he noticed Cadence and Mika exchanging a glance.

When she felt his eyes on her, Mika looked to him.

"I don't have to avoid it because I don't have the avenues to run into it, but I really don't care what people say about me," she shared.

"Mom's all about complete immunity," Cadence said.

Tom found this unsurprising.

It was part that shell she'd erected.

It was part who she was.

"And you, honey?" Tom asked Cadence.

"Well, that was extreme, and felt unsafe. But people have been 'Poor Cadence Merriman this,' and 'Poor Cadence Merriman that,' since I was born, due to, you know, losing Dad." She shrugged. "So, I kinda don't know another way it could be."

At that demonstration of maturity, Tom and Hale exchanged a glance.

Though, Tom was far from a massive fan of "Poor Cadence Merriman" anything.

She lost her dad, but she was so much more than that.

"Though," Cadence carried on, "it's all kinds of crazy that people who do that kind of thing have complete immunity to the concept that the people they're doing it to are actually *people*."

"Absolutely," Hale replied.

Within fifteen minutes, they hit Saks.

They waited maybe five minutes before they got the go ahead.

And Hale and Tom angled out of the car to make sure the handoff went smoothly.

They left one of Jamie's cars for the women, Jamie took another to his office, and Judge and Tom went with Hale to the airport so they didn't have to say goodbye with an audience on the sidewalk.

Once they'd dropped Hale, on their way to Jamie's to regroup and discuss what they were going to do as they waited for the women, Tom asked, "Have you and Chloe ever faced that kind of attention?"

Judge shook his head. "Elsa has her spies in Prescott. She throws a picture of us out on her show every once in a while. It keeps the interest up, so there are shots of us elsewhere. But it's never been that bad."

"Cadence thinks it's about me and Mika."

Judge nodded. "Chloe dove into her phone, and she thought the same thing."

Tom looked out the window.

"She's worried," Judge said.

Tom looked back to Judge.

"About you and Genny. Also about Bowie and Genny. She intends to broach it with her mom. She's not hiding it from you. She just doesn't want anything weighing on you because you seem happy with Mika."

"Nothing that concerns my daughter is ever a weight I can't carry," Tom returned.

Judge smiled.

"I'll talk to her," Tom said.

Judge nodded.

Tom sucked in a breath through his nose and let it out, releasing everything else with it.

One thing he knew, outside taking precautions to keep the ones he cared about safe now that they knew the attention had intensified, and he was going to have a longer conversation with Hale about getting a security team in place, there was nothing he could do.

They just had to live with it.

It was frustrating.

And it was infuriating.

But it was out of his control.

---

### *Hale*

HALE SAT ALONE ON HIS PLANE, TRYING NOT TO THINK NOT ONLY ABOUT how alone he felt, especially after how alive the cabin seemed with all the company he had when they flew out.

But also, what a waste of fossil fuel it was for him to be flying back west by himself.

He should have pushed his meetings and waited to take his family back with him.

If those meetings were pushed, however, other meetings would need to be pushed, and he'd be running to catch up for the next year.

He also had tomorrow off.

Completely.

No meetings. No phone calls. No reports to read, files to go through, numbers to crunch.

It had been so long since he had—he counted—thirty-nine hours all to himself, he didn't even know how to plan what he intended to do with them.

Which meant he hoped to do nothing.

Maybe get some surfing in. A run on the beach. Lose himself in cooking a meal. Or grab one of the three hundred books he had piled around the house that he'd wanted to read and never had the time or headspace to give them.

He set all this aside and pulled out his computer.

He'd made the request before they took off.

He was not surprised he had what he asked for now that they'd leveled off.

His father's team, a team he'd inherited, was preternaturally efficient.

He pulled out his phone, punched in the number he'd been given, and he made the call.

"Hello?" The woman's voice was tentative in answering, unsurprisingly, as his was an unknown number.

And she was who she was.

"This is Hale Wheeler. Do I have Elsa Cohen?"

A long silence, and then, "Hale Wheeler?"

"Is this Elsa?"

"Yes."

"Great," he bit off, making no bones about the fact he did not feel it was great that he had to give her any of his time.

He also didn't intend to waste more of it.

And he set about doing that.

"What would it take for you to lay off my family?"

A long pause and then, "Are you trying to buy me off?"

"I asked a simple question."

"It's my business," she pointed out.

"I hope somewhere inside you, you understand it's a shit business to be in," he stated bluntly.

"Not everyone can be Robin Hood," she returned smoothly. "Someone has to share all Robin does so people know there are good guys out there and maybe inspire them to do something good too."

He didn't hide his feelings for that, and as such, his voice was scathing when he said, "Don't pretend what you do is altruistic."

"You'd know about that," she shot back, then explained her meaning. "So there's no ulterior motive to you giving away all the money your father deserted you your whole life in order to earn?"

Jesus Christ.

She didn't hesitate to go for the jugular either.

"So the answer to my simple question is no," he noted. "You're not going to lay off my family."

"Hale...can I call you Hale?"

"Since this is the only conversation we're ever gonna have, I don't give a shit what you call me."

"Right then," she said quietly. "Obviously, I heard what happened this afternoon. I also knew where you were within minutes of you arriving. And I never, not ever, Hale, divulge the current whereabouts of anyone I cover. For precisely the reasons why you're calling now. It can put people in danger, and I don't want to be responsible for that."

"And she thinks she has scruples," he muttered.

"You don't know me enough to pass judgment on me," she snipped, her famous cool slipping.

"Baby, I don't *want* to know you," he retorted.

"*Baby?*" she asked in an infuriated whisper.

He ignored that.

"Shoot me a deal, Elsa," he urged. "There's practically nothing you can ask that is outside my means to give to you."

"Okay, Hale, for six months of me laying off your family, specifically Tom and Mika, and I know this is about your beloved Tom, so let's not pretend it isn't. And by the way, even if I blackout coverage of them, they're going to get gnawed on. There are still Team Tom people out there who are pissed Imogen moved on. They know the story of her and Holloway and Szabo, and they think she dumped her husband for her childhood love."

Fucking hell.

Hale hadn't heard anything about that.

Elsa wasn't done.

"And Mika just became the new Lisa Bonet, except the tragic one, which makes her all the tastier. Still, her ability to attract the best men hasn't gone unnoticed, no matter the time that has elapsed in between. So I might have broken that story, but it was going to break without me. All of that said, I'll give you six months. In return, I want an exclusive, one on one with you, in person, in your home, or one of them. No pre-approval of questions."

"I don't do interviews," he informed her.

"It's in your means to give," she reminded him.

*Fucking hell.*

"Well?" she pushed.

"Forever blackout, interview via Zoom, pre-approval of questions," he fired at her.

"You're not going to get a forever blackout, Hale," she said, almost gently. "I was being generous with the offer of six months."

"Right," he gritted. "A year."

"I can't do a year."

"A year, Elsa."

She was quiet.

"Well?" he parroted her push.

"A year, but the interview is in your home, your choice of home, no pre-approval."

"Pre-approval and skeleton crew."

"You can't add things, Hale."

"I can do whatever the fuck I want."

It didn't really matter. There wasn't a property his father owned that he intended to keep.

Except the house in LA, because Genny, Chloe and Sasha were attached to it.

Nevertheless, he was feeling surly because of who he had to deal with.

And further, she didn't need to know any of that.

She was going to know too much already with this fucking interview.

"You're based in New York?" he asked a question he already knew the answer to.

"For the most part, yes."

"The New York penthouse. Skeleton crew, Elsa. No pre-approved questions, but I want pre-approval of the broadcast."

"It's the same thing, only different," she returned, and he could tell she was getting annoyed.

It made her sound almost human.

"Final offer," he said.

"I don't have to make a deal with you at all."

"The minute you went after Genny, the minute I saw that you'd sat down with my mother, I bought the building you broadcast from and the building where you rent your apartment."

Total silence from Elsa.

Not from Hale.

"In a week, I could own your web hosting company. It might take me longer to buy YouTube, but it would be a damned good investment."

"Are you threatening me?" she asked, a carefully controlled thread in her voice, probably so it wouldn't shake.

"I'm pointing out what a great deal you're negotiating with me."

"I see you have some of your father in you after all," she spat, now totally riled and not hiding it.

Not the jugular this time.

He felt that arrow hit true, right through the heart, the tip coated in poison.

But he didn't hesitate in replying, "Naturally."

"You have a deal," she capitulated.

"I won't be back in New York for a couple of months."

"They're free game until you get here," she returned.

He'd already pushed her further than he'd wanted.

Still.

"Be good, Elsa," he warned.

"Fuck you, Hale," she replied.

And then she hung up.

# CHAPTER 18

## THE BOMBARDMENT

*Tom*

"It'll be good."

It was the next day, Sunday, and Tom was downstairs in Mika's living room, wandering her domain, checking things out, not taking anything in, considering he was talking to Chloe.

And assuring her all would be fine with her mom.

"Dad, she's in Phoenix," Chloe said.

"I know. I saw a picture—"

"Alone," she cut in. "Without Bowie."

Tom stopped under the picture of Stella Gunn.

And it hit him.

Genny saw Tom and Mika together and ran out.

Her husband was right at her side when she did that.

Duncan adored her. He didn't hide it. He crafted his life around hers. He didn't have any issue with doing that.

But he was still a man.

Genny had not been embarrassed about walking in on Tom and Mika.

She was hurt by it.

Tom knew it.

And so did Duncan.

Well...

Hell.

"Bowie's been in Prescott for weeks," Chloe continued. "Mom's been in the Valley. And I don't think they're talking."

"It'll work out, honey," Tom assured, though he was feeling less assured as the conversation flowed. "She works through things in her own time, but she does work through them."

"Yes, Father, and the last time she took her own time working through things, her marriage ended," Chloe retorted.

Damn, but it might be good to have less intelligent children.

"There were other issues involved with that," he reminded her.

"Indeed," she returned. "You were with another woman. And now Mom's being theatrical about another man."

"There's a difference," Tom pointed out.

"All right, *mon père*, guess what?" she said in an "Okay, Dad, brace" type of way.

He knew his daughter.

So he braced.

And as ever with Chloe, he was glad he did.

"She divorced you," his eldest announced. "You don't have to protect her anymore."

He could tell by the tone of her voice that her mood was deteriorating quickly.

"Chloe, we divorced each other. That was a mutual—"

"Stop it, Dad!" she snapped, loudly.

Tom fell quiet, mostly because, except in a tantrum as a young child, and even those were rare with Chloe, she'd never raised her voice to him.

Chloe had other ways of getting her point across, even, and maybe especially if she was annoyed about it.

"Matt may have missed it. Sasha may be up in her head about her own issues. But I didn't miss it," she carried on. "I did not miss a lifetime of you giving in so Mom could have what she wanted. I'll admit, it hit me too late. But it wasn't lost on me. In fact, I know I'm such a steamroller, it's my greatest fear, being that to Judge. Driving him away because he loves me so much, he'll let me be all I am, and lose himself in the process."

Tom remained silent, now because he was too shellshocked at the bombs she was dropping to say a word.

"I love Bowie. Sasha loves Bowie. Matt loves Bowie. Hell, *you* love Bowie," she continued.

Tom found his voice.

"Your mother loves Bowie more than any of us."

"And she loved you too."

He actually winced, that explosion landed so close.

"Honey, this is not a repeat performance," he informed her. *"This is a different situation.* One, I'll point out, neither of us know a thing about. You need to cut her some slack."

There was a moment of silence before she spoke again.

"You didn't do right. You didn't. I don't have to tell you that because you know it better than I do. But I learned the hard way, through my parents, that there are two sides to every story. You learned your lesson, Dad. Before it's too late, and she screws something else up that's beautiful and has a lot of people she loves involved, Mom needs to learn hers."

"Mom did not screw us up, honey," he said quietly. "Bottom line, she didn't. I don't want you thinking that."

"Dad." She said his name on such a powerful gust of air, he felt the phantom of it brush his cheek. "It's not fair Mom lets you bear that cross on your own. It's not. But it's not my business. It's between you two. That said, I love Bowie. And Sully and Gage. And I found Judge through Bowie. He's family. They're all family. And Mom has got to learn that the world might adore Imogen Swan, but in her family, that world doesn't revolve around her."

"Chloe," he said gently. "You're being far too hard on her."

"I'm done talking about it," she huffed.

"Try to see things from her perspective," Tom urged.

"I'll do that when I'm not this mad. But just to say, you weren't her first in this. Uncle Corey broke them up, and it was absolutely insane how he did that. We were all so blindsided by it when we found out, no one has noticed that way back in the day, out of the blue, Duncan done her wrong, she'd loved him since she was eight, and she didn't fight for him either."

And the shrapnel from that particular shell tore straight through him.

Chloe continued, "I've ranted about this to Judge, and it isn't just because he loves me, and he respects you, and he's a man that he's on my side. He's thrown Mom is being like this. And I've ranted to Matt about it. Matt always takes her side, but he was exceptionally quiet when I was telling him about her latest sulk, and how she's shut Bowie out, her usual modus operandi. And I think he's thinking things through."

"I can't believe you spoke to Matt about this," Tom said, disappointment in his tone.

"It's time he got his head out of his ass. He learned you were human, now he needs to learn Mother is too."

"I'll repeat something I say often to you, Chloe, and share this really isn't any of your business. Marriages have difficult times, and your mother and Bowie's marriage is new."

"It isn't my business now," she concurred. "And I hope it won't be."

He had to agree.

Just not verbally.

"Try to give her some time and grace."

"*N'importe quoi*," she murmured. "I need to get ready. Judge and I are going to a matinee."

"What are you seeing?"

"*Moulin Rouge.*"

"Enjoy it, honey."

"Will do, Daddy. And...Dad?"

"Yes, Chloe."

"You really don't have to protect her anymore." Before he could recover from that detonation and reply, she said, "Love you," and rang off.

He drew in breath and stared at the power of Stella Gunn as he tried to shake off his conversation with his daughter.

Mika and Cadence were in the kitchen, preparing Sunday brunch, all of them fueling up in order to go to Queens to visit MoMA PS1 because Cadence had a paper in modern art due, Mika wanted some inspiration, and Tom had never been there.

He'd come downstairs to take the call in private.

Now he needed to let the call go and get back upstairs.

However, his eyes hit on the microscope as he turned, and he decided finally, after decades, to give himself time to experience it to its fullest and view all the slides.

She had SKY set under the lens. Randomly, he viewed them as JOIN, BROTHERHOOD, US, DREAMER, SHARING and LIFE.

And there it was.

The point.

The beauty.

The meaning of life under a microscope.

Because even after his conversation with Chloe, seeing those words magnified, he was injected with the positivity of them.

Exactly as the artist intended.

And exactly the homage it represented intended the same.

He was smiling when he straightened from the piece, turned and stopped dead.

Teddy was standing in the doorway to the hall.

Tom hadn't heard him come in.

With one look at the man, Mika's PA and friend, Tom braced again.

"So they cook for you, do they?" he asked, either having been upstairs, or probably smelling the bacon.

"Sometimes," Tom replied warily.

He was trying to find the words to negotiate a détente with a man who he shouldn't have to do such a thing with when Teddy spoke again.

Flinging his hand out, he said, "She put that there, pride of place, because of you."

Tom felt his neck get tight.

"Sorry?"

"The microscope," Teddy explained. "When I asked why she placed it there, she said, 'It reminds me of Tom.' And this was before the two of you became a two of you."

Jesus Christ.

That piece was out, placed where it was, because of him?

Teddy wasn't done.

"She bought that place in Arizona, also because of you."

For a second time that morning, with the bombs dropping around him, Tom was struck mute.

"You got divorced, she wanted to be close to you," Teddy said.

Tom opened his mouth but got nothing out before Teddy kept firing away.

"You live there. You like it there. You can play tennis and golf year-round." Definitely a supercilious lip curl on the last. "She'll eventually move there, for you."

Things were becoming clearer as to why Teddy had an issue with him.

However, Tom was feeling exceptionally uncomfortable that Teddy was sharing all of this, and not Mika.

"Listen, Teddy—"

"And you're a cheat," Teddy spat.

Tom blinked and his head jerked as that particular mortar landed at his feet and exploded right in his face.

"Aren't you? You're a cheat," Teddy went on.

"I was wondering how deep you'd dig your grave."

Tom didn't move.

Teddy whirled around.

Mika entered the room from the doorway closer to the front of the house.

She walked to stand in front of a beat-up leather chair, and once there, she planted her hands on her hips.

She was wearing a pair of caramel-colored, wide-legged, silk drawstring pants and a bulky, oversized, cropped, ivory cashmere sweater.

Her hair was a mess on top of her head.

She was makeup-less, had a pair of fluffy slippers on her feet, and she was so pissed, her anger vibrated in the room.

She was also formidable.

Unbeatable.

In fluffy slippers.

Tom was impressed.

"Can you explain," she asked Teddy casually, "what the fuck you think you're doing?"

"I—" Teddy began, his face pale.

Mika swung an arm up in front of her, saying, "Never mind. I don't care." She turned to Tom. "Yes, it's true. Both. That microscope is there because it reminds me of you. And I bought a home in Arizona because I wanted to reconnect with you. Although I'm sure both come as a surprise with the way you learned about them, I hope, when you think about it, they don't. Because I believe I made it clear how deeply I felt connected to you when I met you. And when something like that happens, it just doesn't ever die."

That wasn't a bomb.

That was a miracle balm that felt like it could soothe every hurt.

It felt like it because Tom had had a rough twenty minutes.

And suddenly, he was feeling just fine.

"Mika—" Teddy said quietly.

She ignored him and kept her attention on Tom.

"That's probably a lot for you, but you should know. I would have told you, just maybe not so soon. That said, I needed a change. Cadence is leaving the nest imminently, and I realized I needed space to deal with her loss. I know she's not really going anywhere, but she is. I suspect you understand exactly what I'm talking about. In other words, I was seeking peace. I love the city and you know I'll never fully leave. But I wanted an escape. A new perspective. Therefore, it wasn't only being close to you that made me find that house."

"Mika," Teddy said, having had time to recover, his voice was firm.

She turned to him but said nothing, didn't even raise her brows.

"I only have your best interests at heart," he told her.

"Really? Is that why you shared things with Tom that I haven't even shared yet, and I'm fucking him?" she asked coolly.

"You two became very close very quickly," Teddy retorted. "Mixing families. Him spending the night when Cadence is here."

"And you have a say in this why?" she asked.

"I'm your friend," he retorted. "I care about you. I've known you fourteen years, and I've been working for you for ten."

"Yes, Teddy, thank you for reciting that history. I do remember. Which begs the question why you would share my secrets *and* why you would insult my boyfriend ever, but *in my home*, for God's sake?"

"It isn't just you who's in this relationship, it's Cadence as well," Teddy replied.

"Please tell me why you keep telling me things I know?"

On that, Teddy lost it.

"Because, my dear, *I* happen to be losing her *too*," he spat. "Has that occurred to you? You're in your studio, doing something, ring ring"—he took on a falsetto voice which made Tom very much want to laugh, however, obviously, he did not—"'Teddy? Can you go get my girl from school?' But of course I can, because she's *my girl too*. I've picked her up from school. Brought her home. Fed her. Took her shopping. Took her to dinner. To brunch. To drum lessons. Organized slumber parties for her. Chaperoned that *awful* pizza party fiasco."

Teddy gave a shiver.

And kept talking.

"I had the smell of grease and cheese so deeply bonded to the fibers of my sweater, I couldn't get it out. I had to throw that sweater away. Four hundred dollars of merino wool, probably some homeless person is wearing it, and he's hungry for pizza and he doesn't know why."

Mika sucked her lips between her teeth, and Tom knew what that meant.

She was trying not to laugh.

He understood the feeling.

Teddy was on a roll, however, and as such, didn't stop.

"I bought her Christmas and birthday presents. She was junior attendant at my wedding, Mika. And you know I love her because she stole the damned show *and I let her*. At...*my wedding*."

"Teddy—"

"So, excuse me for feeling like I might have some say in the man you bring into her life."

He'd been gaining traction.

And then he said that.

Tom wanted to let them have privacy, but he had no idea how to extricate himself without turning their attention to him, and in their state, he didn't want their attention.

Not even Mika's.

Because before, she was ticked.

Now, she was ready to rumble.

And she rumbled.

"I love you, Teddy, and I love how you love my daughter. I love how you care for her and cared for her for most of her life. But you do not get a say in who I become involved with. You also do not get to be upset, and instead of using your words and speaking to me like we're both adults, you confront that very man I'm involved with. That is so not okay, I can't even fathom how to explain how not okay it is, because you should already know."

"Has it occurred to you that I love you too? I care about you deeply. I consider you my dearest friend. And yet *Nora* is in Arizona, mixing drinks for Mr. Tennis Star"—he flung a hand in Tom's direction—"and soaking up the sun, and I'm in New York, getting texts about your food orders."

And the truth comes out.

"Again, *use your words*," Mika retorted.

"You *use yours*," Teddy struck back. "To call me and tell me you had *a man in your life*."

"I didn't keep Tom a secret," she shot back.

"And I didn't get to taste *le Poire Surprise de Nora*," he sniped.

"Okay—" Tom began.

They both looked to him.

Yes, he didn't want either of their attention.

But he had it, and this was ridiculous.

All of it.

"You stay out of it," Teddy ordered Tom.

"You do not tell my boyfriend what to do," Mika bit off to Teddy.

"You two do realize you're fighting over how much you love each other and Cadence, don't you?" Tom asked.

Teddy's perfect beard bulged at the jaw.

Mika snapped her mouth shut.

"I'm going to leave you to it," he declared and moved to Mika. He kissed her temple and said, "It's not a lot. It's everything. And I mean that in the best way imaginable." He turned to Teddy and said, "I'm new, but I care for them both too. Very much. And I'd like for you to like me, and give me some reason, no matter how thin, to like you too. Because you mean something to both of them, and it'll be awkward as fuck if you don't."

With that, he left the room, climbed the stairs and went to the kitchen.

Mika's kitchen was like the rest of the house. Overstuffed. There was a crazily designed black and white tile floor. Some busy wallpaper that had a backdrop of black. Teal cabinets. The countertops were covered with everything a cook would need, and more. There were plants and cookbooks shoved in nooks and crannies.

And now it was a mess because brunch was clearly not going to be French toast fingers, but instead, a much grander affair.

"Are they having it out?" Cadence asked, like this was not the first time what was going on downstairs happened.

"Yes," he answered.

"Teddy's being a snot because you're threatening his territory."

"Yes," Tom repeated, his lips twitching.

"Mom's not super hip when Teddy acts like a snot."

"Nope," Tom agreed.

"It gets worse before it gets better," she warned. "Teddy doesn't like to admit when he's wrong or show he cares. He'll go home, complain about all of us to Faunus, his husband. Then Faun will tell him to sort himself out because Faun doesn't like it when Teddy acts like a snot either. Then he'll come back, and he'll act like nothing has happened." She pointed at Tom with a whisk. "Just so you know, like us, you're going to have to learn to pretend Teddy didn't act like a snot. We've found it's the best way forward."

He chuckled and leaned against the counter, crossing his arms on his chest. "I can probably do that."

"Sometimes it's hard," she told the bowl she was now beating something in with the whisk.

"What's for breakfast?" Tom asked to move them away from this subject.

"Mini cheese and herb quiches in hashbrown cups. Blintzes with blackberry compote. Fresh fruit. And bacon. Because Mom and I have a rule of never eating anything breakfast-like without having bacon."

Definitely a grander affair.

"That's the best rule I've ever heard," he told her.

She shot him a wide grin.

Mika stormed in, announcing, "Your Uncle Teddy is fired."

Cadence tossed him an eye roll before looking back to the bowl.

"Yeah, right," she said, then shared, "It's time to make the crêpes. Do you want to do it?"

"Don't I always make the crêpes?" Mika asked.

Cadence looked to Tom. "She does. I like eating them, but I split them on the dismount."

"You have to have patience, kid," Mika said, moving in and taking over at the bowl.

Breaking off in a practiced dance, Cadence pulled open a drawer, and out of it she unearthed a crêpe pan she put directly on a burner.

Because even if the kitchen wasn't all that big, it was bursting at the seams due to all the stuff they had.

Including a crêpe pan.

"Spreader and spatula," Mika called out, like she was a surgeon demanding an instrument.

"Gotcha," Cadence said, opening another drawer.

And now here it was.

A demonstration of the reasoning behind the Arizona house.

These two were so embedded in each other's lives, the loss of one would feel like the loss of the whole.

Tom had a wife and three kids when they started leaving the nest.

It sucked so exorbitantly, he could barely cope with it.

Peace and a new perspective, if you had the means to find either, was the only way to roll.

"Can I do something?" Tom asked.

"You can *mise en place* the filling for Cadence as we get these rolling. I'll call out the ingredients. The *mise en place* bowls are in that drawer over there." Mika pointed to a drawer with her foot. "Let me know when you're ready."

Tom opened the drawer and found it was not chaotic, like he was expecting.

It was almost pathologically organized, the space maximized to its fullest.

It was also the explanation as to how they had *mise en place* bowls and a crêpe pan in a narrow New York brownstone's kitchen that shared a floor with a dining room, a family room and a small room that was used as Cadence's study.

He grabbed the bowls.

Mika and Cadence both took turns calling the ingredients to him.

He helped stuff when it was time.

Cadence couldn't make the crêpes, but she fried the blintzes.

They all carried to the dining room table, and the room was less crowded than at dinner, but it wasn't less electric with the company he was keeping as he ate brunch.

They had a ton left over, even if they were leaving in the morning, but Mika said blithely, "Don't worry. Teddy will be pissed at me for at least a week. But he'll still come over and get the food. Faun is six four, plays flag football on the weekend, though the flags are for show, and they tackle without pads, so I'm not really sure why they don't call it rugby, but whatever, and he loves our leftovers, mostly because neither he nor Teddy cook."

"At least, not very well," Cadence put in before she told them she was taking off to get ready to go to the museum.

Then she took off.

Tom and Mika sat back with another cup of coffee.

"It's going to be okay with Teddy?" Tom asked.

Mika stretched her head to the side and explained, "He doesn't communicate well. His family is very religious, and very old-fashioned, and they chose not to accept him and his supposed 'lifestyle.' He hasn't spoken to his mother or father in at least fifteen years. He loves them. It's a daily hurt, the kind you get used to the pain, but it's still there. We're his family now. This means I get why he's concerned we're breaking up, when we're not. There was dysfunction with his family before he came out, and that shows in how he communicates, or doesn't, and instead lashes out. Faun will have a few words with him, and Teddy will pretend it didn't happen."

"That's what Cadence said."

Mika confirmed this with a nod.

Carefully, Tom asked, "Does he usually go that far?"

She took a sip of her coffee and shook her head. "No, but then he's not usually worried he's going to lose the two most important women in his life either." She studied him closely. "I'm sorry he was an ass to you."

"He guessed what he guessed, and I would assume that would make him even more concerned about us being together."

"It's not his place."

"It still an explanation."

"Agreed. But it's not his place."

Tom sat back and took a sip of his own coffee.

"Are you okay with what he said?" she asked.

"Not particularly," he answered.

"You looked like you'd been sucker punched."

"I had."

Her lips thinned.

"Mika, I can take it."

"Sneak attack too, that little minx," she groused.

"Mika, honey, I'm fine," he said firmly.

"I don't want you to be freaked about the fact I bought a place in Arizona because you were there."

"I'm not," he returned. "I'm thrilled."

She studied him again.

Then her lips twitched.

They stopped twitching when she asked, "Chloe okay?"

"She's pissed at her mom."

Mika made no response.

"It's none of her business," Tom pointed out.

"I'm not sure daughters think that of their mothers...ever."

Tom took another sip of coffee because he had no reply.

When he was done, he shared, "She's scared she's going to steam-roll Judge."

Mika lifted her coffee cup to him. "And there's why a girl pays close attention to her mom."

"I wasn't steamrolled. I made my choices. That isn't on Genny either."

"I don't know anything about it, sweetheart, except your side of it," she said as she got to her feet.

She bent over him and gave him a kiss.

When she pulled way, she finished, "I do know I like your girl a whole lot. She has an amazing personality, and she lets it shine, and she doesn't care much what people think about it. That doesn't mean she isn't self-aware. She is. There are those who are doomed to repeat the mistakes of their ancestors. And there are those who are not. The ones who're self-aware are not. Now I'm going to go get ready. Don't do the dishes. Just let them soak. We'll sort them out when we get home."

She kissed him again.

And Tom watched her walk away.

# CHAPTER 19

## THE AMBUSH

*Mika*

*Give me a call when you have a second.*

I sent that text to Nora, who, since we returned from New York a week and a half ago, had been less available than her norm.

It was strange and gave me an unsettled feeling.

Not that she should be at my beck and call.

Just that she always was, and now that she wasn't, and I didn't know *why* she wasn't, I was feeling weird about it.

I was also hoping it wasn't a Teddy situation insofar as she was hurt I had someone new in my life who was getting a good deal of my attention.

Teddy had since reverted to his uber professional self, was doing his job splendidly, doggedly, even pathologically, but doing it while holding a grudge. He'd melt when Faun had had enough of it. As ever, I just had to wait for that to happen. And considering I was a pretty patient person, and Faun adored Teddy and had all the patience in the world for his mercurial personality, that could take a while.

But I'd never had a man in my life during my relationship with either of them.

Not really.

Rollo seemed like a blink in my existence, or more like a brilliant blinding flash, as shattering as that was. My relationship with Nora had bloomed to what it became because she'd been my rock through his loss, but it wasn't as deep before that.

However, I knew, when a friend who didn't have a man got a man, relationships could become strained.

I needed to be sure both of them felt my love and attention.

On their part, they needed to understand I was happier than I'd been in nineteen years.

With this in mind, in an effort to keep that love and attention flowing, as well as speed things up in regard to Teddy getting over it, I sent a text to my Teddy/Faun/Cadence group, *When are we planning for you gents to come out here?*

I got an immediate reply from Cadence, who was at the Heard Museum in the city because her modern art essay had veered toward Native Americans producing modern art with a traditional bent, *Yay! Yeah! When?*

It took a while, but not long, for Faun to say, *We're looking at our calendars. But soon. We'll let you know.*

Teddy (it was no surprise) didn't reply.

Still, I smiled.

Then I heard the doorbell.

My smile turned into a frown because I wasn't expecting anybody.

One could say the situation in New York with the paparazzi and fans had rattled me. I had security systems in both my houses, and they were robust (or at least I thought that at the time they were installed). But it meant a great deal Jamie had one of his security team stationed at the house after that incident, also the man followed us around while we enjoyed our final day there.

Here, I didn't have that.

My house was remote, but it was accessible.

Practically the minute we landed from New York, Tom had called my security company and demanded an upgrade that included cameras. He also used his Tom Pierce pull to have the installation of those fast-tracked.

Which was why I went to my iPad to check to see who was at the front door.

I stared at Sasha Pierce standing there in all her youthful, glowing, blonde glory.

Yes, she was this even through a grainy feed.

I was not a fan of the ambush.

That said, I couldn't let Sasha stand outside then eventually leave because I didn't answer when I was at home.

I checked the cats, of which I had all five due to Tom being away. We were assessing their ability to travel and be in new environments, considering three of them would permanently be that way very soon. Clay (and Pris and Brayton) had taken care of them while we were in NYC.

They were all sleeping in a pile in their bed.

I closed the door behind me to contain their area, made my way downstairs and opened my front door.

Chloe was Tom in female form, and this included being elegant, sophisticated and chic (and yes, Tom was the male version of that).

Sasha was Imogen, but with a California girl twist.

Tan, blue-eyed, and boho. She was wearing a simple crew tank in heathered gray, faded pink short-shorts and a cream lace duster. A long necklace with an oversized pendant at the end, a slim chain belt and a pair of short-rise Uggs completed this picture.

That and a big head of semi-ratted, disheveled hair that looked like she hadn't washed or brushed it in days, but it wasn't about her being anything but intentionally unkempt.

And it worked.

She was stunning.

"Sasha," I greeted.

"Uh, hey, Mika. This is...um, weird. But...is Dad here?"

I was surprised at the question. Since it was my house, I thought she'd come to see me.

"See, I need to talk to him," she carried on. "And he's not answering his texts. I went to his house, but he wasn't there. I thought he might be here."

"He's not answering his texts because he's flying to North Carolina with Judge. They're meeting with Sampson Cooper."

"Oh, right," she muttered, likely thinking this meeting was about Cooper's interest in Trail Blazer.

It was, but it wasn't.

Cooper was a retired NFL player. Cooper was also a beloved American hero, and that had nothing to do with his playing football.

And Cooper was one of the people they'd decided to approach about the Core Point situation.

I studied Tom's girl.

Then I asked what any mother would ask with what I saw standing on my doorstep, "Do you want to come in?"

She seemed grateful, but this quickly melted to uncertain.

She started hedging back, but I reached out, took her hand and put gentle pressure on to pull her forward.

"Come in, Sasha," I said softly. "Let's have a drink in my courtyard and get to know each other a bit."

"This is...you weren't expecting me. This isn't cool," she replied, resisting my pull.

I was glad she thought that way.

Even so.

"You have something important to talk to your dad about?" I asked.

"He's mad at me, and I don't...I don't like it when he's mad at me."

"Please come in, honey," I urged.

It took her a beat to make the decision, and then she let me guide her in.

She glanced around as I led her to the kitchen.

She stopped at the island as I moved to the fridge, and noted, "This place is awesome."

"Thanks."

"Chloe says your place in New York is amazing."

"That's nice to hear," I replied warmly. "Now, what do you like to drink? I could make us some iced lattes. Or iced chais. I've got San Pellegrino. A few flavors of La Croix. Regular ole filtered tap water. A variety of juices. Or are you feeling an early afternoon cocktail?"

"I...cocktail," she said in a rush.

She immediately looked like she regretted saying it. Maybe because it had just gone two o'clock and she didn't want me to judge about day drinking.

However, I'd offered.

"I'm glad we agree," I replied quickly so she wouldn't feel awkward.

We decided on a mimosa take that included a splash of cranberry juice as well as a hint of Nora's pear and headed to the courtyard.

"This is really...uh, *wow*," she said as she stepped out with me, taking in the adobe fireplace and the stream of water that plunged over a ledge that had a potted tree on it and ran across some cobalt blue tile into a pool on the opposite side of the courtyard.

There were additional potted plants, as well a table and four chairs, plus a seating area in front of the fire that had a loveseat and two chairs angled around some tables with mosaic tile tops.

I led her to the seating area.

"Dad's totally going to move out here," she breathed, then her face turned crimson. "God, I'm sorry. So sorry. You guys are new and that's..."

"It's okay," I promised her, beginning to become alarmed at how unsure of herself she was.

Chloe knew who she was down to the well-shod toes of her feet.

Sasha couldn't have been more different.

Chloe was the oldest, at twenty-five, soon to be twenty-six.

Sasha was twenty-one.

But even Cadence was more comfortable in her skin than Sasha was.

"Do you really think he'd want to live out here?" I asked as I sat in an armchair and motioned to the loveseat for her to join me.

She sat too. "Yeah, he's like...I mean, his place in Scottsdale is totally *him*. But he likes space. I was surprised he didn't buy something with land around it, so he could put in a putting green or even a court."

I would not in the slightest be averse to a having a court added to this property so I could watch Tom Pierce putting himself through his paces. In fact, finding someone to do that was penciling itself on my mental to-do list.

A putting green, not so much.

"His pad is very him, but if we get there, I'd prefer he move in with me," I told her.

"Are you, I mean...are you moving out here, to Arizona, like, permanently?"

I shook my head. "No, but I figure I'll be flipping things, and once my daughter Cadence moves on to whatever it is she's going to be doing, I'll probably spend more time out here than in New York."

"Cool," she mumbled.

"It's too bad Cadence is in town. I'd love for you two to meet."

"Chloe says she's the bomb."

"Chloe's right."

Finally, saying that, I'd coaxed a small smile on her face.

It was time to try to get her to open up.

"You and I have just met, but I care about your dad a lot, he speaks of you all the time. He loves you completely. He's worried about you, as you know. And I'm a mom. I'm also a woman. So if you have something to share, and you want to share it with me, I might get it."

"You might...I think you..." She swallowed, shook her head. "I've been, you know, checking out your stuff. Chloe was a big fan back in the day. I didn't have time for...I was into other things then. Big into volleyball."

Tom had told me this.

I didn't share that. I nodded my head to encourage her to keep talking.

She took a sip from her flute, looked to the cold fireplace, then back to me.

"So, you know, I wasn't into it back then, but, once you started seeing Dad...I watched one of your documentaries. The one you did about women's hair? You know, from Bo Derek appropriating corn rows from Black women to the differing beliefs of Muslim women as to what the hajib is, worn over hair only, to covering the entire body."

"Yes?" I urged when she said no more.

"It was really good. I learned a lot."

"That makes me happy to hear."

"And I read that book of your poetry," she kept at it. "*Spring to Summer to Autumn*, all your thoughts through those seasons. It was really...personal. And beautiful. And powerful. I never got into poetry. I thought it all had to rhyme and it just wasn't my thing. But you made little things, like sitting in front of a mirror to do your makeup, and suddenly discovering your face, realizing you hadn't truly looked at it for forever. Finding every change since the last time you paid attention. Not knowing who you are for a split second, and how terrifying that was. Then realizing a soul stays the same from birth to death, and the lines on your face don't matter. I was...that was a really good one."

"That makes me happy to hear too," I said.

"The soul part," she replied.

"Mm-hmm, the soul part," I prompted.

"I really liked that part."

And suddenly, there was something about her that made me frightened.

"Sasha—" I began.

"I wanted Dad to know I got a job," she blurted.

Well, that was good.

"Okay, but—"

"He's going to think it's silly. But I...I really like it. It's at a coffee place, but they do really good food too, and it's attached to a bookstore and yoga and meditation studio. It's a whole like...*thing*. A complex. It has a courtyard too. Not like this one. Total Zen. The vibe is awesome."

"That's good," I replied.

"I don't make a lot of money."

"Money isn't everything."

"Yeah, we can say that because we have it."

She had me there.

"And I got my own place," she continued. "It's kinda weird. Loft apartments downtown. The walls are mostly concrete and it's not my thing at all, really. But the footprint is minimized. I don't think I ever want to live in a house. No offense, to each their own. But it's just not cool anymore with the way the population has exploded. But I needed to find my own zone, and it was the only thing I liked when I was looking, so I'm in a year lease."

The mother in me resurfaced, and I asked a practical question, "Do you have any furniture?"

That coaxed another smile.

"Yeah. There are a lot of vintage and reclaimed and repurposed stores in Phoenix that have super rad stuff. I don't have very much yet, I'm being picky. But I've been spending a ton of time in those stores and found some really cool things. Who knew decorating could be so fun?"

I smiled back. "It's pretty awesome, isn't it?"

She nodded, took another sip, as did I.

And she spoke again. "I just wanted Dad to know that I heard him. It bugged me, the whole semi-intervention thing. It felt like they were ganging up on me. But I heard him. And Mom. And all that. They were right. It was when I talked to Gage about it, and he said everyone was flipping their shit about me, it made me think on it. I didn't like people were flipping their shit. It hurt to think they were upset. I just didn't want to come to Dad without, you know, having a plan. Getting it together. I don't know what's next. I like doing it, but I'm not going to work in a coffee shop my whole life. But Gage said I couldn't figure it out if my mind was filled with where I was going to sleep that night. You know? Or I was always driving back and forth to Prescott. I had to be settled and have some rituals so my head could be clear. And he was right."

"Sounds like Gage is very wise."

That brought forth a giggle.

A giggle she explained.

"Gage is a frat boy without the frat or the asshole parts of frat boys. What I mean is, he likes a good time and isn't about settling or rituals at all. Though I think he's finally getting good grades. I just realized we're both figuring out how to grow up." She shot me a rueful smile. "It sucks that Gage figured out that was where we were at before me, but whatever. He did, and he gave me some real so I would too, and there we are."

"I think your dad will be very relieved to hear this," I shared. "He should be landing soon. I'm sure he'll get your text and call. And Cadence will be back in a couple of hours, and that'll bring us close to dinnertime, so I hope you stick around. We can keep chatting. You can meet the cats, Tom's brought them here. You can help us make dinner and stay and eat with us. And I'll show you around the house and you can have your pick of a private place to talk to your dad when he calls."

"Do you think Dad'll be mad, me showing up here?"

She should know him better than me.

However, I assured, "I think he'll understand you were looking for him to share something important that would ease his mind. And he's getting to know me pretty well, and he knows I wanted to meet you, so I don't think he'll be mad."

She tipped her head. "Sure?"

Yes, she loved her dad.

Yes, she was upset she worried him.

Yes, she was a good kid.

A little lost, but who wasn't in one way or another?

"Yes, honey, I'm sure."

She rubbed her lips together then nodded her assent.

I'd known her not even twenty minutes, so I didn't know how to broach my concern about what I felt coming from her.

On the one hand, it seemed she was getting her shit together.

On the other hand, something was very wrong.

"I had difficulty finding my way too," I shared.

That visibly shocked her. "Wow. From your stuff, you seem to have it all together."

"Well, I'm twenty-seven years older than you," I pointed out.

"Yeah, but you did that documentary on women's hair when you were, what? Twenty-five? I mean, that stuff is a big deal now. People are talking about it a lot. And you were talking about it decades ago."

"I also lived in New York and had a lot of friends from many different walks of life, and I was a good listener," I said. "And you might not know, but that documentary got zero attention when it was released. It's only now that people have discovered it and are taking onboard what it had to say."

"But you had it together like Chloe has it together."

Okay, maybe some sibling rivalry issues?

"I did," I agreed. "Because I walked right into where I knew I needed to be when I left Philly, and a dad who didn't get me, and a mom who encouraged me. Though, you know, people don't make as big a deal of it, but girls need their dads just as much as boys do."

Her face grew gentle, and I knew why—Cadence and Rollo—before she replied, "Yeah. They do."

"So I was dealing with some issues and I was lost. I had itchy feet all my life. I think I wanted to impress him. I wanted him to know, even if the path he chose for me, college, a solid career, marriage, children, was not the path I decided to take, I was a worthwhile human being."

"I bet he knows that now."

"You'd bet wrong."

She blinked.

"He doesn't understand anything I do," I shared. "He was infuriated I didn't find another man to fill Rollo's shoes, though, at the time, when Rollo was alive, he didn't approve of my choice for a husband. Since I lost Rollo, my father feels I opted to raise Cadence as a single mother just to spite him. I didn't respect him, and that was my way to prove I didn't respect him or any man."

"Oh my God," she snapped. "It's totally not about him."

"Some men live their entire lives thinking everything is totally about them. My father is one of those men."

She made a face that said *Gross*.

That made me laugh, and I assured, "It's okay. Cadence is great.

My mom died too young, but they had time together. They were close. My girl had a lot of her before she was gone. And I learned early that I didn't need anyone's approval. Only one person on this earth had to love what I did, and that's me."

"That's you," she whispered.

"Yes. Only me."

"Wow," she said quietly.

"You're going to walk right into where you need to be, Sasha," I told her. "I promise, honey. It happened early for me. Cadence is graduating, and I worry about her, because she hasn't found her joy either, but I know she'll find it when it's time, when she trips over it as life's path leads her around randomly. You will too."

"Chloe was like, always, you know...*Chloe*," she said.

"This doesn't surprise me," I replied.

"And Matt has always been his own entity. He's like an island. Only people invited get to come there. And when he's done with you, he kicks you off for a while. It's not ugly. It's just him. He retreats into himself, and you have to wait until he's ready to let you back in. Do you know what I mean?"

I wasn't sure.

Though, it sounded like what Imogen was doing...and it could explain why Matt cut his father out of his life for so long.

Thus, I nodded.

"I always wanted to be that way," she said, like she was talking to herself.

I gave her time.

She took a bit of it and came back to me.

"Mom and Dad split, and I was...you know, I was his. Dad's. We moved to Phoenix, and I was still in high school, and everything got messed up for me. And I was kinda mad, because Mom wanted to move, and Dad didn't, and I didn't either. Then they split, and I was mad because, why the move before if they're gonna end things? But I was mad at Mom, and I thought I should be mad at Dad because... because..." She trailed off, appearing horrified.

"I know all about it," I said softly.

"Okay," she whispered. "I was supposed to be mad at him. And I wasn't. And I felt, you know, like, *bad* because I didn't completely take Mom's back. Like Matt did. I'm a woman. I should have done that, right?"

"In this instance, you were their child. Both their child. And you are yourself. And what you feel and how you process what happened between your parents is yours, and only yours. There are no 'shoulds' here, Sasha. I can't say that strongly enough. You aren't supposed to feel anything but what you actually feel."

She stared at me, and I was a woman, I was a mother, I'd just heard all she said.

And I still wasn't ready for it.

But it came abruptly, gushing from her in wailing floods.

She dissolved into sobs so fierce, I had to set aside my glass, and take hers, get on the loveseat with her and pull her into my arms.

"Nobody...n-n-nobody gave me permission to feel," she sobbed into my neck.

"Oh, honey," I murmured, holding her close and rocking her.

"I know I should have just d-done it, b-but I didn't know how," she continued.

"It's confusing. Of course you didn't," I soothed.

"I th-thought being Dad's, b-b-being like Dad would make Mom hurt. So I s-stopped b-b-being like Dad."

Oh, this sweet beauty.

"I get it."

"I miss volleyball," she wailed.

"Okay, sweetheart."

"I miss Dad...and Mom."

"Okay."

"I'm m-m-messed up. Chloe and Matt aren't messed up."

"It's theirs to share, and not mine, but your father has told me some things, and you're wrong about that."

She pulled away and really...

The young.

She looked gorgeous with a tear-stained face and brilliantly flashing eyes.

"Really?" she asked.

I nodded.

"I want to be a nutritionist," she announced.

"That sounds good."

"Not just sports nutrition. Or weight loss, 'cuz I have issues with that, and how people profit off it. Or any of that kind of thing. You know, diets can help manage disease, and not just normal stuff, like eating right. They've used the ketogenic diet for years as a kind of last-ditch effort to assist in seizure control of uncontrolled epileptics."

"Whoa. I didn't know that."

She nodded and swiped at her face. "Is it too late? I mean, I'm twenty-one. I'll be like, *old* if I go to college."

I smiled big at her and said, "Sasha, darling girl, people go to college at any age. I've known seventy-year-olds who got their law degrees. You are far from old."

"So that sounded stupid, huh?"

Okay.

Enough.

I grabbed her wrists and held strong. "Nothing is stupid. Be yourself. Have your worries. Ask your questions. Share your thoughts. *None of it is stupid.* Not a single human being on this planet knows everything. But not a single human being learned anything without questioning, then finding the answer."

Those pretty, wet-spiked-lashed eyes got wide. "Wow, you're wise."

"You will be too in twenty more years."

It was shaky, but she grinned at me.

It was a sweet, happy, uncomplicated grin, the first I'd had from her.

So I relaxed.

And grinned back.

TOM CALLED WHEN I WAS IN BED, READING.

Sasha was in Nora's room.

She and Cadence had gotten on like a house on fire.

They had then gotten drunk.

This had included a FaceTime call, and on a phone screen I got to meet Duncan Holloway's handsome son, Gage.

I feared Cadence would regret meeting Gage while she was slurring, snorting and giggling, but that was a worry for another day.

Between our courtyard time and now, we'd not only had the cats meet, the daughter meet, made dinner, ate it, and they got drunk, Tom had called Sasha.

She sat in my back garden and talked to him for an hour and a half.

Which might be one of the reasons she got so drunk, living it up after the big release.

She'd come in from that to say, "Dad said to tell you he'd call you later."

And now it was later.

I answered his call with a soft, "Hey, baby."

"Honey."

He said no more.

I felt his emotion beat into me from the phone.

I gave it time and then I shared, "She's spending the night. She and Cadence tied one on."

"Good," he replied. "I don't want her alone in her new place tonight." A loaded pause and then came the explosion I was expecting, "*Fuck!* I feel like the world's shittiest goddamn father."

I knew that was where he'd go.

Because that was where I'd go.

"Tommy, I'll point out she wasn't forthcoming she was wrestling with these things."

"Chloe had a meltdown. Matt shut me out. I should have known."

"You did. You showed patience. And then when you couldn't break through, you tried another avenue to get her to open up. I'll point out, Tom, even if I'd feel precisely like you do right now, that avenue worked. She not only started to get her shit together, she let out what was messing it up in the first place."

He didn't respond to that.

He said, "She told me she wants to go back to school to be a nutritionist."

"She shared that with me too."

"I think she thinks that'll make me happy."

"I think you might not be exactly correct about that," I contradicted carefully. "She was very emotional when she shared that with me. Lots of stuff was pouring out. I believe that's her genuine desire, and she lost track of it in all the rest. It's lovely it'll make you happy, but it's also incidental. It'll make *Sasha* happy."

"I shared my concerns with her that she was doing it for me, and she said much the same thing, just not that way," he replied. "She also said something odd. She said she tripped over where she needed to be when she came to you. Do you know what she means by that?"

Oh, I so very much did.

I was choking on emotion, so I couldn't answer at first.

"Mika?" he pushed

My voice was husky when I replied, "It means she wants to be a nutritionist, honey. Don't worry. It's for her. It's just a bonus that it's also for you."

"Why do you sound like you're crying?" he asked gently.

"Because I really like your daughter, and I'm so fucking glad she was looking for you, but she found me."

There was another loaded pause before he replied, "I am too."

We both let that sit for a moment before I changed topics.

"How did your talk go with Sampson Cooper?"

"He's pissed as shit about Core Point, and he's all in. He's got a lot of friends in athletics. Judge and I are bringing him in. We'll knock out a plan tomorrow, then be on a plane tomorrow night."

"I'll pick you up."

"Honey, that's a drive for you."

"I'll pick you up, Tom."

He gave in easily. "You're spending the night at my place."

I loved my bed. I loved my bedroom.

I did not like it that I was in it alone.

I could do alone, I knew that all too well.

But it was so much better having Tom with me.

"I so totally and completely am."

He chuckled.

It died when he said, "Thank you for being there for my girl."

"It's already one of my life's most precious treasures, honey. So the gratitude is coming from me."

"Fuck, you're everything," he growled.

Oh yes.

So totally and completely spending the night with him tomorrow.

"So are you."

"Then you're more than everything."

I smiled and did it wide before I said, "I'll let that lie, because if Nora ever found out we started to get gooey-lovey, she'd never speak to me again."

And at that, he burst out laughing.

---

I TOOK HIM DEEP.

"Mika," Tom snarled. "Up. Here. Now."

Tom being bossy while I was sucking his cock, I released him and clambered into his lap.

It was less I bore down on him than he impaled me.

He also smacked my ass for being a bad girl.

I came instantly, and hard.

It was bonus time for me, I knew, because even though I took him close while I was going down on him, Tom had control and stamina, and he got grouchy when he didn't get his way during sex, like...*immediately*.

Therefore, he retaliated in the most delicious ways.

This time, I was pulled off him and planted on my hands and

knees. I then felt his palm between my shoulder blades, and I was forced to genuflect in front of him while he drove in from behind.

Unsurprisingly, not long later, I came again.

And *hard*.

I was essentially an ooze of flesh by the time he climaxed inside me, which was probably why, after he used my pussy to milk himself dry and then used it more to stroke through the loss of his erection, and he finally pulled out, I collapsed on the bed.

I felt his lips touch my ass cheek, he was gone, then he was back with a warm wet cloth between my legs.

That felt good, but I didn't do anything but release a low moan.

He was gone again, and when he came back that time, he rearranged me in bed so he was on his back, I was draped down his side, and the covers were over us.

I really, really loved that I got the monster fucking me, and the gentleman who took care of me at all other times.

It rocked.

"You need to touch yourself when I'm away," he advised.

"Not a chance," I mumbled against his chest.

"You clamped on so tight when you came, both times, I thought I was going to lose an important appendage," he teased. "And we only had one night apart."

"Stop flattering your own damned self."

"I don't have to, you were so hungry for my cock, I thought you'd asphyxiate yourself with how deep you took me when you got it in your mouth."

It took effort, but I expended it to lift my head and glare at him.

He was grinning.

Widely.

Incidentally, my glare had no effect.

"Cocky is not attractive," I warned him on a lie.

"Bullshit," he called me on it.

I was too mellowed out for this.

The fact I loved the way he fucked me was not news to me or Tom.

If I could take a comment about the documentary I'd spent four years researching that I'd made about women in the workforce from the war effort to Anita Hill of it being called "sophomoric tripe" (by a white male septuagenarian whose favorite film of all time was *American Beauty*, I would add), I could take Tom teasing me.

I collapsed into him again.

He sifted his fingers through my hair to pull it away from my face and then did it again just because.

I closed my eyes and melted deeper into him.

"I'm glad you missed me," he murmured. "Because I missed you."

"Yeah," I muttered. "Sleeping alone sucks."

"Agreed."

I expended more effort to kiss his chest.

And when I'd settled back in, I said, "Welcome home, baby."

"Thanks, honey."

I would have liked to talk to him, learn more about his trip, seeing as I'd picked him up, we stopped by Blanco for some Mexican and we mostly talked about Sasha, Matt's imminent arrival, Chloe still being ticked at Genny, and not about his trip or what was happening with Core Point, then we came home and fucked.

I didn't.

I passed out.

I knew Tom didn't mind, because when he shifted me so we were tangled face to face, I woke just enough to see he did it in his sleep.

So, as ever, he'd been right there with me.

# CHAPTER 20

## THE AMBUSH PART 2

### *Mika*

"Honey, you're fidgeting." I glanced over at my daughter then masked the surprise when I asked, "Are you nervous?"

"Yeah, I mean, we're meeting Matt tonight."

And we were.

Sadly, I'd just had another two nights without Tom.

This was because Matt had arrived Saturday. They'd spent that day and Sunday together, playing tennis and doing other man things.

Now it was Monday, and Cadence and I were going over to Tom's for dinner.

Sasha, Chloe and Judge were going to be there too, and now Cadence and Sasha were thick as thieves.

Before, I couldn't get my daughter to focus on her studies.

Since Sasha showed a little over a week ago, nearly every day, Cadence had been in the courtyard where Sasha's coffee shop was located. She was there because "That place is dope as hell, Mom!" She was also there studying.

They hung out after. Sasha was showing Cadence the cool, hip, young people's Phoenix and Cadence was loving it.

She hadn't seemed nervous at all about Sasha, or Chloe, or Judge, and especially Tom.

I didn't understand her response right now to Matt.

"I mean, sons are important to men, yeah? Like, fathers are really into their sons, am I right?" she asked.

"They're into all their kids, kid," I replied. "Like I'm super into how cool you are."

"Yeah, but if his son doesn't like us, that'll be a big deal, right?"

What on earth?

"Where's this coming from, Cadence?" I asked carefully.

She didn't answer me directly.

She said, "I mean, now I have two big sisters and...and...Tom and, I mean, we don't want to mess this up."

The "two big sisters" thing.

Shot to the heart.

"There's no way we can mess it up, honey," I said gently.

She didn't reply so I glanced at her again.

Her vibe was not good, and she was looking out the side window.

"Talk to me," I ordered.

"He likes me."

"Who?"

"Tom."

"Of course."

"He said I was a natural."

"What?"

"When I went to the courts with him and Clay the weekend before last. He taught me how to serve. I got into it, and he said, 'You're a natural.' And he's like, *Tom Pierce* and he said that *to me*."

No.

It wasn't Tom Pierce, famed tennis star who said it to her.

It was Tom, a man who taught her how to serve. A man with whom she shared meals. A man she watched movies with and went to museums with and talked about books with.

A man who was, for a short time, and with every day that time grew longer, the only semi-kind-of-real father she'd ever had (Teddy and then came Faun didn't count—with the bottomless pit of his vanity, Teddy set himself up as the older brother right from the start, which was beautiful since she hadn't had one of those either).

Tom had kids. Tom being fatherly to my kid would be second nature.

And he'd been being fatherly to my kid.

Oh shit.

That wasn't a shot to the heart.

I was dead.

I was also going to start crying.

Last, I was *oh so totally* building a tennis court at the house.

"Mom?"

"Matt is going to love you, baby," I said, my tone husky.

"Are you okay?"

"I just really like Tom, and it's a huge relief, my darling girl, to know you do too."

"I do," she said softly.

"I'm so glad," I replied.

She fist-bumped my thigh.

I got myself together and shot her a smile.

We made it to Tom's, and I loved it for him that his driveway was full of cars.

I hadn't seen him since Matt showed, but we'd texted and talked, and he was thrilled with how things were going.

*I have my boy back*, was one text.

And I was thrilled for Tom.

But he was like Cadence (also like Rollo). He liked people. He liked to be around people.

And people he cared about being close was his Nirvana.

Tom was very excited about tonight, and not nervous at all.

I suspected between him, Chloe, Sasha and Judge (and hopefully Matt), they'd smooth away Cadence's nerves, and fast.

We were barely in the door to the utility room when Chloe was bearing down on us (I had a garage opener, and Tom had a lot of space in his forecourt, so everyone had parked to give me direct access to the parking spot that was now mine in the garage, so there was no coming in the front like a guest for us, this being Tom's decree).

"My lovelies, you are *not* going to *believe*," Chloe announced.

With Chloe escorting us along the way, we made it to the kitchen, and my eyes found Tom first.

He looked happy and handsome, and best of all, seeing his gaze soft on me, finally—*finally*—he was *mine*.

His smile made my stomach melt, and my panties get wet, and my heart swell, all at the same time.

I then found Matt, who was Tom to a T. Maybe a little leaner, and younger, but he looked like his dad.

I gave him a smile, he returned a cautious one, and I was about to break away to go give Tom a kiss and then meet Matt, when Chloe demanded, "Mika, you must watch this."

"Chloe—" Tom began.

"*Shh, mon père*," she shushed him.

I felt my eyes get big at this.

Tom loved his kids, but he was not a pushover to be shushed.

"It *is* kinda a thing you have to see," Sasha said as she approached our huddle.

She was giving Cadence a greeting smile.

She gave me one next.

And then we all looked down at Chloe's phone.

"*I don't know, my wonderful watchers,*" Elsa Cohen was saying on the phone. "*I think I like this?*" she asked.

And then I gasped.

Because a picture came on screen of Jamie Oakley in an attractive suit and tailored overcoat, escorting Nora Ellington—*my* Nora Ellington—who looked to be wearing something fabulous and semi-formal, but her wrap was hiding it, into somewhere I couldn't tell where it was.

But wherever it was, it was fancy.

He had his head up, looking where they were going, his hand on the small of her back.

She was being Nora, that being coy. As such, she was showing a great deal of shapely leg at the end of which was an amazing shoe. She did this by lifting up a skirt she didn't need to lift to ascend the steps she was ascending. She also did this with her head ducked down, like she was avoiding the photographers.

However, she was absolutely not avoiding the photographers.

Elsa came back onscreen, sitting in her velvet swivel chair, looking into the camera.

*"I mean, Jamie is one of Tom Pierce's best friends, and the little we know of Ms. Ellington, she's one of Mika's. So Tomika segueing into the bestest besties of a Janora might be glorious. Truth, it is time for Jamie to heal after losing his lovely wife, Rosalind. And I'm sure you'll all agree, my wonderful watchers, we want that for him. Of course, only if the woman he finds is the right one. And one must never discount Ms. Ellington's delicious* wrap *and her fabulous* shoes. *And I do not discount either. The woman's style is sublime. But as you know, my wonderful watchers,* j'adore *our New York Oakley almost as much as I love our Arizona Oakley. So I absolutely* must *be certain who he's with is worthy of him. Don't worry. I promise to do some digging into Ms. Ellington. And as ever and always, I'll report all about how I feel during a future episode."*

Chloe swiped her screen.

I pulled my bag off my shoulder.

"I kinda...*love* that?" Cadence asked Chloe uncertainly.

"I cherish it with every fiber of my being," Chloe declared, not uncertain in the slightest.

I had my phone out.

I was about to make a call to Nora when Tom's fingers wrapped around my wrist.

I looked up at him.

"Judge already connected with Jamie," he shared. "Jamie says they're just friends. Dru tends to be his plus one to events he has to attend. There've been some concerns, because they lost Rosalind some time ago, and those two seemed to be forming a co-dependency that wasn't very healthy. Jamie admitted to Judge he was concerned about the same thing, and he wants Dru to feel less tied to taking care of him and freer to do things young women her age should be doing. He and Nora got together after we left New York, he shared this with her, and Nora volunteered to fill that role."

"She hasn't told me this," I pointed out, confused at all I was feeling, but what was winning was hurt.

"Maybe because they *are* just friends and there wasn't anything to tell?" Tom suggested.

Oh, there was something to tell.

With Nora, there was always something to tell.

And Nora told me everything, so her *not* telling me this meant there was seriously something to tell.

I just didn't know why she didn't tell it.

"How about we set that aside and you two meet Matt?" Tom asked.

Shit.

That was more important than Nora being Nora.

I started to pay attention to what was happening in Tom's kitchen, not with my friend, and saw Matt was now close.

He also looked amused.

I didn't know how to take that because I was horrified I'd gotten sidetracked when both my daughter and I should have been all about meeting Tom's son the second we arrived.

"Don't worry," he said, offering his hand for me to take. "Chloe's always been about sucking all the attention."

"*Excuse moi?*" Chloe demanded in full affront.

"Oh my God, don't pretend you're not all about that," Sasha said on an eye roll.

Chloe opened her mouth.

Before she could say anything, Judge called out, "Not everyone has a drink. I'll play bartender. Mika, Cadence, what can I get you?"

Chloe shut her mouth.

I glanced at Tom, and with what I saw, I felt a settling in me.

He liked Judge, very much. I knew that from the beginning.

However, I suddenly felt that in a much deeper way.

I'd never really thought about Cadence finding a partner. She dated. She had so much going on, she wasn't about having anything serious. She'd once had a boyfriend that lasted a few months, and she was bummed when that didn't work out, but she wasn't heartbroken.

Seeing Tom's face, the calmness there, the understanding that he knew his girl had found the man who loved her for who she was and could handle all that was her, and Tom could feel safe in that.

I loved that for him.

And I hoped when Cadence found her person, I'd feel the same for her.

Cadence and I gave our orders, Judge got us our drinks, and we adjourned to the living room to sit around a charcuterie board and nosh while we did some getting-to-know-you chatter.

I watched Matt closely through all of this.

He didn't appear as comfortable in Tom's space as Chloe and Sasha (and even Judge) were, but I wasn't sure that was about his recently ended estrangement with Tom. It was more that the girls lived close, but he'd been away at school, so they'd spent more time there.

I sensed it was also just...*him*.

He wasn't awkward, as such.

But Chloe was about oodles of love and drama. Sasha was also about oodles of love and effervescence.

Matt was neither of those.

He might have been like Corey Szabo (I'd never met the man).

But strangely he reminded me of, well...

Me.

He was an observer. He enjoyed being around people, and he was clearly happy to be spending time with his family, getting to know the two women who had entered his father's life.

But he was also detached.

Not quiet, or shy, or rude.

Just aloof.

And the beauty of that was, he knew it about himself, and he seemed comfortable in it.

He also knew it about me.

I understood this when Chloe, Cadence and Sasha were clamoring on about something, talking over themselves in that way young women do where they were all able to follow everything that was said even though it was being said all at once.

Judge was slouched beside Chloe, his arm along the back of the couch behind her, grinning into his beer, but he would interject occasionally when there was an opening to do so.

Tom was much the same with me, and he was almost glowing, he was so happy his living room was filled with people he loved and cheerful chatter.

But Matt caught my eye, and we shared a look of understanding so astonishingly profound that early in knowing each other, something else settled in me.

That feeling got better when I smiled at him.

And Matt smiled back.

An important aside, I could also see why Matt's calling was to be a vet.

Perhaps it was that his voice sounded a lot like Tom's. Perhaps they smelled something alike.

But the kittens adored him.

Eventually, it got to the point that Tom needed to go back and forth to the kitchen to make sure dinner was coming along, and I helped him.

We were in the kitchen, the prime rib roast out and resting, minutes from calling everyone to the dining room table, when Tom got close and murmured, "It's going well, don't you think?"

I nodded enthusiastically and shared, "Cadence was really worried."

His brow furrowed. "She was?"

"She was worried Matt wouldn't like her."

His consternation cleared and he nodded. "I can understand that. I see she's past it, but I'd probably have the same worry."

"Tom," I called, even though he was right there.

"Yes, honey," he answered, even though he was right there.

"I think she's falling in love with you."

Tom grew completely still.

I continued speaking.

"I figure you know that on some level, but I feel it needs to be out there. She's never had a father, and I've been so involved with how I feel about having you in my life, I haven't realized how she's blossoming for the same reason. I knew she really liked you, and us together. I just didn't—"

"Please be quiet," he whispered.

I shut up.

I also stared at his face.

And then I felt the tears prick my eyes.

Eventually, he broke our silence in order to promise, "I'll handle her with care."

"I never doubted that."

"That means everything, sweetheart, you saying that. But I feel it needs to be out there."

All right.

At any moment one of our kids could walk in.

But I didn't care.

I threw myself at him.

We were making out, lightly, the easier to break it off if someone walked in, when the doorbell rang.

We had to break it off then, because Tom drew back with another furrowed brow.

I understood this one too, because he wasn't expecting anyone.

"I'll deal with the roast, you—" I started to offer.

I was cut off by Chloe saying very loudly, "Oh my *God, you* have a nerve."

Tom let me go and his long legs took him quickly to the living room.

My legs weren't short, but he made it there before me, and I nearly ran into his back because he'd stopped dead on the landing that ran along the area at the front of the house.

I stepped to the side and knew why he was immobile.

Imogen Swan stood in the door, and I'd seen her only twice in real life.

And both times, she'd worn the same look.

Pale.

And pained.

---

### Tom

"CHLOE, COOL IT," MATT ORDERED.

"I will not!" Chloe retorted hotly.

"Chloe, baby, maybe you should take a breath," Judge suggested.

"It really isn't a good time, Mom," Sasha noted.

"I know," Genny said, appearing agonizingly uncomfortable and now standing only a step inside the door. "That's why I shared I'd leave you to it and Tom and I could talk later."

"No, I really rather think you should stay," Chloe put in. "And explain to *all of us* why you've been behaving the way you have."

"This isn't the time, Chloe," Matt bit out.

"It isn't," Judge agreed.

"When's the time?" Chloe demanded. "*Her* time? Is it always going to be *her* time this family does *anything*?"

"I gotta admit, that's valid," Sasha muttered.

At Sasha's words, Genny's face, which had turned pink with embarrassment, lost all color again.

Chloe swung an arm toward her sister, but her gaze was on Matt. "See? We all deserve an explanation." She turned her attention to her mother. "In fact, it's high time we had one."

"Stop it," Tom said low. "Now."

And then what happened anytime in their lives Tom used that tone, silence ensued. It was uneasy and vibrating with emotion, but none of his children said another word.

He turned to Genny but felt Mika's hand on his arm, so he looked down to her instead.

"Cadence and I will go sit out by the pool," she offered.

"No, really," Genny said quickly. "As I said earlier, I'm so sorry to intrude. I didn't see your car. Enjoy your evening. I'll talk to Tom later."

Tom watched Mika look at his ex-wife.

And it was soft, but firm, when she replied, "I think your family needs to talk to you now. And Cadence and I care about everyone here, so we're happy to give you the time." She lifted her gaze to Tom's. "I'll go deal with the food to keep it warm and then we'll—"

"Actually," Genny began, and Tom and Mika looked her way to see she'd taken two more steps in, "maybe you should stay. Maybe you should hear what I have to say too. It really isn't just for Tom."

Tom felt his stomach roil so badly, he worried the bile would force its way up his throat.

"Gen, let's—" he started.

"I haven't spoken to Duncan in two weeks," Genny declared.

Tom blinked slowly.

"I was..."—she took another step forward—"my career was for all intents and purposes over. My children were leaving home and starting a new life. I was a middle-aged woman, and I was reminded of it everywhere I turned. By that I mean I was reminded I was unneeded. Unnecessary. Unvalued. I felt twenty years old, with just as much energy and just as many dreams. But the world deemed me invisible. Or worse, it shoved me into this room all the other washed-out, worn-out, useless females inhabited, all of us wondering how it ended so fast when we felt it had only just begun, and we had so much more to give. And you," she said to Tom, "you had it all. Your practice. Your contract with the network. Your tennis career never had to end. It just morphed into something new. You hadn't changed. You loved talking about tennis. You loved medicine. You were charismatic and vital and *wanted*, and I'd turned down a role that was offered to me playing the mother of a man who was seven years younger than me."

"That whole Forrest Gump thing, totally gross," Sasha groused quietly.

"I really think—" Mika began.

Genny interrupted her, and looking right in Tom's eyes, she asked, "I lost you before I lost you, didn't I?"

"Let's go, Cadence," Mika said, and Tom felt her move away from him.

"We're all going," Judge announced.

"I'm not—" Chloe started.

"You are, baby," Judge decreed.

Tom felt all of them leave the room, but he kept staring at his ex-wife.

When they were gone, he said, "Because you're dealing with something with Duncan, I'm not going to let you take responsibility for what happened with us. Whatever is going on with Duncan, that's between you two. Don't project that on us."

"He was very hurt that I had the reaction I had to seeing you with Mika," she noted.

"Then he doesn't understand what it's like for a woman whose husband cheated on her to see that husband, even if he's now her former husband, with another woman, even if it isn't the same woman," Tom returned.

She shook her head. "It wasn't that, Tom. It hurt you'd moved on. It hurt you were with someone else, and you looked happy. It...*hurt*."

She was losing it; he knew from years of knowing her.

So he moved, took her hand and led her out of the fishbowl that was his living room down the hall into his study.

For privacy, he closed them behind the door. He then sat her in a chair, and he shoved the books aside on the coffee table so he could sit in front of her. Once there, he leaned her way and took her hands.

Her voice was rough with unshed tears when she asked, "Is Mika going to be upset that I'm here when you guys are obviously having an important dinner?"

"Mika doesn't jump to conclusions or read anything into anything that isn't actually there."

"I could learn from that," Genny muttered.

"That doesn't mean this isn't shit timing, Genny," Tom pointed out.

"I just don't want whatever is happening with you and Duncan to have transference from what happened between us."

"I still love you."

He was so shocked, and frankly unnerved by that declaration, he let her go and sat back.

"You still love me too, I know it," she pushed.

"We're—"

She closed her eyes and shook her head slowly in a forlorn manner which made it bobble on her neck.

She then opened her eyes.

"What we had was forever lost, Tom. I just held on to you through it, and I hadn't realized I hadn't let you go."

"Okay," he said cautiously.

"I needed space to let you go," she shared.

"And you shut your husband out while you did that, and since what you were doing was letting go of your ex-husband, he wasn't thrilled about it," Tom surmised.

"We had a very big fight," she admitted.

"And you haven't spoken to him since," Tom said tonelessly.

"Tom—"

He could tell in how she said his name, she hadn't spoken to Bowie since, and it frayed his temper.

"Fucking call him, Genny," he clipped. "Right now."

"This isn't about me and Bowie," she retorted. "This is about putting closure on me and you. This is about me taking responsibility for my part of what went wrong between us."

"And that means something," he told her. "But what went irrevocably wrong between us was that I turned to another woman before I separated from you. That fact will never change. *That* is what ended our marriage, not anything you did."

"I think that's an interesting way to put it, except for the word that's missing. 'Officially.' We were separated, it just wasn't officially. And I was the one who separated us."

Tom couldn't argue that because she was not wrong.

Instead, he said, "Then you must realize you're repeating a pattern here."

"I—"

"Call Bowie."

"But I—"

"For fuck's sake!" he exploded, Genny there, interrupting such an important night, a night he felt content—genuinely, down-to-his-bones content with his family, his life, himself for the first time in years, all the shit coming out, all he was feeling, it was too much. He straightened from the coffee table and took a step to clear himself from her. "*Call him!*"

She stared up at him, face ashen, eyes haunted.

"I lost you before I lost you," she whispered.

"Yes," he agreed. "You did. And then I acted like a complete and utter piece of shit, and instead of being an adult and ending it, I lashed out."

Genny stood too. "Tom—"

He interrupted her again, lifting a hand her way and shaking his head.

"No, Genny. We're regurgitating history. This isn't about us. This is about you calling Duncan and telling him you're coming home and working things out. Tonight."

"I can't do that until you know—"

"I know. God, do I know."

"Tom, stop fucking interrupting me!" she snapped, losing it too. "You know, when it happened, when I found out about you and her, not Mika, the other one, one of the wildest things that ran through my head was, 'He's never going to forgive himself for this.' After I thought that, I was pissed at myself for giving that first shit about how you'd feel about what you did to me. But you were my husband. I loved you. I still love you. I also knew you, and that was what I thought. And"—she threw both hands out to her sides to indicate where they were in that moment—"I was right."

Tom said nothing again because she was, indeed, right.

Genny did say something.

"Do you understand that, before I can go back to Bowie, I have to be here and say these things to you?" she asked. "I have to admit to my part in what happened. I have to hear from you that I'm right. I need it *validated*, Tom, so I *can* move on and when I do, not repeat a goddamn pattern."

"Then yes, Genny, yes," he snarled. "You shutting me out hurt. It hurt a fuck of a lot. I was ready to leave you. I was done with our marriage because you were ghosting me while still sleeping at my side. And I was pissed as fuck at you for throwing us away like that, so I stepped out on you to get mine back. Yes. That is what happened. You're validated."

They stood, staring at each other, both breathing heavily.

Tom didn't know how this was making him feel, outside of shitty, dredging it all up and being backed in a corner to say things he never wanted Genny to know.

"Okay, I can tell you don't like this," Genny said slowly. "And you have company, and you're right, this is the worst timing. I get that, Tom. I do. But we're here, now, saying things we should have said ages ago. In order that we can put this behind us, you can move on free of it, and I can begin rebuilding what we had with all of us together, something that began eroding because I was being me, it all needs to be out there."

Tom braced, certain she was going to blitz him with how he'd injured her with his affair.

And he needed to take it.

She didn't do that.

She said, "You never had your time."

Tom felt his entire frame twitch in confusion. "Sorry?"

"I pulled out my calendars. I looked back, Tom. It was devastating to be reminded of what I already knew. What I ignored. What I refused to remember. And I...I..."

She turned her face away.

Tom waited.

When she gave it to him again, her expression was tortured.

So tortured, Tom's chest caved in.

"I watched you play in the US Open when I first met you," she said.

"Didn't miss a match. I flew to London that next Wimbledon. It was a big deal, me being there. Us being together. I was worried, the paparazzi were all over us. I thought it'd affect your game. It didn't. But that wasn't....it wasn't..." She shook her head, and when she spoke again, it was in an agonized whisper. "It wasn't why I never saw another match of yours. I didn't go to see you play once." She swallowed, and it looked so painful, Tom felt it in his own throat. "And the kids didn't either."

Tom stood still as a statue.

"They were too young to travel on their own," she continued. "We prided ourselves that we didn't have a full-time nanny like all of our friends. We were a 'real' family. We went to work, came home and took care of our kids. We cooked for them and bathed them and read them bedtime stories. When you had to go, I couldn't take them to your tournaments. I was working. Or...I could, but I didn't. Not even to New York. You couldn't take them and look after them and play. I..."—another shake of her head—"not one of your children ever saw you play professionally."

Tom said nothing.

He couldn't.

He couldn't speak.

He'd buried how he'd felt about that for so long, he'd forgotten how deep he'd dug so he could put it somewhere it wouldn't destroy him.

He remembered seeing the other players' girlfriends, wives, children in the stands during their matches.

Not his.

Not once.

Not since the beginning.

Not Genny.

Not his children.

Not until he'd hit the senior tour and then, it just wasn't the same.

"Mom and Dad offered to take the kids," she carried on. "Your parents did. Your parents never missed a match. Dad rarely missed them. But I refused. I was...it was all about me. I wanted to be the real deal. Look at Imogen Swan, famous actress, perfect mother, out buying groceries with her children while her husband's away playing tennis. Mom told me. She was so angry with me. She said I'd regret it. I told her they were too young. There was no point in unsettling their routine. They wouldn't even know what was happening. But Mom was right. I regret it. I can't even...I don't even know why I did it."

Tom did.

It was the Genny Show.

Perfect Imogen Swan, out buying groceries (and she did, as famous as she was, even to this day, she went to the grocery store herself), looking after her babies.

But again, at the time, he didn't push it.

However, he had matches to win and getting up in his wife's face about whether or not she or their children were there was not on the agenda along with taking care of his family, seeing to his wife's needs and enduring the intense and constant training it took to win trophies and purses.

Tom found his voice.

"You were right. They were too young to understand what they were seeing."

A funny smile hit her face and her words were weighted with melancholy when she said, "That's my Tommy. Making it all right for me to be me. Even when I'm being selfish and awful."

"You aren't selfish and awful, Genny," he replied gently. "You were a young mother with a stressful, high-profile career and a marriage and a family. You were doing your best."

"And there he is again."

Tom shut up.

They stared at each other.

And it happened.

They had it all.

They didn't pay attention.

They lost it all.

And now, it was done.

"Fuck, I'm so fucking sorry I did what I did to you," he whispered.

"I know," she whispered back.

"You're going to have to sort things with Chloe," he advised.

She nodded. "I know that too. I will."

"Sasha's getting it together. She's shared, yes?"

"She's texted a few things. She's been busy with all of that. I'll sit down with her. Get the whole story."

"Call Bowie, Gen."

"I'll call him on the way up to Prescott."

"Go tonight."

This smile was small, but not funny, when she said, "I'm going to leave from here."

"Good," he murmured.

A moment passed. Two. Another. And more. Each heavier than the last.

And then she asked, "She's the one, isn't she? Mika?"

"Yes, honey," he said quietly. "You'll like her, though."

"Does she...think I'm terrible, all this drama?"

"She's protective of me, I'm not going to lie."

Genny winced.

Tom went on, "But if I'm good, she'll be good."

"Her daughter's adorable."

"You'll love her."

Bright hit her eyes, and Tom felt that emotion closing his throat.

They had it all.

They lost it all.

And now, it was done.

It didn't hurt as much as when it happened.

It still fucking stung.

They didn't move for long moments.

It was Genny that broke it, but she didn't go to him. He wasn't hers to have, as she wasn't his.

That stung too.

She headed toward the door.

Tom was still unable to physically function.

She stopped at the door and turned back.

"I allowed Corey to take Bowie away from me," she declared.

Evidence was suggesting that Genny had been taking the subsequent weeks to think things through, and thoroughly.

"But I let you slip though my fingers all on my own," she finished. "I'm sorry, Tom."

That got him moving, his body jolted, and he turned more fully to her.

"Don't—" he began.

She lifted a hand his way. "Yes, I know. You bear the brunt of it and there's nothing I can say to make you stop feeling that way. You're that man. That was the man I married. He was loving and fun and talented and fair and he took responsibility for himself. But I played my part in breaking us. And honestly, honey, I couldn't bear it, thinking you didn't understand I know it, and it hurts to know that I did."

He could give her that.

So he did.

He nodded.

"I've interrupted your night enough, I'm going to slip out," she said. "I'll find a safe place to pull over and text the kids so they know I'm okay, and I'll be talking to them soon about all of this."

Tom nodded again.

She took in a deep breath.

And then she said, "I've loved him as long as I can remember. He was my first and he'll be my last. But you were the love of my life, Tom Pierce. That will never change. Please know that not only as the father of our children, but just as the man I was happy to call husband for a long, long time."

"Stop it, Gen," he said gruffly.

She shot him a teasing smile that was more sorrowful than playful. "Yes, honey. I know you love me too."

And then...

Tom's chest heaved...

His wife was gone.

"Did that really happen? Her getting offered a role to play the mom of someone she could have been dating?" Mika asked.

They were out by his pool.

Dinner, due to Mika performing some kind of miracle, had not been ruined.

The kids were now around the coffee table playing Cards Against Humanity.

"It happened," Tom confirmed.

"Jesus," she muttered.

But she was watching him closely.

"I'm fine," he assured.

"This night has been intense for you," she noted.

"It has. And I'm fine."

"Like, good, glad that's done, it needed to happen fine? Or past hurts resurfaced and you're totally full of shit for saying you're fine, fine?"

Tom smiled at her. "The first one."

She reached out. Took his hand. Leaned into him. Then pressed the backs of his fingers against her forehead.

"I'm not harboring any unrequited love for my ex-wife, honey," he assured.

She looked to him, pressed his knuckles to her lips, then settled back into her chair, but didn't let his hand go.

"I promise, I don't think you are," she said. "All you said that you both shared, that was big. But I got where she was coming from with what she said in your living room. Those are things men just can never understand, but women can't avoid. We're routinely reduced. It's something we live with and struggle with and fight against. But once we hit a certain age, what we're allowed to be significantly diminishes. I'm an anomaly. I spent my entire career being accused of being famous for who I fucked or who I was seen with, and trying to ride the coattails of that, only for it now to be occurring to people I had any talent or anything to say. For most women, it isn't even the other way around. They don't get that part where anyone feels they have anything to say. But for her, I can't even imagine the whiplash. I mean, for all the actresses we grew up watching, there are very few Imogen Swans and Nicole Kidmans and Sandra Bullocks who remain relevant and sexual and dynamic even into their forties, much less past them. Instead, you see TikTok morphs of Phoebe Cates or Bridget Fonda then and now, like it's a shock that people actually age. Like those women bear some responsibility for the passage of time and what it does to every living being. Like they need to answer for allowing themselves to be human."

"I thought you weren't on TikTok."

"Cadence showed me. She was ticked."

"I can imagine, that's revolting."

She smiled at him, bright and...

Jesus Christ.

*Loving.*

His chest caved in again, but this time it felt a fuck of a lot better.

"I'm glad you both had it out, no matter how emotional it was," she declared. "I know at first your kids were worried and watchful, but they eventually seemed relieved. Especially after they got her texts, and you were being you."

"If I'm not giving you what you need, or you have something that's eating at you and you need space to deal with it, don't let me give up on you," he warned, and her hand squeezed his.

"I'm not her, baby," she said softly. "I don't get in my head. I'm pretty communicative."

"I've noticed," he teased.

She smiled at him, and said, "But I promise to let you know."

"She needed me," Tom told her.

"Yeah, she did. And she has the excellent timing of an actress to squeeze out every ounce of drama. But I'm happy all of that has happened and it's behind the both of you, and soon the kids can move on from it too."

"Agreed. But that wasn't what I was talking about. I was talking about Susie."

He felt her hand twitch around his, so this time he held her tightly.

She knew who Susie was.

"She had a shitty life, and a lot of it was her doing," Tom shared. "We were both in the throes of an identity crisis. I've thought a good deal about this, and I realize now I liked how I made her feel when I looked at her. I liked that in all her life, and she's our age, she'd never been seen, until she met me. I liked that she cared what I thought of her. I liked that she trusted me to lay all her shit on, and she did, and some of it was really ugly, and the ugly part of it was what she'd done. But she gave it to me. She didn't hold back. She was fully mine when, from the beginning, I was only ever Genny's. Gen was never really mine. Am I making sense?"

She nodded.

"I'm not making excuses," he told her. "I'm explaining."

"I get that," she said.

"It was wrong, but I honestly thought I might have a relationship with her after Genny and I were done. It wasn't a fling. I cared about her."

"I would be shocked as hell if you didn't."

"It wouldn't be right, for her or the family, if I went there. It was Susie who pointed that out to me."

Mika nodded. "No. I'm sure they would all have found a way, but you and she deserve more."

His smile to that was broken.

"You do," she asserted.

"Well, someone in the universe thinks I do, because they gave me you," he replied.

That bought him a beam and she leaned into him again, fake-lamenting, "Oh my God, you're being gooey again. I wish I could hate it, but I hate how much I love it."

Tom chuckled and his gaze wandered to the pool.

"Does it feel strange that it's now completely over?" she asked quietly.

"It hurts," he said honestly. "But there's no going back." He looked to her again. "And I like what I have in my now and see in my future. The hurt will fade."

"Yes," she whispered.

"Matt likes you," Tom changed the subject. "I think he's found a kindred spirit."

"You noticed that, did you?"

"I don't know how I didn't see it before."

"Sometimes it has to be right in front of our face."

"Mm."

As if the universe also knew their focus had changed, a great burst of laughter came from the house.

Tom looked over his shoulder to see inside.

Everyone there was either still laughing or smiling.

He took in a deep breath, and seeing what he saw, let everything else go as he exhaled.

Mika shook his hand, and he turned his attention to her.

"You need to go in there and be with your boy."

Tom shook his head. "No. Right now, what's happening is what should be happening. The kids are bonding without us being around. They can be more themselves. We need to give them more time."

"True, true," she murmured, then tipped her head. "Do you think Matt would come out for dinner, see the house, let me cook for him before he goes? I know it's a lot of driving, but it'd be great if Chloe and Judge could come too. They haven't been out."

"I'll talk to him. He knows we're serious, so he'll likely want to come. See where you live. Have more time with you and Cadence."

"Is that what we are? Serious?" she teased.

"Yes," he stated, not close to teasing.

Her gaze grew sultry. "God, I want to jump you right now."

"I hope you're taking care of yourself. I don't fancy any medical emergencies when we can have sex again."

"I wish that wasn't a viable fear. No wait, I don't."

Tom burst out laughing.

Mika laughed with him and leaned deep to kiss his neck in the middle of it.

And five sets of eyes watched as five sets of ears listened.

And for the first time in a very long time everyone was happy.

# CHAPTER 21

## SHE HAS YOUR HAIR

*Tom*

"You'll go directly there?" Tom asked into his phone while setting up the gates so the kittens would be contained in his kitchen while he was at Mika's.

He was getting ready to head out. He was also talking to Matt on the phone.

"Yeah," Matt replied. "We just passed Black Canyon."

This meant, if Tom left soon, he'd have a little under an hour with Mika and Cadence before his kids got there.

Since Cadence was there, in that time they couldn't make love, which was disappointing. They'd had nowhere near this long of a break since their beginning.

More disappointing, Cadence wouldn't be there for long, and neither would Mika. Cadence's spring break was the next week, and then she and her mom were heading back to New York.

This was not something Tom was looking forward to.

That said, he already had plans to spend two long weekends with them next month and his assistant was clearing his calendar so he could spend a good portion of time with them around Cadence's graduation in May before he had to head to Paris for the French Open.

But Mika was going to be in New York at least until Cadence graduated.

The long-distance thing was not something Tom was looking forward to, but if they couldn't handle a few weeks apart, they were doomed before they'd really started.

Since neither of them was going to let that happen, he reckoned they'd handle it just fine.

Nevertheless, as time was running out, he wanted to get there early and have some of it with them.

He'd been all about Matt during his son's visit. Rebuilding their relationship, rediscovering common ground and making up for time lost. Matt had been all about it as well, spending nearly all of his time with Tom, not his mother or sisters.

They understood this, considering recent history. And Genny herself had mentioned it was Tom's turn, since she'd had most of him since their breakup.

However, Matt and Sasha, at Genny's invitation, had gone up to Prescott for brunch that day. Since they'd already made plans to spend the afternoon at Mika's and have dinner there, they were turning right back around to come back down after brunch.

Matt would be leaving the next day. Tom would miss him. It was the first time since the divorce he felt a sense of bonding with his son.

But more, it was the fact that these times would be few and far between as Matt got deeper into vet school, and living his own life.

If something like this ever happened again.

A fact of life.

One Mika was imminently facing.

She now had Tom.

It was still going to be a blow, and Tom wasn't about to fuck it up this time.

He'd missed facing an empty nest was just one more thing weighing on Genny's mind, taking it away from her marriage and Tom.

He wasn't going to miss supporting Mika through it.

"Are Chloe and Judge on their way too?" Tom asked.

"They left Mom and Bowie's when we did," Matt said.

His phone buzzed with another call.

He took it from his ear and looked at it.

Not Chloe.

A number he didn't recognize.

He declined the call and went back to his son.

"We lost them somewhere around Bloody Basin," Matt was finishing.

Bloody Basin was maybe ten miles down I-17 after leaving Route 69 half an hour out of Prescott.

In other words, they barely hit the highway before Matt put his sister and future brother-in-law in his dust.

"This is because you have a lead foot," Tom joked, though it wasn't entirely a joke.

Matt was quiet and levelheaded unless there was a risk to take. He was a wild man on a tennis court, completely unpredictable with his game. He was an athlete, and an academic, but he didn't date the cheerleaders, debate team members or sorority girls, he dated the emo girls, and later, the local bartenders. He'd hike deep into a forest or jungle to ride a zip line before he'd contemplate a game of golf.

And he drove too fucking fast.

"If I have somewhere to go, there's no point dicking around in getting there," Matt joked in return.

Once a dad, always a dad, so Tom didn't hesitate in replying, "Just remember two of the most important people on earth are in that car, so behave accordingly."

"Right," Matt replied, sounding amused, a tone he'd assumed whenever Tom pulled the dad card after Matt turned eighteen.

Tom's phone buzzed again.

He glanced at it, same number, so he declined.

"I'm headed over to Mika's now. I'll see you when you get there," he said.

"And this Brayton and Priscilla and Clay are coming too?" Matt asked.

"They'll be there later. For dinner."

"I can't wait to meet them!" Sasha chimed in. "Cadence says they're the bomb!"

"They are," Tom confirmed.

"Great. Cool. See you soon," Matt put in, and Tom could now tell by his tone Matt was done talking.

Tom wasn't.

"It might be nice to have some clue as to how things went with your mother and Duncan," he noted.

"They're fine, Dad. And Mom was super honest with us. They're all good. *We're* all good," Sasha said.

"Matt?" Tom prompted.

"They're lovey-dovey again. I think they worked it out," Matt shared, now with a tone like he was about to vomit, which meant Tom heard Sasha's giggle and Tom himself smiled.

Genny and Duncan were very affectionate. They tried to hide it in front of Tom, but he'd caught it a few times.

They clearly didn't hide it in front of the kids.

This meant Genny and Duncan were good.

Tom ascertained the cats had plenty of water, and their beds and blankets were accessible for naps, as his phone beeped with a text and he said, "Good news. I'll let you go, and I'll see you soon at Mika's."

"You got it," Matt replied.

"Later, Daddy," Sasha added.

"Love you both," Tom finished it.

He got two "love you mores" in return, and on his way through the utility room to the garage, preparing to hold back the furballs who always wanted to follow him wherever he went, and they were following him now, he checked his texts.

The one that came in while he was talking to his kids was from the number that had called twice.

*Please phone, Tom. It's urgent I speak to you. It's about Miranda.*

Seeing that name, Tom stopped at the door to the garage and called the number.

It was answered immediately.

"Tom?" a man asked.

"Who's this?" Tom asked in return.

"It's Andrew. Andrew Winston. From the tour. It's been a while, buddy."

*Buddy?*

Tom's saliva glands were working overtime as he walked back into the kitchen, doing this carefully, due to the gaggle of kittens at his heels.

"Why are you calling, Andrew?" he inquired, stopping at his island, leaning a hip to it and gazing at the serenity of his pool.

He'd need that serenity because he knew whatever this was from Andrew was no good.

"Listen, this is awkward," Andrew stated.

And that was it, he said no more.

But Tom didn't like this for a number of reasons, not least of which was that there was no reason Andrew should be calling him.

In his conversations about Core Point, Tom had named no names. No one would know Andrew was one of the actors in that farce. That information wouldn't be divulged until Georgiana and Kateri had completed their work and the story broke. And with the limited updates he was getting, it was his understanding that wouldn't be for some time.

As suspected, Georgie and Kateri had discovered the First Four were the tip of the iceberg. AJ Oakley had left a swath of victims not only in his years sitting on boards, but also in how he dealt with his own businesses. There was so much work to be done locking down the entirety of the story, it would be months— and Georgie had warned, it could even be over a year—before they were safe to go to press on it.

"Andrew, I have plans today and I was on my way out the door. Why are you calling?" Tom prompted.

"Listen, this is crazy, and so uncomfortable, once you hear it, you'll understand how it's hard to broach. But apparently, Miranda has been spouting some seriously slanderous shit about me." Pause, and when Tom didn't say anything, he went on, "I mean Miranda Trainor. You know, Patsy's friend."

"I remember Miranda," Tom replied coolly.

"It's this whole MeToo witch hunt shit, Tom."

Tom said nothing.

"She's saying I was inappropriate with her."

"Again, Andrew, I'll ask why you're phoning me," Tom repeated.

"Why am I phoning?" He sounded incredulous.

"I haven't seen you in twenty-five years. So yes, why are you phoning?"

"She's saying it was that time, decades ago, when we were at Wimbledon."

"Andrew—"

"And you and I were having drinks at that pub."

This motherfucker.

"Andrew, you and I never had drinks at a pub. Not only did I barely know you, and from what I'd learned, I eventually avoided you, I didn't drink when I was competing."

"We did, Tom. We had drinks."

Jesus Christ.

"How many players have you approached with this bullshit who told you to go fuck yourself before you came to my name on your list?" Tom demanded.

"We were friends. We haven't talked for a while, but we *are* friends."

"I'm not your friend. I've never been your friend. And not talking for twenty-five years is not 'a while,' Andrew. It's the definition of two colleagues who barely knew each other, and on my part, I couldn't stand being around you, going their separate ways when they stopped competing professionally."

"This is some serious shit she's burying me in," Andrew bit out.

"Is it? Is it shit *she's* burying you in, Andrew?" Tom asked.

"What the fuck does that mean?"

"If I were you, which, thankfully, I am not, I'd have to ask myself, after all this time, when she retired from the tour, and you retired from the tour, why anything like this would surface now?"

"Because women are doing this fucking everywhere," Andrew spat. "It's their way to make money or settle scores or remain relevant."

Fucking hell.

"We're done," Tom said.

"Tom! Fuck!" Andrew shouted into the phone. "There are legal implications with this."

"Goodbye, Andrew."

"Tom, if this shit hits, I'm naming you as my alibi," Andrew threatened.

His vision blurred, his hand tightened on the phone, and it took a moment for Tom to get his shit together.

When he did, he said evenly, "If you do that, Andrew, if you drag my name into your mess, I will unleash a shitstorm on you that will bury you. You'll be eating shit and breathing shit for the rest of your fucking life."

"Half the world thinks you fucked around on your wife, Tom. They won't blink, thinking you partied with me back in the day."

"Part of that shitstorm will be Imogen taking a tour of every morning show on five continents, sharing the opposite."

"She was never at any tournament."

"Patsy was. Rod was. I could name five dozen others who knew my focus when I was competing. People who knew I didn't go out and party. People who knew, once I learned what type of man you were, I had nothing to do with you. People who knew, even before I was with Imogen, I didn't touch a drop of alcohol, not only during a tournament, but weeks before while training for it."

"Nobody's gonna believe Patsy. Those bitches are sisters in crime with this shit."

"Were you inappropriate with Miranda?"

"We had a thing. It was consensual."

"Your version of that word? Or the actual definition of that word?"

"*Christ!*" Andrew burst out. "If we can't stick together, what's our future, Tom? It's never gonna be safe to get laid."

This...

Fucking...

*Motherfucker.*

"I do not count myself in the 'we' in that scenario, Andrew. Your desperation during this phone call smacks of guilt to me. If that's the case, then you're not a man. You're a predator. Real men should have no problem finding partners to enjoy spending time with, their partners enjoying that time as much as they do. *We* are weeding out the predators, Winston. Get ready to be archived. There's no place for your kind in this world. There never was. It's taken too long to get to this juncture. But now that we're finally here, I'm pleased as fuck to see the good work being done."

"Fuck you, Tom."

Tom didn't reply.

He disconnected.

The first thing he did was text Mika to share he'd be delayed considering he'd already texted to say he was almost out the door.

The next thing he did was block Andrew's number.

He then had to decide who was his next call.

He hadn't shared this situation with Rod yet.

After retiring, Tom had gone into the senior tour and commentating. Rod had started his own club in his hometown of Glasgow, and now he had five coaches working with dozens of kids. Rod, himself, was coaching a twenty-year-old Scottish phenom who, to the home crowd's delight, and then despair, almost won Wimbledon last year.

Tom had decided the chats about Core Point needed to be face to face, so he was going to discuss it with Rod in a couple of months when they were both at Roland-Garros.

Winston did sound desperate. If he hadn't already approached Rod, he was likely going to.

Due to that only being "likely," Tom wasn't sure of the wisdom of a preemptive call.

On that thought, he phoned Jamie.

His friend picked up on the third ring.

"Hey, Tom. How are things?" Jamie answered.

"Andrew Winston just phoned, sharing something was up with Miranda, there were legal implications, and he was going to lie and throw me under the bus, saying I was his alibi."

"Fuck," Jamie muttered.

"I can definitively prove him wrong. I still do not want his name linked with mine."

"I can imagine," Jamie replied. "And Kateri did tell us that Core Point is far too colossal of a player in the retail and sports worlds for our investigation to go entirely under the radar. I don't believe Georgie is ready to reach out to either them or Winston or any of the other athletes who have been protected by Core Point to give them a chance to tell their side of the story. So Winston contacting you means we've been made. I'll tell Kateri and warn Georgie."

Tom found this concerning. "When it gets to this point, other journalists breaking these kinds of stories have had some significant issues with being threatened."

"Apparently, Georgie's husband is a member of a motorcycle club. They're a large one and a famous one. They had a documentary made about their history. Kateri tells me they're not men to mess with. And Georgie's a tough nut. This isn't the first sensitive story she's broken. Core Point may think they can mess with her, but anyone they send will be disabused of that notion pretty fucking quick."

"And Kateri?"

"I have her back, though I would imagine you'd know that won't be hard work. She can take care of herself."

Tom could imagine that.

"This doesn't mean we shouldn't gag Winston when it comes to you," Jamie noted.

"My attorney is my next call."

"I have a firm on retainer. They'll have a letter delivered to him by tomorrow, outlining just how intricately they'll dissect him if he even whispers your name in this."

"And that firm can be traced to you. Then you'll be exposed."

"I can't even describe how few fucks I have to give if Winston, or Core Point, find out I'm involved in exposing them."

"And your father?"

"It wouldn't be optimal that he has a heads up I'm pulling at a new string to unravel his security blanket. But I have very few fucks to give about that either. In fact, I like the idea that will enter his headspace and he'll have to worry about it. So let me get my legal team on it."

"Appreciated."

They shared a few more words before they rang off, and Tom managed the herculean task of getting out to the garage without one of the cats following him.

He was halfway to Mika's before his phone rang again.

He didn't have a good feeling about the fact it was Rod. And not only because it was after nine at night in Glasgow.

He took the call. "Hey, Rod."

"Well, fuck me ten ways to Sunday, guess who just called, sharing he's been caught in some MeToo moment, and when I told him I was surprised it took this long, he told me he was going to tell everyone he was out drinking at some pub with me when it happened."

So...yes.

Winston was going down a list of players, hoping one of them would commiserate and take his back.

And if that didn't happen, feeling out the threat that he'd take them along for the ride anyway, and going with the one who caved.

"He must have called you right after me because he did the same thing to me half an hour ago," Tom shared.

"Jesus Christ, I didn't think that asshole could get worse. But I guess he could. He screwed with Miranda?"

"We need to talk, not on the phone."

Rod sounded cautious when he asked, "Why would we need to talk, Tom?"

"Because this is bigger, and uglier, and sponsors are involved, and I'd rather not talk on the phone."

"Core Point," Rod said.

Rod saying that so quickly made Tom's neck itch.

"Why did you say that?"

"It was a rumor that turned into a joke," Rod explained. "You know how everyone had a blast talking shit about that Weinstein guy, when Weinstein was tormenting women for-fucking-ever, so it wasn't fucking funny, but no one had the balls to say anything real to anyone who could put a stop to it. I heard stuff about Core Point. How they'd look after you. Then there was that kernel that just dug in and it always bugged me. This is why none of my players have accepted CP sponsorship. It's an unpopular decision, they pay big money, and I had nothing real to hang my hat on as to me banning them from my club's players. But it felt like biding time until that situation blew up in everyone's faces, and I didn't want any of my kids anywhere near that kind of explosion."

"There was a reason it bugged you."

"And how do you know this?"

"I'd like to tell you face to face."

"France is two months away and Winston is making waves now. Give me a hint, Tom."

"First, I'm having a letter sent to Winston that will shut his mouth. I'll be sure to add your name to it. Second, my daughter is marrying Jamie Oakley's son. Jamie's dad is AJ Oakley. AJ was on the board of Core Point during the time they sponsored Winston. And that's all I can say right now."

"Jesus, you're thorough in checking out the in-laws," Rod muttered.

He wasn't.

But Corey sure as fuck was.

"I'd be obliged you put my name on that letter, mate," Rod said.

"It's done."

There was a heavy pause before Rod asked, "Did he hurt Miranda?"

"That's not mine to give you, Rod," Tom said.

"He fuckin' hurt her, that fuckin' *piece of shite*," Rod gritted.

"We'll talk more."

"We will. I reckon you can't hit Spain next month, what with you seeing Mika Stowe and all?"

Christ, Rod was such a gossip.

"Mika's going back to New York with her daughter in a week. I'm heading to her house now. I'll talk to her about it."

"I like her for you," Rod said.

At least that made Tom smile.

"I like her for me too."

"I have a lot more to say, but my wife is fretting after Winston's call. I'll let her know I'm not the only one, and you're gagging him. But we'll talk more, yes?"

"We will definitely talk more, Rod. My love to Freya."

"I'll give it. Speak soon."

"We will."

They rang off and Tom called Jamie again to share that news.

He was not in the best mood when he hit Mika's house, but he hid it when he walked into her kitchen and Cadence was there, making herself a coffee.

"Hey, honey," he greeted, going to her and giving her a sideways hug and a kiss on the side of her hair as she leaned into him and replied, "Hey, Tom. Want a coffee?"

He wanted a vodka rocks.

He didn't share that.

"I'm good. Where's your mom?"

"In her studio. She told me to tell you to go on up when you get here."

"Right," he murmured, turning to head out, but some papers sitting on the island had him stopping. "What are these?" he asked, touching his fingers to the papers that had photos of clay tennis courts on them.

Cadence glanced over her shoulder at the papers.

"Mom's getting quotes on what it would cost to put in some tennis courts," she said offhandedly, like her words didn't rock Tom's world. Cadence gave him her full attention, which included a radiant smile.

"If she has one put in, we can play right here. And Clay can come out too."

"Yes, sweetheart," he replied.

She kept beaming at him before she went back to the espresso machine.

Tom headed up to Mika's studio.

He found her curled into a rocking chair, knees to her chest, staring at the long workbench that took up one side of the sunny, colorful space.

"You okay?" he asked instead of offering a greeting.

Mika didn't curl into herself. She lounged. She sprawled. She strutted.

This felt...*off*.

"I'm fine, Tommy," she mumbled. "Kiss?"

He went to her, bent deep, and they kissed deeper—wet and warm and familiar, and Tom suddenly felt a lot better before he pulled away.

"Sure you're okay?" he pressed.

"Yeah, I'm okay. Nora and I finally talked. She, too, says the whole thing with Jamie is just friends."

"You don't believe her?"

She shook her head. "It isn't that. It's just that I don't want her to get hurt."

Tom could understand that, but knowing Jamie, he knew it would never happen.

"Or the other way around," she continued, and then teased, "It might surprise you to know Nora can be a viper."

He chuckled. "That wasn't lost on me. But she likes Jamie. Men and women can be just friends, honey."

"Hmm," she said, and he read from that not that she didn't believe him, just that she didn't believe it pertained to what they were discussing. Regarding him closely, she tipped her head to the side. "Are you okay?" Her brows drew down. "You were delayed. Are the kids good after having brunch with Imogen and Duncan?"

"They left a while ago. I got a call about an hour ago that they were about an hour and a half out, which means Matt and Sasha will be here in five minutes, considering how Matt drives."

Finally, her lips tipped up.

"But yes. They report things are 'lovey-dovey' with Gen and Bowie, so it seems that's all good."

She nodded while murmuring, "Awesome."

He moved to the other rocking chair that sat angled across a long, low table that, considering the notebooks and papers and pens and other bits and pieces scattered across the top of it could only be described as a desk.

He sat and said, "The reason I was delayed was that Andrew Winston called me."

She came directly out of her curl, putting her bare feet to the floor and twisting to him.

"Say that again," she demanded.

He did, and added more, including what Winston said, and the calls to Jamie and from Rod.

"He just mentioned Miranda," she noted.

Tom nodded.

"But there were four women he attacked," she went on, and added, "That we know."

"I don't know why he knows Miranda is talking, I didn't ask. I didn't want the call to go on as long as it did. As far as I'm concerned, Jamie's letter will be the end of my interaction with Andrew Winston."

"It's going to get ugly from here, isn't it?" she asked quietly.

"Just as long as most of that ugly is aimed at the people who earned it, it doesn't matter."

"That isn't how this normally works, honey," she reminded him.

Tom didn't have anything to say to that, because she was woefully correct.

"Can I show you something?" she asked.

He nodded.

She reached a hand to him as she pushed out of her rocker. He took it, and she pulled him out of his chair.

She then led him to the worktable.

He saw the bones of what it was immediately. He wasn't sure what she intended the end result to be. But he saw the poems. The short pieces. The pictures of wildflowers, cacti, desert rock and dirt, all of them beautiful, all of them seeming desolate, lonely, fragile.

Tragic.

And then there were other pictures.

Of Mika.

And Rollo.

And the two of them together.

Tom wandered the table, seeing the beauty, but feeling the pain.

"At first," she said softly, "the idea was...I just wanted her to know. She'll be leaving me soon, and before she does, before she goes out into the big, wide world, before she finds herself, I wanted her to know, truly and completely *know* her roots. Who made her. What she was. How much I loved him. How much he would have loved her. How much he and I loved each other. I also wanted to let him go, give him to her. It grew from there. To something I wanted everyone to see. I wanted everyone to see how much we loved each other. How much Cadence lost. Make him live again in people's minds. And maybe give people who experienced the same as we did a place to feel their own pain reflected to them. So they'd know they weren't alone."

Tom stopped and stared at the table.

"Each section is a page of the book," she said. "There's more I completed before in folders. But today, I finished it. It's done."

Tom didn't take his eyes from the table.

"And now," she whispered, "I've let him go, so I can give all of me to you."

Tom dropped his head and closed his eyes.

*I can give all of me to you.*

He'd loved Genny, Christ, to his soul.

But he'd never had all of her.

Never.

Corey never had it.

They didn't because Duncan did.

*I can give all of me to you.*

"He'll always have a piece of me, Tommy," Mika said gently. "A special place that's just his. But the rest…"

She trailed off.

Tom opened his eyes, but he didn't see anything when he said in a thick voice, "Not that photo. The one in your home. Keep that for you two. For the cover, use the one with the cat on his chest. It says everything about him."

"You're right, yes. Tommy. It says it all. I'll use that," she whispered.

Tom focused on the paper in front of him.

*She Has Your Hair*

"Hey!" they heard Cadence call up the stairs. "Matt and Sasha are here!"

His son.

Lead foot.

Risktaker.

Beloved.

Tom read:

*She bubbles.*
*And froths.*
*And rushes to greet the day.*

*She has your hair.*

*The stick twirls in her fingers.*
*She doesn't notice it.*

*She has your hair.*

*The beat pounds*
*through the house.*
*Her beat. Yours is gone.*
*I close my eyes.*

*She has your hair.*

*In the beginning*
*I lay in our bed*
*with her tiny baby body on your pillow.*
*I never washed the case.*

*She has your hair.*

*The coils spring back*
*if tugged.*
*Bouncing.*
*Alive.*

*She has your hair.*

*You never heard her cry.*
*You'll never hear her voice.*
*You'll never see the light that dances in her eyes.*
*Your eyes.*

*She has your hair.*

*Every day*
*an agony*
*that you will not meet.*

*She bubbles.*
*And froths.*
*And rushes to greet the day.*

*She has your hair.*

Tom, gutted, stripped raw through those words, looked to Mika.

And after reading beauty and tragedy written by a master of costuming emotion in the shroud of words, he spoke simply.

"I'm in love with you."

Tears filled Mika's eyes.

"Part of me has been in love with you since the microscope," he admitted. "You have all of me now."

Mika, so Mika.

She gave it back and didn't make him wait.

"I'm so glad I'm not the only one."

They were only three feet away from each other.

They collided in the middle.

He tasted her, he smelled her, he felt her, warm and soft, pressing against him.

Steady and strong, anchoring him.

It was what he'd been searching for all his life.

We were all adrift, everyone was searching for an anchor. It could be a person. It could be a career. It could be a place.

For Tom, it was Mika.

She knew what he could do at his worst, and she'd fallen in love with him.

He broke the kiss that tasted of salt and smoothed the hair away from her face, gliding his thumbs through the wet on her cheeks, as he looked into those sparkling aquamarine eyes.

They could do long distance.

She could live on the moon, and he'd go to her there.

"I'll build the tennis court," he said.

A laugh exploded from her almost like a gasp, and she was kissing him again.

"Shit. First Mom and Bowie, now this," they heard Matt complain.

"See! I told you! This studio is *life!*" they heard Sasha exclaim.

"I hope I find a guy who kisses me like that," they heard Cadence whisper.

Tom broke the kiss, touched his lips to Mika's cheeks, looked into her eyes and told her what he needed to do next.

He did this without words.

She nodded.

She'd written that poem.

She knew.

He let her go and walked right to Sasha.

*She has your hair.*

He took her head in his hands exactly like he'd been holding Mika, and he looked in her eyes.

"Daddy," she whispered, those eyes now wide, staring alert into his.

"I'm sorry I allowed you to flounder," he said.

"Dad, it was me who—"

"I love you more than my own life, Sasha. And that will never change. You can come to me with things you need to unburden, or you can find your way to carry them, knowing I'm always close at hand to share the load. It's your life, and now that you're grown, the only reason I'm in it is to love and support you. Do you understand me?"

A tear fell through her lashes, gliding down her cheek as she nodded.

He pulled her fiercely to him, pressed his lips hard to her skin and kissed her forehead.

He then let her go and turned to Cadence, who was standing in the circle of her mother's arms, staring at him and Sasha.

"You have that now, do you understand?" he asked her.

Her answer trembled. "I think so."

"We'll have time and then you'll understand."

She sucked in her lips as wet hit her eyes.

Mika pulled her closer and kissed the side of her head.

He moved to his son.

*She has your hair.*

Rollo never had it.

Tom did.

He did.

Three times.

Fuck, how lucky was he?

Matt took a step back like he was trying to escape.

Tom caught him by his head.

Matt groaned like he was in pain.

Tom's voice was harsh when he said, "I'm so fucking sorry I disappointed you."

"Dad," Matt whispered.

"Thank you for forgiving me."

His son shut his eyes.

"It won't happen again," Tom vowed.

Matt opened his eyes.

"Here you all are. Good grief, it was—" Chloe's voice came from the doorway.

"I'm bi," Matt's voice, jagged with hesitancy, came from right in front of him.

"Holy shit," Judge whispered.

"Whoa," Sasha said.

"*Je suis désolé, qu'avez-vous dit?*" Chloe asked.

Tom said nothing.

He just took his hands from his son's head so he could wrap his arms around his body.

# CHAPTER 22

## THE OTHER ONE

*Rhys*

*A few years before...*

HE SAT SILENT, PATIENT, WAITING FOR THE MAN BEHIND THE DESK TO speak.

This happened often.

Rhys had noticed how people clamored for his attention. They wanted to impress him. They were impatient for his wisdom.

He also noticed how shutting the fuck up and letting the man think things through was the only way to roll with Corey Szabo.

Finally, the man broke his silence.

"You're sure?"

There was very little emotion Rhys ever allowed himself to show.

Except when he was with Szabo.

His employer took in Rhys's annoyed expression and one side of his mouth minutely lifted.

"Stupid question," Szabo muttered. He sat back in his chair. "You'll need to muzzle any man he fucks. Until Matt is ready to share, if that ever happens, nothing is shared. I want Matt protected, Rhys. At all costs."

When it came to his family—that being Imogen Swan's family, and, of course, Hale—"at all costs" were words Szabo said a lot.

Rhys nodded.

"Susan Shepherd?" Szabo asked.

"She won't talk," Rhys assured.

His boss didn't question that.

He asked a different question.

"Do you like her for Tom?"

"I'd need to do more digging. She seems broken. Pierce is not a fixer. He's a shelter. You go to him in a storm. You stay close to him when you need to feel safe. But he's never faced that challenge being with his wife. So he might have other talents."

"Alternate candidates?"

Rhys shook his head. "None. The cheating was an anomaly. Before, he was pathologically loyal. As far as I can uncover, not even a flirtation."

"Hmm," Szabo hummed, reaching out and twirling his Smythson pen on his desk blotter.

Rhys had a bad taste in his mouth when he said, "I'll stay on it and guide Chloe when the time comes."

Szabo's fingers ceased their activity and his eyes narrowed on Rhys. "This is a great deal for you to take on."

Rhys said nothing.

"If you need assistance," Szabo started, "I'd want to vet them before I carry on."

This was what put the bad taste in his mouth.

By "carry on," he meant take his own life.

That was what all this shit was about.

At least, the current shit. Rhys had been looking after Szabo's loved ones for years.

But now...

Now, the only man in Rhys's life...fuck, the only person he had any respect for was going to die by his own hand.

It wasn't Rhys's place in Corey Szabo's life to talk him out of it.

It was his mission to let Szabo do it knowing everything he needed to take care of was taken care of for years to come.

"I don't need assistance," Rhys told him.

"You—" Szabo started.

"You don't have to say it," Rhys interrupted him.

He watched something he'd seen often, though it was rarely directed at him.

Lips thinning. The sides of his eyes tightening. Skin over cheekbones stretching.

Impatience at being interrupted.

Rhys had seen the man sack someone on the spot for interrupting him.

That wouldn't happen to Rhys.

"Don't silence me," Szabo said low. "Not now."

Rhys flicked out a hand, indicating his boss should proceed.

The impatience disappeared, and Szabo's lips tipped up, a rare indication he was amused.

This didn't last long, and he was dead serious when he said, "You mean a good deal to me, Rhys."

"I'm aware," Rhys murmured.

"Knowing I have to do what I have to do, not speaking against that when you understand you're the only person I trust and would listen to, there are no words."

Rhys was silent.

"We have to talk about Sasha," Szabo perpetrated a sneak attack.

"I'll keep a close eye," was all Rhys would say about that.

"Very close, Rhys, do you understand me?"

It was one of the only times he wasn't sure he did.

He knew what he wanted that to mean.

He didn't know if that was what was meant.

He also wasn't going to ask for confirmation.

"I understand."

Szabo studied him for long moments.

Then he nodded and said, "We'll talk more."

That meant he was dismissed for now.

Rhys stood and walked to the door of Corey Szabo's office.

"Rhys?" Szabo called.

Rhys stopped and turned around.

"I'll go with one of my sons not knowing how much I loved him, I won't go without the other one knowing."

Rhys stood, statue still, staring at a man he not only respected, but admired.

The only person on the planet he'd ever loved.

Corey said no more.

But then, he'd just said it.

Rhys jutted up his chin and walked out the door.

# EPILOGUE

## THE FIRST AND THE LAST

*Tom*

*A*pril...
*New York City*

TOM WAS SITTING WITH MIKA AT THE BACK OF HER LIVING ROOM IN New York under the portrait of Rollo Merriman.

She was flipping through some paint samples (apparently, it was time to redo the entryway of her brownstone).

Cadence was three floors up, but they could hear the distant pounding of drums.

Tom was on the phone with his son.

"So, I've been thinking about it since I came out to you, and, well... everybody, and I need you to know that was why I was such an asshole to you," Matt was summing up what they'd been talking about. "I knew you wouldn't care. Mom wouldn't care. But I got up in my head about it. I study medicine and I've studied sexuality. But I was convinced it was just a thing that guys did. A phase. Many men have same-sex experiences, even repeatedly, without them being homosexual. So I didn't understand why it didn't go away. Why I enjoyed being with women so much if I enjoyed being with guys so much. I understood the concept of bi, but even in the LGBTQ community, until recently, and there's still an issue with it with some people, there's a mono-centricity. You like guys, or you like girls. You're trans, but you aren't fluid. I was stuck in my head that I was supposed to like one, or the other. And I was into both."

"And that was frustrating," Tom deduced.

"And I took that out on you."

"No, Matt," Tom contradicted. "I'd fucked up and you were angry at me, and you were dealing with an identity issue on top of that. Don't confuse the two. Because being angry at me meant you didn't have me to come to in order to talk about this. So you had two reasons to be angry with me, and both were valid."

There was quiet on the line, and then a soft, "Yeah, Dad."

This did not feel good.

But at least they were on the other side of it. He'd hold on to that, mostly because he could hold on to it, seeing as Matt was sharing with him again.

And that did feel good.

"So where are you at now?" Tom asked.

He heard Matt chuckle. "Well, Indiana isn't exactly a hotbed of open-minded thinking, so it's not a free-for-all. But Indiana girls have it going on, and farm boys are nice to look at. I won't settle here. But for now, I guess where I'm at is, I'm having fun."

That made Tom chuckle too.

Though, of course Matt wouldn't find another vet student or someone in architecture or engineering or even forestry.

He was into something else.

That was the father thinking about his son's future, unwelcome if spoken out loud, so those thoughts were always kept in his head.

Because in the end, the only thing that mattered was that his boy was happy.

Nevertheless, Tom *was* a father, and there was some thinking that had to be spoken aloud.

"I hope I don't have to tell you to be safe," Tom warned.

"Jesus, Dad, I'm nearly twenty-five years old, and I lost my virginity at sixteen. You know that. You kept me supplied in condoms through high school and undergrad."

He did know that, and he did do that (with Gen's blessing).

Fortunately, he'd forged a relationship with his son where Matt shared.

And Tom was pleased as fuck they both had that back.

"Be safe," Tom repeated. "Girls, guys, whatever."

"Yeah, yeah," Matt muttered. "I gotta study."

"Right, I'll let you go. Love you, Matt."

"Me too. Later, Dad."

"Later."

They rung off.

Tom looked to Mika.

She had a cornucopia of shades of red held up toward him that almost gave him an instant headache, but he knew no matter which one she picked, the entry would be magnificent.

"Crimson Quarrel?" she asked, pointing a perfectly arched fingernail to one horizontal strip on a longer vertical one. "Or Rouge La Rue?" She pointed to another one. "And by the way, I'm giving up my day job and spending the rest of my life making up names for hues. Not only for paint, but makeup, wallpaper, fabric, you name it. On my tombstone, it'll read, 'She knew how to ridicule color with words, and someone paid her for it.'"

He grinned at her.

What he didn't do was pick a color.

This was why she declared, "Your silence, of course, indicates you agree that we *have* to have a wall painted in a hue called Rouge La Rue."

*We* had to have it?

She read his reaction.

"Please, Tom. Don't pretend this isn't your house as well as mine at this juncture. I have you now. You love me. Do you honestly think I'm ever letting you go?"

Christ.

If those drums weren't sounding, in about five minutes, he'd be fucking her on the floor.

"Honey," he replied, "you've been living here for twenty years, and I've spent, all told, about a week and a half here."

She lifted a shoulder in a shrug, her eyes sparkling, like it was nothing to her, when Tom felt that shoulder shrug and sparkle dive deep into his heart.

They heard the front door open, breaking their moment, and Teddy and Faun strolled in.

Faun tipped up his chin to Tom.

Tom returned it.

Teddy homed in on the paint chips, and instead of offering either of them a greeting, he exclaimed, "Oh my God! I told you *no red!*"

"Teddy—"

Teddy interrupted her. "Red has bad juju."

"It does not," Mika retorted.

Ringo made an appearance and slunk through Faun's ankles.

Faun picked him up before he sat in a chair opposite Tom, all while throwing Tom a look advising him to settle in, because this was going to take a while.

Ringo settled in too. Tom could hear him purring from where he was curling himself into Faun's lap.

Faun was a huge man, tall, built, fit, dark, with Italian ancestry, and Tom had recently learned he had a great sense of humor and a supremely laidback demeanor.

Which meant, fortunately for Teddy, he had a lot of patience.

Mika, for some unhinged reason, offered a paint card to Teddy, announcing, "We're going with Rouge La Rue."

Teddy swiped it out of her hand, stared at it, then rolled his eyes and clicked his tongue, declaring, "It's hideous."

"It is not," Mika returned.

"Come with me," Teddy demanded, then stalked out of the room.

Mika, ready to rumble, only glanced at Tom and Faun before she got up and followed him.

They could be heard carrying on their argument in the entryway.

Tom looked to Faun. "How's things?"

"Can't complain."

"My God, Teddy! Can't I paint a wall without a drama?" Mika cried.

Faun slouched deeper in his chair, going for the gusto with his big hand buried in Ringo's fur, and Ringo's purrs grew louder, before Faun asked, "Care to take in a Mets game while you're here?"

"Mets?" Tom asked in disbelief.

"Yankees are bullies," Faun replied.

Thus, a much less animated, but no less fascinating conversation sprang up in the sitting area at the back of Mika Stowe's living room, Rollo Merriman forever smiling above them.

Smiling because, when he was alive, Rollo knew without a shred of doubt that he was the love of Mika Stowe's life.

But now, Tom knew he was her first.

He also knew he'd be her last.

---

*STILL APRIL...*

*Scottsdale*

"ARE YOU GOING TO BE OKAY?"

Tom looked down at Priscilla standing beside him.

They were watching Clay, who was using the greatest of care while loading the cat carrier in the backseat of Brayton and Pris's car.

Nala was going home.

"It's never fun letting one go," Tom said.

Her eyes grew soft, she wrapped her fingers around his forearm, and her voice was quiet when she replied, "I'm dreading it."

She was not talking about pets.

He moved his arm so he could take her hand and give it a squeeze.

"Ready, baby?" Brayton called.

She nodded then looked to Tom again.

He kissed her cheek.

Clay dashed to him and gave him a hug.

Brayton shook his hand, murmuring, "We on for Saturday?"

Tom nodded. "I'll text the tee time."

Brayton clapped him on the shoulder, joined his family in the car, and Tom followed as they backed out.

He then stood at the end of his drive, watching until he couldn't see their car anymore, as another of his kids left him to go and live her happy life.

———————

*May...*

*New York City*

*Graduation Day*

"The minute the last one left, I called the workers to tear down the walls. I lost two bedrooms but gave myself a *glorious* bathroom and an *enormous* closet," Nora drawled, sipping champagne, her eyes on Cadence who was holding court across the room.

Tom and Jamie, standing with her, chuckled.

But Tom was learning how to translate Nora Speak.

That meant she was devastated when her children left home. Therefore, she threw herself into a project that would take her mind off it, at the same time it reassured her children she was okay they were going off to live their lives, even when she was not.

Tom noticed Teddy walking in, carrying a huge bouquet of exquisite blush roses, an occurrence of the like that had been happening the last few days as Cadence got flowers and gifts and cards with checks in them from her and Mika's large family of the heart and cadre of acquaintances.

However, carrying that bouquet, Teddy had a funny look on his face.

This meant Tom watched as Teddy set it down on one of the final available spaces and made a beeline to Mika, who was sitting with Chloe.

All of Tom's kids came, with Chloe, being Chloe, having already bought tickets for her and Judge before they were officially invited.

Only Sasha was staying with Tom, Mika and Cadence (Chloe, Judge and Matt were at Jamie's).

But they all made a point to come.

It meant everything to Cadence.

And Mika.

And Tom.

However, now, Tom watched as Teddy whispered something in Mika's ear.

Mika promptly shared it with Chloe, who immediately turned to look at the flowers Teddy had just brought in.

Shit.

What did that mean?

Mika got up and made her way to Tom.

He kissed her cheek and slid an arm around her waist when she got close.

She was proud but vulnerable. This was a happy day, and an excruciating one.

She was letting Cadence see the former of both.

She was giving the latter to Tom in private.

But now, he wanted to know about the flowers.

As usual, she didn't delay in giving it to him.

"Those pink flowers that just came in?" she asked.

He nodded, wondering at the look on her face and worried they came from her dad, who had been invited to not only the actual graduation (to which they'd only had four tickets, so Mika, Teddy, Faun and Nora went while Tom let those closest to Cadence have that experience, and he and his kids took care of setting up for this party). Her father had also been invited to the party.

The man did not respond, and so far, had not shown or given any indication he knew his only grandchild had hit an important milestone that day.

Rollo's parents, both still alive, now retired and living in Florida, sent a heartfelt card, a generous check and the tassel from Rollo's high school mortarboard in a satin-lined box (a gesture which was sweet, and made both his girls cry).

But sadly, this came along with a bullshit apology of why they couldn't attend.

A belated piece of news that, in the newness of them, Tom had not had the time to ask after, but he'd recently learned was that Rollo's parents never got over his death, particularly the grisliness of it. At first, they were very supportive of Mika and thrilled she was carrying Rollo's child. But once Cadence came into the world, and grew older, bearing such resemblance to their son, they backed off.

It was insane.

Tom couldn't wrap his head around it.

Mika described the relationship as "exceptionally loving, but distant."

Tom called bullshit on that, but he didn't speak those words out loud (though, he did share his thoughts with Matt, who agreed with his father).

It just made him doubly happy his kids went out of their way to show up.

"They're from Imogen and Duncan," she told him.

Tom looked to the flowers, his throat suddenly feeling tight.

They had yet to intermingle the families. He hadn't seen Duncan since that day they'd walked into his house and Genny then raced right out. Family texts were good. Duncan had politely declined a game of tennis when Tom knew he was in Phoenix. He'd joked in a text, thanking Tom for not saddling him with another cat as the kittens were dispersed.

But it wasn't like it used to be.

Those flowers said that Gen and Bowie intended to put in the work to make them like they used to be.

"It's a good thing," he assured Mika.

"Yes," she agreed. "I'm touched. Cadence will be too."

Tom let out a breath he didn't know he was unconsciously holding and had been for months.

"Oh my God, guys!" Cadence shouted to her friends. She was standing at the flowers, Teddy, as ever, hovering near. "*Imogen Swan* sent me these!"

She then rounded them with her arms like she wanted to hug them and gave them an exaggerated sniff.

Tom smiled and caught Chloe's eyes.

She was smiling too.

---

### *Mika*

*STILL MAY...*
*New York City*
*Day After Graduation*

MY HEART WAS FULL.

And so was my table.

Chloe, Judge and Matt had come over for brunch at my place that morning, Cadence, Sasha and Tom had helped me make it.

Teddy and Faunus were there.

Nora had texted. She was going to be late, but she'd be there soon.

This day, just months ago, it would probably have been Nora, Teddy, Faun and me.

Lots of love, for certain.

Just not that many people.

Now, my daughter had a noisy table filled with people she loved, all of them there to continue celebrating her awesomeness.

We would always have had a crush during the open house yesterday, no matter what. That was our life. It was full.

But this...

This was family.

We'd never had a big one of those.

Now, we did.

This beauty cut through the low hum of melancholy that now, my girl's life was hers to do whatever she wanted.

I stopped myself from laying a happy kiss on Tom to share my gratitude that he'd given us this bounty just as Nora swept in on a cloud of Boucheron perfume and a sway of the ends of her scarf collar, sleeveless Givenchy blouse.

"Finally! You're here!" Cadence cried.

My eyes narrowed.

My daughter was full of life, and sometimes she let that out through her decibel level.

But what she just said sounded annoyed and accusatory.

It wasn't like we'd waited on Nora to arrive.

It was brunch. You dove in when you showed up. And if food got low, we made more.

We were all eating.

"Darling, you know I'm always late. You can't make an entrance if you're *on time*," Nora replied, saying the last two words like they tasted bad.

"Sit down," Cadence demanded.

Again, that was not Cadence.

I exchanged glances with Tom.

"May I have coffee, *Herr General*?" Nora requested.

"Huh," Cadence said, then left her own seat and ran into the kitchen to make Nora's coffee.

It was then, Nora exchanged a glance with me as she took her seat.

When my daughter brought in Nora's coffee, I opened my mouth to ask if she was all right, but I closed it when I watched her bounce on her feet, side to side, rather than retaking her seat.

Okay.

What on earth?

Again, I opened my mouth to say something, but then Cadence

looked me right in the eye and announced, "Okay, Mom. I want to make a movie with you."

I shut my mouth.

"I've got it all blocked out in my head," she went on nervously. "It's called *Mothers and Daughters*. Like, we go all over the world, and we film the stories of mothers and daughters, like us. Either the dad died, or he left or whatever, but they have to get on. They have to make a family. I want it to be powerful, like we are. I want it to be hopeful, like we are."

Oh God.

I was going to lose it.

She looked to Judge. "I want...I want...I wanna ask you if I can talk to your aunt. Chloe was telling me stories yesterday and she'd be perfect. Because, when she divorced your uncle, she started her own cattle ranch with her daughter. They...I mean, I googled them, and they're a force to be reckoned with."

"Reid and Greer?" Judge asked.

Cadence nodded. "I know it's awkward. Your uncle left them high and dry. But I just, they made it, like doing"—she lifted her hands in air quotation marks—"'man's work,' and, like, they're super respected and most everyone working their ranch is a woman."

My daughter returned her attention to me.

"Like that. Stuff like that. I don't know, two or three in-depth stories, and four or five smaller ones. Not just in the US. Not just women doing stereotypical men's jobs. Just mothers and daughters who made it. I want to show how beautiful we are. Not like"—she anxiously glanced through Tom, Matt, Judge, Faun and Teddy to look back to me—"women don't need men. This isn't anti-men. This is just really, super, double, extra, pro-mothers and daughters."

She sucked in a huge breath.

Then said in a rush, "And I wanna talk about Dad. I wanna talk about us. Knowing, even if he wasn't here, we were stronger because at one time, he was. He helped make us. It's not about erasing men. I..." She swallowed. "I wanna talk about Dad."

"Honey," I said softly, my voice husky.

She talked over me.

"I'm gonna use my graduation money and the money you set aside for me for college and I'm...yeah, I'm going to use all of that. I don't know how to budget, but I'll figure it out. I know it might sound crazy or stupid, but I believe in this idea. I see it in my head. I have it all blocked out. But I want you with me. Like, we'll be co-producers. You'll be involved. Openly. On camera. So will I. We're mother and daughter. But it'll be only me who directs. Still, you'll teach me."

Cadence went quiet.

No one said anything.

All I heard ringing in my ears was, *Still, you'll teach me.*

So Cadence said, "And that's it. That's what I want to do now that I've graduated."

With that, she plopped down in her chair, spent.

"So it's not going to be *Adventures with My Mother*?" I noted.

"It's gonna be kinda that too," Cadence said. "I want us to be funny and awesome, like we are. Like we're the springboard. We lost him and it was like...like...it wasn't nice how we lost him. But"—she threw a hand out to indicate the table—"here we are."

"Here we are," I whispered.

She looked upset when she asked, "Do you think it's stupid?"

"I think I wish I'd thought of it."

Her face brightened.

"When do you want to start?" I asked.

Tears shimmered in her eyes.

"I need to show you my ideas," she said. "But I thought, when we're in London with Tom during Wimbledon, we'll find a mom and daughter and start there."

"I'll have a look and you can share your plan. And that's where we'll start."

Cadence stared at me and then said fiercely, "I love you, Mom."

"Same right back at you, kid."

"You will all notice," Nora cut in, and everyone looked at her to see she had both hands, fingers ramrod straight, pointing at her temples, or, rather, the tears brimming her eyes, "the works of art I have achieved with this eyeliner, as per usual. *However,* I would appreciate a warning in future if something is going to occur that will threaten this gargantuan achievement. Say...*tears.*"

Cadence burst out laughing.

The emotion hanging thick in the room lessened as everyone joined her.

But I sought Tom's hand, running into it because he was seeking mine.

He took firm hold, and with his strength seeping into my skin, I was able to hold it together rather than losing it after my daughter shared her dream.

A beautiful dream.

An ambitious and creative and interesting dream.

A dream that was a part of me.

A dream that involved me.

But a dream that was all hers.

Chloe drained her champagne flute then proffered it to Judge, stating, "I'll take it *without* the pomegranate juice this time, *mon beau.* And maybe with a splash of gin, simple syrup and lemon."

Sasha followed suit, after saying, "I hear that."

I held Tom's hand and found my daughter's eyes.

She smiled radiantly at me.

And all I could think was, I loved that happiness, I loved the excitement she had to go forth and tackle her life. I loved she knew what her path was and was raring to follow it.

I loved she was going to do that.

And she wanted me with her.

Last, I loved that Rollo and my creative legacy would live on through the most brilliant thing we ever created.

Yes.

I loved that last part most of all.

*Still May...*
*Roland-Garros*
*France*

"I think we're all a little surprised to see that performance on clay of Rod McMurtry's protégé, Dougal Baldwin, aren't we, Tom? He's a grass court player. Just twenty-one. And now he's in the semifinals here at Roland-Garros."

"Agreed," Tom replied. "What we've seen this year from Baldwin means the top players need to watch their backs. He's not simply getting better fast, he owned that court today. He looked like a man on top of his game. Confident. Not once losing focus. Straight sets against the number two seed? Even with Baldwin making the quarter finals in Australia, I don't think anyone imagined that would happen here in France."

Dave, his co-commentator, watched the monitors and chuckled. "Well, there you go. Red-blooded Scotsman, he has his win, and he's found a favorite in the crowd."

Tom frowned at what he saw on his monitor.

Specifically, Dougal Baldwin, who was known on the tour as enjoying female company on his off times, going right to Cadence, who was sitting by her mother, both of them standing and clapping after Dougal's win, and Dougal was extending a hand toward Cadence.

Beaming, she took it and shook it.

"You don't look happy," Dave joked.

Tom glared at him.

"Oh-ho," Dave said jovially. "Stepdad is not a fan."

*Cut it out*, Tom mouthed.

Dave gave him a the-audience-is-going-to-eat-this-up look.

"Let's get back to the match," Tom said. "That break serve in the first set clearly threw Giamatti. He never recovered from it. Baldwin saw it and went in for the kill."

When they finished the commentary, Tom yanked off his headset and went right to their producer.

"He pulls that shit again, he calls alone. I walk."

"Tom," she murmured placatingly.

"You're very aware I don't need this job, Sue," he reminded her. "I'll buy myself out of my contract. My family isn't up for discussion on-air."

Dave bellied up.

"It was all in fun, Tom. Relax," he said. "And I'm sure this isn't news to you, but you're again seeing one of the most famous women in the world. People are going to expect you to talk about it. Especially if she and her daughter are sitting courtside, so damned close, because you wangled those seats, her daughter can shake hands with the players after the match."

"I'm calling tennis, not hosting a gossip show, Dave," Tom returned. "And in no way is my private life something people expect me to talk about when I'm calling a goddamned tennis match."

"You're high-profile. You've always been high-profile," Dave shot back.

Tom was surprised, and annoyed. He'd been working with Dave for years. They were friends. So it didn't need to be said they'd never had this issue or any issue.

"You're high-profile too, Dave. Shall I mention your daughter's DUI on-air?" Tom asked.

Dave's face got red.

"She's not courtside," Dave gritted.

"I've been sitting beside you for a decade. You've not once mentioned Genny, Chloe, Matt or Sasha. So what the fuck?" Tom demanded.

"Dave, that was off. You know it. Don't do that shit again," Sue waded in.

She turned to Tom.

"Tom, you're dating the coolest chick on the planet. I'm sorry, if she shows at a match, and the cameras find her, and you're calling, it's going to be noted. We all know, if you're dating her, the cameras are going to find her. When it's no longer new, if she comes regularly, she'll just be expected to be there. But even when it's not new, she's Mika Stowe. The cameras are going to find her. Now, it's new, Tom, and because it is, it's noteworthy. So a mention and some on-air, good-natured ribbing *will* be expected. You've been in this business long enough, you know that." She went back to Dave. "But the daughter's off-limits. Jesus, Dave. What were you thinking?"

"He does it again, he's calling the match alone. I'm walking," Tom reiterated.

"You're heard," Sue said. "Is he heard?" she asked Dave.

"He's heard," Dave muttered.

"We have a problem here?" she asked.

Dave looked to Tom. "I didn't know you were that close to her. But I blew it. Won't happen again."

Tom let out a breath of relief.

Dave could be a blowhard, but he wasn't a dick.

"Appreciate it," Tom replied.

And because Dave wasn't a dick, and Sue didn't put up with any shit, and Tom was high-profile, and so was Mika, and they were used to that shit, that, both fortunately and unfortunately, was that.

---

"ARE YOU A TENNIS FAN NOW?" TOM ASKED MIKA THAT NIGHT IN BED.

Mika lay naked, sprawled on top of him.

"Okay, I'm not going to lie, that was pretty cool."

He smiled and teased, "Now I bet you're wishing you two went to matches last week."

"I can't say you're wrong," she admitted. "Cadence is hooked, and my mind has been expanded today, Tommy. Totally coming with you when you have to work, if you want me to."

Tom rolled her so he was on top. "I want you to."

She traced his cheekbone, her eyes following her movements.

"I watched you, back in the day." Her gaze found his. "Even when I was with Rollo, I watched you." Her finger stopped at his bottom lip. "He knew about you."

"What did he know about me?" Tom whispered, matching her mood with his tone.

"Just that he was the one because you couldn't be."

"Did that upset him?"

She smiled. "No, because I was fucking him and not you."

Tom chuckled.

She touched her lips to his while he did.

When she dropped her head back to the pillow, she said, "Thank you for taking Cadence's back today."

He'd told her about the situation with Dave.

"My job."

This smile was warmer, sweeter, but she said, "She's not old, but she's not young. She knew the cameras were on us several times during the match. It was wonderful, you did that. But she knew what she was doing and the consequences."

"She's off-limits," Tom said firmly.

And he got another smile.

After this one, he said, "I'm gonna eat you until you have another orgasm before we go to sleep."

Her brows shot up. "Do I have a say in this matter?"

"Do you want one?"

"Not really."

"I didn't think so," he murmured, beginning to move down her body.

"Tom?" she called, and he stopped and looked up at her. "I'm going to be moaning a lot soon, then I'll probably pass out. So, before that happens, I have to say, love you, baby."

He kissed the skin of her midriff.

He slid down and kissed the skin of her belly.

She opened her legs for him, and he kissed somewhere else.

And Tom made sure Mika knew he loved her too.

*July...*

*Everywhere*


"LONGTIME RUMORS SURROUNDING CORE POINT ATHLETICS EXPLODED *today in an incendiary piece released on the Internet news outlet,* The Worldist. *Reports of no less than sixteen women sexually harassed or assaulted by executives at Core Point, as well as athletes they sponsored, have surfaced.*

"*In the article, the company's 'Catch and Kill' policy of these cases was exposed in alarming detail. Spearheaded by the late Doyle Martin, founder of Core Point, and continued by his son, Cyrus, the current CEO, they were allegedly masterminded by a board member, AJ Oakley.*

"*Oakley is an outspoken oil man from Texas who is known by some to be a colorful character and considered by others to be a highly objectionable one.*

"*Information detailed in* The Worldist's *article alludes to further being shared in future pieces in the series about Mr. Oakley in regard to these activities. Organizations with which he served on their board and Mr. Oakley's own companies are already responding.*

"*Mr. Oakley has been removed from the boards of two organizations after emergency board meetings were held today, clearly in an effort to distance themselves from the eighty-eight-year-old, beleaguered, once-giant oil magnate.*

"*Oakley's own companies were unavailable for comment. However, all the other organizations with whom he's affiliated have shared they're internally reviewing this issue and their boards will decide soon regarding Mr. Oakley's future involvement.*

"*It has been reported of late that Mr. Oakley is in the midst of already significant financial troubles with mismanagement of not only the family's multi-national company, Oak World Oil, but even their large Texas cattle ranch. Mr. Oakley's son, Jeff, who's had a history of bad behavior and deci-sions, including serving jailtime for an assault in a bar years ago, runs the ranch. Jeff Oakley recently fell afoul with the Lone Star Cattle Ranchers' Association. Though exactly what happened has been sealed by the Asso-ciation.*

"This isn't all the bad news that befell the senior Mr. Oakley today. AJ Oakley's wife, a twenty-four-year-old social media influencer, self-styled 'life coach' and former beauty pageant contest, Margaret-Sue Faber-Oakley, announced today she's filing for divorce.

"In news related to this story, ex-tennis star Miranda Trainor contacted New Scotland Yard in order to bring forth a criminal investigation into her rape by a former colleague, an athlete sponsored by Core Point, Andrew Winston. Today's Worldist article shared her story, as well as those of three other women who were raped or sexually assaulted by Mr. Winston in his tenure as a professional tennis player.

"As Mr. Winston's sponsor, it's alleged that Core Point Athletics paid these women to remain silent on these allegations, something the women have done for decades, until this story broke today.

"After it did, singer and ex-model Luna Bevin announced on Twitter that she, too, was a survivor of a sexual assault by Winston.

"British authorities have already said they will be seeking extradition of Mr. Winston to stand trial for his assault on Ms. Trainor some years ago.

"Mr. Winston has denied all of these allegations.

"The sports world's response to this article has been swift and aggressive, with several professional organizations releasing statements that they're reviewing Core Point sponsorships and activities with players, teams and owners. Sampson Cooper made a statement that Core Point gear is banned at his famous camp for troubled youth in North Carolina. Rod McMurtry did the same, banning it from his tennis club in Glasgow, Scotland. Hale Wheeler stated that none of the upcoming services of his outdoor not-for-profit, Trail Blazer, will allow Core Point gear to be used or worn. Dozens of other athletes, both still competing and retired, have made statements denouncing Core Point and these activities. And some have even posted videos on TikTok of themselves burning Core Point gear. Social media has since begun swarming with nonprofessionals doing the same, calls for stores to stop stocking Core Point products and even calls for picketing of stores, should they continue to carry Core Point on their shelves.

"Mr. Oakley has become the face and target for most of the hostile fallout, likely because The Worldist article describes this as 'the tip of the iceberg.' We shall see what details emerge next."

. . .

"*In a shocking twist to the evolving Core Point Athletics and AJ Oakley story that has been emerging the last few days, with more women all over the globe coming forward with allegations of being silenced by money or threats from the besieged athletics organization and companies with ties to octogenarian businessman, AJ Oakley...*

"*Jameson Oakley, the senior Oakley's youngest son, in league with Hale Wheeler, the heir to the fortune left behind by his father, tech billionaire Corey Szabo, have announced their purchase of Core Point Athletics.*

"*Mr. Jameson Oakley and Mr. Wheeler have released a statement that they plan to abolish the company, wiping clean its multi-national executive branches and reporting any wrongdoing uncovered to the authorities. Scores of executives were dismissed today and escorted from their offices, with security teams entering Core Point buildings in twelve different countries to lock down records in order to launch a clean and thorough investigation.*

"*The younger Mr. Oakley and Mr. Wheeler have also shared they will assess operations, and if viable, which they feel will be the case, they'll relaunch under a new name as a social for-profit. This would mean the company would carry on with its current activities with a volunteer board, and all profits would be funneled into social causes, including Mr. Wheeler's Trail Blazer program.*

"'It's a perfect fit,' Mr. Wheeler was quoted as saying. 'If we can clean the stench of past management from it. However, we hope we can keep as many people employed as possible as we attempt to turn this company around. We'll be working swiftly in order that loyal employees not embroiled in this sordid matter will be able to keep their livelihoods. We'll carry on paying salaries, with benefits intact, while we're investigating.'

"*In other news involving this still unfurling story, the senior Mr. Oakley has been removed from all boards on which he once held a seat. This campaign of distancing themselves from AJ Oakley is so widespread, it's reported that even his own company, the family's floundering flagship, Oak World Oil, is considering his removal as CEO and Chairman of the Board."*

---

### Jamie

*STILL JULY...*
*New York City*

WHEN HIS PHONE RANG, JAMIE CHECKED THE SCREEN, SHOT A HALF-smile to his companion and didn't hesitate to take the call.

But he did get up from the couch and move to the window as he answered, "Hello, Dad."

"Pipsqueak, momma's boy, sumabitch, little motherfucker," AJ replied.

"You don't seem in a good mood."

He heard a sultry laugh come from the couch.

Even though Jamie was smiling, he didn't look in that direction.

He studied his verdant back garden, lit now with precisely placed lights, positioned to make it appear welcoming as well as show off its lavishness.

And he thought about the news he'd heard from a board member not ten minutes ago that the vote had been cast, and his father had been removed from his own company, effective immediately.

"My commiserations on Maggie-Sue's lawsuit fighting your prenup," Jamie pretended not to know what was really pissing off his father. "Pain and suffering, marital misconduct, infidelity, those don't sound good."

"That prenup is unbeatable."

"I hope you're right. You don't have much to give her. The creditors are circling the ranch. They own more of it than you do at this juncture. To save it, I'm going to be forced to pay them and assume their markers. But don't worry. I have no interest in ranching. Though, Reid's been in touch, and she's expressed interest in a buyout. I'm considering a family discount."

"You let that bitch anywhere near my land, I'll shoot you dead, I don't care the years I have left I'll spend behind bars," AJ threatened.

"I don't understand the hostility. It'll stay in the family."

"You're going to regret this, boy."

"Dad, I really will not."

"You think you got this?" AJ scoffed. "You think city boys know how to play dirty?" His father blew a breath out like a bull. "You been wet behind the ears since you been born. You take on me. You take on Jeff. We'll show you dirty."

"You've underestimated me since the moment I was born. You're a Billings. You're an Oakley. But *I* am a Jameson. I'm a Morgan. And we learned a long time ago that it's the stupid fucks who enjoy wallowing in the mud. It's a lot more fun to crush you from my penthouse office. That leaves me much better prepared when it's over simply to go out and have dinner."

"It's shit like that makes me wish I didn't plant you in your mother's belly."

"It's shit like you, Dad, that made her not want it."

Silence.

Then AJ demanded. "What did you just say?"

"You know," Jamie growled dangerously, "I think my favorite part of this is not going to be taking everything you love. It's going to be you figuring that out."

He disconnected and then blocked his father.

By the time he looked up from the phone, Nora was standing there, offering him his Scotch.

He noted she'd refreshed it.

"Thank you," he said, taking it.

"Are you all right?" she asked, watching him closely as he took a sip.

He swallowed the warm, rich, woody liquid that cost ten thousand dollars a bottle.

Money he earned.

Not a penny of it was touched by the filth behind Oak World Oil.

"I'm perfectly fine," he stated the obvious.

"Jamie—"

"He's never been my father, Nora," Jamie said. "Even before I found out he actually is not my father."

"I think you need to be careful," she advised. "What's that saying about an animal being cornered?"

"He has no weapons left at his disposal."

"Right then, what's that saying about a desperate man?"

Jamie shook his head.

"He doesn't have a penny or a piece of property he hasn't leveraged. This recent divorce is going to break him. He has nothing to give her. She's not going to stop until blood leaks from that stone. Every wife before her did the same, he just had the funds to pay them off. Now, he doesn't. And my brother is an imbecile. Dad has no allies. None. The only thing he had left was his reputation. Now, even geezers who insist on calling their assistants secretaries won't take lunch with him. He's a pariah. And to be a pariah in that bunch takes some doing. Honest to Christ, six months ago, even having nothing to strike a deal, I wouldn't have put it past him to do exactly that and get his ass out of the sling he'd put it in. Now, Nora, he's done. And there's no coming back."

"If you say so."

He smiled a comforting smile at her. "I say so."

"Mm," she hummed, lifting her martini glass to her lips.

"I'm supposed to feed you," he noted.

"I *had* realized how famished I was and wondered when you'd be seeing to that chore," she replied.

Jamie smiled again, offered his hand and said, "Turkey sandwiches?"

She took his hand even as she replied, "You will never see me again if you lead me to your kitchen and serve me a sandwich."

"Can't have that."

And he couldn't.

He liked her.

She was hilarious. She knew herself and was comfortable in her own skin. She was loyal and loving, just in her own way. Dru got a kick out of her. Judge did too. Chloe worshipped her.

He hadn't smiled as genuinely or as often as he had with Nora since Rosalind died.

And she was fantastic to look at.

His daughter was now doing her own thing, resting in the knowledge that Jamie had someone with whom he liked to spend his time. Dru had even talked to him about renting her own apartment in Brooklyn and moving out of the house she grew up in with Jamie and her mom.

And miraculously, sometimes, he'd forget the gnawing ache of the empty hole Lindy had left in his life.

Then he'd go to bed alone and remember.

But Nora was terrific. He'd known her as an acquaintance for years, but he wished he'd become her friend much sooner.

Rosalind liked her, but if she'd known her better, she would have liked her much more.

They enjoyed each other, and Jamie was remembering how good it felt to have a female at his side, one he trusted implicitly.

It would never go there, not for him, he'd had his one great love, and he didn't intend to look for anything like that again. And Nora had openly shared she didn't want that either.

If they needed to deal with baser human instincts, they'd find it discreetly elsewhere.

Now, it was a deepening friendship that he was beginning to count on.

Even treasure.

And since Nora adamantly did not cook, including refusing to learn when he'd offered to teach her, Jamie enjoyed making her chicken Kiev with sauteed green beans and rice while she watched.

Nora smiled.

She laughed.

She joked.

The conversation was easy and interesting, with Nora's delightful sharp edge.

And they ate their meal together, then had drinks after while watching a movie, before Jamie put her in one of his cars to take her home, and he went up to bed, feeling at peace with his night.

And for the first time since they lost Lindy, with his life.

HE DID THIS NOT HAVING ANY IDEA NORA ENJOYED HER NIGHT TOO.

But she did not go home feeling peaceful and serene.

She didn't because she was falling in love with her host.

And she knew she'd never get that in return.

But she would never leave him.

Not until he found someone to replace her (which she knew, with a man as good to the soul and with as much love to give as Jamie, he would do).

When that happened, she'd go back to her exquisite but quiet apartment.

And go back to living her life.

Alone.

---

### *Hale*

*STILL JULY...*
*Tokyo*

IT WAS EVENING HIS TIME, MORNING HER TIME, AND HALE SAW THE name on the phone.

He had no fucking clue why he took the call.

But he didn't hesitate to take it.

"Elsa," he greeted.

"You buried the lead, handsome," she purred.

He felt his lips tip up as he loosened a couple of buttons on his shirt and headed to the window of his hotel that had an amazing view of nighttime Tokyo.

"Please tell me that was as *insanely* delicious as it seemed," she begged.

"I don't know what you're talking about," he lied.

"Well, I'm not talking about you and Jamie Oakley taking over Core Point. I'm talking about you and Jamie Oakley already having a substantial stake in Core Point before news broke about Core Point, so, within days, you could assume control of Core Point."

Hale did not find that amusing.

They'd done that under the radar.

Or that was what they thought.

"How do you know all this shit?"

"I do not divulge my sources."

"Elsa—"

"If you gave me an exclusive on that months ago, I would have left Mika and Tom alone for *years*," she said.

Right.

That was why he picked up.

She occasionally featured Jamie and Nora. Chloe and Judge. Genny and Duncan. Rix and Alex.

But his people informed him she'd only twice done short features on Mika and Tom. During the French Open and Wimbledon.

While everyone was feeding on the only dad Hale knew, and the woman he'd fallen in love with, Elsa had been silent.

"I appreciate you laying off them," he said quietly.

"I like my apartment, my studio and my job, Hale," she said coldly. "Did I have a choice?"

"That wasn't meant to silence you."

"Wasn't it?"

"You can talk all you want about other people, just not my family."

"So, it was meant to silence me about things *you* want me to remain silent about. Can I request silken cords for my puppet master so his pulling at them won't leave marks?"

Hale sighed.

"I'll accept that as your confirmation of my statement," she declared. "And a yes on silk."

Silk cords and Elsa.

Hale put that out of his mind.

"Did you call to bust my balls?" he demanded.

"No, I called because, even though *I very much do not like you,* regardless of what you think, I do like your family. They're perversely perfect, which I don't trust, but I will be right there if that happens to be a façade, and it slips."

When she said no more, he asked, "You called me to tell me you don't like me, but you do like my family?"

"Please hear me correctly, Hale. I said I *very much* do not like you. This isn't simple dislike. It's me *very much* disliking another person, that other person being *you.*"

Hale had the unusual feeling of wanting to laugh and being annoyed along with something else he didn't allow himself to contemplate.

"Got it," he said. "You very much do not like me."

"But I do like your family."

"You're repeating yourself, Elsa."

"Then I'll share something new. Paloma Friedrichsen has a grudge she's been carrying. And she is very, *very* close to stumbling upon a woman named Susan Shepherd."

Hale's body, top to toe, grew solid.

"So I'd get on that, handsome. *Tout de suite,*" she advised.

"Let me get this straight," he said, sounding as incredulous as he was feeling. "You're phoning to warn me before a story breaks?"

"I have an advanced copy of Mika Stowe's book that's releasing in September," she stated. "Have you read it?"

"Not yet."

"You will. Trust me. Don't miss it. Though, I doubt I have to remind you that Rollo Merriman's head was severed from his body in that accident."

He flinched. "Jesus, woman. No. You don't have to remind me."

"She waited a long time for happiness, Hale. You're the rabidly loyal and protective family man. See to it nothing fucks that up, yes?"

With that, she hung up.

Slowly, Hale took the phone away from his ear and stared at it.

As he did, a text came through.

From Elsa.

*Oh, and when you're done taking care of SS, set Nora Ellington on Paloma. Don't ask. Just trust me.*

He texted back, *The CP situation is off the table during our one on one.*

He was bare chested when he received, *So he remembers our deal.*

*Is it likely you'll let me forget?*

He was in his pajama bottoms, brushing his teeth when she returned, *Never. Shall we set a date now?*

*It's late in Japan. I'll get back to you.*

And for some reason, it just made him laugh when he received, *Yes, I VERY MUCH do not like you, Hale Wheeler.*

He left it at that and turned off his phone because that would drive her nuts.

Then his mind wandered to being sprawled in one of the velvet chairs on her set while she was on her knees between his legs, and he allowed it to remain on this visual as he took care of himself.

He came particularly hard.

But after he cleaned up, he unusually had no trouble falling asleep.


WITHIN TWENTY-FOUR HOURS, HALE HAD SEEN TO IT THE LINE BETWEEN Susan Shepherd and Tom Pierce had been forever erased.

He then called Nora Ellington.

---

*Tom*

*AUGUST...*

*Cave Creek*

. . .

TOM GRABBED THE MAIL AND SAW SOMETHING REDIRECTED FROM HIS old address in Scottsdale.

He'd sold that house.

His commute to his clinic was longer, but at least Mika and Cadence had cats at home.

He recognized the handwriting and opened it immediately.

*Tom,*

*I wanted you to know, I've moved back home. It's safer. Cal and Colt said they'll look after me. And it feels good to be home.*

*I didn't think it would. But it's closer to those who deserve amends. It's not as hard as I thought it would be. It's not like they're inviting me to dinner, but Cal will sit with me if I'm having a drink at J&J's. Feb is civil. And Cher and Merry are becoming friends.*

*I've been keeping an eye, and I'm happy you're happy, Tom. You deserve it.*

*I know what you're thinking.*

*I deserve it too.*

*I've got good news.*

*I no longer think you're wrong.*

*Be happy and take care,*
*Susie*

He let that settle, and it settled nicely.

He considered contacting her, letting her know he was glad she was moving on in her life and it seemed it was the right direction.

Then he thought better of it.

Their break was clean, and although it was her idea, it was mutually agreed.

No going back.

He was relieved to know she was good.

But now, that too, was done.

Then Tom set the letter aside to show to Mika when she got back. She and Cadence were in Texas, filming the piece about Judge's aunt by marriage and cousin, Reid and Greer Oakley.

Tom got himself some water from the fridge.

And then, keeping Ace and Serena back with his foot, because they still followed him everywhere (at least he had two kids at home who were never going to leave him), he went out to check on the men who were building his tennis court.

---

### Elsa Cohen

*"The Elsa Exchange"*
*Celebrity News and Interviews*
*YouTube Channel*

"MY WONDERFUL WATCHERS, I HAVE JUST SPENT THE EVENING WITH greatness. Yes, as reported earlier, not only did I get an advanced copy of the coffee table tome, Mika Stowe's latest, *Our Creation*, a collection of extraordinary and *ultra-personal* pictures, short stories, vignettes and poems as well as new photographs by the great Ms. Stowe chronicling her adoration and grief for her shooting-star love affair with Pissed-Off Hippies drummer, Rollo Merriman. And an aside, *you must buy it. Immediately.* It is *divine.* But I digress, I was also invited to the book launch party."

*Picture on screen of Mika Stowe, resplendent in burgundy satin with large, bright, embroidered flowers, deep cleavage and a hem of fringe, standing next to tall, dark and handsome Tom Pierce wearing a Tom Ford suit. On Tom's other side, also in the curve of his arm, was Mika* and Rollo's daughter, Cadence, who was wearing a simple pink strapless shift.

Cut back to Elsa.

"How's that for adjusted? New man at the book launch party celebrating your lost love. But of course, as ever with this crew, there's more."

Picture on screen of Mika and Tom standing and chatting with Imogen Swan and Duncan Holloway.

Cut to photo of Judge Oakley, Chloe Pierce, Jamie Oakley, and Nora Ellington talking with Tom and Mika.

Cut back to Elsa.

"All in the family, as ever, but I must pout." [Close-up shot as Elsa pouts at screen, before the camera pulls back.] "I have *no news* of Judge and Chloe's impending nuptials. Not that first snippet. They are being very stingy. I hear this, and that, and I fear it's close, and I…know…*not one thing*. But! What's this?"

Picture on screen of John "Rix" Hendrix with his arm around Alexandra Sharp, both of their heads were bowed, seemingly in deep conversation with Alexandra's father, Ned Sharp.

Cut back to Elsa.

"It wouldn't be a Pierce/Swan/Holloway/Stowe event if the Sharps, and one of our favorites, the handsome hero Rix Hendrix didn't make an appearance. It seems all is, as ever, astoundingly well with our favorite family as it grows and spreads. But this leaves us with a question. I know you know what it is. Who's next?"

Photos flashing on screen of Cadence Merriman with tennis player Dougal Baldwin. Another with Cadence and Duncan Holloway's youngest son, Gage. A third with Drusilla Lynch and Sullivan Holloway. And last, one of Hale Wheeler and Blake Sharp.

Cut back to Elsa.

"I, for one, will be waiting with bated breath. And watching. Watching. *Watching.* When I find out, you'll be the first to know. Now, until our next exchange, keep it positive. Elsa is signing off."

The branded Elsa wink and blowing of kiss.

Sign off.

## *Elsa*

SHE STEPPED OFF THE SET AND MOVED TO THE SPACE WHERE THEY DID hair and makeup.

Her set was only hers. She'd gotten to the point they didn't break down so someone else could use it.

A win.

However, the actual set was tiny, as was the space around it.

There was a cage where they locked their equipment, since it wasn't the greatest part of town. Elsa also had a small office where she could work and take calls and field tips and decide on what pictures to buy. Further deciding what would go on-air, and what she'd put on her website (and then putting it on her website, at that point, she couldn't afford someone else to do updates, her posh set and comprehensive, carefully branded website were smoke and mirrors, she didn't like to think of how much they cost, but it had been worth every penny).

Her followers were exploding. So were her sponsors. So were her website hits, and from there, affiliate advertising.

If this kept going in a way she could trust, she'd be able to move, expand, have a bigger office, a dressing room, maybe an assistant.

This was a seat-of-her-pants operation.

But soon, it wouldn't have to be.

However, she knew even if she traded up, Hale Wheeler would follow her.

Elsa had to scrimp and save and find designer dresses to appear on her show on online resale sites, or consignment stores, handing out money to her beloved little ferrets who scurried everywhere to bring her tidbits, and shelling out even bigger money to maggot paparazzi when one of her team couldn't get a shot.

But Hale could buy the building where she set up a new shop without blinking.

"Good show, babe, see you later," her one and only cameraman, Chuck, said as he headed to the door.

"Thanks," she replied.

"You good to lock up?" he asked.

She had to change. She wasn't walking through this neighborhood in a Prada dress.

"Yes. See you tomorrow."

Chuck gave her a salute as he walked out.

Elsa grabbed her phone from the dressing table.

She had two new texts.

Text one: *What's with the avoidance tactics? I'm in New York. We were at the same goddamn party last night. You didn't even say hello and you took off every time I approached. The last time I came your way, you booked it so fast, you dropped your bookmark, which I have, by the way, and now I'm holding it ransom. I've texted you repeatedly to set this shit up. What the fuck, Elsa? What's with the games? Are we doing this interview or not?*

The second one said, *Just saying, you don't get your bookmark until we get that interview done and in the rearview.*

That was from Hale.

And the bookmark he was talking about was worth a ransom (kind of). It was a Tiffany's Elsa Peretti heart bookmark. It came with Mika's book for the big splash launch party.

Elsa had loved it the second she saw it. It was something she'd want to have, but not something she could buy for herself. She'd been upset when she'd noticed she'd lost it.

Now it was worse because Hale had it.

Her bookmark in his possession.

A shiver slid over her skin.

She went to her pictures, the series she, herself, took of him at Mika Stowe's book launch last night.

Hale with Blake Sharp.

The smiles.

The laughs.

The flirting.

Her heart squeezed.

Then she did the same with her eyes.

This...

Was not.

*Good.*

She ignored Hale's text (again), changed clothes, carefully folded the Prada and stowed it in a duffel she bought at Target, turned out the lights.

And she was sure to lock up when she left.

---

SEPTEMBER...

*New York City*

AS THE COUPLE LAY ENTWINED IN THE BED UNDER THE MURAL OF flowers in a thronged room two floors up, the book lay open to its last page on the table next to a microscope, that instrument's sole purpose to magnify hope.

Along the opened spine of the book lay a drumstick.

On the left page was a photo of the vivid orange and shadowed clouds of an Arizona sunrise through the dark frame of a wild but tended desert garden. It was taken from low, pointing up, the sun seeming less of an inevitability and more of a destination. Less of a dawn, more of a launch.

On the right page was a picture of five kittens, their adorable heads tipped back, staring at something that had them in thrall.

Also on that side was a poem.

*And Then Came You*

*And then came you.*
*But you were first.*
*Disarming me with devotion.*
*Leaving me.*

*Leaving me.*

*Lonely.*

*And then came you.*
*But you were always there.*
*Right there.*
*Far away.*
*Leaving me.*
*Leaving me.*

*Broken.*

*And then came you.*
*The first and the last.*
*Charming me with kitten fur.*
*Sticking.*
*Staying.*
*Making her bright eyes shine.*
*Giving.*
*Sharing.*
*A monster, gobbling me up,*
*Making me beg to be your meal.*

*And then came you.*
*Just through a touch,*
*And I had strength.*
*A look,*
*And I understood.*

*And then came you.*
*Disarming me with devotion.*
*The first, the last.*
*There you were,*
*In the sunrise.*

*There you were,*
*When it set.*
*There you were,*
*In my bed.*
*There you were,*
*In her life.*

*There you were.*

*Disarming me with devotion.*

*And then came you.*

**The End**

*The River Rain Series will continue...*

# AFTERWORD

Educating yourself all your life is crucially important.

And the moral of this story is, taking responsibility for yourself is too.

As such, I will say, early in my life, and even later in it, I misunderstood Yoko Ono.

I knew so little, but I still had an opinion about her.

I listened to those who had opinions (and I cannot stress this enough, in this day and age of podcasts and news commentary shows, go beyond listening to other's opinions about something and *find the answers yourself*), instead of listening...*to her*.

When I did, and further, when I listened to others who loved her, understood her and spent time with her, including interviews with John Lennon, I realized how colossal my mistake was.

Even as a feminist, I did this.

There's a documentary about John Lennon and Yoko Ono that has quite a bit of very personal footage.

Striking to me were two things.

One, John admitting that he took credit for "Imagine" when it was Yoko's. (Google it, it will say SONG BY JOHN LENNON because he copyrighted it, but he said himself, he wished he'd given her credit, because it was hers.)

Two, a man who worked with them saying something like (and I paraphrase), "If you listen to those words, John didn't talk like that. It was all Yoko."

Imagine something else.

Imagine creating something so profound, it has moved generations of people, and will continue to do so, likely for eternity, and not really having much respect for doing it.

Then imagine what that was was the song "Imagine."

Not once to my recollection have I seen Yoko Ono do anything but hold her head high and behave with the utmost confidence of a woman who knows exactly who she is, and she has no apologies for it.

Think of that and think of being the scapegoat for the demise of the world's most favorite band. Even before that, and certainly after, being roundly derided and ridiculed.

She was and still is an unusual, introspective, quiet, uniquely talented, tremendously hopeful Japanese woman with a tragic past who clung to positivity in her art and life who fell in love with the most popular rock star in history, and he fell in love with her too.

She was bound to be unloaded on.

But she carried that weight without once appearing to feel its burden.

I'm copping to landing my stone on her.

And here, in this book, through Mika, I endeavored to take it away.

Life. Sky. Dreamer. Sharing. Join. Us. Brotherhood.

I think that says it all.


Rock on,
Kristen Ashley

# RIVER RAIN TEAM

## SHOUT OUTS

For those who know this series, you know from the start I've written these books with my readers. At first, it was something to do, banding together in the first throes of the COVID-19 pandemic.

But I enjoyed the experience so much, I decided, if the publication schedule allowed, I'd work with my team to write the rest.

As such, I had a ton of help with this book.

In fact, the River Rain Team's fingers are all over this, it was just that mine were the ones that struck the keyboard.

I wanted to make mention of those whose ideas made it directly into this book.

Here we go:

Dena Kendig – gave Tom and Clay their box of kittens.

Susan Kowalksi – gave me the idea of Ace chasing after Tom's tennis balls.

Karen Bartholomew – offered up Steffi and Marti (Martina) as possible names for the cats, an idea I gave Mika.

Mary Kent – gave kitty Ace his name.

Ruth Stromberg – gave Venus and Serena their names.

Dee-Lanya Hunter – gave our bad guy the name Cyrus.

Ginger Conti – offered up the name Martin.

Anna Zadroźna – suggested the name Doyle.

Colleen Hinesley – gave Eleanor and Nora their last name, Ellington.

Aimee Jenkins Butler – gave Judge's aunt the name Reid.

Kirha Rodriguez (formerly McMullen ☺) – named Judge's cousin, Greer.

Kristal Dalgetty – gave Tom's sister her name, Teresa.

There were so many fabulous ideas for the character of Kateri True Arrow, it was mind-boggling. I wanted to give Jamie a team of kickass female investigators. But Kateri pushed through in my head. However, a Native American future heroine was a big winner with my River Rain Team, so the team helped her come to life in this book.

I might have missed some folks, the writing can be fast and furious and my notetaking not so great, but hopefully I recorded all of the above without error.

Even so, my gratitude is no less to all my Team who jumped on board to be a part of this book.

Until next time...

Rock On!


PS: If you want to become a member of my River Rain Team, join the group on Facebook. All are welcome!

# BOOK CLUB/REFLECTION QUESTIONS

1. In previous books in this series, it seems Tom has done the unforgiveable: he cheated on his wife. However, this book is a study of how both partners in a marriage need to pay attention to their relationship and keep it healthy.

Even if what he did was not right, do you feel you understand Tom more after reading this book?

2. Mika is a talented woman with a wide repertoire who has a lot of things to say, but when she introduced those, no one paid attention, and many even derided them. It would take decades before she was taken seriously.

Madonna has spoken about how much people commented about her and her work but none of that commentary mentioned that she had any talent or anything interesting to say.

On the other hand, Dolly Parton is famous for continuing to dress and wear her hair in a certain way in part so people *would* underestimate her. While they were distracted with that, it made it easier for a woman of her generation to build an empire.

This is not a phenomenon from the past. Female artists and voices are often reduced, all the while looks and attire are pulled center stage.

Can you think of a female artist who you might have dismissed, then realized later their fuller message or depth of talent? Has it opened your mind to how you perceive new artists?

3. As this series carries on, the interest from paparazzi and gossip machines is increasing. In this book, we see Tom, Mika and Genny dealing with speculation and people taking sides. Seeing what's happening from the perspective of fictional characters, does it make you rethink how you view the personal lives of celebrities?

4. Even after everyone has moved on in forgiveness for Tom's betrayal of Genny, Tom won't allow himself to do the same. He understands he's become "That Man," a man he doesn't want to be, but his affair has inescapably defined the man he is.

Do you think this is healthy? Do you think it's deserved? Do you think it's necessary so Tom won't do something like this again? Or do you think Tom needs to forgive himself?

Onward from this, is there anything you've done in your life that makes you feel the same? Do you feel maybe you should forgive yourself? Or does having that history help you to carry on with your life and relationships in a more thoughtful way?

5. With Sasha's revelations, we're confronted with more fallout of Tom and Genny's divorce. Were you surprised when Sasha shared what she did with Mika? Do you feel there's more to the story?

Along this line, do you feel Tom, Genny and their family handled the situation with Sasha appropriately?

6. It's clear Nora and Jamie have grown close over the course of Tom and Mika's story. Rosalind was the love of his life and Jamie has closed himself off to romance since he lost her. Nora seems very lonely, but she's also still holding a great deal of animosity toward her ex, which could mean there's still a spark. Do you think Jamie and

Nora will begin to see each other with different eyes? What are your thoughts on later-in-life love or love after loss at any age?

7. Did Matt's big announcement take you by surprise? Considering that, what do you think would be the perfect pairing(s) for Matt?

8. Were you surprised at the interactions between Hale and Elsa?

9. If you had to pick one home where Mika and Tom would live, would it be the Arizona adobe or the New York brownstone?

# DISCOVER MORE KRISTEN ASHLEY

**After the Climb: A River Rain Novel, Book 1**
By Kristen Ashley

They were the Three Amigos: Duncan Holloway, Imogen Swan and Corey Szabo. Two young boys with difficult lives at home banding together with a cool girl who didn't mind mucking through the mud on their hikes.

They grew up to be Duncan Holloway, activist, CEO and face of the popular River Rain outdoor stores, Imogen Swan, award-winning actress and America's sweetheart, and Corey Szabo, ruthless tech billionaire.

Rich and very famous, they would learn the devastating knowledge of how the selfish acts of one would affect all their lives.

And the lives of those they loved.

Start the River Rain series with After the Climb, the story of Duncan and Imogen navigating their way back to each other, decades after a fierce betrayal.

And introduce yourself to their families, who will have their stories told when River Rain continues.

## Chasing Serenity: A River Rain Novel, Book 2
### By Kristen Ashley

From a very young age, Chloe Pierce was trained to look after the ones she loved.

And she was trained by the best.

But when the man who looked after her was no longer there, Chloe is cast adrift—just as the very foundation of her life crumbled to pieces.

Then she runs into tall, lanky, unpretentious Judge Oakley, her exact opposite. She shops. He hikes. She drinks pink ladies. He drinks beer. She's a city girl. He's a mountain guy.

Obviously, this means they have a blowout fight upon meeting. Their second encounter doesn't go a lot better.

Judge is loving the challenge. Chloe is everything he doesn't want in a woman, but he can't stop finding ways to spend time with her. He knows she's dealing with loss and change.

He just doesn't know how deep that goes. Or how ingrained it is for Chloe to care for those who have a place in her heart, how hard it will be to trust anyone to look after her...

And how much harder it is when it's his turn.

## Taking the Leap: A River Rain Novel, Book 3
### By Kristen Ashley

Alexandra Sharp has been crushing on her co-worker, John "Rix" Hendrix for years. He's her perfect man, she knows it.

She's just not his perfect woman, and she knows that too.

Then Rix gives Alex a hint that maybe there's a spark between them that, if she takes the leap, she might be able to fan into a flame This leads to a crash and burn, and that's all shy Alex needs to catch the hint never to take the risk again.

However, with undeniable timing, Rix's ex, who broke his heart, and Alex's family, who spent her lifetime breaking hers, rear their heads, gearing up to offer more drama. With the help of some matchmaking friends, Rix and Alex decide to face the onslaught together...

As a fake couple.

---

### Wild Wind: A Chaos Novella
By Kristen Ashley

When he was sixteen years old, Jagger Black laid eyes on the girl who was his. At a cemetery. During her mother's funeral.

For years, their lives cross, they feel the pull of their connection, but then they go their separate ways.

But when Jagger sees that girl chasing someone down the street, he doesn't think twice before he wades right in. And when he gets a full-on dose of the woman she's become, he knows he finally has to decide if he's all in or if it's time to cut her loose.

She's ready to be cut loose.

But Jagger is all in.

---

### Dream Bites Cookbook: Cooking With Commandos
Short Stories by Kristen Ashley
Recipes by Suzanne M. Johnson

From *New York Times* bestseller Kristen Ashley and *USA Today* bestseller Suzanne M. Johnson...

See what's cooking!

You're invited to Denver and into the kitchens of Hawk Delgado's commandos: Daniel "Mag" Magnusson, Boone Sadler, Axl Pantera and Augustus "Auggie" Hero as they share with you some of the goodness they whip up for their women.

Not only will you get to spend time with the commandos, the Dream Team makes an appearance with their men, and there are a number of special guest stars. It doesn't end there, you'll also find some bonus recipes from a surprise source who doesn't like to be left out.

So strap in for a trip to Denver, a few short stories, some reminiscing and a lot of great food.

(Half of the proceeds of this cookbook go to the Rock Chick Nation Charities)

Welcome to Dream Bites, Cooking with the Commandos!

---

### Wild Fire: A Chaos Novella
By Kristen Ashley

**"You know you can't keep a good brother down."**

The Chaos Motorcycle Club has won its war. But not every brother rode into the sunset with his woman on the back of his bike.

Chaos returns with the story of Dutch Black, a man whose father was the moral compass of the Club, until he was murdered. And the man who raised Dutch protected the Club at all costs. That combination is the man Dutch is intent on becoming.

It's also the man that Dutch is going to go all out to give to his woman.

**Every 1001 Dark Nights novella is a standalone story. For new readers, it's an introduction to an author's world. And for fans, it's a bonus book in the author's series. We hope you'll enjoy each one as much as we do.**

---

### Quiet Man: A Dream Man Novella
By Kristen Ashley

Charlotte "Lottie" McAlister is in the zone. She's ready to take on the next chapter of her life, and since she doesn't have a man, she'll do what she's done all along. She'll take care of business on her own. Even if that business means starting a family.

The problem is, Lottie has a stalker. The really bad kind. The kind that means she needs a bodyguard.

Enter Mo Morrison.

Enormous. Scary.

Quiet.

Mo doesn't say much, and Lottie's used to getting attention. And she wants Mo's attention. Badly.

But Mo has a strict rule. If he's guarding your body, that's all he's doing with it.

However, the longer Mo has to keep Lottie safe, the faster he falls for the beautiful blonde who has it so together, she might even be able to tackle the demons he's got in his head that just won't die.

But in the end, Lottie and Mo don't only have to find some way to keep hands off until the threat is over, they have to negotiate the overprotective Hot Bunch, Lottie's crazy stepdad, Tex, Mo's crew of frat-boy commandos, not to mention his nutty sisters.

All before Lottie finally gets her Dream Man.

And Mo can lay claim to his Dream Girl.

---

### Rough Ride: A Chaos Novella
By Kristen Ashley

Rosalie Holloway put it all on the line for the Chaos Motorcycle Club.

Informing to Chaos on their rival club—her man's club, Bounty—Rosalie knows the stakes. And she pays them when her man, who she was hoping to scare straight, finds out she's betrayed him and he delivers her to his brothers to mete out their form of justice.

But really, Rosie has long been denying that, as she drifted away from her Bounty, she's been falling in love with Everett "Snapper" Kavanagh, a Chaos brother. Snap is the biker-boy-next door with the snowy blue eyes, quiet confidence and sweet disposition who was supposed to keep her safe...and fell down on that job.

For Snapper, it's always been Rosalie, from the first time he saw her at the Chaos Compound. He's just been waiting for a clear shot. But he didn't want to get it after his Rosie was left bleeding, beat down and broken by Bounty on a cement warehouse floor.

With Rosalie a casualty of an ongoing war, Snapper has to guide her to trust him, take a shot with him, build a them...

And fold his woman firmly in the family that is Chaos.

---

## Rock Chick Reawakening: A Rock Chick Novella
### By Kristen Ashley

From *New York Times* bestselling author, Kristen Ashley, comes the long-awaited story of Daisy and Marcus, *Rock Chick Reawakening*. A prequel to Kristen's *Rock Chick* series, *Rock Chick Reawakening* shares the tale of the devastating event that nearly broke Daisy, an event that set Marcus Sloane—one of Denver's most respected businessmen and one of the Denver underground's most feared crime bosses—into finally making his move to win the heart of the woman who stole his.

Sign up for the Blue Box Press/1001 Dark Nights Newsletter
and be entered to win a Tiffany Lock necklace.

There's a contest every quarter!

Go to www.TheBlueBoxPress.com to subscribe!

As a bonus, all subscribers can download FIVE FREE
exclusive books!

# DISCOVER 1001 DARK NIGHTS COLLECTION NINE

DRAGON UNBOUND by Donna Grant
A Dragon Kings Novella

NOTHING BUT INK by Carrie Ann Ryan
A Montgomery Ink: Fort Collins Novella

THE MASTERMIND by Dylan Allen
A Rivers Wilde Novella

JUST ONE WISH by Carly Phillips
A Kingston Family Novella

BEHIND CLOSED DOORS by Skye Warren
A Rochester Novella

GOSSAMER IN THE DARKNESS by Kristen Ashley
A Fantasyland Novella

DELIGHTED by Lexi Blake
A Masters and Mercenaries Novella

THE GRAVESIDE BAR AND GRILL by Darynda Jones
A Charley Davidson Novella

THE ANTI-FAN AND THE IDOL by Rachel Van Dyken
A My Summer In Seoul Novella

A VAMPIRE'S KISS by Rebecca Zanetti
A Dark Protectors/Rebels Novella

CHARMED BY YOU by J. Kenner
A Stark Security Novella

THE CLOSE-UP by Kennedy Ryan
A Hollywood Renaissance Novella

HIDE AND SEEK by Laura Kaye
A Blasphemy Novella

DESCEND TO DARKNESS by Heather Graham
A Krewe of Hunters Novella

BOND OF PASSION by Larissa Ione
A Demonica Novella

JUST WHAT I NEEDED by Kylie Scott
A Stage Dive Novella

THE SCRAMBLE by Kristen Proby
A Single in Seattle Novella

*Also from Blue Box Press*

THE BAIT by C.W. Gortner and M.J. Rose

THE FASHION ORPHANS by Randy Susan Meyers and M.J. Rose

TAKING THE LEAP by Kristen Ashley
A River Rain Novel

SAPPHIRE SUNSET by Christopher Rice writing C. Travis Rice
A Sapphire Cove Novel

THE WAR OF TWO QUEENS by Jennifer L. Armentrout
A Blood and Ash Novel

THE MURDERS AT FLEAT HOUSE by Lucinda Riley

THE HEIST by C.W. Gortner and M.J. Rose

SAPPHIRE SPRING by Christopher Rice writing as C. Travis Rice
A Sapphire Cove Novel

MAKING THE MATCH by Kristen Ashley
A River Rain Novel

# ON BEHALF OF BLUE BOX PRESS,

Liz Berry, M.J. Rose, and Jillian Stein would like to thank ~

Steve Berry
Doug Scofield
Benjamin Stein
Kim Guidroz
Social Butterfly PR
Kasi Alexander
Asha Hossain
Chris Graham
Jessica Saunders
Dina Williams
Kate Boggs
Donna Perry
Richard Blake
and Simon Lipskar

CPSIA information can be obtained
at www.ICGtesting.com
Printed in the USA
LVHW041723261022
731633LV00001B/53

9 781957 568010